THE
HAWKWEED
PROPHECY

THE
HAWKWEED
PROPHECY

IRENA BRIGNULL

WEINSTEIN
BOOKS

Printed in the United States of America.

Cataloging-in-Publication data for this book is
available from the Library of Congress.

ISBN: 978-1-60286-300-2 (print)
ISBN: 978-1-60286-301-9 (e-book)

Published by Weinstein Books
an imprint of Perseus Books Group,
a division of PBG Publishing, LLC, a subsidiary of Hachette Book Group
www.weinsteinbooks.com

Weinstein Books are available at special discounts for
bulk purchases in the U.S. by corporations, institutions and other
organizations. For more information, please contact the Special Markets
Department at the Perseus Books Group, 2300 Chestnut Street,
Suite 200, Philadelphia, PA 19103, call (800) 810-4145, ext. 5000,
or e-mail special.markets@perseusbooks.com.

First edition

10 9 8 7 6 5 4 3 2 1

For Theseus, Athina, and Phoenix

PROLOGUE

The babies were born as the clocks struck twelve. As they finally slid from their mothers' bellies, wet and sticky, their tiny faces scrunched up with the effort of being born, their fists clenched and eyes shut tight, a dark cloud crossed the full moon, and out in the forest the sky turned black. A bat fell from the air midflight. A silver salmon floated dead to the surface of the river. Snails withered in their shells, moths turned to dust on the night breeze, and an owl ate its young.

The spell had been cast.

This is how it came to be that two children, born at the same second of the same hour but on opposite ends of the land, changed places. It happened in the blink of an eye, as magic does. Too fast for anyone to possibly notice. The newborns spun through the ether, passing each other perhaps as they turned, and then arrived in different arms being handed to a different mother.

And when the two mothers—one at home on an old, sagging mattress, the other in a sterile hospital delivery room—first set eyes on those babies, they simply had no idea that it was not their own flesh and blood they were putting to their breast. They gazed at their bloodied, wrinkled infants and saw perfection. Miraculously, they recognized features and family traits that existed only in their imaginations.

"She has my mother's nose!"

"My sister's chin!"

"Your smile!"

A whole winter they'd been waiting patiently to see their child, and now they savored every detail. The bond had been made many months before. The love was already there. There was no chance of suspicion or doubt.

The witch, Raven Hawkweed, knew this. She'd been brewing and scheming and summoning every wicked thought and fear and feeling from deep inside her since the day her younger sister, Charlock, had told the coven that she was expecting a daughter. Until that day, Charlock had been cursed with boys.

No witch from their coven had sons. Not now, not ever. They stilled those babes in their wombs with a poison. The few who survived until birthing day were so weak and feeble that more than a few hours in the brightness and noise of life proved too much for them to bear. They closed their eyes and slipped back into the familiar darkness until they breathed no more.

But this time it was a girl growing inside Charlock.

Charlock had trembled as she told Raven. She had tugged on Raven's sleeve, steering her away from the others. Her eyes were bright and her cheeks so red that Raven had put a hand to Charlock's forehead.

"You look sick. Are you tired?" Raven fretted as she pulled down the skin beneath Charlock's eyes to peer into them.

"I'm well, Raven. I'm more than well." Charlock's voice was almost breathless.

"Stick out your tongue," Raven commanded.

Charlock opened her mouth to reply and Raven's fingers instantly pulled out her sister's tongue to examine it. Her eyes narrowed. Her forehead wrinkled.

"You're pregnant?"

Charlock nodded.

With a slight shake of the head, Raven turned away. "I'll prepare the mixture."

"No . . . no poison." Charlock had spoken so softly, almost a whisper, and yet the words thundered in Raven's head. She stopped in her tracks, her whole being focusing on Charlock's next words. "Not this time."

Raven could feel Charlock's smile. She could feel the warmth of it on her back and she knew what it meant.

"It's a girl?"

"It is."

The certainty hit Raven like a blow. A blow so hard that her teeth bit into her lip and she tasted blood. She pretended to busy herself at the washing tub. A drop of blood fell and mingled with the dirty water.

"A *girl*, Raven. At last. I wanted to tell you first. I knew how happy you'd be."

Her sister had always been a simpleton, but for the first time ever, Raven hated her for it.

"You are happy, aren't you?" Charlock asked.

Raven wiped the blood from her mouth onto her hand as she turned. "How could I not be?"

Charlock beamed. "I know—it's a surprise. But think, you'll have a niece and Sorrel will have a cousin."

Spells were whirring inside Raven's head, the kind that bubble with rage and desperation, and she had to use her breath to quell them. This was her sister. The sister she had cared for since she was born, to whom she had sung and told stories and taught to read. The sister who was so much softer than she, so weak that the edges of life knocked and bruised her, and it had been Raven's job to mop up the tears. The tiny heartbeat of a niece she could hate. But not her sister. She loved Charlock, perhaps more than herself.

But not more than Sorrel.

Sorrel was a tall girl, all bones and angles, the spitting image of her mother—and Raven's only child. Having endured pregnancy and birth once, Raven had determined never to try it again. One daughter was enough for her. Sorrel was all she needed.

From behind, mother and daughter were often mistaken for each other. Sorrel had inherited Raven's crooked walk and hunched shoulders. They had the same long hair too, which they braided down their backs each night and again every morning. When they walked, the braids swung behind them like tails. Sorrel liked to chew hers, but the ends collected in her throat and it took Raven's strongest brew to disintegrate the ball of hair that gathered there. Both wished their coloring was bold and dark like the witches in storybooks. But their hair was the dull gray-brown of mice fur, not black as coal, so it was only by length that they could distinguish it.

When her daughter was but a babe, Raven had presumed Sorrel would stand out, that everyone would be stunned by her talent and ability. It hadn't taken long for Raven to realize Sorrel's powers were not much more than ordinary. Taking a big gulp, she had swallowed the rancid disappointment, let it cramp in her stomach, and then vomited it into the compost heap by the old oak tree. As soon as she straightened, she decided to take matters into her own hands. What nature had denied her, nurture would supply. Sorrel would have to *learn* to be brilliant.

For Raven's daughter was destined for greatness.

Or so the prophecy told.

It was centuries before that the die had been cast and the prophecy made—back in the day when witches flitted through the sky on whittled, wooden brooms and boiled their potions in heavy iron pots and when, if discovered, they were burnt at the stake on bonfires or tied to chairs and drowned in lakes and rivers. The coven that had the revelation was a hunted, persecuted bunch of spinsters and widows. But under the cover of darkness, out in the thick of the trees, together they decreed that the Hawkweed sisters, in three hundred and three years hence, would deliver a queen who would govern all of her kind.

The bones of those witches now lay lost in the earth under thorny brambles and hedges, their skulls full of sand under the water, their burnt ashes long since swept to the corners of the land . . . but their words lived on. The Hawkweed prediction passed from generation to generation until Raven and Charlock, as little girls at their mother's feet, heard it for themselves.

One of their daughters would be queen.

Raven could still remember the thrill that had shivered through her when she first learned of the prophecy. The pulse pumped in her wrists and neck and the blood flooded through her veins. She was only six but suddenly she felt taller, older. Never before had she looked forward or back but had just been content to exist in the present. Now, suddenly, her future was mapped out before her and she already saw, far in the distance, signs with directions for her to read. Charlock had been too young to fully understand their mother's words. She had looked at Raven with questioning eyes, wanting her older sister to explain, just as she had explained that cobwebs come from spiders, feathers from birds, and honey from bees. But this time Raven didn't want to help Charlock. She didn't want to discuss what their mother had told them. She didn't ever want to talk about it. Her hopes and fears stirred inside her with the same steady rhythm with which her mother stirred her bubbling pots. She couldn't let them splash and spill.

As the two sisters grew, Charlock overtaking Raven in height but not in speed of mind or skill, Raven brushed off Charlock's questions just as she might crumbs from the table.

"Will she wear a crown?"

"Who?" asked Raven, pretending not to know what her sister was talking about.

"Our daughter."

Charlock was yet to comprehend what Raven had grasped immediately—that it could no longer be "we" or "us" or "our." The ropey knots of sisterhood had been unraveled and lay in coils around them, ready to trip them up.

"Will she have a castle?"

Under her breath, Raven muttered a spell and Charlock started to sneeze—once, twice, thrice. Raven handed her a cloth to wipe her nose. "Mother says you have to forage this evening," she lied. "But wash your hands after picking the nightshade," she added, to soften the falsehood.

"Aren't you going to come with me?" asked Charlock in a voice scratched with disappointment.

"I have to study."

"You're always studying," Charlock complained, turning away to mask her hurt.

It was true that Raven had turned from a wild, ungovernable child into the most industrious student. The coven was always remarking on her hard work. She had by far surpassed the other girls in her knowledge of plants and poisons, spells and curses. She read every book and text she could get her hands on, turning the pages well into the night. She drew diagrams of insects and reptiles, learning through her own experiments which eye of which newt and which leg of which toad would most enhance her spells. She knew which berry made your stomach ache so bad that your bowels broke and emptied themselves down your legs, and which caused rashes that itched and burned for days. There were weeds that made your eyes redden and water, toadstools that made the hair fall from your head, and snake venom that would take so long to kill you that you'd wish for someone to put you out of your writhing misery.

The more Raven learned, the less popular she became with the rest of the young sisters. More often than not, her success in lessons showed up their failings. She always had the right answer, and the other girls would roll their eyes and mumble curses that she would have to block and spin back at them. Without intention, Raven became a loner. She found herself an outcast from the circle of friends who laughed and played tricks and gossiped wickedly about the coven. Only Charlock wanted to spend time with her, and Charlock was the last person Raven wanted for company.

For all Raven's studies were for one purpose: to ensure her daughter would become queen. And to ensure she herself became so strong and powerful that she could guarantee it. Without arousing any suspicion, Raven knew she must eliminate all other contenders. Killing Charlock would be the most obvious solution, but despite it all, she still felt a deep and ceaseless love for her sibling. Besides, murder was the way of the chaffs—the common people—crude and without magic. This was not the sisters' way, and Raven was determined to be the best of witches—the mother of a queen, no less. She would concoct a spell that would astound any witch with its power and complexity. For witches judged not the act but the method.

So Raven dedicated her youth to finding the magic that would stop Charlock from giving birth to a girl. And it had worked. A drop of tincture measured to the exact milliliter and warmed to just the right degree, then slipped into Charlock's tea, together with the right curse incanted at the desired second when the moon was at its slightest slither, and all of Charlock's babies became boys.

But then the sickness struck. It came one winter when the ground was hard as stone and the grass crunched and crackled with a frost so cruel that the worms froze like sticks, then snapped in two. The coven told them it had been sent by the South, retaliation for a slight made against the eldest of that clan. For thirteen days they were plagued. Boils oozed with pus and blood trickled from their ears. Then it was over as suddenly as it began. Not a scab or a scar to prove it had even happened. Every woman and girl was just as they had been, as if they had never been sick at all.

Apart from Charlock.

She was pregnant—and this time it was a girl.

The rest of the coven celebrated the news. As with every prospective daughter, they lay Charlock down on the wooden slats and, with her bare belly exposed, formed a circle around her. They bent their heads over her, young and aged, handsome and ugly, all united by the same purpose.

Raven held the ring, suspended from a string, inches from Charlock's womb. The ring, though centuries old, had been polished so it shone like new. It was the wedding ring of some hapless peasant girl who had thought to cheat a gray-haired, toothless peddler woman and who had paid for it with her fingers.

The witches started to chant. The whisper became a murmur, became a din. The faces had stopped smiling and were now distorted by their fierce intensity. The sets of eyes were like opaque glass, the mouths gaping open like wounds.

Then the ring began to move. Only slightly. First this way. Then that. Backward and forward, as if undecided. Charlock shut her eyes. Her body was tense with anticipation. The chanting was now a deafening percussion. *"A girl! A girl! A girl!"*

Raven hoped against hope. She said the words but willed them with all her might to be a falsehood. Then the ring seemed to make up its mind and it spun. Slowly at first. Then faster and faster until you could hardly see it spiral, it was so quick. Suddenly the thread snapped. The ring dropped, landing on Charlock's belly, scalding her, hot as fire. The chanting stopped immediately. The room was silent. Raven's mind and body hardened, both as still as stone.

Charlock opened her eyes and smiled.

CHAPTER ONE

The uniform felt like a straitjacket, secondhand and too small. Poppy's father had learned long ago never to invest in a brand-new one. When she was a child, Poppy had been nervous about starting at a school, daunted even. Now, as a teenager, she was numb to all that. It was just the uniforms she hated—the idea that by wearing the same clothes, you're on the same side, like a team, or an army, all with the same sense of purpose. *More like inmates*, Poppy thought to herself bleakly, as she regarded her reflection in the mirror. Maroon—the bright ones were the worst. It was like she was donning a disguise. But she knew she was different, always had been, and no uniform could hide that. For this was going to be Poppy's eleventh school.

Poppy finally found her shoes in the bottom of a box that hadn't been unpacked yet. Outside the window, litter and leaves were lifting in the air, leaping across the street, and she stopped and watched them for a while, wondering dispassionately how long she was going to last at this next place. A whole year was her record. Something always went wrong. Either intentionally or by accident, Poppy would break too many rules, cause too much disruption, or lose her temper, and disaster would strike. Like the time Mrs. Barker, her science teacher, slipped and fell, fracturing her wrist. Mrs. Barker had sworn Poppy had tripped her, and despite Poppy's protestations that she'd merely looked at her teacher, this offense had been the last straw. Her father had been called from work, and Poppy had been expelled in disgrace. Other schools had been more kind about it, suggesting gently but firmly that theirs was not the right environment for Poppy and that she'd be better suited elsewhere.

John Hooper, Poppy's long-suffering father, had tried everything. He'd sent Poppy to the most expensive, traditional boarding schools, to the most progressive and nurturing day schools in the country, and even once to a convent. (That had not ended well—a broken stained-glass window dating back centuries and a vast restoration bill.) But the last expulsion had been the worst yet—a series of prank fire alarms that unleashed the wrath of the fire brigade and the local police department.

Poppy remembered seeing her father emerge through the smoke. There was no rush or panic, just the slow, heavy footsteps of a man resigned to disappointment. In all the heat, his eyes were cold blue ponds; when he saw her, they iced over. On the way home Poppy tried to deny the pranks, but he didn't want to hear it.

"Stop! Just stop!" he ordered.

"But I—" Poppy didn't get a chance to finish.

"Not another word."

And she knew he meant it.

They drove back home in the most itchingly uncomfortable silence. Poppy stared out of the car window at all the people busying themselves with the mundanities of life and wondered if a single one of them could understand her. Had any of them ever felt as she had? For Poppy hadn't touched the alarm. And she hadn't started the fire. Yet she knew as an inexplicable truth, deep down inside of her, that somehow she had been the cause of it.

She had been frustrated, angry, sad . . . the desperate urge for the day to stop had rushed up and out of her. She had needed a break, just a moment of change, and the next thing she knew, the alarm had been blaring and the teacher had stopped her tedious testing and kids were jumping out of their seats, and she had been outside in the fresh air, and for those next few minutes, she'd felt calm.

"I give up," her father uttered suddenly after he'd pulled into their driveway. He was facing straight ahead as though he couldn't even bear to look at her. They sat there, both as motionless as the car, and then the door was open and he was out, marching toward the house, keys clenched in his fist. Once he was inside he immediately fetched their suitcases and told Poppy to start packing. And that was how Poppy now found herself living in a new house, dressed in yet another school uniform, and about to start her eleventh new school.

Her father had left for work already. He and Poppy were beyond the usual niceties of father and daughter. No kiss on the cheek, breakfast on the table, no good luck or even good morning. Poppy knew he was trying hard just to tolerate her. He had already started his new job, the only one he could get at such short notice, one with an even lower salary than before. Their standard of living had been gradually reduced with each new move—but they had never traveled so far away from her mother before.

Poppy was more than used to her parents living apart. Her mother had spent so much time in and out of different treatment centers and rehab facilities that Poppy had stopped associating her with home a long time ago. Yet this move felt different, as though family ties would snap under the strain of all these miles between them. She packed her school bag in the quiet, empty house and admitted to herself how much she would love to turn and see her mother there, like other mothers, reminding her not to forget her books and to wrap up warm because it looks cold outside. And then Poppy felt like a fool for even imagining such a thing. She doubted her mom would even miss her. She probably wouldn't even be conscious that she'd gone.

Melanie Hooper had been awake when Poppy and John went to say their good-byes. She had spent most of the last few years asleep or in a medication-induced stupor, but on this occasion, she was alert and even dressed in something other than pajamas. She was still lying on a bed—Poppy tried to think when she had last seen her mother upright—but the curtains in the room were open, and the light offered some hope in the otherwise dull and austere atmosphere.

John broke the news they were moving up north and Melanie shed a tear. Like a child, she repeated after John that it was "for the best" and she promised to be brave.

When John stepped out for coffee, Melanie grabbed Poppy's hand. "What was it this time?" she asked feverishly.

"A fire," Poppy mumbled.

"It's not your fault," her mother said urgently, squeezing Poppy's hand more tightly.

Poppy couldn't breathe; the sudden prospect of understanding had caught in her throat. She looked into her mother's eyes and let her limp fingers softly squeeze back. Melanie's nails dug into Poppy's palm. Her lips pursed.

"It's the devil in you," she whispered.

Poppy flinched like she'd been struck and pulled her hand away just as her father walked in and passed Melanie a glossy magazine that she cooed over with delight. The intensity in her face vanished and her usual misty expression returned.

What Poppy didn't know was that, after they left, Melanie woke in the night with tears running down her face. It took three members of staff to restrain her.

"My baby! My baby," she wept in despair, and the tears kept falling until she was sedated and the drowsiness took hold.

As she fell back asleep, the dreams became hazy, less real—memories from a life long ago, lived by a person she could hardly recognize . . .

A woman with soft, blonde hair and pretty features was watching a baby as it lay in a crib. Herself and Poppy, Melanie realized faintly from the depths of her dream. She'd been watching Poppy for hours, she remembered, unable to pull herself away. The phone was ringing in the distance, but she chose to ignore it. She had dark circles beneath her blue eyes. She had pins and needles in both feet. Her lower back ached. She was tired—she'd never felt so tired.

Poppy, however, never seemed tired at all. Dressed in a pink vest with a bunny on the front that clashed with her dark, wild looks, Poppy stared back at her. Only a few weeks old and she showed not a trace of emotion—she seemed so in control, so independent.

A storm of thoughts tossed around Melanie's mind.

She's only a few weeks old and she doesn't need me!

Is she normal? She's not normal.

Why don't I love her? Of course I love her!

Then, guiltily—*what kind of mother am I to even think such a thing?*

The next thought came out of her mouth as a scream. The words followed, words of shock yelled down the stairs, through the house: "John! John! Poppy's eye just changed color."

Melanie sprang to her deadened feet and, ignoring the pain, picked Poppy out of her crib, holding her at arm's length so she could look more closely. Sure enough, one of Poppy's blue eyes was now green and a black dot had emerged from it, a satellite to the pupil. She gave a shiver, quickly put Poppy down, and backed away from her daughter. Her husband was at the door, out of breath.

"What's happened? What's wrong?"

"John! You've got to come and see this."

The pediatrician hadn't been able to explain it. It was a strange phenomenon, but apparently babies' eyes do change color, and Poppy's had merely turned more quickly. Different color eyes were rare but not unheard of and, she suggested, rather an attractive feature to possess. Melanie smiled weakly, unable to express why she felt so unsettled by this development. The doctor, a young woman so polished that her hair and skin seemed to reflect the light and cast a shadow on Melanie, scribbled something down on Melanie's notes.

"Are you getting enough sleep? Any sleep?" she asked with a smile.

Melanie wondered whether to come clean and then decided she was too exhausted to try to explain. "Sleep's not really the problem," she sighed.

It was only a white lie. Poppy never disturbed them. If she was able, Melanie could be having twelve hours of uninterrupted sleep a night. The brand-new baby monitor had never picked up a sound. So Melanie would lie in bed each night, the long, long minutes ticking by, wishing for just one cry from her baby.

The doctor added another sentence to the notes. "Isn't your mom lucky to have you?" she said to Poppy in that voice grownups reserve for young children.

Melanie didn't begin to weep until she was outside.

It wasn't their last visit to the doctor, merely the beginning of a series of appointments that were to become more and more regular over the following months. Poppy did not smile. She didn't laugh . . . or gurgle . . . or even cry. Other mothers envied such an easy baby, and their compliments made Melanie doubt herself even more. How could she ever tell them that Poppy wasn't easy—she was different, strange, not . . . not normal?

Melanie would look into Poppy's contrasting eyes and try to make some connection, but Poppy would stare back, unblinking, giving nothing away. Melanie loved her baby. She really did. But she knew it to be absolutely true that her baby did not love her.

And no amount of baby books and teddy bears and musical toys seemed able to change that. The only thing that inspired a reaction from Poppy was the cats.

They came at night. At first just one, then a few, then more and more. They would sit on the roof and the windowsills and meow to the moon as if heralding Poppy's arrival into the world. They left mice on the doorstep as an offering to her, even on one occasion a baby squirrel. Melanie screamed when she saw it and sent John outside to dispose of it. If ever a cat got inside the house, it would climb into the crib, and Melanie would find it curled around Poppy, encircling her head protectively. Poppy would look up at Melanie, and her eyes would be shining bright, happily almost.

So Melanie went back to the doctor with these various complaints, and the doctor would nod and jot things down and then ask again how she was coping and if she was getting enough sleep, until one day she prescribed her some mild antidepressants and sleeping tablets just to help her through this difficult time. Melanie wanted to protest, but the prescription in her hands felt like a relief. If she couldn't find a remedy for Poppy, at least she could find one for herself.

So when the flies dropped dead onto the beige carpet in Poppy's room, black and dry so they crunched if you stepped on them, Melanie didn't scream. She just simply vacuumed them away. And when Poppy wrote strange signs on her dolls' stomachs, or made the taps turn on and off while she sat trapped in her high chair, or hummed tunes Melanie had never heard of but that made spiders spin webs across the ceiling like a lace shawl, or screamed so piercingly high that glass would crack—Melanie just reached for another little pink pill to beat the baby blues.

John remonstrated with her. He pleaded and begged, grew angry and violent, wept with despair.

"She's not ours," Melanie kept repeating. "She doesn't belong to us."

John punched the wall, then called for the doctor. An ambulance arrived and took Melanie away for treatment until, a few months later, she returned, bright and clean and repaired. However, it didn't take long before she broke down again.

"Where's *our* baby?" she would cry. "Where can she be?"

The doctors diagnosed postnatal depression and told John in grave voices that this could be an extremely serious condition. He would need to keep a close eye on his wife and be extremely patient with her. John tried his best, but as his wife's mind slipped away, it took with it his future, and he found it impossible to keep his anger to himself. When he yelled at Melanie that she'd "gone mad," Poppy—a toddler by then—looked at him sympathetically. When she saw him packing a suitcase full of her mother's clothes, she brought him the book Melanie was reading and her perfume and face cream. Things, in fact, that he would have forgotten.

Before long, it was just the two of them.

CHAPTER TWO

Before leaving for her new school Poppy placed food for the cats under the hedge at the side of the house. They weaved in and out of her legs, rubbing their fur on her skin in gratitude. There was a chill in the early autumn air, and Poppy relished the warmth of their touch. It had felt cold ever since she'd arrived up north to this far edge of the country, like she had left the sun behind forever. This piece of land, jutting out to sea, felt like the precipice of the world, like there was nowhere to run but into the icy waters to drown. At first Poppy had wondered how she would survive in such a desolate place, the town barren of charm or interest, the hills and their forests on one side and the bleak gray sea on the other. Then, just as she was about to despair, the cats had appeared. It had taken them seven days and several hundred miles to reach her. Her spirits had soared when she'd spotted them on the rooftop, making themselves at home.

As if sensing her thoughts, the ginger cat that Poppy called Minx gave a meow, and Poppy reached down to stroke her. Minx was the cat she felt closest to. She'd known her since she was a tiny kitten, fitting so lightly in the palm of her hand. Minx wasn't the sleekest or the strongest of the group, but for some reason, Poppy had connected with her. A few years ago Poppy had tried to take her indoors, thinking she might persuade her father to keep Minx as a pet. But Minx had wriggled and squirmed and run back outside. She wasn't happy within the four walls of the house, and Poppy didn't persist because neither was she. Occasionally Minx would climb in her bedroom window in the dead of night and lie above her head like a fur hat, but then she'd slink away again before dawn would break.

Poppy scratched Minx's chin and heard her purr contentedly. She wished she could huddle up with the cats and spend the day in their company, away from all the people and all the stress, just as she'd done when she was small. They were her only real companions, but she had to keep them a secret if she wanted to avoid her father's suspicions. As Poppy had grown up, she'd learned to hide the things she guessed would bother her father. So for a long time now, the cats had sensed they must stay away, only coming to her when she was alone. The spiders would also scurry out of sight when John returned home, and the insects would flitter into the shadows.

In this way Poppy had managed to deceive her father into believing there was nothing mysterious or unnatural about her. And as she'd grown from a little girl into a teen, it became easy for John to blame Poppy's troubles on her mother. On the odd occasion Poppy would reason this too. She told herself her mother's breakdown had been a traumatic event, that she must be scathed by it even if she wasn't conscious of it. She lacked a female role model, a mother's love. No wonder she had anger issues. But then something truly weird would happen—like how she knew Uncle Bob was going to die before the summer came, and how two days later he announced he was terminally ill. He died at the end of May, and the day after his funeral the sun began to shine.

After that, Poppy stopped making excuses for herself and tried very hard to accept that she was different. So much felt beyond her control or understanding, but as long as she kept her head down at school and as long as she kept covering her tracks at home, her dad would choose not to look too closely at any evidence she might have failed to hide. Denial was a powerful thing, and a part of Poppy admired her mother for not having been held under its sway. It was lonely, though, all this pretense. There was no hiding that.

Poppy looked around the classroom. On the far side, middle row, she could see one empty desk. It was next to the window. Outside stood a tree almost near enough to touch. Its branches swayed in the wind, beckoning Poppy closer. She moved quickly and quietly to the seat, her head bowed, eyes fixed ahead. She was about to sit down when she felt the hairs on her arms bristle.

"What d'you think you're doing?" The accent was harsh this far north, the vowels spiky and serrated like the thistles that spread across the fields.

Poppy straightened. "Sorry," she mumbled without looking up.

"Find somewhere else to sit."

Poppy glanced at the girl, taking in her angry, narrowed eyes and lips pursed in confrontation. "It's all yours," she said in a low voice as she turned away.

"Too right!"

The other kids started to laugh. A gust of wind shook the tree and rattled the windows. Poppy glanced around her, hoping and praying for another desk.

"Got nowhere to go?" the girl taunted.

A skinny boy with long hair pulled out his chair. "She can have mine, Kelly."

Poppy stared at the boy, trying to decide whether to trust him. Past experience told her not to. From the girls, she got dislike and aggression. But from the boys, she sensed fear. She didn't understand why. She was small, unthreatening. They were so much stronger. But she saw it now in this boy's eyes, underneath the bravado and the posturing.

"Do you want it or not?" he challenged, holding onto the back of the chair and moving it so she could sit.

Poppy felt all the eyes in the room upon her and realized that she didn't have much choice. She walked past some other girls, and the overpowering scent of perfume, gum, and Diet Coke made her want to gag.

"Thanks," she muttered to the boy.

As Poppy sat down, there was the scrape of chair legs on flooring and a heavy thump as she hit the ground. A pain shot up her spine. The kids broke into laughter, some embarrassed with their hands over their mouths, others in unfettered delight. Poppy stared at her shoes. Her voice was loud in her head, trying to drown out the uproar—*ignore them . . . just ignore them . . . don't get angry . . . breathe . . . just breathe.* Hot tears stung her eyes as the voice tried hard to calm her. She blinked them back. She looked up at the boy, who shrugged belligerently but then blinked nervously. Poppy scanned the room, taking in all the grinning faces, monstrous in their howls of laughter.

The tree branch slapped the window and the kids flinched. The crack it left in the glass seemed small but it spread, slowly at first . . . then ripping along the windows until they shattered. The glass splintered, and tiny shards dropped like hail onto the class. The kids screamed and tried to cover themselves.

"It's in my hair!" yelled Kelly, the desk girl, her hands picking frantically at the glinting sparkles in her hair. Unbeknownst to her, a trickle of blood ran from her forehead to her ear. "What are you looking at?" she yelled at Poppy.

Without replying, Poppy got up and sat down at the boy's seat, pulling it firmly behind the desk. He stepped away from her, and she began to coolly and calmly unpack her bag. She set out her books so they lined up neatly and opened her pencil case, carefully laying out a pencil and pen. The boy just stood there, his mouth open, watching her numbly.

"Got nowhere to go?" Poppy asked pointedly. Looking spooked, he backed away further, tripping over someone's backpack as he went.

Kelly was brushing the glistening specks of glass from her skirt. "You're a freak!" she accused.

"Tell you what," Poppy picked up the pen and clicked it open, "you stay away from me, and I'll do the same for you. How does that sound?"

Kelly raised her eyebrows challengingly.

"And you might want to wipe that blood off your face," added Poppy in her most matter-of-fact voice.

Kelly dived for her bag and rummaged through it, grappling for the hand mirror buried in its depths. She flicked it open and shrieked when she saw the blood. Poppy shook her head. She'd encountered tough girls like Kelly before—they liked scratching and punching with words, talking a fighting talk, but anything resembling a real wound, and they crumbled. Kelly ran out of the room, clutching her head, barging past the teacher as he was walking in. He watched her go as though such scenes of hysteria were utterly to be expected, then entered the room and saw the damaged windows. At that moment the wind shook the building and surged through the remaining jagged glass so that, inside the classroom, papers rippled, skirts billowed, and hairdos ruffled.

"Mark," the teacher yelled to the chair boy. "Don't just stand there looking foolish. Go get Mr. Harding."

Mark, relieved to get away, sprang into action instantly. The teacher looked around.

"Okay, everyone. Settle down." His eyes rested on Poppy. "New girl, right?" He looked down at a list on the top of his folder. "Poppy Hooper?"

"Yes, sir."

"You picked quite a day to start. I see you found yourself a desk all right."

Poppy gave the smallest hint of a smile. "No problem, sir."

Chapter Three

I t took two to extract venom from a snake. Sister Ada, whose cracked, leathered skin resembled that of the adders in her basket, instructed the girls to split into pairs.

Ember glanced around at the girls sitting cross-legged under the shelter of the wide-branched ash tree in the northwest corner of the camp. All of them were now getting to their feet and making a beeline for their chosen partner. Ember sat and waited, but as always, no one picked her. It still hurt to be alone and last, even after all these times, especially since today it meant partnering with Sister Ada. She was one of the elders who, despite her respect for Charlock, found it hard to hide her deep aversion for Ember, always with a pointed word or stabbing look, crossing the camp to avoid her. Now Ember had to stand next to her at the front of the class, so close she could see the hairs on Sister Ada's chin and study the loose, reddened wattle skin hanging from her neck.

Sister Ada picked up one of the adders, holding it firmly in her hands and pointing it toward the old, glass jar on the weather-worn table. Ember wanted to run from the lesson, but she wasn't sure of whom she was more frightened—the adder or Sister Ada.

"The fangs must pierce the membrane that covers your glass jar. This will induce the snake to bite." In one deft move, Sister Ada had her snake in the required position, fangs inserted through the membrane.

The snake eyed Ember beadily as if blaming her for its predicament. Ember tried to stop shaking.

"Seems this feller doesn't want to cooperate." Sister Ada looked at Ember suspiciously. "I'm sensing deep discomfort."

Ember, who never thought she'd have something in common with a snake, felt a brief pang of sympathy for the creature. It didn't want to be here anymore than she did.

"Ember, rub your finger between its eyes. Snakes detest that. Should make him angry enough to bite."

Ember willed her hand to move, but it wouldn't. She started to feel sick.

"Sister Ada, she's going to vomit again!"

Ember couldn't tell which of the girls had made this announcement, but there was tittering and chattering from the mass of them.

"Ember Hawkweed! You will touch this snake this instant," spat Sister Ada, spraying Ember with spittle.

Ember's arm obeyed and lifted. The index finger of her right hand uncurled and pointed. Her shoulder stretched in its joint . . . her fingertip was less than an inch from the snake's brow. The snake watched, waited, then twitched.

And Ember fled.

"Ember Hawkweed! You pitiful excuse for a witch. Come back here!" shrieked Sister Ada.

But Ember kept on running—out of the camp, past the wooden caravans with their peeling, faded paint, along the vegetable patches, between the boulders that encircled everything, into the bushes, through the great forest, and out into the fresh air of the river bank. There she stopped. She always stopped there—too scared to continue but too mortified to go back.

An hour later, when the shame had receded, Ember was scooping the cold water into her palms and splashing it under her arms. She had goose bumps all over and her teeth were chattering. The bar of soap she always kept in her skirt pocket was a thin, translucent slither. It still smelled of lavender, though, she noticed with a fleeting sense of pride. For while the other girls brewed up vile medicinal stuff every day, she created soap.

It hadn't been easy. The first slabs were flaky, then mushy, before she got the ratio of oil, lye, and water just right. Since then, Ember had tried her hand at perfume too. Where the others took the roses' thorns, she took the petals. She'd dab a few drops of the fragrance on her pillow at night and bury her head in the sweet, floral scent. The camp didn't smell good. There were too many animal carcasses and fish bones. The ancient skills of witchcraft seemed to require the most hideous of ingredients. Ember worried that the rancid smells had coated her hair and become ingrained in her skin. So she slipped away to the river whenever she could and scrubbed at her body until the soap lather foamed upon her, washing the traces of her odorous existence away.

Ember watched as the last bubbles of her soap were carried downstream by the river. She wondered, as she always did, where the river led, and wished for the umpteenth time that she was brave enough to carry on, to follow the river around the bend and onward, away from her life to a world beyond. If only she were less fearful, she would dip her toes in the water, step out into the deep, lie back in the water, and let the currents take her.

But she wasn't brave. Not one bit. She was a coward, a pathetic thing, soft and weak. Ember had been told it enough times, and she had stopped taking offense long ago. It was the truth and there was no point denying it. So many things scared her—nettles, mice, owls, spells, curses, snakes. The list was endless. She wished she was like the others. She had tried to be. But she bruised easily and tears always came to her eyes before she had a chance to blink them back. To fit in with her clan, you had to be strong and coarse like rope—but Ember's curves were plump and soft as pillows. And if you wanted to fit in with the night, your hair had to be dark. Ember's was like a lamp, lighting up her inadequacies for all to see.

Despite all this, Ember secretly cherished her looks. She knew she should want to look more like her cousin, Sorrel, but she just couldn't make herself. She'd grown up in a community of women who paid no attention to their appearance. They scorned such feeble concerns and put their minds to greater pursuits. Ember had tried so hard to follow their example, but she loved to brush her fair hair until it shone; she liked her fingernails clean, not lined with black earth; and she disliked it when the hair grew long on her legs and sprouted from her armpits. Ember appreciated the pretty things in life, like the delicacy of a dragonfly's wings, the first burst of blossom on a fruit tree, and the sheen of the colors on a drake's neck. And she knew instinctively, though she had no way to prove it, that she was pretty too.

By all accounts, it was evident from very early on that Ember was a useless witch. It wasn't just her looks—Ember had been told that those would have been accommodated if she wasn't so squeamish and sentimental. The plain fact of it was Ember showed no predisposition for magic whatsoever. Never had there been a member of the coven so lacking in talent and skill. Over the years, the elders had waited for some gift, just one, to emerge. Most girls in the coven showed magical tendencies before they could even walk. Even the least able had a flair for one aspect or another. Some had "the sight." Others had an aptitude for spells—they only had to concentrate and chant in their heads and something strangely magical would occur. And all had an affinity with nature. Every youngster could predict the weather by simply smelling the air and rubbing the earth between her fingers. Even babies could attract the birds so they'd flutter down and perch on their small hands and let their feathers be stroked. For so many years Ember had tried to master this one basic skill, and yet the birds still flapped away from her in fear, as though she were foe, not friend.

Ember had nothing to offer the coven. Her spell chants would end up as little songs that she would hum to everyone's annoyance. She was allergic to animal fur and would faint at the sight of blood. And she was known to puke around anything reptilian. The only lesson Ember enjoyed was history, as she loved hearing stories about the past and learning of her courageous ancestors—independent women who were often cast out from society and many of whom sacrificed their lives to stay true to themselves and their calling. But then, at night, the nightmares evoked by these legends would be so vivid that she'd wake up screaming and have to take refuge in Charlock's bed. With her head in the crook of her mother's arm and her cheek upon her bosom, she'd listen to the rhythmic beating of Charlock's heart and be soothed back to sleep.

Ember turned from the river and all that it promised and headed home. Her mother would be waiting. She would have heard about the snake incident and guessed where Ember had run to. Charlock knew Ember's habits and tolerated them, covering for her with the others. Since Ember was a baby Charlock had spent most of her time overcompensating for her daughter's deficiencies and protecting her from criticism. Ember felt her mother's love like a quilt, its warmth keeping the chill of scorn from icing her heart.

Her aunt, too, was her defender, and no one dared question Raven. The elders of the clan had chosen Raven to sit at the head of the table, a position never given before to one as young as she. For Ember's aunt was the most powerful witch in the north and not to be crossed unless you wished to suffer the consequences. She produced spells no one had heard of before, let alone believed were possible. Her reputation echoed across lands far and wide, and Ember's cousin, Sorrel, loved to gloat about it, basking in her mother's glory.

Charlock kept a lower profile. She was sister to the great witch but never drew attention to the fact. Perhaps she thought she would suffer in comparison, but Ember didn't think that was the reason. Her mother was simply humble and uninterested in the notoriety of the family name. She was a talented healer, but while her knowledge of plants and cures was extensive, her witchcraft and sorcery were limited. The family prophecy that Raven so zealously promoted, Charlock shied away from. She was happy for Raven and Sorrel to be the chosen ones. And Ember was just as relieved not to be a contender. Either she or Sorrel would be the next queen, or so the prophecy said, and everyone knew it would never be Ember.

As Ember wandered back into camp, she saw her cousin, Sorrel, with some other young witches and quickly ducked behind a washing line to avoid them.

"Too late, Em!" shouted Sorrel.

Ember felt a familiar stomach churning.

"We can see your legs," declared another.

"Heard about you and Sister Ada, Em. You can't hide forever." That was Sorrel's voice again.

Ember considered making a run for it, but Charlock had made her promise to stand up for herself. So Ember stepped out from behind the washing and stood. The girls advanced.

"Doesn't she smell sweet?" Kyra, Sorrel's chief cohort, taunted.

Sorrel bent her head and sniffed. Her nose twitched and then she sneezed. The girls burst out laughing, and Ember couldn't help joining them. As a reprisal, Sorrel gave a lock of Ember's hair a sudden tug.

"Ouch. That hurt!" cried Ember.

"Oh, poor little Em. Shall I make it better?" Sorrel said, imitating Ember's higher-pitched voice.

"No," Ember pleaded, trying to lower her tone. "Please, Sorrel . . ."

Ember tried to stop herself from shaking, but the panic was setting in. Usually Sorrel's offers of help ended in further injury for Ember. She had the scars, pockmarks, and burns to prove it. Sorrel's whole face narrowed to a point as she concentrated on her spell. Ember shut her eyes and shielded her face with her arms. She didn't know why she still had the instinct to do this, as her arms offered no protection. It wasn't a physical blow that Sorrel was conjuring up but something more virulent. Still, Ember braced herself for whatever was coming her way.

"Sorrel Hawkweed. No mischief make for mischief's sake." It was Charlock's voice, loud and clear with authority.

Ember's eyelids flicked open to see Sorrel's face contort with irritation before putting on a fake smile and turning toward Charlock.

"Of course, Aunt. Never our power abuse, never the craft misuse."

Ember glanced at her mother and saw that her head was cocked to one side and her eyebrows raised. She wasn't fooled. But when Charlock turned to look at Ember, her eyes were guarded. "Come along now, Ember," she chided. "Stop dawdling. There's work to be done."

Ember scuttled past the girls, hurrying to her mother's side. Her skirts swept Sorrel's as she passed, and she heard her cousin murmur, "You're an embarrassment," and Ember glanced at her almost apologetically.

Ember always forgave her cousin's bullying, for she knew how hard it was on Sorrel having a relative like her. When they were little, Sorrel had treated her like a pet, and Ember would follow her cousin around, looking up at her adoringly. But then it had dawned on Sorrel how inept Ember was, and she had tried to distance herself from Ember's failures. Now, to save face, she would tease Ember and hurt her before anyone else could, and in that respect, Sorrel was doing her a favor. Ember could take Sorrel's punishments, curbed as they were by family connection, over what the others might inflict instead.

It was hard on her mother too. Charlock never told her so, but Ember could feel it. The only member of Ember's family who didn't make her feel like a burden was Raven. She seemed to accept Ember for who she was—she had neither expectation, nor disappointment. Her mother had plenty of both; she just kept them stored inside.

As they walked back to the caravan, Charlock stayed silent. Ember could tell she was too enraged to talk and knew her anger wasn't just directed at Sorrel and the others but at her also. She had let her mother down once again. Later, to try to make amends, Ember would cook the supper with the vegetables she'd dug from their patch and brew some tea with the mint she'd gathered, sweetening it with the last of the honeycomb just as she knew her mother liked it. It was far from magic and took no special skill or power, but it was the best that Ember could do.

CHAPTER FOUR

There was a bee buzzing in her brain. At least that's what if felt like. It happened from time to time, unexpectedly and without warning, like Poppy's frequency to the world shifted and all she could hear was static. This time was worse than ever, though. Poppy tried lying down and shutting her eyes, but that just raised the volume. Her room, this house, this town—all of them felt stifling. Her father was out. Poppy didn't know where, only that it was the weekend and she was alone and that the empty house wasn't empty enough. She needed to move, to breathe.

She took the quickest route out of town. She walked so fast and with such focus that she didn't notice how the buildings were thinning out and how the pavement had become a verge, grassy and nettled. She climbed a gate into a field. Up the hillside she strode, toward the forest that rose like a giant fortress guarding whatever hid within. According to her father's map, the ocean lay beyond these trees that stretched high and wide for miles and miles, an uninhabitable and inhospitable expanse of land that people left well alone.

As she traveled, Poppy was tuning in and out of various sounds as if trying and failing to receive a message. All of a sudden the noise got so sharp—like nails on a blackboard—that Poppy put her hands to her ears, forgetting the sound was within not without. She crouched to the ground, making herself small as though that might minimize the pain. Rocking back and forth on her heels, Poppy made her ears search for other, better sounds. The call of the birds in the sky; the wind sweeping through the grasses, jangling the buckles on her boots; the distant lowing of the cows—as this medley came to the fore, the buzzing became a background track, and Poppy could once more raise her head and open her eyes.

Her vision was blurred at first, so she had to squint to see the animal as it approached her. Poppy rubbed her eyes in dizzy disbelief, but forward it came, and then Poppy realized it was real—a real hare: long legs, thin face, twitching nose and whiskers. The hare tipped its head to one side quizzically. Then it nodded in the direction of the forest. It took a few steps and looked back at Poppy, waiting. Poppy turned toward the town, as if to check it was still there, gray as ashes in the glossy green. The hare bounded forward in a sudden leap to recapture Poppy's attention. Again it stopped and seemed to beckon her. Poppy stumbled to her feet and felt her head spin. The hare twitched impatiently.

"Okay, okay," Poppy grumbled. "I'm coming."

She followed the hare all the way to a steep dip in the forest floor. It wasn't far into the woodland, but the dell appeared unexpectedly. Even more surprisingly, this tiny valley was not just full of trees but, in amongst them, old furniture and rusting household machinery lay cluttered and upended. Even if her head weren't so muddled, Poppy knew this image would still look surreal.

The hare scampered down the sheer slope, then looked up at her.

"Really?" questioned Poppy. "This is where you bring me?"

Gingerly she picked her way down the hill. Her head was still hurting from the noise and now her legs were aching too. When she reached the valley floor, Poppy slumped down and lay back weakly against an old, tatty sofa.

"Is this it?" she slurred, closing her eyes. "Is this all?"

Ember thought it was one of the others at first and felt a rare surge of outrage. The dell was her place. Her secret. Then she saw the girl's hair was dark but short, far too short for her to be one of the coven. There was a hare at her feet, watching her. Ember took a step, and the hare sped away in a flash. The girl turned and looked at her. Then her eyes searched for the hare but it had gone.

"Sorry. Were you trapping it?" Ember asked shyly.

The girl didn't say anything for a moment. "Trapping it for what?"

Ember was confused. "For your supper."

The girl burst into laughter, then stopped. "You're serious," she said in wonder.

Ember just stared at her. "You're a chaff," she thought out loud.

"What?" the girl queried.

Ember knew she should turn and walk away. It was what she had been taught since infancy. The childhood rhyme sang in her head:

Heed the berries of the holly and yew,
The ivy and the nightshade too.
Beware the false widow spider's bite,
But most of all a chaff in sight.
Do not mingle, do not mix,
For trouble bring that none can fix.

Yet even as the words played out, Ember's curiosity grew stronger. The girl must come from where the river led, from where she herself had always yearned to go. So Ember didn't walk away, but stood there taking in every detail of the girl's appearance.

"Are you all right?" the girl asked, and Ember caught the concern in her voice and it made her more daring.

"Who took your hair?" she questioned. She had heard of spells that made the locks fall from your scalp and always feared them. As the girl's face scrunched in confusion, Ember felt a quiver of doubt. "You are a doe, aren't you? Not a stag?"

There was a long pause in which the girl rolled her head around her neck in a circle and then gave it a shake, as though rattling her brain. Her eyes widened and she blinked and smiled. "The noise," she said. "It's gone." Then her smile broadened further, using up her cheeks, taking over all of her acorn face. "It's gone!" she gasped with delight, though only a second later her lips fell into a frown. "I'm not asleep, am I? This isn't just some crazy dream I'm having?"

"Pinch yourself," suggested Ember. "That's what my mother would say."

The girl pulled back her sleeve and pinched her arm so hard

that it left a red mark on her skin. "Well, I think I'm awake," she said dryly.

"What's that on your nails?" spotted Ember.

The girl put a finger to her lip. "Don't spoil it. Not yet," she hushed.

"What?" Ember whispered.

"The silence. Can you hear it?"

They both sat there motionless for a few moments. The girl's thoughts flickered in her eyes until finally she opened her mouth to speak. "Is it this place? That made the noise stop?"

Ember wasn't sure of her meaning so she searched for a truth with which to answer. "I come here for the quiet too."

The girl seemed satisfied with this as she began to study Ember closely, as if reappraising what she saw. Then she held out her hands, palms down, fingers stretched to show the chipped shock of blue on the tips. "The nail polish? Is that what you mean?" she said.

Ember nodded. "The color. How'd you conjure that?"

The girl rummaged in a big, leather bag and pulled out a little glass jar of the same liquid blue. She tossed it over to Ember. Ember reached for it in surprise but dropped it and had to stoop to pick it up. She felt the cool glass in her hand and stared at it before unscrewing the bottle and pulling out a little brush.

"You paint it on," the girl explained.

Ember tried to figure this out and, becoming impatient, the girl gestured for her to come over. Tentatively Ember began to step across the pieces that filled the dell. She didn't know what half of this stuff was, but she loved it here among these treasures, all clues of another land.

The girl patted the ground next to her and Ember sat down. "Give me your hand."

Ember held it out nervously and the girl took it and placed it on her knee. Then she took the little brush and did what she had said—she painted each nail until they shone with color. Ember stared down at her hand like it didn't belong to her, lying there so detached on a stranger's leg. She could feel the girl's arm touching hers and she could hear her soft, concentrated breathing. The girl was a chaff, but Ember didn't care. Sitting next to her like this seemed a consolation for all the hours she had spent sitting alone. Friendship felt even better than Ember had imagined. It was as many hued as a sunrise, turning black to brilliance, and full of promise of a warmth and light to come.

When the girl finished, Ember held her fingers up in wonder, moving them in a little dance.

"Careful. You don't want them to smudge."

Ember froze, then lowered her hands to her lap. The girl positioned her hands to match. "See . . . twins."

Ember felt a glow inside her and it spread to her cheeks and she blushed. The girl looked at her inquisitively. "Where are you from, anyway?"

Ember looked away, not knowing how to answer and feeling self-conscious about her long skirt and battered boots. She hoped she didn't smell.

"Yonder," she replied. She had broken one rule by conversing with the girl, but the clan was sworn never to reveal anything of themselves or their camp. This was sacred.

The girl's eyes widened again. "Yonder? . . . What are you like?"

Ember wasn't sure how to respond to this, but then the girl asked a simpler question and she found herself answering even though she shouldn't.

"What's your name?"

"Ember."

"I'm Poppy."

Any guilt Ember felt at disclosing her name instantly evaporated. The chaff was called after a summer flower, bright and red and welcoming. And the witches used its extracts in their healing, sparingly but to great effect. Somehow this name felt like a sign that all was well. The girl, Poppy, placed the brush back into the pot and screwed the lid back on, then she handed it to Ember. Ember glanced at her, not daring to take it.

"Go on. I've got more at home."

Ember grinned like her cheeks would split. "Really?!"

Poppy nodded. "So, Ember from yonder. What are you doing down here?"

"Escaping."

Poppy looked up quickly, and in her eyes Ember saw something unusual, something like understanding.

"Well, Ember," she said. "That's what I'd call a happy coincidence."

It was dusk before the girls parted. They had spent all afternoon there in the dell among the homeless objects. Poppy had explained to Ember what each of them was. Some of them sounded more magical than anything that the coven created. A television for watching stories brought to life; a sofa for sitting on when you watched television; a vacuum cleaner for sucking up the dust; a washing machine; a toasted sandwich maker; CDs—tons of them, holding music on their shiny dials; a microwave for cooking food in seconds.

Ember was amazed. These miracle inventions would hardly fit in her and Charlock's tiny caravan. The most their single room had space for was their two small beds, a chair, the chest with their clothes and bedding, and their kitchen shelves. The meals they ate were cooked in the wood-fired oven outside or on spits over fire pits dug into the earth. And the food was eaten fresh or pickled, boiled and jarred. As Ember traced her fingers over an old lawn-mower, she dreamed about a world of houses full of all these marvelous contraptions and gardens with neat, short grass called lawns.

Poppy had a question now. "Are you in some kind of religious cult?" Ember turned to look at Poppy. "I won't tell anyone."

"I don't know what that is."

"Are you being held against your will?"

Ember pondered this. "No. Are you?"

Poppy gave a harsh laugh. "No. Though it feels like that sometimes." She looked down at the books poking out of her bag. "Do you go to school?" she asked Ember.

"Kind of. We're taught by our mothers and sisters."

"Oh, I get it. You're homeschooled. No wonder you're weird."

"Can I see?" Ember pointed at the books, and Poppy nodded.

Ember took one of the books and opened it up. In it were lots of numbers in rows and columns. She squinted at them but they made little sense. Like the symbols in her own books, they were a foreign language to her. She reached into Poppy's bag for another.

This one had writing. She scanned it at first, then started reading out loud.

Art thou pale for weariness
Of climbing heaven, and gazing on the earth,
Wandering companionless
Among the stars that have a different birth,
And ever-changing, like a joyless eye . . .

Poppy finished the rest for her, knowing the words by heart. "*That finds no object worth its constancy?*"

"Is it a spell?" asked Ember.

Poppy looked at her. "You're even stranger than me, you know that?"

And Ember smiled.

Later Poppy gave her some chocolate. It was so sweet that it clogged in Ember's throat and she had to gulp down water to flush it away. In return she shared the dried fruit and seeds she always kept in her pockets. As Poppy nibbled on the seeds, Ember looked around the dell and wondered why anyone would want to escape a home that was filled with all these incredible, life-enhancing things. Then it occurred to her that she could ask, and she said, "What is it you're trying to escape?"

Poppy looked surprised but answered with a shrug, "Just my life. My family. I don't know. Myself!" Ember leaned her shoulder against Poppy's in recognition. Poppy didn't shift but let her rest there. "What about you?"

"It's hard feeling like a failure all the time. So I come here. Just to have some respite for a while."

"And then you go back?"

"Where else would I go?"

"I'm glad I met you, Ember from yonder."

"Me too."

Before she reached the camp, Ember stopped to remove the blue from her nails. It was stuck there. She scratched and gnawed but it wouldn't come off. So she kept her fingers tucked into her palms, or behind her back, or deep in her pockets so no one would see. But Raven had eyes in the back of her head.

"Ember Hawkweed!" Her aunt's voice was low but had a force to it that made Ember stop in her tracks. She looked around and saw no one. Then, suddenly, her aunt was there before her. "What are you carrying, niece?"

Ember gulped. "Nothing," she replied, praying that the truth of this might spare her any further investigation.

Ember wasn't sure whether it was in disappointment or irritation, but Raven slowly shook her head. "Come hither."

Ember took two steps forward so that their feet almost met. Then Raven took Ember's clenched fist and uncurled it, holding the fingernails right up to her face as she peered at them.

"It's paint," explained Ember in a small voice.

"I know what it is, kitten."

Ember felt a chill down her back. "I found it . . . in the forest," she said hurriedly. Under Raven's scrutiny, she felt her cheeks blush at the fib she had told.

"An interesting shade," Raven added. She never smiled, but Ember could tell from her eyes she was joking. Ember felt a rush of relief. Her aunt wasn't angry after all. As if to confirm this, Raven asked, "Do you want to leave it on or shall I vanish it for you?"

Ember shifted from one foot to the other in indecision.

"One more night?" Raven conspired.

"Oh, thank you, Aunt," Ember gasped.

"It'll be our little secret," Raven whispered, and Ember nodded gladly.

When she woke the next morning, Ember's nails were clean. The paint had gone, and even the bottle was nowhere to be found.

CHAPTER FIVE

That evening Poppy and her father sat eating Vietnamese food out of cartons. They ordered takeout a lot. Whenever they moved, Poppy would collect the flyers that came in the mail, and her father would order from each one until they narrowed them down to their favorite few. Poppy had eaten a lot of dodgy curries, stodgy pizzas, and gloopy stir-fries in her time. Tonight was a soupy noodle dish that slipped down your throat before you had a chance to bite at it. Sauce trickled down her father's chin as he slurped the noodles into his mouth. Poppy giggled. The sound surprised her as much as it did her father. He instantly glanced up at her.

"What?" Poppy challenged.

Her dad shrugged and, as he did so, a noodle that had been resting on his shirt fell into his lap.

Poppy giggled again.

Her father tried to wipe it off but it clung to his trousers. "God!"

Poppy laughed, actually laughed out loud. She laughed so hard that her mouthful of noodles came tumbling from her lips.

Her father looked up at her in astonishment. "Poppy! That's revolting!" But that just made Poppy laugh some more. He shook his head and smiled. "Haven't I taught you any manners?"

"No!" Tears were falling from her eyes, she was laughing so hard.

Poppy went into the kitchen and got her father a dish towel. He watched her warily but took it from her with a thank you and started wiping gingerly at the stubborn noodle.

"I can wash them if you want."

Her father looked surprised. "I'll have to order from"—he picked up the menu and read—"Little Saigon again."

Poppy wrinkled her nose.

"No, not a keeper?"

"Throw it away."

Her dad crumpled the paper into a ball and tossed it toward the wastepaper basket. It landed right inside. "Yes!" Her dad pumped his arm in victory, then looked at Poppy with a grin. "How's the new school?"

"Okay, I guess."

"Okay?! Really?!" he said, raising an eyebrow. "Don't tell me you made a friend?"

"I did, actually," she replied. "Don't look so surprised. I am capable of it."

"I'm not surprised, just impressed. I know you didn't want to move all this way."

Poppy felt herself blush and she looked away. Sensing her discomfort, her dad moved the conversation on.

"What's this school like?"

He hadn't asked her that in years.

"Oh, you know. It's school." Her dad seemed disappointed, and Poppy sensed their chat would be over pretty quickly unless she said something. "How's the new job?"

"Fine."

"You don't sound too sure."

Her dad half-smiled. "It's a job."

And there it was. A moment of connection that came and went but, for Poppy, that made two in one day. Later, as she lay curled up in her bed with Minx, she realized she had walked out into the hills alone but had returned having made a friend. Her first. Maybe it was the headache or the hare that made her act so out of character, but she had achieved a proper conversation with another girl. It had been so easy with Ember, as though she were not human but, like the hare, another wild creature from the woods. There had been no glint of criticism in Ember's eyes, no hint of artifice or hostility in her voice, and now Poppy found herself wondering, if she went back to the dell tomorrow, whether Ember might appear again. Then immediately she felt silly for thinking such a thing and determined not to go.

Sorrel tripped up the steps and banged her ankle on the door-frame as her mother pulled her inside. She knew well not to complain. Raven's eyes were burning, fire within the black. Her lips were twitching, chanting soundless words. She started pacing back and forth, lost in frantic thought. Only Sorrel got to see such scenes of her mother's private self. In front of the coven Raven maintained constant calm and control.

"The real magic is to make it look effortless," she always told Sorrel when it was just the two of them, after lessons and away from the other girls.

"Mother?" Sorrel prompted, and Raven snapped her neck around so she faced her. "You wanted to talk with me?"

Raven's eyes focused and the fire dimmed. "Follow your cousin."

Sorrel groaned inwardly but her mother heard it; nothing escaped Raven.

"I mean it. I want your eyes on her. Something doesn't bode well."

"It's Ember. Nothing ever bodes well," replied Sorrel.

"She's happy. Listen to her step—it's lighter. Look at her eyes—they're brighter. Her heart is beating faster. She's straighter, taller. Use your senses, Sorrel. All of them."

Sorrel nodded. Her mother was always right. "Why is she so happy?"

"That's what you must find out. See if she ventures into the town. Check she isn't talking to any chaffs. Who knows what the simpleton might say."

Sorrel nodded, though she could scarcely believe her timid cousin capable of such rebellion. Every decade or so there was a witch who would be seduced by the outside world. They would disappear into the dead of night, covering their tracks to avoid all detection. Then the inevitable betrayal would begin. They'd confess their past and admit to witchcraft, telling of the coven out in the forest, forsaking all they had once sworn to protect. Usually they'd leave for love . . . or so they said. But then they'd come back weeping and begging to come home.

It never worked—a witch and a chaff. However learned or open-minded, the people of the outside world lived smaller lives. They saw only what was visible and believed only what could be proven or what was preached. They were missing a sense and were so handicapped without it that the witches almost pitied them. For a witch would rather lose their sight or hearing than the sixth and most precious of senses.

The males were the worst. For centuries they had owned their womenfolk as though they were mere belongings, not beings like them with an independent mind and voice and a right to determine their own lives. Sorrel's ancestors had sought another way to live, but they had been persecuted for it. Men rode across the land, taking bits of idle gossip and jealous sniping and using it to put any woman they feared on trial, relishing their screams as they burned at the stake, the flesh melting from their bones. In the years after, many of these women had gathered, forming sisterhoods and covens, living separate from the rest of society and practicing their craft in hidden safety. They swore never to forget those who had been slaughtered so mercilessly. Men, they decided, were to be shunned. They needed them for daughters, but nothing more. Just one of their kind would weaken the bonds of loyalty and trust between the witches. It had been proved time and time again. Even Sorrel, in her short life, had heard one such renegade witch weeping over her broken heart, regretting her betrayal and grieving for the loss of her clan. To watch her helpless, heaving sorrow had been horrifying, and Sorrel had hidden behind her mother's skirts until Raven had pulled her away and left her. For Raven had to work through the night to mop up the damage, cleaning the chaffs' minds of what they'd heard, wiping away all evidence of this witch's existence.

Sorrel tried to imagine Ember in such a state. The more she strived to picture it, the more unlikely it seemed. But Raven had charged Sorrel with a task and she must complete it. Besides, Sorrel liked having a mission. It made her feel important. She liked having a chance to prove her worth. It quieted the nagging voice in her head that told her she wasn't good enough, not to be queen anyway.

What Raven didn't tell Sorrel was that the owl from the western oak had circled three times around the camp and then settled on the roof of Charlock's caravan. A cloud shaped like a wolf had passed the moon, and the soot from the fire had formed seven peaks before a northeast wind had swept them away. All these omens would have incited too many questions from her daughter, and she didn't want Sorrel knowing too much. Raven longed to investigate herself, but her sister was so attentive to Ember, so sensitive to her frailties, that Raven's presence or any spell she cast might easily arouse Charlock's suspicions. Sorrel, however, was often in Ember's vicinity and Charlock was used to her meddling. Raven must, for now, be prudent and let Sorrel do the work.

That night Raven dreamt that the great yew tree yanked itself from the ground and walked with earthy, fibrous limbs to warn that her life would be uprooted too. In Raven's nightmare, she saw all her buried secrets come trailing out like worms and centipedes, exposed in all their ugliness by the light of the sun, defenseless against the pecking beaks of hungry birds.

The next morning she found the great yew toppled, its ancient branches crushed. Its needles were scattered far around, and its trunk that had survived a thousand years was now lying prone like a giant corpse, its roots like entrails spilling out and dangling helplessly into the gaping, empty grave that once had been its home. The women and girls of the coven were gathering around and falling to their knees in grief at such a dreadful sight. They had thought this tree would outlive them all, as it had done for countless generations before them. They stroked its bark and gathered its needles, the ululating song of the eldest of the sisters a harrowing funereal dirge.

Later the whisperings began. It was their enemy of old again, the witches of the East.

"They wouldn't dare," claimed one sister.

Another suspected the Southerners. She had heard they'd suffered a rot that attacked the heart of their trees and killed whole thickets in days. Perhaps they'd sent it here. Two of them went and inspected the center of the yew but reported back that it was healthy.

"It is an omen. An omen of disaster and ruin," the blind one said.

The others hushed. They all looked to Raven. She held a piece of bark in one hand and the needles in the other and appeared to be divining a truth of great significance. Her eyes shut and her arms stretched out in supplication. The sisters waited silently. Then Raven spoke.

"It is the Eastern mountain clan. They struck the great tree to make us fear such an omen. For our future is golden. We have the next queen among us. And they mean to tarnish that."

Sharp as a sword were the words, steely as truth. It was, Raven told herself, the most likely conclusion.

"We must have retribution," a younger sister cried.

The voices rose around Raven and the talk turned to plots and schemes of reprisal against their bitter rivals. The Eastern sisters had fought with the Northern since long before the Hawkweed prophecy was first foretold, but the battles had escalated in more recent times. Three hundred and three years hence, the prophecy claimed. The day was drawing ever closer, and the enmity of other witches had heightened as they readied their own challengers to the throne.

Since Sorrel was a baby Raven had cloaked her daughter in protection. Much of her energy went into creating a barrier around Sorrel that magic couldn't penetrate. It took such focus and discipline that Raven had partitioned a corner of her mind to deal only with this. Such was the connection with Sorrel that Raven could sense and feel potential danger to her. This invisible shield made Sorrel seem and feel far stronger than she actually was while making Raven more tired and older than her actual years. The effort was so vast and relentless that it had sapped Raven's youth, drying and wrinkling her skin, hollowing her cheeks and stiffening her joints. But it had to be done. For even though there were those who scoffed and scorned at the prophecy, Raven knew that there were plenty who would kill to gain the throne for themselves.

Raven was not alone in noticing the change in Ember. Charlock had heard Ember singing in her bed, her clear, high voice trilling like a bird. Normally Charlock would hush her in case the sisters complained, but that night Ember had sounded so contented that she let her continue uninterrupted. *Let her be happy today, for there is plenty of sorrow on the way*, thought Charlock. Later, through the darkness, Ember asked her mother how far she had ever traveled beyond the camp.

"Not far," Charlock answered.

"Further than the blackberry bushes at the edge of the meadow?"

"Yes."

"Further than the bluebell wood?"

"Yes."

"Further than the top of the waterfall?"

"No," Charlock lied as she always did. Charlock had become so good at lying that it was now easier than telling the truth.

"Did you ever want to?"

"Yes."

"Might you go further one day?"

"No."

"Why not?"

"Because it is not by steps that I measure the journey of my life." Charlock heard Ember's sigh. "Might *you* go one day?" Charlock asked her daughter.

"No, I don't think so." Ember was not a good liar.

"Why not?"

"What if I couldn't come back?"

Charlock felt a pang in her heart for this sweet, fragile song-bird with her clipped wings who longed to take to the skies.

"Tell me about you and Raven when you were young," Ember asked pleadingly.

Charlock laughed. "Again?!"

"Again!"

Ember's favorite stories were those of Charlock and Raven and their childhood days before Raven had tied herself to her books and was still eager to play and cause mischief. Charlock told of the time when she and Raven rode the hog like a horse, how it charged through the camp, trampling everything in its path, and how they had laughed, even when they had been scolded by all the elders. As she spoke, Charlock remembered what life was like before they knew of the prophecy. The naiveté of it felt weightless as a dandelion seed spinning in the air. Charlock's spirits lifted for a moment as she recalled their lost innocence, and then it struck her what a vast shadow the prophecy had cast over them, dimming their light, lowering the temperature of their lives.

Ember's breath had steadied, and Charlock knew she was asleep. As she studied her child's soft features, she marveled at Ember's grip on hopefulness. It could not be prised from her. No matter the mockery or contempt, Ember had a purity that none of the rest of them could ever find within themselves. She was an oyster with a pearl. All her life, Ember had been criticized for being different, but maybe, thought Charlock, maybe it was because she was better.

CHAPTER SIX

The next morning Poppy opened her curtains and her room remained dark. The sky was not to be seen that day. It was as though a white sheet had shrouded it, leaving the world colorless and drab. Her father had left for work already. The dregs of his coffee slumped in a mug on the counter; a few soggy cornflakes sat seeping in a bowl. Beside them was a note informing Poppy that he'd be home late. Only a few perfunctory words, no trace of the moment they had shared last night. Poppy mentally kicked herself for feeling let down. The flicker of hope that had been lit yesterday in the dell and then fanned by the laughter with her dad was suddenly snuffed out. *So much for a new start*, she thought, and she left the dirty breakfast things on the counter to sour.

❦

"Double, double toil and trouble . . ." Poppy hated reading out loud to the class. She had kept her hand down while plenty of others had shot up, but Mrs. Walters had chosen her anyway.

"Speak up!" Mrs. Walters was now demanding in a shrill voice that demonstrated her desired volume.

"Fire burn, and cauldron bubble . . ." Poppy raised her voice, and the words seemed to echo around the classroom.

"Like a witch, Poppy. Not a moody teenager."

The class broke into laughter. Poppy's eyes flashed and she quickly looked back down at the text. She took a deep breath to try to slow the blood gushing through her veins. Only two more lines to go.

"Cool it with a baboon's blood, then the charm is firm and good." She finished with a flourish, relieved it was over.

"Okay. Talk to me about the weird sisters, Poppy. Enlighten us with your analysis."

Poppy's relief vanished. Mrs. Walters smirked at her, enjoying Poppy's discomfort.

"Come on. You just read it out . . . you must have understood something."

Poppy shrugged. She stared at Mrs. Walters, perched on the table so condescendingly. There was a smudge of lipstick on her teeth, noted Poppy, and the shop label was still stuck on the bottom of her shoe.

Mrs. Walters rolled her eyes at the class in an exaggerated expression of exasperation. "No? . . . Nothing? . . . Nothing at all?" The teacher gestured to the heavens despairingly, an actress on her classroom stage.

Poppy took a breath, then raised her eyes to Mrs. Walters and stared at her intently. "I think the witches see Macbeth," she said angrily. "He's all smug and superior, looking down on them and

thinking they're just ugly, old hags and they're glad they're messing with him, showing him how he and his Mrs. Macbeth are
more ugly and evil than they'll ever be . . . and maybe that's why
they hang out on the moor and not in the town or up in the castle with the rest of the deluded bunch of hypocrites who think
they're so civilized."

There was silence, then the snickering started.

Mrs. Walters uncrossed her legs with a flick of her toes and
sprang up from her desk. "I'm not entirely sure that's what Shake-
speare had in mind, Poppy, but colorfully put. Jamie, why don't
you continue—go down to where Macbeth enters?"

Jamie started stammering and stuttering his way through the
speech, and as she listened, it dawned on Poppy that nothing had
gone wrong. No one was hurt, nothing was broken. She hadn't
been ordered out of the classroom or sent to the principal's office.
She had simply said what she thought. Perhaps it was a new start
after all.

Poppy took the long way back that evening. She was in no rush
to reach home. She wandered past the uninspiring shops and fast
food places in what was fancifully known as the town center—a
small bit of street, closed to cars, where the stores kept their doors
open, heat and music wafting out, trying to tempt people in from
the cold, damp air. Groups of kids gathered, talking loudly, utterly
unaware of anyone around them. Girls bitching, their strident
voices interrupting and overlapping so no sentence was finished

before another started. Boys pushing and pulling one another, exploding into laughter, chasing one another down the street. Couples clinging to each other, lips locked, like they were one four-legged, two-faced being. At least that's how they appeared to Poppy as she glanced at them curiously, trying to imagine herself as one of them, wanting to but finding it inconceivable.

She passed them unnoticed, hidden by her hat, lost inside the baggy folds of her coat. Then she stopped suddenly outside a pharmacy as the nail polish on display in the window caught her eye, a rainbow of glistening colors. She walked inside the store, and when she came out it was raining hard, the groups had dispersed, and people weren't lingering anymore; they were rushing past, underneath umbrellas. Poppy tucked the small shopping bag into the wide pocket of her coat. She didn't want it to get wet. Inside was a manicure set, the first she'd ever bought. Not for herself—her nails were bitten to the flesh—but for Ember. *Just in case*, she told herself. Just in case she ever saw her again.

Rain from the awning above Poppy's head overflowed and spilled onto her hat with a plop. The sound made her smile.

CHAPTER SEVEN

Leo was sheltering in a doorway, cursing the weather. He had stuffed his bag between his legs, trying to shield it from the rain, and was wondering where he was going to sleep that night when a bike zipped past on the pavement and its wheel sprayed a dirty puddle over him. As he looked up angrily, a girl on the pavement caught his eye.

She was alone but she was smiling. The smile laid her bare, stripping her from all the usual disguises people wear to cover up how they really feel. And she was standing still. If she had been frowning like everyone else, or hurrying on her way like everyone else, or under an umbrella like everyone else, Leo wouldn't have paid any attention. Instead, he noticed her and he saw not just her smile but the shape of her lips, the line of her jaw, the length of her neck.

Then the girl stepped out from under the edge of the awning, took off her hat, and raised her head to the sky. The cool rain hit her face, gliding over her skin, pooling in her collarbones, and trickling down beneath her coat, under her clothes.

Leo became conscious of how huddled he was on the doorstep, hiding from the elements while she embraced them. He bent his head, contrite somehow, and when he looked again, she was walking away. Her hat was pulled down low on her head and her big coat flowed behind her so that Leo had to search for a last sight of the girl within. Then he saw them, her fingertips, just visible beneath the long sleeves, the tiniest glimpse revealed before the girl was gone.

He had been living on the streets for nearly a year now. It felt like forever, though. Occasionally he'd see a newbie roaming around the train station, with a cheek bruised and swollen or a gash on his head. As he witnessed them being kicked away from the usual hangouts, not knowing where to curl up for the night or which shops gave away the "past their sell-by date" food, he'd remember what he had been like when he first ran away. Defiant by day, terrified by night. Now he knew to keep his head down. He'd marked out his small piece of turf, and he'd found out who was all right and which crazies to steer well clear of. Life was all about survival, day to day, hour to hour sometimes.

When Leo felt sorry for himself, he often thought about the kids who had trod the same piece of land all those centuries before him—-working in the fields, or down in the pits, or in the mills, or homeless just like him. Perhaps things weren't that different after all. Food, water, warmth—still the essentials, and still hard to come by for someone like him, someone without a home or a family or anyone who gave a damn.

Yet among the alkies and the druggies, the psychos and the pervs, there was kindness to be found too. Not just a favor or a bit of sympathy, but real, big gestures that humbled him. The woman at the gym—Kim—who let him sneak inside to take a shower after closing time. The librarian who let him spend hours in the warmth of the library, reading books, and told him when the new ones came in. The antiques guy who, without asking questions, found odd jobs for him to do and paid him in hot meals and spare change so that Leo left with his stomach full and his pockets clinking. The old-timer who had fought off a group of boys who had been about to attack him in the middle of the night. His friend from school, who never told a soul where Leo was, despite a grilling from the teachers. So life was tough, but it wasn't all bad.

When you're on the street, you hone your instincts. You learn to pay attention. You see how arguments erupt, how romance sparks, how betrayal wounds and love heals. You see the same people day after day, stepping from the bus to the road, stepping over the cracks in the pavement, stepping from the highs to the lows of their existence and back again. Leo had seen tears, tantrums, brawls. He'd seen a proposal under last year's Christmas tree in the shopping center, the ring glinting under the fairy lights. He'd seen a heart attack on a pedestrian crossing, an elderly lady giving mouth-to-mouth to an elderly man. He'd seen a teenage girl go into labor outside the supermarket, clutching hold of a shopping cart for support. And he'd seen a mother lose sight of her child, screaming as she ran up and down the road until she found him, hitting the toddler over the head before clutching him tightly to her.

Sometimes it was far more subtle, no obvious drama. Even then, if you observed carefully, you could witness life turning on a single moment. So Leo recognized it when such a moment happened to him.

He had seen a girl smiling in the rain and he had felt himself change direction. Call it luck, or serendipity, or fate, but Leo knew that he would see this girl again and that their paths would cross and twist and entwine until they were hand in hand, journeying together. He knew this without a doubt. It was simply a matter of time.

CHAPTER EIGHT

Ember didn't come to the dell that next day, nor for the next few days after that.

Poppy kept returning, though. She never meant to, but she liked the walk—her legs crossing the grassy slopes, treading through the bracken, past the russet trees, avoiding the prickle of the thistles. And she liked it in the dell. She found peace in the soft sounds of the countryside and took comfort in the warm glow of the sun as it slouched into the hills. Each time she meant to leave the gift somewhere Ember might find it and save herself another trip. But as the sun slid from sight and the light faded, Poppy's troubles seemed to fade with it, and she didn't leave the gift in case it got tossed by the wind or soaked by the rain. Instead, she came back again, day after day after day, finding solace there and hoping Ember might come to find some too.

The paper bag in Poppy's pocket that held the present had crumpled and ripped. Then, on the Saturday morning when the day was starting, Poppy carried on past the dell, into the woods. She went where her feet took her. She had no idea where she was going or how she'd get back, but this didn't seem to concern her. She felt strangely at home in the speckled light, dwarfed by the tall trees that swayed and rustled, bending their branches in greeting. The ground was supple under her feet, cushioning her tread. She pushed through nettles, past brambles; she climbed over tree trunks, her hands reaching to stroke leaves overhead as twigs snapped underfoot. She felt a part of life here in a way that she never had in any town or city. Squirrels stopped their climbing and looked at her with interest. Small birds flew past as if on reconnaissance, chirping the news of her arrival. Poppy felt like they were welcoming her into their home.

She saw Ember by the stream, the water singing as it sashayed over stones.

"Ember?" she called.

Ember looked around, startled. Then she beamed. "I was hoping you'd find me."

"You weren't at the dell."

Ember looked apologetic. "My mother told me I must stay away from there." Poppy raised her eyebrows and Ember quickly added, "I wanted to come, though." She reached down into a leather satchel by her feet. "I've been carrying this in hope that I might see you." She pulled out an old, cloth-bound book. "I wanted to bring you something to look at. To thank you. You showed me your book of learning, so . . . " Ember trailed off nervously, then held the book out to Poppy, shutting her eyes as if in fear as she did so.

"Are you sure?" Poppy asked.

Ember opened her eyes and nodded. "I want to."

Poppy took the book and opened it carefully. She flicked through the first few pages. There were dried flowers stuck to the paper, labeled and detailed. Later on she found drawings of reptiles and mushrooms and berries.

"You mustn't tell anyone I showed you, though. Not ever," Ember added.

Poppy quickly glanced up and saw the gravity on Ember's face. "I promise. I brought you something too." Her hand felt in her pocket and she pulled out the crushed bag. "Sorry."

Ember took the bag eagerly and looked inside. She pulled out the manicure set and gasped. "Oh . . . thank you . . . thank you! This is the best gift I've ever received."

A thought suddenly struck Poppy. "Do you know what it is?" she asked.

"No," admitted Ember with a big grin on her face. "But no matter. I love it."

"It's for your nails. If you want to shape them and buff them and paint them." Poppy shrugged. "If you like that kind of thing." Ember's eyes widened with amazement. "Don't get too excited. It's only a manicure set."

A sudden look of worry crossed Ember's face. "The paint!" she despaired. "How will I get it off?!"

Ember sat against the rocks, beautifying her nails with such artistry and attention, it was as though she were creating a masterpiece. She had been instantly placated by the knowledge that the set contained a liquid, like an antidote, to remove the polish, and so had set to work immediately. Meanwhile Poppy had spread her coat wide, laid down, and begun to read.

Ember's school book was an epiphany. Its curious mix of biology, astrology, chemistry, and poetry had Poppy captivated. She marveled at the intricate drawings of a bird's wing, a frog's leg, a newt's tongue; the study of the night sky's constellations; the rhythm and vocabulary of old recipes and sayings. She was enthralled by it like she had never been by any book before. It felt foreign yet familiar, though Poppy couldn't fathom how. She just let her brain soak in the facts and the diagrams, memorizing them so she would never forget.

"You're so lucky," she murmured to Ember, who was appraising her handiwork.

"I wish I were you," whispered Ember to Poppy, as she realized it was time to head home.

They made a pact to try to meet every afternoon. As soon as Poppy would leave school, she'd jump on the bus heading out of town, get off at the stop at the foot of the hill, and then start her climb toward the dell. With her she'd bring gifts of shampoo and conditioner, toothpaste and a toothbrush, and other such tiny luxuries. She'd arrive with her bag stuffed full with books, newspapers, and magazines, and Ember would flick through all of them, her eyes darting over the words and the pictures of presidents and foreign countries, of vast cities and oceans, of architecture and sports. She devoured it all like it was food and she hadn't eaten in weeks. She said the names of the places out loud, committing them to memory—Rome, Tokyo, Sydney, and, her favorite, Paris. Eiffel Tower, the Louvre, Notre Dame—these she whispered as if casting a wish.

Ember scrutinized the faces on those pages as though they were an alien species, especially the models and celebrities whose loveliness she studied every detail of. Poppy had to stop herself from being scornful. She had to remind herself that Ember didn't see how they were fawning at the camera; she didn't realize their eyes were too shiny, skin too smooth, and smiles too forced to be genuine. She didn't know better. Not about that, or about wars, or starvation, or crime, or climate change. And Poppy didn't want to be the one to spoil it for her. *Let it be lovely for as long as it can*, she figured.

In turn, Ember brought Poppy more books, older ones this time, their paper dry and yellowing, their chapters more dense and detailed. And she brought ingredients, tools, and tonics to make remedies for ailments—cuts and sores, headaches and belly aches, rashes and stings.

It was like all of Poppy's birthdays and Christmases rolled into one, only the gifts were just what she wanted, not all those dolls and toys and clothes that had been left untouched and ignored over the years. So Poppy became a chemist of sorts, and for the first time, she felt like she had found her place in the world. For that, she could never thank Ember enough.

Animals often joined them in the dell, keeping their distance but not at all wary, just going about their business as though Poppy and Ember were merely another part of forest life to be accepted. The hare made an appearance, not coming over but catching Poppy's eye while nibbling at the grasses that sprouted between the strings of an old tennis racket. Then, one day, a flock of birds settled on the branches of the trees all around them and watched them like an audience on high.

Ember seemed delighted with their arrival. She stood in front of them with her arms held up and muttered strange words that seemed to be her way of trying to tame them. When that had no effect, she began whistling and breaking off bits of bread that she held in her fingers to entice them. She even threw the crumbs in the air in a shower of temptation, but the birds wouldn't budge.

"I don't think they're interested," Poppy told her, looking up from her work.

Ember's face looked so crestfallen that Poppy longed for one of them to fly down to her. The birds called in conversation across the tiny valley, and Ember sang back as if trying to join their gang.

"I'm pathetic," she finally sighed.

"Don't say that!"

"It's true though." Ember slumped to the ground, giving up her efforts. Just then a bird, the nearest to her, flapped from its perch and swooped down and pecked at the bread at her feet. Ember gasped, and Poppy could see she was so stunned that she dared not speak. Poppy smiled and Ember beamed back at her. Twitching its tail feathers, the bird fluttered upward and landed on Ember's head. "Oh," she cried. "It's the first time this has happened to me!" Then she saw the confusion cross Poppy's face and quickly added, "My family, they like birds." The bird skipped down onto Ember's shoulder. "Oh, how I wish they could see this!" She held out her arm, and the bird hopped along it before taking to the air and retiring to the treetops. "I think it's you," Ember announced, and Poppy blinked, then felt her body tense. "You're my lucky charm."

Poppy's smile returned to her face. "I've never been called that before."

But Ember was full of insistence. "It's you! How I wish I could take you home with me."

"Me too," Poppy replied softly. "It's not me, though. It's this place. There's something magical about it, don't you think?"

As the mellow autumn afternoons turned colder and darker, Poppy busied herself dissecting and experimenting while Ember lay back, her eyes soaking in the photographs, her imagination carrying her far, far away.

"Are they wed?" Ember asked dreamily of a couple kissing in a magazine.

Poppy glanced up from her pestle and mortar, her fingers stained orange from the turmeric. "I think they're just dating."

Poppy had mentioned marriage a few days before, and ever since, Ember had been picking up the idea like an object, turning it over and examining it from all sides. Ember glanced back down at the photograph. She seemed lost in thought, and Poppy hoped no other questions would follow. After a while, though, Ember's voice piped up again.

"What's dating?"

Poppy ground hard at the spices in the mortar as she tried to think of the most simple definition of boyfriends and girlfriends.

When she spoke, it didn't sound so simple, though Ember sat there riveted by every word.

"So do you have one of these boyfriends?" she asked after Poppy finished explaining what happens when a boy and a girl like each other and want to be more than just friends.

"No," replied Poppy.

"Do you want one?"

"No," Poppy answered with not a drop of doubt.

"Because you don't like them?" Ember asked.

"Do you ask everyone this many questions, or just me?" Poppy replied, her eyes fixed on the water she was adding to the paste.

"Just you."

Ember's answer was so sincere, no sign of cynicism or sarcasm, that Poppy responded alike.

"Look, boys just don't like me. I can't tell you why. Girls too, really. But boys—it's different with them. They shy away. Can't even look me in the eye." Ember was staring at Poppy, mouth open. Realizing this was the most she had ever revealed about herself, Poppy felt her cheeks begin to heat up. "I think I creep them out," she finished rather hurriedly, just wanting the whole conversation to be over.

"It's because you're so strong and powerful," Ember responded in a matter-of-fact voice.

This wasn't the response Poppy was expecting. She looked at Ember in surprise. "Why do you think that?"

"I've been told. By my mother. By everyone I know. The males—they fear a powerful woman."

It sounded so simple. Simple enough to be of comfort. Perhaps even simple enough to be true.

It was later than usual when Poppy got off the bus that night. The October sun had disappeared without any good-bye, and suddenly it was dark already and the street lights were glowing.

Poppy had stayed at the dell to finish her attempt at herbal remedies. Arriving back at the town made her time in the forest almost feel like a dream. As if to check it was real, she sniffed at the lapel of her coat and smelled the smoke of the fire she'd lit. Then she looked at her hands. Today they were stained with the red of berries and rosehips. She had brewed a cure for headaches and made a poultice for an infected wound.

Ember had been her patient. She had a headache from Poppy's constant grinding of the pestle and mortar and the chopping of the wood—that and the smell of the concoctions as they boiled. Ember had no wound, though, and refused to have one inflicted for the sake of Poppy's medicinal education. Poppy had felt a sudden, searing urge to persuade her, sensing she had the power to do so, but she had resisted.

To make up for such a wicked thought, she had summarized the next chapter of *Jane Eyre* for Ember, who was now hooked on the love story between Jane and Mr. Rochester, whom she kept referring to as boyfriend and girlfriend. Poppy didn't have the energy to correct her. Ember had so many questions as it was, ones that Poppy couldn't begin to answer.

"It's just a story," she said.

For Ember, though, there was no distinguishing between fact and fiction. Her mind accepted the inexplicable and mysterious as a young child's would.

Poppy had taught Ember money too—dollars and coins and how to buy things in a store. They had acted it out—Poppy as shopkeeper, Ember as customer. It took a few attempts before Ember stopped trying to bargain. When finally they had said good-bye, Ember hugged her, and Poppy, so unused to such affection, had stood there like a statue. On the bus home she replayed the moment in her mind, practicing wrapping her arms around Ember and squeezing. It felt too big, too showy, but Poppy kept reimagining the scene until she felt more used to the idea.

She knew the four boys would follow her as she passed them on the corner. She couldn't understand it at first. Interest from any guys of any sort was so unusual to her. But she felt their eyes upon her, and it made her squirm and then she sensed why. They were drunk and they wanted a fight. Not knowing how best to react, Poppy kept her head down and kept walking, pretending she hadn't noticed them.

"Hey! Hey, wait up!" one of them called out.

Poppy kept on walking.

"We just want to talk to you."

She didn't reply.

"C'mon . . . why don't you show us what you got under that coat?"

Poppy clenched her jaw and sped up. She was walking so fast, she was on the brink of running. But she knew she shouldn't run. That would make it a chase and they would be faster. She crossed the road instead. They followed. She could hear them laughing. Then one of them caught up with her. He reached out and pulled at her arm.

"Hey, freak show. We're talking to you."

Poppy turned and saw them. A scrawny mean-looking bunch with cheap chains around their necks and bad tattoos. Suddenly they were around her, encircling her like a pack of flea-bitten wolves.

"You've picked the wrong girl," Poppy said defiantly.

"Yeah? Why's that?" the leader growled.

"Because you'll get hurt. You don't want that, do you? To be hurt by a girl."

The guys snorted and sniggered. One of them spit, his phlegm foaming on the pavement. The sight of it made Poppy's stomach turn. She wanted to retch but stopped herself. Then the most curious thing happened. The boy who spat clutched his stomach and made a noise like he was going to be sick.

"Pete! Gross, man!" The guys beside him stepped away in disgust.

Poppy seized her chance and went for the gap in the ranks, trying to break free, but one of the guys grabbed her and swung her around.

"Where you going?" His breath stank of cigarettes and beer. Poppy turned her face away, but he took hold of her chin. "We only just got started."

Poppy glared at him, the hatred shooting from her eyes, and he started coughing. His chest convulsing, he let go of her as he struggled for breath. The others stared in horror as smoke began to billow from his mouth and nostrils. Poppy barged past him and started to run. There was a moment's silence before a crescendo of feet on pavement as they all sped after her.

Poppy was running faster than she knew she could. She raced across the pavement and swung around the lamp post. She was

outrunning them. Then one loosely paved stone and she was flying through the air. Her hands came up to shield her face, and the
pain shot into her knees and then her shoulder. The guys loomed
over her, panting like hounds having caught their prey.

"Back off!"

Poppy glanced over to where this new voice had come to her
rescue and caught a glint of metal, sharp and silver.

"What the—" objected her attacker.

Poppy heard a shove and a thump and saw the two of them—
attacker and rescuer—up against the wall.

"You heard me." The words were delivered hard like a punch.

Keeping her eyes low, Poppy saw the cluster of feet start to
back away, then cross the road until she could see them no longer.

The voice was next to her now, arms around her, helping her. "I
got you. Can you stand?"

"I'm okay," mumbled Poppy.

As she stood, she felt a creeping sensation on her left leg.
The instant she recognized that it was blood trickling along her
skin, it started to sting. She forced herself to ignore the hurt and
straighten. Looking up for the first time, she saw the face before
her and the pain disappeared. Just like that.

The boy helped her to a low wall and sat her down.

Poppy felt helpless and didn't like it, but sort of liked it all at
the same time. "I can look after myself, you know," she said gruffly.

The boy regarded her thoughtfully with night-dark eyes. Poppy
looked away. He was thin and scruffy, with matted hair and torn
jeans that seemed authentic, not just for effect like some of the
boys at school. But, most of all, he was handsome. Too handsome
for her to look at.

"I expect you can," he replied. The same voice that had intimidated and menaced with such authority was softer now, protective.

"Thank you," Poppy whispered, glancing back at him.

The boy smiled as if he knew how unused she was to saying that. "Where does it hurt?"

Poppy remembered her knee and opened her coat. Her tights were ripped and soaked with blood. The boy gently pushed the material away. Then with one quick movement, he tore the rest so he could peel it down to her boot. Then his fingers touched around the wound as he examined it. Every nerve ending in Poppy's leg was firing . . . cold, hot, pain, pleasure.

"The cut's deep. You might need stitches."

"No," Poppy retorted quickly. It would mean her dad knowing, and she couldn't face that. The boy looked surprised but didn't argue. "My bag, could you get it?" she asked.

Her bag was lying close to where she fell. Some of the contents were scattered around, and Poppy watched as the boy carefully picked up each item, returning them to the bag. While he was distracted, she took her chance to study him, her eyes straining to make out his features in the darkness. He was much taller than her, but it was hard to judge his age. His appearance made him look older, but she felt instinctively it was only by a year or two. His hair was long and shaggy, his cheeks hollow, and his cheekbones high, and he was olive skinned, his face glowing gold and bronze when caught in the glimmer of the street light.

The boy turned and Poppy quickly looked away, wondering if he'd felt her stare. As he walked back toward her, Poppy glanced at him, and his eyes locked on hers and she felt herself flush. Then she realized—there was no fear in him. His eyes looked straight at her, freely, without inhibition. Silently the boy handed over the bag and Poppy looked inside until she found the jar with the poultice she had made. He raised his eyebrows, and Poppy shrugged as she scooped on the paste, then covered it with a leaf that she pressed to her knee. She felt a tinge of pride as it actually began to work, the relief spreading through her knee and down her leg.

"It's helping?" the boy asked, and Poppy nodded. "I could do with some of those," he added.

Poppy's eyes flicked to him. He had a scar on his forehead. "You fight a lot?"

"Not if I can help it."

"But you've got a knife."

The boy hesitated as if not sure whether to lie.

"You don't have to tell me," Poppy quickly added. She didn't want him to lie. She'd prefer him to be a knife wielder, not a liar.

"Yeah. I have a knife."

"You ever stabbed anyone?"

"Not to death."

Poppy blinked. His tone was wry, but she knew he was telling the truth.

"So you make medicine?" he asked, and it was Poppy's turn to hesitate. "I saw the book in your bag," he explained. "Natural remedies?"

"Oh, that. A friend lent it to me."

The boy studied her face, searching for clues to her sincerity. "It looks old," he said.

"I think it's like a family heirloom. I'm supposed to be taking very good care of it."

He seemed to be waiting for her to say more, but when she didn't he pressed on. "I grew up with all of that. My mother was into it, herbs and healing stones. Tarot cards too."

He gave a half-laugh and Poppy touched his arm without thinking. "I'm sorry," she said, and suddenly her hand on his arm felt momentous and she quickly removed it. "She died, didn't she?"

He shut his eyes for a second before answering. "A few years ago. She wasn't my real mother," he said, like he was confessing a secret. "But it felt like it."

Poppy kept her hands in her lap, fighting the impulse to touch him again.

He insisted on walking her home, even though it wasn't far and Poppy told him she'd be fine on her own. She was limping, and he took her arm and she leaned on him. Despite the pain in her leg, Poppy took him the longest route. They walked without words, as if not wanting to puncture the promise that floated in the air. The silence was soft and silky, and they glided through it, letting it caress their skin. She got used to the boy's warmth and felt the chill as soon as they parted. They stood there outside her house, looking at each other. Suddenly the silence seized them, tethering them too tightly.

Say something, Poppy wished to the boy. And then she couldn't bear the wait and spoke herself. "So now you know where I live."

The boy smiled, and she saw a hint of satisfaction there.

"What about you?" she continued.

He shifted from one foot to another, and Poppy couldn't work out what was wrong but then he answered, "I live in town," and she thought nothing more of it.

The boy was looking at her like he wanted her to read something in his eyes, but Poppy tried and found herself illiterate. All at once she felt overwhelmed and she turned to go.

"See you around, then," she muttered, but he reached out and took her hand in his. She glanced back at him apprehensively. But they just stood there, her hand in his until everything became about their two hands, joined, melded. Poppy looked from their hands to his eyes, and this time she could interpret what she saw there and her heart beat faster.

"I just wanted to know what it felt like," he said. Then he let go and Poppy felt bereft. "Good night, Poppy Hooper."

"How d'you know my name?"

He was walking away but he called out, and the word hung in the air: "Magic!"

It was when Poppy put her bag down on her bed that she saw her name tag hanging from it. She shook her head, smiling to herself, then realized she'd never asked the boy his name. As she fell asleep, she focused her mind away from the dull ache in her shoulder and knees to her hand until she felt his hand there once again. She slept a dreamless sleep and awoke feeling truly rested and content and knowing, somehow, that his name was Leo.

Chapter Nine

Sorrel and her friends were picking the last of the autumn fruit when one of the younger girls came running up.

"Your mother's looking for you." There was trepidation in the girl's face, and Sorrel tossed her an apple in thanks for the warning.

Her friends looked at Sorrel with concern.

"Don't worry," she reassured. "It'll be nothing important." But Sorrel knew it must be and wondered what displeasure she'd caused now. She crossed the orchard and headed down the forest path, preparing herself for the onslaught to come.

Raven was plucking a goose when Sorrel reached her, her wiry arms working fast, the feathers collecting at her feet to be stuffed into a cushion, the bird becoming balder by the second. Sorrel placed the basket of fruit in front of her mother like an offering to a god.

"Not near the bird," Raven complained, and Sorrel quickly moved it. Her mother didn't stop working while she talked, her hands and mouth both plucking away. "Where's Ember?"

Pluck.

"With Charlock."

"No, she's not."

Pluck.

"She told me she was baking bread with her mother today."

"Oh, she told you, did she?"

Pluck. Sorrel's skin began to smart.

"And what has she been telling you these last three weeks?"

"She's been unwell. Charlock kept her inside."

Pluck. Pluck. Pluck.

Sorrel looked at her arm and saw the red pores emerge. "Mother!"

Raven stopped and looked at Sorrel. "You said you would follow her."

"She didn't go anywhere." Sorrel could hear her voice whining.

"How would you know? You weren't following her."

"What was I supposed to do? Sit outside her caravan all day?"

Before Sorrel had a chance to regret taking such an indignant tone, Raven had flung the featherless bird down. Its long neck, loose and limp, flopped heavily to the ground. Sorrel looked into its pink, glassy eye with a feeling of empathy as her mother rose roughly from her stool.

"That's *exactly* what you were supposed to do. Do I have to stop all my work and trail the girl myself? What do you think your aunt would think about that?"

Sorrel wanted to argue—what about lessons, what about food, what about me?! But she hung her head and said nothing.

"Get some calendula for your arms," her mother ordered.

That was typical of Raven, first doling out the injury, then the salve. Realizing she was dismissed, Sorrel stomped away, swearing she wouldn't eat a mouthful of that goose. But by dinner, the smell of it roasting was wafting in the air, and she couldn't resist just a taste, then a second helping.

Ember sidled onto the end of the bench and put her bowl down on the table. The coven tried to eat together whenever the weather allowed. Ember remembered brushing the snow off the bench last winter and eating with frostbitten fingers, her spoon hardly finding her mouth past her scarf. Tonight was mild for this time of year, though. A golden autumn day, where the ambers and bronzes of the trees blazed in the light. The powder-blue sky had darkened now; lamps hung from the lower branches of the trees and the tables were lit with candles. Tomorrow the frost would fall, promised the elders. Today, it was agreed, was a last encore of summer's show before winter took the stage.

"Did you have a good bake, then, Ember?"

Ember looked to her left and saw her cousin's sharp features cutting into view. "I did, cousin." She started to eat, hoping that might be the end of the conversation. It wasn't like Sorrel to address her at these gatherings. Her cousin rarely even sat near her if she could help it.

Sorrel cracked open a bread roll and fished out the middle, dipping it into her sauce before plopping it into her mouth and chewing audibly. "Mm-nn. What is it I can taste? What did you put in this one, Ember?"

Ember felt a rising panic. She forced herself to carry on with her meal as if unaffected. "I'm not sure which batch you are trying from," she replied, rather proud of herself.

"I think it is the taste of truth. That's what it is. Honesty and truth. Delicious."

Ember willed her hand to stop trembling. She stared at Sorrel fearfully.

"Eat up, little cousin. Your goose is getting cold."

The meat stuck to Ember's tongue, clogging in her throat and making it hard for her to breathe. She gulped down some water to help her swallow, but with Sorrel's eyes on her, she had to lift her fork to her mouth once more and begin to chew again. She must do nothing to cause suspicion. For that afternoon Ember had broken the greatest of the clan oaths. She had told Poppy who she was and where she came from, and it had felt good. Even now, sitting here, feeling scared, she was glad she had done so. She would never regret confiding in her friend, no matter what might happen.

Ember hadn't intended to tell Poppy. The two girls had decided to leave the dell that afternoon, and it had felt like an adventure, hiking through the bracken and along the stone wall that stretched uphill and down, stitching the landscape into a vast patchwork. Poppy had asked about her family, and Ember found herself describing each of her three relatives—her mother, aunt, and, lastly, her cousin. She left out Sorrel's harsher traits, trying only to mention her more flattering characteristics. It hadn't been easy, but Ember had made sure to expose nothing of their craft.

"So you're an only child, like me?" Poppy said as she marched up the flank of the hill, Ember hurrying to keep up.

"All of our clan are supposed to be sisters. That's what we call one another," Ember replied, her voice breathless from the exertion. "But I don't think any of them see me like that and . . . well, they're not my real family, not like my mother and Raven and Sorrel."

"What about your dad?" Poppy asked.

"We don't know our fathers. None of us do."

Shocked, Poppy stopped and turned to look at Ember. "There are no men in the camp?"

"None," Ember answered emphatically. "It's forbidden."

"So you've never met a man?!" Poppy uttered in amazement.

Ember shook her head. "Not close up. I told you what my family think of men."

"I know, but I didn't realize . . . I mean . . . " Poppy paused as if to give herself a chance to take this in. "No wonder you want to leave," she tried to joke. Then she added more seriously, "Not that I know much about men either."

"What about your father? What's he like?"

"He's . . . he's simple."

"What do you mean?"

Poppy pushed herself up onto the wall behind her and sat there with her legs dangling. "I don't mean he's stupid. He's actually really smart. It's just he doesn't understand much . . . not about what people feel, anyway. He wants things to be straightforward and easy, and he tries to pretend they are."

Ember searched Poppy's face, but she lifted her head to the sky, avoiding Ember's gaze. Up there on the wall she seemed so remote and unreachable. "Does a father not love as a mother does?" she asked, but Poppy didn't answer. She just shut her eyes, the air hitting her face, fanning her hair. "I'm sorry," Ember apologized quickly. "I don't know much about . . . about anything."

Poppy nudged her with her foot. "Hey. You do too. You just know important stuff, not the useless trash that the rest of us fill our lives with."

Ember smiled up at her, relieved Poppy wasn't mad at her.

"So why are men forbidden?" Poppy questioned.

Ember trailed her fingers across the rough edges of the stones lodged in the wall, some gritty, others smooth like satin. "I don't think men have been so good to my clan over the years. At least that's what I've been told." She smiled ruefully. "Maybe the sisters are trying to protect themselves. Or maybe they just prefer to do without. They don't trust any chaffs."

"Chaffs?" Poppy retorted, and Ember tensed, realizing she shouldn't have used that word.

"The wheat and the chaff—it's what we call those . . . it's what we call everyone else."

Poppy made a face and jumped down from the wall. "Like me, you mean?"

"You call us worse," Ember retaliated, hearing with surprise the "us" come out of her mouth.

Poppy looked hurt for a second and then hit back. "When are you going to tell me?"

"What?" Ember felt her cheeks flushing as she tried to feign ignorance.

"Who 'us' is? You and your clan and your sisters living up in the hills away from the men and the . . . the chaffs."

Ember couldn't speak and she couldn't move. She simply stood, stock-still, waiting. If she had an ounce of magic in her, she might conjure up some spell as her escape, but she had none, and her mind felt like the sludge that lined the riverbed.

Poppy seemed to take her silence as refusal. "Forget it," she snapped. "I shouldn't have asked. I don't even care, you know. Whatever you guys are, it makes no difference to me . . . to me and you." She strode away and the wind whipped up, causing the autumn leaves to crackle and lift around her like a fiery coat of armor.

Ember's eyes widened. She held out her fingers, wondering if this display had come from her and searching her mind for any subconscious spell. "Come back," she called, but her words were lost on a gust of air. Released from her trance, Ember chased after Poppy, pulling at her arm. "Stop," she begged. "Stop!"

Poppy turned and the leaves were carried off by the breeze like a flock of burnished birds.

The truth tumbled out of Ember, fast, before she had a chance to hold it in. "We're witches. That's who . . . that's what we are."

"You're a witch?" Poppy asked, and Ember nodded quickly, hardly able to look Poppy in the eye for fear of her reaction.

"I'm not a very good one. In truth, I'm a terrible one. But the others, they have great powers."

Now it was Poppy's turn to stand and stare.

"Say something," Ember pleaded.

Poppy looked across the hills as though seeking a distant truth. Finally she responded. "I think I knew that," she said. "I think somewhere inside me, I knew that all along."

"And it makes no difference still?"

"What . . . that I'm a chaff?" Poppy retorted with a smile, and Ember's heart sang to see it forming on her face.

"I'm not like the rest of my clan," Ember told her.

"And I'm not like my clan either," Poppy replied.

It felt like a vow of sorts, and Ember threaded her arm through Poppy's and they started walking again, their steps matching each other's as they trod over the flinty fields.

"Will you tell me?" Poppy asked so quietly that Ember nearly didn't catch it. "About the magic, I mean?"

Ember nodded. Above them a flight of swallows peppered the sky, each bird so light and tiny but swirling together in a colossal kinetic cloud. They both stopped and looked up at them, watching in amazement.

"They're off to Africa," Ember said. "That's the very last of them. They read the stars, you know, to help them find their way," she explained.

"Can you read the stars?"

Ember shrugged. "The sisters have tried to teach me. I know some of the constellations."

"Will you show me?"

"You need someone better than me to teach you."

"I'd like to know everything. If you'll tell me."

"But what about you? I'd like to know everything about your world too."

Poppy started to walk again, and Ember moved with her, staying by her side.

"You can ask me anything you want," Poppy said, but Ember sensed a slight reluctance that belied her words. Suddenly she felt unsure what question to pose first.

"Well," she said. "You told me a little of your father. But your mother—what is she like?"

Ember realized her mistake before Poppy even replied. Poppy's body had tensed imperceptibly and there was an edge to her tone.

"You don't want to know."

"But I do," Ember said encouragingly, trying to make everything right.

"She's brave and . . . and true to herself."

"Like you."

Poppy looked away before she spoke and Ember had to strain to hear.

"I don't think I'm either of those things."

Sensing she had done some damage and not knowing how to remedy it, Ember searched for something positive to say. "She sounds like my mother."

The slope had suddenly turned steep, and out of nowhere and without a word, Poppy just started to run, faster and faster, all the way to the bottom where the earth was dark and muddy. Ember watched her from up high, thinking Poppy would take off with her coat flapping in the air and lifting around her like wings. She was shrieking like a banshee as she went, and her cries were caught by the gusts of wind and lost in the hills. When she reached the bottom, she turned and looked at Ember, her cheeks flushed.

"Come on! What are you waiting for?" she yelled through gasping breaths.

Ember ran, and soon it was like she couldn't stop if she tried and her legs were moving without her saying so. Her hair whipped around her face and her organs jolted inside of her as she hurtled downward. She had almost reached Poppy when she slipped and careened into her. They both squelched into the mud. Ember gulped down air as Poppy laughed and laughed until it hurt, and then Poppy was crying and crying. Big sobs from deep inside took hold of her, and Ember pulled her up so she was sitting and put her muddy arms around her.

"I'm . . . sorry," Poppy bawled. She wiped her nose and eyes on her sleeve so that her face was streaked with mud. "I don't know what's wrong with me. I never cry. Never."

Ember felt the tears form in her own eyes and she blinked them back. "I cry all the time."

Poppy hiccupped a laugh and then sniffed and wiped her eyes again. "Can't you find us a spell to turn us into swallows? Then we could fly away."

"To Africa."

"To Africa."

The mud dried, then cracked upon them as they made their way back to the dell. They lingered there for a while, waiting for the light to fade, neither girl wanting to return home. Ember collected chestnuts from the horse chestnut tree, holding up her skirt to make a pouch to store them in. Poppy watched as Ember made her selection, tossing aside the ones she didn't favor. She was studious and rapt in her work. Then she straightened and held one out proudly, and Poppy realized the effort had all been for her.

"For you," she said. "It's the best. The strongest one."

It was a simple gift, but Poppy felt lucky and grateful and happy all at once. It was only a chestnut, but it felt glossy in her fingers and it gleamed so richly in the last of the autumn light.

The two girls sat on an old, damp sofa and Poppy put her headphones over Ember's ears. Ember flinched at the sound but then raised her hands to press the music closer. Poppy could read the song on Ember's face: intent on the verse, a blink at the refrain, a twitch of a smile at the chorus, a nod of the head at the bridge, then a softening of features at the end. Holding the headphones to her ears with painted nails, Ember looked like a regular girl, part of the modern world.

An image suddenly came to Poppy of Ember dressed in jeans, face made up, hair cut and styled, hand in hand with her boyfriend outside a café. Poppy gasped; it seemed so clear and intense. She felt a deep sadness come over her. That girl wouldn't run down hillsides or be interested in the migration of birds or marvel at songs. That girl wouldn't have Poppy as a friend.

"I'll see you tomorrow?" Poppy asked, but Ember didn't hear her through the music. Poppy pulled one of the headphones to the side and Ember looked up at her. "Tomorrow afternoon again?" Poppy said, and Ember beamed and nodded, putting Poppy's fears to rest. That other Ember was just a thought, as thin as air, a product of her imagination.

❦

When she reached home, Ember scrubbed at her muddy clothes and wrung them until the dirty water ran clean and her hands were red and raw from the effort. As she worked, she sang the song Poppy had played for her. She had listened to it over and over. Poppy had said she had hundreds that she could play instead, but Ember had only wanted that first one. To listen to another would be to dilute it, to break the spell. Ember held every note and every word in her memory like it was the code to her survival.

"What's that you're singing, Ember?" asked Charlock.

Ember spun around. "It's nothing. Just something I made up." She hung her dress on the rack to dry, hiding her reddening cheeks from her mother's gaze.

"It sounds angry. That's not like you." Charlock handed her a mug of tea and clasped Ember's hands around it. "Where were you today?"

"Up in the hills," Ember answered, glad for the truth of it.

Charlock cocked her head and surveyed her daughter's face, the washed clothes, the filthy boots.

"I slipped in the mud."

Charlock went to the chest, lifted the lid, and got out Ember's spare skirt and sweater. She had knitted it three years ago when Ember had suddenly grown two inches one summer and could no longer wear her winter clothes. Handing the garments to Ember, she said, "Get changed quickly now. Clan supper tonight. Raven's roasting one of her geese."

CHAPTER TEN

When Poppy got back, Leo was waiting outside her house. It was already dark, and from the top of her street, she could only see the outline of his shape against the fence. But she knew it was him. She stopped and looked and he stepped out under the street light. He didn't wave but just stood there waiting for her, and she went to him, forcing herself to walk slowly and steadily and not break into a run. When she reached him, he didn't smile or say hello. He just looked at her, then said, "What took you so long?"

And Poppy smiled and said, "It's only been a day."

A moth came and fluttered around her hair. She brushed it gently away. Then another came and another until they formed a halo around her head. *Go away*, Poppy yelled inside her mind. *Not now, not in front of him.*

"They seem to like you," Leo commented.

He wasn't freaking out. But then Poppy saw the cats emerging from bushes, climbing down from trees, balancing along fences. Minx appeared from behind a car tire and hurried toward her, purring in anticipation.

"Let's go inside," Poppy proposed quickly, trying to stop the panic reverberating in her voice.

She saw Leo blink with momentary surprise. "Inside your house?" he checked.

Poppy took Leo's arm and pulled him toward her door. She tried to signal to Minx with her eyes, but the cat just looked confused. Poppy begged forgiveness in her head, and Minx seemed to understand as she sat on her haunches and started to lick her paws.

"What about your parents?" asked Leo a little nervously.

"Well, one's in the loony bin and the other isn't around much, so don't worry—you won't be meeting them."

Leo nodded. "O-kay . . ." he said hesitantly. "You sure you don't want to go out some place?"

Poppy unlocked the door. "I've been out all day."

"How's the knee?"

"What?" Poppy could see the other cats coming up the path now.

"Your knee? Remember yesterday?" Leo was sounding perplexed.

"Oh . . . oh, it's fine. Honestly, it's all better."

Leo looked at her doubtfully.

"Magic!" Poppy joked, then tugged him across the threshold and slammed the door before the first of the cats could slip through.

They stood inside the hallway in the dark. Now that Poppy felt safe, she didn't know what to do.

"So we're inside."

"How about some light?" Leo suggested in a bemused tone.

"Light . . . right . . ."

And Poppy flicked the switch. She looked up at Leo and stopped breathing. He reached out a hand and touched her cheek lightly. She had to tell her brain to tell her lungs to exhale.

"You've got mud on your face," he said softly.

Inside the bathroom Poppy looked at herself in the mirror, her cheeks streaked with dirt, her eyebrows caked in mud, one green eye terrified and one blue eye excited, staring back at her like they belonged to two different people. *Oh God*, she thought. *This is hopeless. This is impossible.*

Leo heard the water running from the taps in the bathroom and imagined Poppy washing her face as he looked around the kitchen. It was smart but bare, like a show home that had never been used. There was a note on the table addressed to Poppy, telling her there was leftover pizza in the fridge and to please clean up afterward. It was signed "Dad," and Leo's heart went out to Poppy as he understood where her mother must be and he wished he could tell her he knew what that kind of hurt felt like. He opened the cabinets looking for coffee. Coffee in a proper mug—he hadn't had one of those in such a long time.

When he turned, he saw her in the doorway. Her face was clean and fresh like a child's. She was wearing an old kid's T-shirt with her jeans, and he saw her shape and had to look away. He felt like he should leave, like he should never have come in here anyway. It was clean in the house and so normal—he didn't fit. Then Poppy came over and reached up to a cabinet and pulled out two mugs. He could smell the soap on her and stepped back, wishing he could go and shower and wash the streets away. She put the mugs on the counter, put the ground coffee and water in the cof-feemaker, turned it on, and they waited.

"I didn't think I'd see you again," she said, and Leo felt puzzled.

"Why not?"

"I guess if I let myself think it, then I'd hope it, and then I'd just be disappointed . . ."

Leo slowly smiled. "I'm happy to see you too."

There was a crackle and a spark from the coffeemaker and they jumped back. Then the water started to bubble furiously, rising out of the top.

"Careful!" Leo called out as Poppy quickly unplugged the cord. He was the one to take the pot and pour the coffee into the mugs, adding the cream, and handing it to her, his fingers brushing hers as he did so.

They sat at the table and talked, and he found himself asking her inane questions, like his brain had stopped functioning, like he didn't know who he was anymore. If he just kept talking, maybe she'd overlook the fact that he was wearing the same clothes as last time, that his hair hadn't been washed in weeks, that he didn't have a house or a chair or a table or a coffeemaker. That he'd never be able to make her a cup of coffee. *I should never have come inside*, he thought again. Outside it was his world and he could be him-self. Next time he wouldn't come inside. Next time.

Poppy was answering his questions in a small, quiet voice. Leo found out she had moved around a lot, that she'd only arrived in town a couple of months ago, that her dad had got a job at a local factory, that she hated school as much as he did—not the subjects or the work but the institution and the timetable and the bells ringing, telling her when to stop and when to start. When he asked about the other kids at school, she got to her feet and took the pizza out of the fridge and they ate it cold out of the box. They both went for the same piece and their skin touched accidentally, and he could swear he felt a charge of electricity and she felt it too as she sprang back.

He took the pizza slice and gave it to her, then grabbed her wrist and held on. Her eyes fixed on his but she didn't pull away. Slowly she put the pizza down so their hands could entwine. Leo reached for her other hand too, so they sat there, both fists locked, holding on, waiting, not sure what would happen next. The light bulb flickered above their heads. Leo tensed, tightening his grip on Poppy's hands, and she squeezed back. Then all the lights went out. He could hear Poppy breathing, fast, in . . . out.

"What's happening?" he murmured, hardly daring to speak.

"I don't know," she whispered.

He bent his face toward hers through the blackness, and now he could feel her breath on his skin, in . . . out. If he moved just an inch, their mouths would meet. As if reading his mind, she tipped her head, just a tiny movement, and he felt her lips about to brush his.

Suddenly the lights came on and the glare was blinding. Both of them sprang back. They let go and the gap was back between them, like it had never been closed.

Poppy's cheeks were burning. She grabbed the mugs and took them to the counter, turning her back on Leo and all that had happened. She couldn't do this. It had already felt weird having

Leo in her house, like the whole place changed when he was in it, his presence filling the room so that everything else felt small and dim, like only he was in focus. They had sat there having coffee as people do all the time, but it had felt like they were faking it, pretending to be two ordinary people making conversation when really there was something else going on between them that they couldn't utter but made Poppy's pulse race and her heart pound. Then the blackout. Poppy couldn't bear to imagine what Leo must be thinking about that.

"Hey," she heard. His tone was soft, purposefully so. "You know I never even told you my name. Sparks are flying, and we never even got introduced."

Poppy couldn't turn around. Not yet.

"I'm Leo."

"Hi, Leo," she said, her voice hoarse and cracked.

"Thanks for the coffee, Poppy, and the pizza," he replied. "And thanks for letting me in. Not many people would have done that."

Later Poppy remembered that last comment and felt confused, but right now she was just relieved to feel him walk away, to hear the door close behind him. When she was sure he had gone, she loosened her grip on the kitchen counter and made herself turn around. The room felt desolate without him. She gathered up the pizza box and threw it away. When she picked up his mug to wash it, it was still warm. She wrapped her hands around it, then brought it to her mouth and put her lips where his had been.

CHAPTER ELEVEN

Leo ran back to the town center, the burn in his ribs and stitch in his side offering a welcome distraction from everything else he was feeling. He hadn't even said good-bye. She probably wouldn't want to see him again. He should have gone up to her and held her. He should have turned her around in his arms and kissed her and shown her that he wasn't freaked out or scared like she was. He had no idea what had happened, but on some level, it didn't surprise him. All that electricity just seemed to confirm the connection between them. He sensed it the same way he sensed Poppy wanted him gone, that she was struggling and couldn't ask him to go but was praying he would. So he had left but now wished he hadn't, not without reassuring her at least. Leo bent over his legs and waited until the pain eased and his breathing slowed.

Early the next morning he went to the market and gathered some flowers that had been discarded. He picked the best of them, snapping off the broken stems, and took them to Kim at the gym who let him use the shower. She looked at him like "not you again" but then noticed the flowers and rolled her eyes before unlocking the door.

"Be quick," she said, and took the flowers before he had a chance to give them to her.

She threw him a towel and Leo ran to the changing room. Turning up the water as hot as he could take it, he watched the glass steam up before stepping inside. He used almost half the container of soap, piling it on his head until his hair was white and slick with lather. When he finished, he saw Kim had left him a neat pile of clothes from the Lost and Found. Leo picked them up off the bench and held them out. They looked brand new. Leo marveled at how much people must own that they could leave these behind and never come to claim them. Once Kim had given him a pair of sneakers, and Leo still wondered how it was that someone could forget their shoes.

He quickly got changed and then looked at himself in the mirror. His hair was soft to touch. His skin tingled clean. The tracksuit changed his whole hunted, hungry, feral demeanor. He held himself differently in it. *Almost like an athlete*, he thought, then felt like an idiot for thinking so.

As Leo left the gym, he saw the flowers in a vase on the reception desk. Then a guy spoke to him, a gym member who was arriving as Leo was leaving.

"Didn't know they opened so early," was all he said, but he addressed Leo like an equal, like he too had a job and could afford to join a gym. Leo found himself too stunned to answer, but he carried those words with him all day.

His new, clean image wasn't to last long, though. Behind the bakery, one-eyed Mike tried to snatch his breakfast. Leo wouldn't let him. No way. He'd learned the hard way that if he did, they'd all be on him every time. Easy pickings. Mike was in one of his crazes, though, and kept coming for him. In the end, Leo had to fight him just to keep him off. Mike was wild, throwing punches and biting with his cracked, yellow teeth until Leo went for his blind side, bringing him down. When he had him on the floor, Leo kicked him a few sharp ones for good measure. Teach him not to come back. Leo knew he should feel sorry, but he didn't. He just wanted it finished.

The manager of the bakery pulled Leo off Mike, hurling him to the ground.

"Get lost, you scum. Beating up a cripple. That all you good for?"

Leo didn't bother trying to explain. It never got him anywhere. He was young and the young ones always got blamed. He got to his feet, picking the now-dirty bun from the gutter and stuffing it in his mouth before taking off. He wouldn't be able to go to that bakery again—that was a real loss. And his arm was stinging where Mike's teeth had broken the skin. But what hurt most was the rip in the new tracksuit and the feeling of the torn material flapping against his knee as he ran. Who am I trying to kid? he thought to himself.

Later that morning he got his friend Ben to shave his hair off. All of it. Leo sat on one of the fat, rusting pipes that ran from the factories into the murky waters of the river. The sweet-smelling locks of hair fell softly onto the slick shore. They didn't look like they ever could have belonged to him. Leo thought of that story of the man who cut his hair for a woman—Delilah, he remembered—and how that guy lost all his power. But as he looked at his reflection in the oily water—his head shaved, his face stark and unadorned—Leo felt stronger. This way he would never have to worry about keeping his hair clean. This way he could never even try to look like the boy he used to be before the streets, before the trouble, before he had to escape.

Poppy ran her fingers over his head, feeling Leo's skull under her hands.

"I like it," she said.

He had been waiting for her outside her school, leaning against the wall in a tracksuit and sneakers. The other kids stared at them as they passed.

Kelly Fletcher's jaw dropped when she caught sight of them together, her eyes lingering on Leo. "Weirdo," she barbed at Poppy under her breath, and the girls who linked arms with her whispered and giggled, managing to make the sound of laughter grating and nasty.

Mark Shaw spotted Poppy and Leo out of the corner of his eye. He kept his distance but spat on the ground, then looked the other way.

"They don't like you much," Leo said matter-of-factly.

"They think I'm weird." Poppy shrugged, and Leo laughed, so she added, "I am weird, I guess."

"Who isn't?" Leo retorted, and Poppy felt like hugging him but didn't.

Instead, she said, "Let's get out of here," and they walked side by side down the road, past all the other kids, like they were a regular couple and she, Poppy Hooper, wasn't a freak but the cool girl with the handsome boyfriend.

"How did you get out of school so early?" Poppy suddenly thought to ask.

"I have my ways," he said enigmatically and then took her hand in his so she only thought of that.

They went to the back of the churchyard, treading carefully between the graves and past the headstones, through a small door hidden in an ivy-clad wall. It opened onto a wild garden where the long grasses reached their knees and the brambles and blackthorns, hawthorns and holly bushes grew unfettered. The meadow sloped down to a stream that reflected the dappled sky. All sound of distant traffic was drowned out by the trickling of the water as it hurried on its journey. If Poppy listened hard, she could hear the birds and the squirrels in the trees, the insects in the air, the croak of a frog, and the imperceptible sound of duck legs paddling below the surface of the water. She could tell this was Leo's place, his find that no one else he knew strayed upon.

Leo got two apples from his pocket and they crunched away in silence, looking out across the water to the fields beyond. The road that circled the town was just visible in the distance. From where they sat, it looked like another stream, a concrete one reminding them they were still within the confines of society. They threw their cores into the water and watched them bob away. Then the church bell rang, its chimes reverberating across the town, reminding Poppy of the time.

"I should go," she said apologetically, causing Leo's face to fall. "I'm sorry," she went on. "It's just I promised I'd meet a friend."

"It's okay," he told her, but he looked so crestfallen that Poppy couldn't bring herself to get to her feet.

"I *want* to stay," she murmured, and he looked up at her with eyes so urgent that they held her there, fixed in that spot.

"Don't go then," he said gruffly.

Poppy thought of Ember waiting at the dell as they had promised and all that she must be wondering. Grimacing with guilt, she looked at her watch. She was already late. Even if she rushed, by the time she made it there, Ember would have to leave soon after anyway.

"I'll see her tomorrow. She'll understand," Poppy resolved, and she was rewarded with the sincerest smile from Leo.

"You'll stay?"

Poppy nodded, consoling herself with the thought of how much Ember would love to hear her news and how she'd hang on every word of her description of Leo and make her tell their conversation over again.

Poppy lay back on the grassy bank and Leo did the same, their eyes looking upward to the limitless sky, and Leo talked, this time about himself. He sounded like he was joking when he confessed he didn't know where he came from. And he laughed when he told her that he didn't think much of parents, having been abandoned twice, first by his father, then by his mother. But he turned serious when he said he never missed them because he had never known them and, besides, he had had Jocelyn, and she loved him enough for both of them.

"The tarot card reader?" Poppy remembered.

"Yeah, not sure how good she was at reading them. But she was the best mother to me. You'd have liked her. She was a strange one too."

"Oy," objected Poppy, elbowing him in the ribs. "I thought you said everyone was weird."

"Everyone I know. But you and her—you're in a different league."

Glad to be paired with someone Leo loved, Poppy decided to take that as a compliment.

"We were happy when it was just me and her. But then she met Evan." Leo gave a bitter laugh. "The joke of it is that I think she thought it'd be good for me. Having a father figure."

"What did he do to you?" Poppy's voice dropped to almost a whisper.

"It wasn't just him. He had his boys. Two sons. The spitting image of him. Heads like potatoes, all of them. But their fists . . ."

Poppy's finger went to the scar that ran through Leo's left eyebrow, but she flinched as the sensation she got from it was fiery like a burn.

"Ashtray, that one."

"How many are there?" Poppy asked.

Leo pointed to each of the scars they'd given him over the years, like they were props to a good story—on his forehead, his chest, his hand, his arm—his mementos of family life. Poppy hid the pity from her face, though it had caught inside of her and she couldn't dislodge it.

"There was no escaping them. Our apartment was tiny. Three

growing boys, I guess, with no room to grow. I get why they were violent, but him . . . he would goad them into it. He'd enjoy it."

"What about Jocelyn?"

"She used to shout and pull them off me. But then she got sick. She just faded away. Every week there seemed to be just a little bit less of her. After she died, that's when I got the knife." Leo kept his eyes gazing long into the distance, as though looking back in time before he spoke again. "She saw her death in the cards. She knew it was cancer before the doctors told her, but she thought all her herbs and crystals might buy her more time." Leo gave a short and bitter laugh, like a fist hitting wood. "She didn't stand a chance." He hung his head then and picked at the grass. "She kept telling me it was going to be okay. Even when she couldn't sit up anymore, she still kept saying so." Then Leo looked at Poppy and tried to smile. "That's optimism for you."

He gazed back out across the field and went quiet. It felt like prying to look at him, so Poppy stared ahead too, wishing she could think of something to say that didn't sound empty and trite. She sensed Leo retreating inside of himself and very gently she prompted, "What happened after? With them?"

"You don't want to know."

His voice had changed, like he couldn't keep the lightness in it any longer and the words were too heavy to trip off the tongue. Poppy turned and looked, despite herself. His features were so very still. He sensed her looking and finally turned his head, and she caught a flash of what he'd suffered in his eyes. Then he blinked and it was gone and a stranger's eyes were looking back at her.

"Leo?" Poppy whispered.

"Forget about all that," he said. "We're here . . . now . . . alone."
He looked at her flirtatiously, like it was all a bit of fun, but it felt
like an act and Poppy didn't buy it. He reached out and touched
her hair, twisting his finger around a strand that fell on her cheek.
"You're gorgeous, you know that?"

He leaned forward to kiss her and Poppy put her arm out to
stop him. The words—they sounded wrong. They sounded empty,
like a lie, like they belonged to someone else. Poppy rapidly replayed them in her mind, but no matter which way she phrased
them, they jarred. Why did he have to say gorgeous? It wasn't
him. And it certainly wasn't her. Leo was looking at her warily.
She pulled away, just out of his reach.

"I'm sorry," she mumbled.

"C'mon," he coaxed, trying to pull her back in. Poppy resisted
and he said harshly, "What? You want me to tell the rest of my
sob story first? Is that it?"

"First?" Poppy flashed fiercely.

Leo froze, and Poppy instantly felt ashamed.

"I'm sorry," she said again, but Leo shook his head angrily.
"What are you sorry for? Me? Them? Yourself?"

Poppy didn't answer and sat there for a moment. She knew she
should try to hold him, kiss him, and make him feel better. But
she just didn't know how to start. Instead, she got to her feet.

"You're going?" Leo said to her without looking up. It was
more of a statement than a question.

"My friend. She'll be worried."

She wished he'd look at her, just for a moment, but he kept
staring at the ground.

"Haven't you got things you don't talk about?" he said accusingly.

Poppy wanted to sit back down and tell him the things were so endless she wouldn't know where to begin. But then she heard him say, "Just go then," and so she did the easiest thing and started walking away.

He didn't call after her. He didn't try to stop her from leaving. He just let her disappear.

Chapter Twelve

E mber waited for Poppy until the bugs filled the dusky air and the moon appeared in a chalk-blue sky that was yet to darken. Waiting time was slow time. The seconds stretched to minutes, stretched to hours, Ember's mind pulling, twisting, and pummeling them like dough. Hope played tricks on her. The crack of a twig and Ember's spirits rose, the rustle of leaves and she turned her head expectantly, the flutter of a bird and she jumped to her feet, each time to be left disappointed. The dell had lost its magic now that Poppy wasn't there. Instead of emblems of a better life, Ember looked around her and just saw broken pieces of wood and rusting lumps of metal. Nature had tried to claim these bits of junk for its own. Ivy trailed over an old fridge, weeds poked through bicycle wheels, woodlice and beetles lived beneath old boxes, and a family of mice nested inside an old washing machine. It was how Ember imagined all the world would be in the end. One giant dell.

Lingering in this lost and lonely place, Ember felt herself begin to languish. No longer certain of Poppy's arrival, other doubts scratched at the scabs in her mind, scraping at her newfound optimism, exposing her old insecurities. Without Poppy, Ember was nobody again. She shivered, not from the cold but from the fear. It could happen so quickly, joy to sorrow, love to loss. Worse still, she had trusted Poppy with the coven's secret. She had confided in a chaff, believing she would never tell. She had been rash and foolhardy, putting herself and the clan in danger, and all for the sake of friendship.

Ember shook her head to try to rid herself of such thoughts. Poppy would never betray her. Surely there was a simple explanation for her absence. Something important must be keeping her away— her school, her family, her health. Ember gasped as another idea took hold: What if some disaster had befallen her friend? What if she was trapped or injured, in need of Ember's help? Ember felt the panic begin to drum a beat inside of her, faster and faster, louder and louder. She looked past the dell, wishing with all her might that she could see beyond the here and now like some of the other girls. For the first time, Ember truly wished she was like them. As herself, she was powerless. Even if she stepped out beyond the dell into the unknown and headed—without permission—toward the town, she had no way of finding Poppy. The extent of her plight hit Ember harder now than it had ever done before. She wanted to run into the town and knock on every door and ask every chaff if they knew her friend, Poppy, with the short hair and the big coat and one eye of turquoise and the other of jade. Instead, Ember waited and hoped until she could wait and hope no longer.

Before she had to leave, Ember left a book for Poppy, tucking it under the sofa, the corner just peeking out so Poppy would see it if by chance she made it to the dell that night. Ember had chosen this book carefully. Poppy had asked to be taught magic, and this had seemed the best place to start. She had imagined that they would read it together, sitting side by side, Poppy listening as she explained the different chapters. Instead, the book lay hidden under damp cushions with no reader to be had, all alone like she was.

Reaching the top of the slope, Ember had one last look back, hoping she would hear Poppy's voice echoing to her and see her arm outstretched, waving through the shadowy light. But the place was still and quiet, only the mist moving, rising from the ground like steam from a cauldron, giving the dell and all its belongings a ghostly hue. Her spirits sinking once again, Ember wandered home with a heavy feeling in her legs, dragging her feet, delaying her arrival when she would have to face another night within the camp without the memories of an afternoon with Poppy to carry her through.

Sorrel followed her cousin from a safe distance. After hours of sitting silently, it was tedious to have to creep along so slowly. She longed to break into a run and catch up with Ember. She wanted to let her limbs stretch, let the bubbling, boiling energy inside her burst out. She wanted to give Ember a shake and a slap and demand to know who it was she'd been waiting for all that time. It irritated her that her mother had been right and her feeble, unadventurous cousin actually had a secret. A big one.

Sorrel and the other sisters had Ember neatly bottled away like one of their potions, labeled as useless and utterly predictable. But Ember had popped the cork and slipped out without them noticing. Only Raven, always Raven, had spotted her evasion. Now Sorrel would have to face her mother and tell her that, despite waiting so long and suffering hours of pins and needles, she knew nothing that Raven didn't already know herself.

"It must be a boy," she told her mother when she got home. "They had arranged a time and place and he didn't attend. Otherwise why would she look so desperate and lovestruck?"

"What did she do?" Raven asked as she rubbed Sorrel's feet in almond oil.

"Nothing."

The grip on her foot tightened. "Tell me everything."

"She paced, she sat, she picked at the grass and tore a fallen leaf into a thousand pieces. She paced some more. On occasion she would jump to her feet and stare, believing that she'd heard a sign of his arrival. Then, when she realized it was not so, her face would fall and she would sit back down and fidget once again. Finally she gave up hoping for his appearance, and came home." Sorrel didn't add that, for sport, she'd caused a stirring in the grass and trees just to see Ember's eyes light up, then cloud again.

"What else?" Sorrel felt her mother's nails dig into her soles. "What else?"

Sorrel was on the verge of making something up just to satisfy her mother when suddenly the memory came to her.

"She left him a book."

"A book?" The claws retracted and the grip lessened.

"She put it under the cushion of the sofa there."

"She left a boy one of our books. Why?"

"I don't know," Sorrel replied nervously. "Should I have retrieved it?"

Raven's hands were still and cold as they waited upon Sorrel's feet. Finally the answer came. "No," Raven muttered. "Let's bide our time for now and let this little mystery reveal itself." She shut her eyes to think some more, then spoke again. "What would some chaff boy want with a book?"

Sorrel realized that this question wasn't for her. Raven was asking herself. Her mother's fingers started to move again, rubbing and pressing, working in time with her mind as it delved, deliberated, and determined.

Sorrel's foot was only released when Charlock knocked on their door and called Raven away. Sister Bridget had heard the Eastern clan was on the move. They hadn't traveled so far in over a hundred years. Sorrel caught a trace of apprehension in her aunt's eyes, and her mother, who usually berated such interruptions, got to her feet instantly and without complaint.

"Get yourself to bed, child," she ordered.

Sorrel watched them slip away, gathering with the other elders by the fire. Long into the night they conferred, and Sorrel felt her ears burn and knew they were talking about her. *The prophecy again*, she thought gloomily. All alone, under the cover of darkness and with her mother preoccupied elsewhere, she allowed herself to wish that Ember was more of a witch so she could share the deadening weight of expectation with her. Sorrel wondered, not for the first time, what her life would have been like if three hundred and three years ago those witches had not looked into the future of the Hawkweed sisters. She would not know the path her life would take; instead, she would meander this way and that until she found the avenue that suited her.

Her mother would love her for the child she was, not for the woman she'd become. Her friends would treat her as an equal, feeling free to tease and tittle-tattle as well as joke and play. Her teachers would not require perfection. They'd commend her for what she could do and not castigate her for what she could not.

As Sorrel dreamed, her eyes shut and she eased into a sleep where her fantasy of anonymity and mediocrity could come true. Her face mellowed, and for the next few hours, she became that other girl—young, carefree, and content.

When at last Poppy reached the dell it was dark and Ember had gone. She found a book tucked under the sofa, sticking out of the cushion. It was old and heavy like the others. Poppy held it in her hands and thought of the generations of women before her who'd held it too. The thought comforted her and she hugged the book to her, wishing she could hug her friend, her life raft, who never made her feel like she was out of her depth, like she was drowning. She left Ember a note saying she was sorry for being late and she'd be there tomorrow. With it, she left her geography book. It hardly seemed a fair exchange, but they'd been studying Africa at school. Ember would like that.

Lying in bed that night, Poppy read Ember's book until her hands grew stiff with cold and her eyes itched from tiredness. She read all night, the house silent but for the faint crackle of thumb on paper as she turned the pages. She read until the dawn broke. This book told of witches through the centuries. Young women who were outsiders; who knew how to heal; who had a sixth sense; who could create storms and make things happen at will, things that couldn't be explained or understood or believed; women whom people were instinctively scared of. Anything bad that happened, they were to blame.

A baby died in its sleep—Ada Swift had cursed it. A farmer's barn burned down—it was Bathsheba Flynn's revenge for being scorned by him. The village beauty fitted and foamed at the mouth—the envious Morwenna Dickinson had put a spell on her. They were the boogeywomen. Every town must have one to make some sense of their woes.

There was one, a girl named Margaret Bryant, who was suspected of witchcraft on account of her eyes. One blue, one green. The left eye had two pupils. Poppy's eyes read about Margaret's eyes. Her brain slowed and dulled so the words became just meaningless shapes on the page. Then she read about the cats who came from villages far and wide to live with Margaret Bryant. The "Cat Caller" the people had christened her.

On cue, Minx appeared at Poppy's window and gave a loud meow, rubbing her body against the glass. In that instant Poppy knew. It was like a dousing with cold water that woke her without warning from a sleepwalk. Suddenly her brain whirred into action and she saw her whole life afresh. It flickered across her mind like a reel of old film, a silent movie without words or colors, the images stark without any special effects. The cats . . . the spiders . . . the sixth sense . . . the weather . . . the accidents . . . the expulsions . . . her mother . . .

Her mad, mistaken mother! She had known. She had tried to tell her, but Poppy hadn't listened. Nobody had.

Poppy opened the window and Minx leapt inside and onto the bed. The cat waited for Poppy to get back under the covers and then stepped back and forth over her stomach before settling on it. Poppy stroked Minx's head, then lifted the book and read over and over again about poor Margaret Bryant who drowned for the sake of her eyes . . . the very same eyes that Poppy saw in the mirror each day. Poppy felt the words crystallize in her mind.

She recognized Margaret Bryant. She recognized all these women, with their old-fashioned names and cats and grisly ends.

These women were her sisters.

Chapter Thirteen

After school Poppy found Leo. She had guarded her news within her all day long, but she wanted so badly to release it. For years she'd existed in a blur of confusion and doubt, but now she had clarity. At last her life made sense. She felt like a whole new person and longed to introduce herself.

Poppy knew where to find Leo, just as she'd known where to find Ember that day in the woods. He looked shocked to see her, but she took his hand and looked into his eyes and this time he didn't retreat. He didn't look away and she saw everything. The childhood beatings, the violence that caused the scars, the tears sobbed in secret at his mother's death, the final fight—one against three, the slash of the knife and the blood, so much blood, the running away and the never coming back; those first few nights on the streets, feeling hunted, cold, scared; the brawls, the danger, the survival. Poppy's heart contracted in her chest as she realized where Leo lived. She felt an acute pain deep inside of her at all he'd suffered and she cried out. Tears pricked in her eyes and emotion clogged in her throat so she couldn't speak.

Leo squeezed her hand. "Poppy?" he said in a voice that was strained and anxious.

"I messed up yesterday," she managed. "I shouldn't have left you." Then she let go of his hand. "I don't want to have stuff that I don't talk to you about," she said shyly. "I want you to know everything."

Without any more delay, she led him to the dell, walking quickly so as not to keep Ember waiting once more. Leo followed her without asking where or why, just traveling alongside her, helping her over stiles and through hedgerows, holding back the brambles from her face. As they went, Poppy's thoughts ripped through her mind. *How would Leo and Ember react to what she had to tell them?* Ember, she hoped, would understand. Witches were all too familiar to her. *But what would Leo make of it?* "I am a witch." Even to Poppy's ears, it sounded laughable. Leo might not even believe her. And if he did, he might not want to. He might think she was crazy or evil.

He might run for his life.

And then he took her hand, and Poppy felt like she could breathe again. As the panic eased, she focused on the warmth in her palm that seemed to spread up her arm and to her heart. Shyly glancing up at him, she saw him smile at her.

"You all right?" he checked. Poppy nodded. "You looked pretty worried there."

"Yeah, I'm good," Poppy said, realizing that she meant it. "It's all going to be okay."

No sooner had she spoken than the path ahead became thick with mud and they had to stop. Poppy took a tentative step, and her boot squelched into the dark, wet bog. She pulled it back, the sticky earth not wanting to let go of her foot.

"I'll carry you," Leo told her.

"You're kidding."

"C'mon. I dare you."

Poppy scanned Leo's face. His eyes seemed to be laughing at her, though his mouth was straight and serious.

"You can't," she said. "I'm too heavy."

"Heavy! There's nothing of you, girl."

"Okay. Piggyback."

"Seriously?!"

"Turn around."

"Yes, ma'am."

Poppy jumped up onto his back, clutching her arms around his neck, her legs circling his waist.

"Okay?"

"Yup, you?"

"Hold tight." Leo started to walk through the bog with long, slow strides. "Not that tight," he muttered.

"What?"

Leo made a choking sound. "You're kind of strangling me!"

Poppy loosened her arms. "Oh God, sorry!"

He almost slipped, and her arms and legs tightened a second. "Don't worry. I've got you." Poppy relaxed and leaned her head on Leo's shoulder, her mouth a moment from his neck. He nearly slipped again and she cried out and clung on. He laughed.

"You're doing it on purpose," she said with mock outrage. "Let me down!"

"Never!" His arms came back and shifted her up higher onto his back. "Don't you trust me?"

"No!" She spoke out loud, but inside she answered with a *yes*. For she did trust him. She trusted him to know her secret and still want to be with her. She trusted him to believe her and not to run away.

***

Ember stopped in her tracks when she saw Poppy. She had worried all night that Poppy wouldn't come today either, that she'd never come, that she'd never see her again. But there she was, standing in her long, familiar coat, her hands buried deep inside her pockets. Ember raised her arm and waved excitedly.

Poppy withdrew a hand and waved back, and it was then that Ember first set eyes on him. He must have been sitting before, hidden behind the old chest of drawers, for he rose up as if from nowhere, as if by magic. Ember couldn't move. Poppy was smiling at her. And the boy, he was looking up at her expectantly. She was supposed to be hurrying toward them, returning their smiles and greeting them. But the boy's black eyes had her fixed and she couldn't release herself.

"Ember!" Poppy beckoned.

Ember's legs obeyed and she found herself tottering down the hill, unstable as a fawn taking its first steps.

"Hey!" said the boy as she neared them.

The warm, low tone of his voice, the likes of which Ember had never heard before, rippled over her like the river in summertime.

"I'm Leo," he said, and those words brought Ember back to life. Her lips spread into a smile and a blush tingled in her cheeks.

She couldn't risk looking at him directly in the eye, showing all she was feeling, so she gazed at him through her lashes and said as sweetly as she could, "I'm Ember."

Leo offered out his hand and she took it, memorizing the feeling for later.

Ember heard Poppy make a sound, a muttered word or a cough, Ember couldn't tell, but it was enough to make her turn suddenly and remember that her friend was there too. Relieved and happy and embarrassed all at once, Ember threw her arms around Poppy and held her tight.

"I missed you," she said. Over Poppy's shoulder, Ember spied the textbook under the sofa cushion and she broke off to retrieve it. "You got the book I left for you?"

Poppy nodded. "I did. It was . . . it was perfect."

A silence fell over the three of them. Poppy opened her mouth to speak, but then paused as if uncertain what to say. "I wanted . . . I wanted to . . ."

Ember glanced for a second at Leo and immediately felt her blush returning. When she looked back, she realized Poppy had stopped speaking altogether.

"Poppy?" Leo questioned.

Poppy swallowed as if nervous. "This is where I first met Ember," she said quietly. "Where we hang out . . ."

"It's a good place," he said.

"Yeah, a garbage dump!" Poppy remarked.

"I'll fit right in, then," he said flatly, and Poppy rolled her eyes like she was cross, but then they smiled at each other and Ember realized they'd been joking. It was as though they spoke a language she had yet to learn.

The dell was Ember's place, but suddenly she felt like the stranger there when it should be Leo who took that role. He seemed so comfortable, so at ease. The light dappled through the trees and a ray caught his face, illuminating him. And in the clear autumn light Ember's mind brightened with understanding. *Poppy has brought him here for me*, she thought. *This is why she didn't make it yesterday. He is the reason. I told her I didn't have a friend, and she gave me her friendship. I told her I'd never even met a boy and she brought me him—the most perfect boy I could ever have imagined.* She felt a surge of love for Poppy and wished she could cry out her thanks. Instead, she stored up all her gratitude for later and stole another glance at Leo, who smiled at her, and this time, she smiled back more openly.

"It is a good place," she gushed. "I come here often. It's like my home. Not where I live—I don't mean that." Ember felt her cheeks reddening. "Just, I feel more at home here."

Ember could hear herself babbling, but Leo was nodding as though he understood completely.

"Can I show you my favorite thing?" she asked him.

Ember didn't wait for Leo to answer but took his arm and pulled him along. He came so easily. It felt so natural, so effortless, being with a boy, like fox cubs learning to hunt or chicks taking flight for the very first time. Pushing the nettles aside with her foot, she took him to the fireplace with the broken tiles and the cracked marble. From the hearth she lifted up the old clock with flowers engraved at the bottom, and he took it from her hands and studied it.

"It doesn't work," she said apologetically.

"I could try to get this fixed for you if you like?"

Ember's eyes were shining. "Would you? Really?" She felt almost breathless. She turned the clock within his hands and bent her head toward him to show the opening at the back. Trapped inside were the tiny metal wheels suspended there like fallen, silver stars.

His long fingers reached and touched them so delicately. "It's beautiful," he said.

Poppy felt like she had run aground and she was sinking. Cold water was icing her from her toes upward. The chill was spreading up her legs, through her stomach, touching her heart. Soon, she thought, she would drown. She had been sailing on the wind, free and fast, until Ember had set eyes on Leo and Poppy's hull had cracked.

I brought him here, Poppy told herself. *I did this.* She thought she had brought them both together so she could tell them her news, her big, life-changing news. She had wanted to share it so much, but now the words couldn't form in her mind, let alone come out of her mouth. For when Ember had stood there before Leo, Poppy had seen the real reason why they were here.

It was not for her. It was for them.

From across the dell Poppy stared at Ember and saw her afresh through Leo's eyes. She was a girl from another time, untainted by the modern age—long, peasant skirt and rosy cheeks and hair that fell to her waist. It wasn't just her locks that were golden; her whole being shone with hope and promise and goodness. Poppy watched as Ember smiled and brushed the hair from her face and tipped her head to look at Leo shyly through her lashes. Poppy had seen other girls do the same. She wondered how Ember knew what to do when she herself never did. And she realized then that it wasn't copied or learned. It was ageless and instinctive.

As she studied the two of them, their heads close together, almost touching while they examined the clock, Poppy felt a surge of anger and a cloud swept across the sky to cover the sun. She wouldn't tell them her news. Not now, not ever. Gloom descended over the dell and Ember looked up at Poppy, trying to catch her eye, wanting to impart something.

It's gratitude, thought Poppy. *She is thanking me, for him.* Just as quickly as it arrived, the anger departed. Poppy felt limp, powerless without it. A squirrel scampered onto her back and settled on her shoulder. Poppy stood up straighter just so it could rest there.

Later, when Leo was gathering bits and parts he could use or sell, Ember linked her arm through Poppy's.

"A boy!"

"I know."

"A real-life boy."

"There are lots of them out there."

"Not like him."

Not like him, Poppy thought, watching Leo as he worked, his hands deft, the sinews in his arms straining as he took apart the

machinery and broke off the pieces he needed, his face so concentrated and serious.

"Will you tell me?" Ember asked.

"Tell you what?"

Ember giggled in a way that Poppy had never heard her do before. "Tell me what he says about me." Poppy raised her eyebrows
and Ember quickly added, "I'm a silly thing. I know."

Poppy wondered what a tough and flinty boy would do with a
girl as soft as gossamer. Then she felt bad and said, "Of course I'll
tell you."

"You never mentioned him before . . ." Ember said with a hint
of complaint.

Poppy looked away from her. "I haven't known him for long,"
she explained.

Ember must have caught the wistfulness in Poppy's voice, for
she suddenly stiffened and Poppy detected a hint of fear in her
voice as she asked, "He's not . . . he's not your"—her voice dropping reverently—"boyfriend, is he?"

"You are silly," Poppy replied, and with those three small
words, she gave away all hope.

CHAPTER FOURTEEN

The shock stabbed Sorrel like a splinter in her palm. She wasn't sure why seeing the boy hurt so much. She had been expecting him, after all. But a boy being there, in the flesh, touching her cousin, smiling at her, laughing, holding her in his arms before they parted—this was something she could never have imagined. He was a good deal taller than Ember and the other girl. His head was shorn so he had a toughness that belied the gentleness he displayed in his gestures and his mannerisms. His skin was warm colored like honey. He was lean, though, his cheeks hollow and arms wiry. *If you sliced through him, there'd be no fat on the meat*, thought Sorrel.

She had watched from the top of the dell, her eyes fixed on the boy—the way he moved, long legs climbing surely over the broken wares; the way he tilted his head before he smiled, his eyes crinkling at the corners; the way the hair grew sleek and smooth on his arms; the way his voice carried low and rich like the dark, damp earth deep beneath the surface. When Ember or the other girl spoke to him, he looked at them so intently as though he was truly listening, as though they were important.

Sorrel wanted him to listen to her like that. She wanted such a smile. She wanted someone—him—to hold her arm to make sure she did not fall. No one had ever shown her such consideration, nor had she needed them to. In the coven she was able and strong. She was independent. Now she felt weak with confusion and longing. Ember was supposed to be the feeble one, but all of a sudden her cousin had something Sorrel didn't. And Sorrel hated her for it.

The other girl looked as Sorrel felt. Confused, hurt, angry. She hid it well, though, from both of them. Sorrel wasn't even sure what that girl was doing there. *Had the boy brought her? Why?* He left with her too, but the girl kept her distance, and Sorrel felt the wall she'd built around her. Ember had no such barrier. Her emotions lived on her outer edge and she offered them out for all to feel, no matter the bruises or the knocks. For those who had the sight, Ember's new elation was like a mist rising around her, the colors of a sunrise. Sorrel possessed just enough power to behold it, but for those without, it could be sensed.

The boy felt it for sure. Sorrel saw how he was drawn to Ember, how when she hugged him, he hugged her back, her light rubbing onto him. Yet when Ember touched the girl, the light deflected back as though she was impenetrable.

Poppy kept a gap between herself and Leo as they walked back through the night, the trees silhouetted against the blue-black sky. She didn't even look at Leo, not that much was visible now, only the shapes of things, not the details. The murkiness seeped inside of Poppy. She had lied to Ember, and now she would lie to Leo. Her body seemed to rebel against the notion, as she didn't sense the broken branch and her foot tripped over it. She would have fallen to the ground but Leo caught her arm and held her up.

As she grasped onto him, Poppy wondered if she'd get to touch him ever again. Blinded by the blackness of the night, all her other senses were on alert and she could feel Leo's energy. She could smell him, hear him breathe, hear his heart beat. She knew he was about to speak.

"Your friend—is that why we came up here?" he asked. He had a backpack full of stuff on his shoulder, but he held Ember's clock in his hand.

"I wanted you to meet her. She's the best person I know. I . . . I would never do anything to hurt her."

Poppy started walking again, more quickly this time. But a couple of steps and Leo was level with her, tugging on her arm to stop her.

"You had something important to tell me, when you came to find me. I know you did."

His voice in the darkness was rough and urgent. All Poppy could feel were his fingers on her sleeve, nothing else. All she could see were the whites of his eyes. The rest was lost in the night.

I am a witch, she remembered. *I am a witch.*

She shut her eyes and breathed deeply until she was ready. She felt the magic stir inside of her, tingling under her skin, rising up through the pores, and caressing the hairs above.

"I want you to be happy," she whispered. "Remember that."

An owl was circling above their heads, its wide wings beating the air, slower and slower and slower. She heard the owl call to her and she answered its call.

"She'll make you happy," she invoked. "She is good and kind, and she will love you and look after you. Remember that."

Leo was still, silent, but Poppy knew he'd heard her. Somewhere in his mind he'd heard her and the magic had touched him. She opened her eyes and time began again. The owl fluttered away to a tree and the clock in Leo's hand gave a tick, then a tock. The tiny wheels were whirring. Tick tock. Tick tock.

"Hey, Poppy! Look at that!" Leo stared at the clock in his hands in amazement. Then he grinned. "Wait till I tell Ember!"

Leo, Leo, Leo, thought Ember. She wanted to say it, sing it, write it, over and over. When they said good-bye, he reminded her about fixing the clock. She ran and fetched it for him, and their hands touched as he took it from her. She watched him walk away with it, carrying it so carefully, carrying a piece of her with him. She hugged Poppy close, trying to convey through her arms how thankful she was. Then she hugged Leo too, impulsively, and he laughed and she felt his body shake.

"Whoa, you're strong!" he said, and then, "It was nice to meet you, Ember."

"It was nice to meet you too," Ember returned, speaking each word as if she really meant it.

Leo looked from her to Poppy and back again. "You know, it's strange," he said, "but even though you look like total opposites of each other, there's something similar about you, too."

Ember gasped. "It's true!" She looked at Poppy, but Poppy's eyes were on Leo.

"Maybe it's because you're both so different from everyone else," he suggested.

Poppy gave a scoffing noise that made Ember flinch.

"What?" she exclaimed. "You know it's true." Ember quickly turned to Leo. "You're right. We might not look it but we are the same." She tapped her heart. "In here."

Poppy was staring at her now, and Ember knew she shouldn't have protested so much. She wished Poppy would just agree with her and then the moment would be over and another gentler one would take its place. In the end, it was Leo who agreed instead.

"Rare. That's the word."

Rare. That was good, wasn't it? He'd made it sound like it was. Like a rare bird or flower. Ember loved spotting those.

Poppy's voice came unexpectedly. It was small and quiet but sounded utterly sincere. "If I'm similar to you, that makes me better than I thought I could be."

And Ember nearly cried as she hugged Poppy close.

After Leo and Poppy left, she returned to the woods. She was so lost in thought that she didn't feel the ground beneath her feet, or the chill in the air, or sense her cousin's presence by the chestnut tree.

Sorrel stepped into the path and Ember almost skipped straight into her. It took a few moments for her to remember to shield her happiness from Sorrel. Then she noticed the harshness in Sorrel's stare and the rigidity of her stance.

"Where've you been, cousin?"

"To the river."

Sorrel kept her eyes fixed on Ember's. "The river's that way." Her arm moved; the rest of her was hard like granite.

"I was just walking."

"That so?"

Ember felt her head begin to itch. She tried to ignore it and focus on Sorrel, but her hand went to her scalp of its own accord. Once she started itching, she couldn't stop.

"No, Sorrel. Please."

"I think you have lice, dear cousin."

Ember cried out. She felt them now, each one of the thousands of them crawling through her hair. She looked at her hands. Her nails were black with them. She started to weep, a downpour of tears. "Why, Sorrel? Why?"

"Because you think you're so fair. The fairest of them all."

Ember started to run, away from Sorrel, to the safety of her mother.

"Thank your stars it wasn't leeches," Sorrel shouted after her. Then, in a lower voice that Ember couldn't hear, "See if he'll think you're so pretty now."

Sorrel gathered her long skirts and ran to tell her mother that she'd been right about the boy. With the utmost caution, she answered

Raven's questions about him. One hint at her own befuddlement would be a catastrophe. Any of her coven would feel great shame at being interested in a male, but for her, the future queen, it was unthinkable. So Sorrel stuck coldly to the facts, watching and waiting for her mother's reaction. She was expecting Raven to be pleased. Sorrel even hoped she might receive some praise for her work. But none came. Instead, her mother's lips pursed with dissatisfaction and lines of irritation crossed her forehead.

"A boy," Raven repeated. "This was all for the sake of a boy?" She shook her head, then scratched at the back of it in puzzlement.

"She may run off with him," Sorrel added, but it was like trying to light a fire with wet kindling.

"Let her go," Raven spat. "You think I would mourn her departure? You think any of us would?"

"She could tell our secrets," Sorrel sparked. "It is forbidden for any of our clan."

"Pffhh!" Raven huffed dismissively. "Omens predicting misfortune and disaster. The great yew fallen. For this?! For such a one as she, and for a boy?! It cannot be."

Sorrel let a moment pass, then spoke quietly. "Perhaps the boy's companion will do her harm. She seemed aggrieved about the boy's interest in our Ember."

Raven spun round. Crouching low to where Sorrel was sitting, she grabbed Sorrel's chin within her bony fingers. "She? Who is this 'she'?" she snapped.

"A girl. Nobody," gulped Sorrel. Her mother's eyes blackened until the pupils were lost inside the darkness. Despite the pressure of the eyes, the fingers, the breath on her face, the body coiled and ready to spring, Sorrel continued bravely on with her testimony. "She was just someone the boy brought with him. She didn't do or say much. She only waited there and watched them."

Raven pulled herself up to standing, and as she did so her body elongated, her limbs stretched and spiked, all branches and twigs, until she towered over Sorrel. A bonfire, she was, all ablaze, her features fiery, a ferocious energy crackling within her.

"And you mention her but now?" Raven's voice burned, and Sorrel flinched and shrank from the roasting.

"It's the boy Ember's involved with. I tell you, she couldn't shift her eyes from him."

"And *your* eyes, you fool? It was the *girl* you should have been watching."

Charlock felt the heat of Sorrel's humiliation from all the way over in her caravan and guessed she must be facing Raven's wrath. She felt a pang of sympathy for her niece despite the distress she had caused her daughter. She understood what it meant to be related to Raven. How, if you let it, it could make you lose sight of yourself and act in ways you were not proud of.

Charlock was washing Ember's hair, combing the lice from her scalp. Their miniature black corpses lay bobbing in the water, like the charred remains of a shipwreck.

"There you are. All gone now," Charlock said gently.

Ember looked up at her with grateful, reddened eyes. "Thank you, Mother. I love you so!"

Charlock wrapped the golden ponytail around her hand and squeezed the last of the water from it. Ember had a habit of wringing her heart this way. When Charlock thought she'd given as much as she was able, somehow Ember would squeeze a few more drops of feeling from her.

"Whatever you did to annoy her, stop it!" Charlock had a last pull on the ponytail before releasing it.

"I don't know what I did wrong, though!"

Ember's voice was high and plaintive, and it irked Charlock. "Think on it, then stop it. Or more mess will come your way, you hear."

Charlock took the bowl of dirty water and threw it with a slosh onto the grass outside. For a moment she stood and watched the water seep into the ground, back from where it came, the nits sinking to their muddy graves. Then she turned back to her child.

"And I won't always be able to clean it up for you."

CHAPTER FIFTEEN

Minx screeched when she saw it, her cry so sharp with shock that it slashed the air. The ungodly creature had emerged through a cloud, as if born of the night, its bluish-black feathers and ebony eyes melding it with the dark sky. It flew past Minx and settled on the highest branch of the tree. Minx crept along the roof, padding closer for a better look. The bird was a huge, hideous brute, all out of proportion, with a beak too long for its head and oversized skeletal wings that hunched and hung at its sides, making it look much older than its years.

As Minx approached, the creature took off again. It flapped through the air, over the house and garden, back and forth, patrolling the area, its beady eyes surveying the surroundings. Minx watched it go and called to the others, alerting them to the danger. The other cats appeared, their eyes flashing in the darkness.

The bird landed on Poppy's window ledge. Minx screeched again, this time for Poppy, trying to tell her to wake up, to be careful, to know something evil was lurking. The winged monster peered inside the room, its hooked beak tapping on the glass. All the cats started to meow now, their voices a warning siren. Minx leapt forward, landing on the gutter just above the window. She swiped a paw at the creature, who looked up at her and cawed an ugly, hellish sound. Minx hissed, baring her teeth, and the bird took flight again, soaring high. Minx trembled with relief. Poppy was safe.

Then suddenly, without warning, the bird plummeted. Talons outstretched, it plucked Minx from the roof as though she were a mere mouse and carried her squirming body off into the night.

Poppy sat up in her bed, her eyes snapping open. Her heart was beating fast, and her breath was coming quick and shallow. She looked around her room. All was silent and still. Swinging her legs out of bed, she went to the window, pushing her curtain aside. Outside she saw nothing unexpected. But something was wrong. She could feel it. She forced herself to get back under the covers and calm down. Shutting her eyes, she tried to fall back asleep, but rest would not come. She was on high alert, and no matter how much she told herself there was nothing to be scared of, she still felt fearful.

The next morning she was exhausted. The adrenalin had sapped away, leaving her feeling low and depleted. Her eyes were bleary, the skin beneath them tinged with shadow.

"Morning," her father said, more chirpily than usual.

From her bedroom, in her sleepless state, Poppy had heard her father's radio alarm, his feet on the landing, the water from the shower hitting his body, the whine of his electric toothbrush, and the sound of his spit in the sink. But now she was up, she was so tired she hadn't heard him enter the kitchen. She turned and murmured a good morning. He looked annoyed.

"For God's sake, Poppy. Miserable already?"

Poppy rolled her eyes and turned back to her toast.

"Eye rolling?" Her dad looked at his watch. "And not even eight o'clock."

Poppy opened the fridge and searched for milk.

"If it's milk you're looking for, we've run out," her dad advised. Then he laid a ten-dollar bill on the counter. "Pick some up after school, will you? And some bread too."

"Why do I have to do it?" Poppy muttered.

"Because I'm working, Poppy. To pay for the milk and everything else in this house."

Even though Poppy now remembered giving the last of the milk to the cats, she felt like taking the ten dollars and running away. Leo had done it. Leo. Why did she still think of him when he wasn't hers to think about? She took the ten and grabbed her coat and school bag.

"Good-bye, then!" her dad called after her in an exasperated voice.

"Bye," she replied quickly as she opened the door.

Poppy's hand flew to her mouth to stifle her scream. Minx was on the step in front of her but she'd been ripped apart, her stomach and chest exposed so that Poppy could see right inside of her. The little cat's teeth were bared in a grimace.

Poppy dropped to her knees. "Minx . . . oh, Minx!" she gasped.

Minx's head twitched and her eyes turned to Poppy. She couldn't move her head but she was still alive. Poppy reached out a hand to touch her.

"I'm sorry. I'm so sorry," she whispered.

Poppy's heart was burning in her chest. The guilt and pain seared through her. Minx had waited all these hours for Poppy to come, lying there in agony while Poppy had sat in bed, wishing she could sleep.

Why hadn't she walked downstairs and looked outside? Why? She had known something was wrong. All those hours she had known and she had done nothing about it. She scooped Minx into her arms and opened the door.

"Dad! Dad!" she shouted.

His mouth dropped when he saw her. "Poppy. What on earth?!"

"You've got to take us to the vet. Please!" Poppy pleaded.

"Where did you find it? Put it down—it's bleeding everywhere."

"We've got to go. Hurry!" Poppy was crying in earnest now.

"For God's sake, Poppy. Look at it—it's not going to make it." Her dad came closer and stared at Minx with an expression of deep distaste. "It doesn't even have a collar. It's just a stray. Poppy, come on now!"

Poppy looked around her wildly. "Give me your keys? I'll drive her myself."

"Are you out of your mind?"

"What are you going to do? Have me locked up like Mom?" Her dad looked wounded. "I'm sorry. Please, Dad. I'm begging you."

"It's dying, Poppy. It'll never make it. Let the thing die in peace." Her dad walked back into the kitchen. Minx gave a whimper.

"I hate you!" Poppy yelled after her dad, the pain and fury of the words raking her throat. "I hate you!"

She stumbled down the road sobbing, her tears splashing onto Minx's fur. Every time Minx shut her eyes, Poppy would call her name and the cat would try so hard to open them until the effort proved too much and her lids sank back down. Her breathing was long and hoarse, rattling in her wounded chest.

"Don't die. Please don't die!" Poppy begged.

Minx looked into her eyes and Poppy stopped.

"I have to try to save you," she insisted.

Minx stared back at her meaningfully, and Poppy shook her head as if in answer: *I can't lose you too.* But then she looked at her friend, savaged and bleeding, and she moved to the wall and sat down on the pavement. Cradling Minx in the crook of her arm, she stroked her head ever so lightly, not wanting to cause her more pain.

"I love you," she whispered.

As soon as she said that, Minx's breathing slowed even further. Then her eyes shut for the last time and the expression on her small face turned from pain to calm serenity.

Poppy went weak, not just with heartache but something more. The spell she had cast for Leo and Ember stopped. Just like that. It was as though the power lines were down and she could no longer reach the witch part of herself. Not that she cared. She simply continued to stroke Minx, knowing her friend was gone but needing to pretend for just a little while longer.

"Who did this to you?" Poppy asked, and then she understood. It was because of her. Someone had killed Minx to hurt her. And with that realization, Poppy's sorrow sharpened to a hard spike and formed a weapon.

*◦

To Leo's surprise, the clock broke again that morning. One second it was keeping perfect time, the next it stopped dead. As Leo examined the clock, his head felt clearer, his vision sharper than it had been since last night. He had slept heavily, despite the noise and the cold, and dreamt deeply, so deeply that when the sun rose, he found it hard to wake. He floated in and out of sleep for some time until a garbage truck stopped close by, and first the clatter and then the smell forced him to get to his feet and move on.

Still the dream lingered in his consciousness like a mist, and Leo was aware he was thinking and moving more slowly than usual. Try as he might to focus, his mind kept returning to Ember, the girl who had entered his dreams uninvited and unexpectedly. She was a hazy figure, the stuff of fantasy, not flesh and blood like Poppy. Leo tried to picture Poppy, her dark, boyish hair and girlish figure, her wild, clashing eyes. So often he had seen her in his mind's eye, but this time her features wouldn't stick. As soon as he captured them, they'd fade away and in her place Ember would appear, hair spun like gold, smiles and dimples and curves, inviting him closer and closer in. Then the clock stopped, and suddenly she was Poppy's friend again, pretty and sweet, but nothing more to him than that.

Relieved that he was now thinking straight, Leo put his mind to the clock. Its workings looked no different from before, and

Leo could see no reason for its hands to freeze like that. He hoped Mr. Bryce, the antiques guy, might be able to fix it, so he set off to see him, passing the church on his way. As Leo glanced over the graveyard toward the hidden garden, thoughts of Poppy came rushing back to him. He felt so relieved to have her back in the forefront of his mind that he decided to stop and visit there. The clock could wait a while.

For the first time Leo found the old, secret door in the wall hanging open. He hesitated but then stepped through, his eyes scouring the garden to find the person who trespassed there. He wasn't sure who it was at first. He couldn't make out the face, just a figure near the stream crouched on all fours, burrowing into the ground with their hands. Leo moved closer and then stopped when he realized it was Poppy. There was something so violent and desperate about the way she was attacking the ground that he wondered whether he should disturb her. Just as he decided to back away, Poppy turned and looked at him. Her eyes were wild through her matted hair. Tear tracks streaked her muddy face.

"Help me," she said.

Leo moved to Poppy's side, and that's when he saw the cat's body. He had seen the corpses of animals before, mostly road-kill, but this was something different, something vicious. Leo's eyes went to the hole in the earth and immediately he understood what Poppy was digging.

"It'll need to be much deeper or the foxes will get to it," he told her.

Poppy looked at her filthy hands and started to cry once more.

"Wait here. Don't move," Leo instructed.

When he returned he brought with him an old spade. Poppy

shuffled out of the way and watched him dig. It was harder work than he expected. The ground was full of stones, and the metal blade of the shovel made painful sounds as it clashed and clanged upon them. Leo's back and arms started to ache, but he made himself dig further and further, just to be sure. When finally he was satisfied with his work, Poppy placed the cat into the hole.

"What about some flowers? Leaves, even?" he suggested.

Poppy shook her head. She knelt beside the grave and murmured words that Leo couldn't make out. It wasn't a prayer, but Poppy seemed in some kind of trance and the soft words took on a rhythm that felt somehow spiritual. Leo stepped away to give her some privacy. Then Poppy took the earth and started filling the grave. He bent down to help her but she shook her head.

"I have to do this."

So Leo waited until all was complete and she was ready. Poppy stood and faced him.

"You don't mind, do you? That I brought her here?" she asked.

"It's where I'd want to be."

"Me too."

Leo took her home. They stopped on the way so he could put the spade back in the shed from where he'd taken it. He jumped back over the fence and landed softly next to her.

"Like a cat," she said.

When they reached Poppy's house, there were bloodstains on the step and Leo asked if she wanted him to call her dad. She looked at him like he was crazy. Then he asked about school. She sighed and shook her head wearily. He knew what it was like to feel too tired and sad to speak. He ran her a bath and told her to get in it. Downstairs he looked through the kitchen cabinets, his stomach rumbling at the sight of all the tins of food. Rifling through the bottles there, he picked one and poured a little in a mug for her. Then he called the school—the number was pinned to the board by the phone—and pretended to be her dad, informing them Poppy wasn't feeling well today.

He put the mug by Poppy's bedside and looked around her room. It held no obvious clues for him—just lots of books, many of which he'd read himself in the library, and one photograph: a blonde woman, holding onto a black-haired baby. Poppy's mother. A smile was on her lips but it didn't reach her melancholy eyes. Poppy walked in, a towel wrapped around her, and Leo froze when he saw her. Then he said gruffly, "You should get some sleep."

"It's still morning," she quibbled, but he pulled back the duvet and she obediently got into bed.

Covering her up, Leo held her head as she sipped at the drink. She made a face but then sipped some more. Then he rested her head back down and Poppy dropped the towel from under the covers onto the floor and Leo had to force himself not to think of her bare skin on the sheets. He shut the curtains and quickly moved to the door.

"Don't go," she asked in a voice so small, like that of a child's.

Leo sat on the floor, his back to the window, a safe distance away.

Poppy looked at him, then closed her eyes. "It stopped again, didn't it? The clock," she murmured drowsily.

"Yeah, actually. It did."

When Poppy didn't say anymore, Leo presumed she was asleep. He was getting to his feet when she mumbled, "I'm glad the spell broke." Then she shifted on her side and Leo knew she was sleeping.

As he walked down the path toward the street, cats started to appear. Leo stopped to look at them. There must be thirty at least, but more were gathering. Maybe even fifty. Later he'd tell himself he must have exaggerated the number. Each cat found a place in the front garden and sat up proudly. Staggered by the sight, Leo had to make his legs start walking again. As he passed the cats, he couldn't help feeling they were acknowledging him. He knew they made a freakish sight and wondered why he didn't feel more frightened. But there was nothing creepy about them. Quite the opposite. They were full of dignity, and he sensed they had come in reverence to pay tribute to one of their own.

When Leo reached the road he looked up at Poppy's window and thought how strange his existence had become since he had met her. His life had never taken an ordinary course, but Poppy had added another dimension to the journey. With her, they seemed to stumble into the truly extraordinary, the realm that his mother, Jocelyn, had so longed to explore. He wondered when Poppy would feel able to talk to him about these sidesteps into unknown territory. Everyone he knew on the streets had a story, all of them bleak and troubled like his. But Poppy's story felt like a mystery that even she had little comprehension of.

The pristine house with bloodstains on the doorstep. The mad mother with the mournful eyes. The otherworldly friend from the woods. The congregation of cats.

And Poppy, standing all alone at the center of it, the axis to the circle.

CHAPTER SIXTEEN

Raven stretched her wings as she nibbled on the last of the mouse liver. She knew she should be getting back to the camp to check on Sorrel, but she enjoyed these rare interludes she spent as a bird and wanted to savor every last moment before the spell wore off. A simple spell to follow the trail left by the girl from dell to city, and she had quickly found the girl's house, then faced the little ginger cat's pathetic attempt to defend her mistress.

Following her attack on the cat, Raven had soared high above the houses for hours, spying on the lives of the city dwellers below, gathering information on their habits and peculiarities. She observed how they rushed from place to place and task to task without taking the time to notice the details of the world that they themselves belonged to. She listened as they talked without saying much of any worth at all. Little lie after little lie. Only the children seemed aware of the life they held within them, caught in the moment, saying what they meant, and doing what they felt.

When at last she tired of the chaffs and their limited ways, Raven flew away from the town. She still had the taste of blood on her tongue and wanted more. She went hunting for mice in the hills and caught a squirrel, but nothing could compare with the thrill of having that cat squirming in her claws, watching its eyes as she cut into its middle. It had taken great control not to go for the kill, instead to inflict injuries that were deadly but not instant.

Realizing her time as a bird was dwindling, Raven now headed out to sea. As a human, she feared the sea and never ventured to its shores, but as a bird she reveled in it. The air was fresh and tangy with salt, the wind gusty, carrying her feathered limbs faster and higher. She felt freer with the ocean beneath her than any place overland.

Raven was not far from the camp now. Reluctantly she flapped down from her branch and let her talons sink into the wet earth. She shut her eyes and bowed her head, waiting for the excruciating agony to begin. Not many witches had the skill to shapeshift, and those who could avoided it, the pain being so hard to bear. Raven felt the narrow, small bird bones in her body begin to stretch and crunch. It was like being placed on a rack but a hundred times worse. Joints dislocated, skin tore, eyes bulged, organs ballooned until it felt like they would pop. Hunched and naked on the ground, Raven gritted her teeth so she wouldn't scream. Around her feet were black feathers with red blood tips. Raven took each one and jabbed it hard into her white scalp. In moments the feathers turned to hair. Then she hurried to the hawthorn bush and collected her clothes, quickly putting them on before anyone might stumble close to her location. Straightening up, she brushed down her skirts, and on hobbling legs, she walked toward home.

Though Raven's body ached, her mind was at ease. Ember's friend, the girl, posed no threat. Anyone possessed of true magic would have been alerted to the danger Raven had threatened. Raven had flown over the child's house three times to see if she would awake. The girl's cat had called and cried to her, but still she hadn't stirred. And then, when Raven made her attack and had the cat dangling in midair, even then the girl failed to make an appearance. She must be devoid of the sixth sense that would have warned her.

Raven's worries were appeased. Perhaps her daughter had been right to insist that the secret Ember had been treasuring was the boy. Raven had always believed that would be Ember's fate—to leave the coven for a man. She might talk to Charlock about it, persuade her to let the girl have her romance and slip away without objection. It would be a relief not to have to watch Ember's inept attempts at witchcraft any longer. Her mess and incompetence had grated and ground on Raven all these years. Charlock loved the girl, but perhaps she might feel reassured that there would be no search parties or recriminations if Ember were to go.

As Raven entered the camp, she saw Ember sitting busily stitching on her caravan steps, Sorrel beside her, folding the washing. At the sight of her daughter—their future queen—wasting her time with that moon-faced, starry-eyed creature, Raven felt a sudden fury. She knew it was unfounded, that Sorrel was merely following her instructions, but every inch of Raven, outside and in, was aching in unspeakable agony, and she was in no mood to be rational. Ember gave a giggle, Raven's eyebrows rose in irritation, and Ember cried out softly as she pricked her finger on the needle.

It was the first time Raven had ever hurt her niece, and already she regretted it. A bead of blood rose upon the tip and Ember looked at it in clueless surprise, like she never knew such a substance flowed within her veins.

Sorrel watched Ember's face crumple. "Suck it," she instructed, and Ember obediently lifted her finger to her mouth. "Better?" she asked, and Ember nodded.

When I become queen, Sorrel thought, *I will banish you. Aunt Charlock may weep and rail, but I cannot have you as a cousin. You can go anywhere, but not to the boy.* The thought of Ember being a wife to him, sharing a home with brick walls and a roof, lying down each night in the same bed, touching him whenever she pleased, her cousin having everything that she could never have—the idea of this twisted in Sorrel's gut. Ember was powerless, and yet now she had picked herself a fruit beyond Sorrel's reach. How was that possible—for Ember to succeed where Sorrel would surely fail?

Before Sorrel ever set eyes on the boy, watching Ember had been a chore, a duty she wished she could neglect. But today she spied on her cousin with a bittersweet relish. For it brought back the image of the boy as though she could see his face reflected in Ember's blue daydreaming eyes.

All day long she had found herself eking out opportunities to be close to Ember. Until recently she had always kept her distance from her cousin, unless to tease and taunt her. Over the years it had become a habit to choose the other end of the table at clan meal times, to make sure she worked in a different group during chores and schooling, and even to turn away if she saw Ember walking in her direction. This morning, however, Sorrel had sat next to her cousin at breakfast and struck up a meaningless conversation about the weather. Sorrel could see Kyra and the others trying to catch her eye, wondering what she was doing, but she ignored them and kept her attention fixed solely on Ember. Later Sorrel offered to help with Ember's errands. Her friends were puzzled, but thankfully they knew better than to remark on it, for Sorrel had no logical answer to give them. For being that near to Ember hurt Sorrel. It was a jarring, jagged reminder of everything she now realized she lacked.

Close up, Sorrel could see the details of Ember's beauty, the beauty she had always scoffed at, that held no worth or meaning within the coven. She observed how Ember's skin was as soft and luminous as the white rose petals that flourished along the wall of Sister Martha's caravan. She noticed the color in Ember's cheeks was just the same shade of the peaches that grew in the orchard, that her lashes were long and thick like a deer's, and that her eyes weren't just pastel pale but had flecks of the bluest summer sky. And when Sorrel inhaled, she wondered how it was that, even in the depths of winter, Ember smelled of blossom and springtime. With a pang, Sorrel knew what she now saw in Ember was what the boy must see too. And with a wrench, she knew any hopes she had for herself with him were utterly in vain. She, with her beaky nose and narrow eyes, her sallow skin and brittle hair, she could never compare with Ember's loveliness.

Sorrel's newfound interest in her made Ember's hands tremble and her voice crack with nerves. When Sorrel had swung her legs over the bench at breakfast and clunked her bowl of oatmeal down next to hers, Ember immediately suspected a trick. She could see the other girls watching curiously and feared what they might have planned for her. But breakfast passed without incident. Her usually caustic cousin was suddenly sweetness and light, offering her milk and honey, pouring her tea. Later Sorrel folded the laundry with her and asked about her lessons, saying she could help Ember with her studies if she'd like. There were no pranks or spells, no mean laughter or taunting from Sorrel's crowd, and as the hours passed, Ember's suspicions began to fade. Her best guess was that Aunt Raven must have forced Sorrel to help her as some kind of punishment. It was impossible to believe that her cousin would seek out her company of her own accord. But whatever the motivation behind Sorrel's sudden affection for her, Ember became grateful for it. It took her mind off Leo. Alone, she had replayed their meeting over and over again until it felt like a fantasy that she doubted could be true.

Lunch came and went, and as the afternoon dwindled into evening, Ember began to worry how she was going to escape her cousin and get to the dell to see Poppy. She had to wait for Sorrel to be called away by Aunt Raven to take her chance, and then she ran for it, making sure she was clear of the camp before she slowed to a fast walk.

"Have you seen him?" she asked Poppy breathlessly.

Poppy was chewing on the side of her thumbnail so the skin had become red and raw.

"Who?" Poppy questioned belligerently without raising her head from her hand.

"You know who. Him! Leo!" Ember wanted to shake Poppy. She'd encountered her moods plenty of times before, but this afternoon she wanted chatter and laughter, not long, weighty silences and monosyllabic answers.

Poppy lowered her hand. "Yes, I saw him."

Ember's heart beat a little bit faster. "How was he?" she said softly.

"He was . . . he was a good friend."

Ember smiled, then spoke. "You would tell me, wouldn't you? If he said anything about me?"

Ember's eyes shone with pleading, but Poppy looked away, across the dell. She didn't reply, and Ember wanted so badly to ask again but didn't dare.

"I need more books," Poppy said at last. "About the coven's magic and their spells. And the ingredients for the spells—can you get me those?"

Ember felt panic climbing up the ladder of her spine. To smuggle such books out of the camp felt a risk too far.

"I'll mention you next time I see Leo," Poppy added.

Ember understood the suggested trade and it hurt her. "You don't have to," she muttered in response.

Poppy glanced at her and her expression changed. "No, I will. I couldn't yesterday, but I will."

Ember looked down at her feet and nudged at a stone with her boot. "I'll do my best," she conceded.

Poppy suddenly took Ember's hand. "Thank you. Just get me what you can."

"Why do you want them? You mustn't give any of the books I show you to anyone. You know that, don't you?" Ember felt the panic mounting again, higher and higher. What if Poppy showed other chaffs? And what if she showed Leo?

"They're for me. No one knows. I swear it."

"Not even Leo."

"I promise, Ember. I thought you trusted me?"

Ember could hear the hurt in Poppy's voice and see it in her eyes. "I do. I do trust you. You just seem . . . different today."

Poppy hung her head and picked on the skin around her nail. "I'm sorry."

"You trust me too, don't you?" Ember whispered.

Poppy looked up, then finally spoke. "I think I'm a witch."

"A witch?" The word caught in Ember's throat and she had to force it out.

Poppy's face had become more animated. There was a light in her eyes. "I think that's why I met you. I think you and I were destined to meet. So you could show me. Teach me." Ember almost choked at that one. There was a sharp taste in her mouth and she wanted to spit it out. Poppy grabbed both Ember's hands. "Don't you see, Ember? My mother knew. She knew I was different and it made her crazy. Look at my eyes."

Ember stared into them. It was like looking into two separate souls. "I know they're different colors, but that means nothing," she argued. "Plenty of witches have the same color eyes." Poppy's mouth opened with a retort, but Ember saw her think twice about it. Ember stared with wide eyes back at her friend, and in a small voice, she added, "Not just me. My cousin Sorrel, my mother, my aunt, plenty of us."

Poppy dropped Ember's hands and looked away. Then she spoke again, just as vehemently. "And the cats? So many of them keep following me every time we move to a new house. And the insects that gather around me. You don't understand, Ember. So much weird stuff keeps happening to me. It always has."

Ember held her arms out in despair. "I know what you're looking for. An explanation for why you're so alone, why you've never fit in. I know because I want one too. But . . . a witch?"

Poppy looked like she was about to cry. "Why won't you believe me?"

Ember longed to walk away, back to the simple, dreary tasks of laundry and wood collecting, but Poppy's desperation kept her stuck in her place, unable to move.

"Why?" Poppy cried again.

"Because I don't want you to be a witch! Not you! Not you too!" Then Ember started to cry—angry, scalding tears.

Poppy took a deep breath. "I can do stuff, Ember. I don't even know how I do it. It just happens." She took a finger and lifted a tear from Ember's cheek. It sat there, a perfect sphere on Poppy's fingertip, and then magically it lifted and spun like a globe. It turned from white to silver to gold and then fell with a splash onto Poppy's palm.

Ember blinked in disbelief.

Then Poppy shut her eyes and Ember waited until suddenly a small flame sprung up from the damp grass beside them. Ember sprang back but the fire spread, drawing a pattern around them until they were standing in the middle of a burning heart. Ember started to stamp it out, but Poppy exhaled as though blowing out a candle and the flames disappeared without a speck of a singe.

"I need your help."

"You're a witch," Ember stated, just wanting to feel the words on her tongue.

"Yes," said Poppy.

Ember thought back to the bird that had rested on her arm in the dell and hated herself for ever thinking she could have summoned it. "It was you," she sighed, letting the disappointment drift out of her. "You sent the bird to me that day."

Confusion traveled across Poppy's face until it finally arrived at the memory. "Oh," she gasped. "I'm sorry. I'm never really sure what's me and what isn't."

"What are you going to do?" Ember asked, her mind picking up speed as it hurdled over the possibilities.

"I'm going to practice and learn and practice some more."

"And then what are you going to do?"

Poppy's mouth twitched unsurely, and as her certainty deserted her, she again looked like the young girl Ember knew.

"I don't know."

"Will you still be my friend?" Ember felt the tears welling in her eyes once more, but Poppy grabbed her and hugged her close.

"Always. Don't ever doubt it."

Ember clung to Poppy, not wanting to let go. The questions fluttered like an eclipse of moths in her mind, but she batted them away, refusing to let them fly out of her mouth and cloud the moment.

CHAPTER SEVENTEEN

Sorrel helped her mother into the hot bath. She had boiled pot after pot of water to fill the wooden tub in the old shack next to their caravan. Raven was stooped, her joints refusing to straighten, and Sorrel could tell by the way her eyelids kept drooping that the pain was worse than usual. She took Raven's weight as she struggled to raise her leg over the edge of the tub.

"Should I pick you up?" Sorrel asked, wondering if her mother's leg would ever reach its destination.

Raven tutted, and spurred on by her annoyance, her leg finally made it into the water. Sorrel lifted her mother's shoulder so the other leg might follow, then helped to lower her down.

"Lie back," Sorrel said softly, "and I'll get your tea."

She watched her mother's bony, loose-skinned body sink into the water. She heard the relief in her long sigh. Then she turned to leave and nearly stopped in surprise when she heard her mother mutter, "Thank you, child." And, "I'll be better tomorrow."

"I know you will," Sorrel said kindly as she slipped through the door.

Sorrel had been angry when she'd rubbed arnica onto Raven's knees and ankles, sullen when she'd laid hot lavender towels across her back. She had ground the fennel seeds for the tea with a desperate vigor so the pestle and mortar scraped painfully together. For when she was called to her mother's side, she knew Ember would take her chance to leave. She knew too where she would be and whom she would be with. She pictured her cousin in the dell—with him. She saw him touching the sunshine hair, smelling the blossom scent, holding the soft, pale hand. She saw their lips moving toward each other. With that, Sorrel had kicked at the wall, hurting her toe. But now, seeing her mother so diminished, Sorrel felt a sense of self-loathing and guilt at her betrayal. She quickly poured the boiling water over the seeds in the strainer and waited until the tea turned green.

As she returned with the tea, Sorrel sensed her moment to ask about Ember.

"Shouldn't I be following Ember, Mother? You'd said to watch her at all times."

"You can leave that to me now."

Sorrel's eyes flickered and she clenched her jaw to stop herself from responding too quickly and revealing how much it mattered.

"What about the girl?" she asked calmly, controlling the shake in her voice.

Her mother turned her head to look at her. "You were right, child. It was the boy who holds Ember's heart."

Sorrel looked to her lap, feeling her cheeks heat up, knowing they'd be red.

"You did well, Sorrel," continued her mother, offering up her praise. "You can leave the matter with me now."

"She might leave."

"Let her fly."

"The girl, though," Sorrel insisted, trying to keep the panic from her voice. "I know you were concerned about her."

"I have my eye on her. As of yet, she is nothing for us to fear." Sorrel looked at the doorway, the tears pricking dangerously at her eyes. "Be pleased, child. Your task is done. You are free." And with that, Raven took a sip of her tea.

"Yes, Mother," Sorrel murmured, dispelling the urge to grab the mug of tea and hurl it against the wall. If only she'd had the nerve when preparing that brew to reach into the cabinet beside her and take down the sleeping tonic from the collection of bottles and add a few drops to the liquid. Then she would have run and run to that dell and feasted her eyes on the sight of them, of him.

Now it was too late. Dusk was darkening, and Ember would be skipping merrily home. Once again her cousin had outwitted her.

Later, when night had crept upon the camp and the air had chilled to freezing, Sorrel took her cousin a bowl of sugared nuts. She'd had to forego her best hat for them. She missed that hat already as the cold crawled inside her ears and stole the heat from her head. It would be worth it, though, if her cousin were to confess all about the boy. Sorrel could not let Ember get away with her crimes so easily.

"They're not poisoned," she said as Ember looked at the nuts with apprehension. Sorrel turned her mouth upward into a smile to show she was making light, and Ember took the nuts gratefully.

"Thank you, cousin," she said, offering Sorrel some.

They both munched on the nuts like squirrels, letting the brittle syrup melt and ooze upon their tongues.

"Do you ever wish you could leave this place? Eat as many sweet things as you please?" Sorrel asked in her most wishful tone.

Ember looked at her in surprise, then lowered her head.

Sorrel pressed on. "I heard the chaffs have so many different types of sugared treats, it would make your head spin and your teeth turn black."

"We'd need money," Ember at last replied. "You have to buy everything there . . . or so I've heard."

"We'd need to study harder at Sister Brianna's alchemy class then." Sorrel was rewarded with a laugh for that. "In earnest, though, do you wonder what life might be beyond the camp? . . . For I do." She whispered the last words even though no one was about, hoping Ember might feel privy to a deeply held secret and offer up her own to balance the scales of confession. She could feel Ember's eyes searching for clues in her face and kept her features steady.

"I am content with what I have," Ember muttered, taking the last of the nuts, then dipping her fingers into the sugared crumbs and licking them. "Especially with such gifts as these. Thank you again, cousin, for your kindness."

Sorrel was seconds away from inflicting a rash of spots across her cousin's pretty face, but she took a long, deep breath and exhaled slowly. "I thought perhaps you might understand me, Ember. No matter." She stood up to leave. "Just don't mention what I said, I beg of you. Not to anyone."

She turned to walk away and heard a rustle as Ember got to her feet.

"Cousin, wait." Sorrel turned, and Ember stepped toward her. Sorrel sensed victory within her reach. Then Ember's hands reached forward. "Don't forget your bowl."

The next day Ember was in the storeroom, her pockets full of dried herbs and pickled eyes and claws, searching for a jar of poisonous berries that were in short supply. It was morning lessons, and she had been excused from Sister Ada's class on account of the toads. Thankfully it was quickly decided that removing the warts that spotted the toads' rough skin would be more than Ember could cope with.

Outside the class the camp had been quiet, and it was easy for her to wait for a safe moment to slip inside the storeroom. She had dragged a step over to the shelves and was standing on her tiptoes trying to reach the highest ledge.

"Can I help you, cousin?" came the voice. Ember turned and saw Sorrel standing there, a crooked smile upon her face. Sorrel couldn't seem to show happiness without her face contorting so, and this made it impossible for Ember to ever know whether she was sincere. Ember glanced at Sorrel's eyes but they were hooded, the gray pupils two tiny, dull pebbles lost in the shade of her brows.

"My mother sent me to fetch some supplies," Ember hurriedly explained, hoping against hope Sorrel would not investigate further. She wobbled as she stepped down, and Sorrel took her arm. "Thank you, cousin."

Sorrel hopped onto the step and looked down at Ember. "What was it that Aunt Charlock requires?"

Ember's mind whirled. No witch would need the berries unless for an emergency. "Erm, arrowroot," she mumbled.

Sorrel scanned the shelves. "It's right in front of you, you dunce."

Ember rolled her eyes in fake embarrassment. She took the arrowroot and placed it in her pocket, feeling the other secret ingredients brush against her fingertips. She glanced guiltily at Sorrel and felt her cousin's suspicion fall upon her shoulders like a cloak.

"Is there anything else I can find for you?" Sorrel asked neutrally.

Ember's mind whirled with what on earth to say and how to say it. Then it came to her. "I've thought about what you said last night. And I do understand what it was you were speaking of." Sorrel blinked in surprise, and Ember, encouraged, continued on. "Wondering of another life, or a different world from ours."

"Sometimes," said Sorrel, "I wish I could meet a chaff, just to know, to ask them what it's like, out there."

Ember held her breath and clocked how extraordinary it felt, such a moment as this. A bond of true friendship with any of her fellow sisters was something she had long since stopped dreaming of. But now the moment was here and the seconds were ticking away, taking it further from her.

Unless she spoke. Now.

She opened her mouth to tell her cousin something true, something secret. Sorrel leaned forward just a fraction in anticipation, so as not to miss a word.

"Ember!" came the call. Then again, more urgently, "Ember!"

Sorrel's face twisted with frustration. Ember's mouth closed. The moment was lost, and she doubted it would ever be refound.

"My mother," Ember whispered as Charlock's head peered around the storeroom door.

"There you are, girl. I was wondering where you had got to."

Ember looked dazed. She'd never been very good at lying to her mother.

"She was just bringing you the goods you asked for. I'm afraid I delayed her, Aunt Charlock."

Her mother's eyes flicked from Sorrel, who was smiling that misshapen smile of hers again, to Ember. Ember couldn't bear to meet her mother's gaze so let her eyes fall shut for a moment.

"Well, let's not dawdle any longer. I'm sure your cousin has better things she could be doing."

Ember heard her cue and hurried to the door, glancing in apology to Sorrel, who stood there stiff and unyielding as a post.

"Thank you, Sorrel," Ember heard her mother say as she stepped into the bright winter light and her lungs gulped down the sharp, cold air.

Ember and Charlock's feet tapped quickly over the hard ground. It was only when they were back inside the caravan, the door firmly shut and the windows checked for eavesdroppers, that Charlock spoke. Ember was grateful for the sound as the silence had been so heavy, she had felt it pressing upon her brain.

"Speak," was all her mother said.

And this was how Ember found herself confessing to most, but not all, of what had happened that autumn. She made no mention of Leo—that she didn't dare—or of any names. She just talked of meeting a girl one day in the dell, a girl who was kind and understanding, a girl who now believed herself—no, knew herself—to be a witch.

"Are you sure?" Charlock asked.

Ember nodded. "She can do things, things even the girls here can't do, and that's without knowing how or why."

Charlock's brow furrowed, and she moved to the kitchen and busied herself heating water on the stove. "And the things from the storeroom? They are for her?"

"She just wants to learn. To practice," Ember said, marveling at her mother's quiet response to this news. "She is one of us, Mother."

Ember noticed a look of hurt cross her mother's features before she quickly blinked it away. The water was beginning to rumble in the pan, the bubbles rising, but neither of them paid attention to it. Instead, Ember watched as her mother reached into her cabinet of supplies, picking deftly and swiftly at different bottles and jars to make a small packet of ingredients. When Charlock was done, she went to the shelves and took down a book, placed the packet upon it, and handed both to Ember.

"Take her these," she said. "And tell her I expect the book back in the state she found it."

Ember hugged Charlock tight. "Thank you, Mother. I am the luckiest of daughters."

Charlock pulled her roughly away. "You are not to speak of this to anyone."

"I know," Ember quickly reassured.

"Not even Sorrel."

Ember flushed under her mother's hot look. "Not even Sorrel," she promised. "Nor Raven," she added for good measure.

"Especially not Raven," her mother said, and then she turned, at last, to the water, burbling so fiercely now that it was foaming up and spilling out over the confines of the pot.

CHAPTER EIGHTEEN

Poppy had intended to look for Leo before now. She had intended to find him, thank him, hold him so he knew how much his help with Minx meant to her. But yesterday had disappeared so quickly. She had awoken late in the afternoon, dazed and distressed. Then her meeting with Ember had left her even further drained, and she had returned to her bed and cried for Minx some more. As she sunk back into sleep, she promised to herself that she would get up early to find Leo before school, but she had overslept and only woke when her father was banging on her door, shouting that she was late.

Poppy spent classtime memorizing spells. She became so lost in them that she didn't hear Mr. Reed ask her a question, then ask if she was listening, then ask if she'd listened to a single word he'd said all class. In fact, she didn't hear a thing until Mr. Reed was right in front of her, hands on her desk and leaning forward until his face was only a few inches from her own. Only then did she hear the class snickering and Mr. Reed furiously ordering her out of his classroom to the principal's office.

After that, Poppy heard everything. The scribble of Mr. Jeffries's pen on paper, the bell ringing, the chairs grating on the floor, the doors opening, and the gossip chiming down each and every corridor, rippling into every room. Each time her name was mentioned, Poppy felt it like a little pinch. It actually made the task of eliciting Mr. Jeffries's sympathy easier as, while Poppy talked of her grief for her pet cat, the constant sting of the pinches caused her to shift in her seat, her breath to catch in her throat, and finally her eyes to actually tear up.

Mr. Jeffries offered up a conciliatory box of tissues, and as Poppy went to take them, their hands touched for the briefest of seconds. Suddenly Poppy knew Mr. Jeffries was a dog lover. She had no idea how she knew. She just did. So as she sniffed into one of the tissues, Poppy talked of her hope that she could now persuade her father to get a puppy . . . a black Lab . . . her favorite breed.

"I have one!" Mr. Jeffries declared proudly, as Poppy knew he would.

In the end Poppy was awarded the rest of the day off so she could mourn in peace, for "A death of a pet is a death in the family."

As soon as she left school Poppy went not to the dell but to the stream behind the graveyard. Calling Leo's name, she searched the garden, and when she didn't find him, she ignored the urge to go and sit by Minx's burial spot. Instead of lingering there, she hurried back through the hidden door, down the church path, and through the gate. Heading directly into town, she scoured the streets for all the spots her eyes usually wouldn't think to stray upon—doorways, benches, under bridges, by the trash cans down the backstreets, along the railroad tracks. There she found an invisible community of old men with beer cans and bottles in paper bags, kids tucked into ratty, old sleeping bags, and a lady with newspapers tied around her feet, pulling a shopping cart stacked high with all her worldly possessions. But no Leo.

Her feet aching, Poppy rode the bus home. She pressed her face up against the window, her breath steaming a small, oval patch onto the glass as she stared out in hopes of spotting him. When she got inside the house she sat cross-legged on the floor and tried to meditate. She thought it might help her reach that place in her mind that could fathom information, impossible information like about Mr. Jeffries's dog. How was it she could know that trivial, useless fact and not know the things that really mattered to her?

Frustrated, she tried to empty her mind of all other thoughts. It was hard to do with everything that had happened recently. She visualized a lake, with waters still and serene, but then a thought would bob up about Leo, or Ember, or school, or the fact that she had missed lunch and her stomach was rumbling. She tried focusing on Leo. She tried to picture him outside in the cold. She tried to see the landscape around him—outside or in, town or country? Nothing came to her at all, just the flat, emptiness of the lake.

Then Poppy remembered how her and Mr. Jeffries's hands had touched and how that had caused her to see into his life. She rushed to the hall to pick up the bag that Leo had touched, then all the items within that might hold a trace of him. She still got nothing, not an inkling. Poppy felt so powerless that it almost made her laugh to think she had proclaimed herself a witch. *What's the use of magic*, she thought, *if I can't control it?*

Poppy was so used to her powers being random and unprompted that it didn't occur to her until much later that night that she simply might find a spell to aid her. As it turned out, Ember's books contained several methods for locating people. Some for enemies, others for strangers, and some for loved ones.

With a deep breath, Poppy went for loved ones. If she wanted the spell to work, she reckoned that she had better be truthful. A couple of the spells demanded ingredients she didn't have. Another required her to boil a concoction in a cauldron over a fire (Poppy hoped a nonstick saucepan on the stove would do). However, the smell was so putrid Poppy had to abandon her cookery halfway through, open all the windows, and flush the vile mixture down the toilet. Finally she thought she'd try to divine Leo's presence using sticks. She didn't have a glass ball, her dad never bought loose tea so she couldn't read the leaves, and they had run out of coffee, but sticks she could collect from the garden.

> *Spin, turn, around and around*
> *If the person must be found.*
> *Quicken, quicken, until you drop,*
> *Then throw your hand to read your lot.*
> *The sticks in their landing show*
> *All it is you seek to know.*
> *Open your eyes and you will see*
> *Where it is your loved one be.*

Poppy spun on the spot like a whirling dervish, arms outstretched, head tilted back, eyes closed, lost in motion. She felt

silly at first, self-conscious, even though she was alone in the
house and had shut the curtains so no one could see her. But then
the sensation of turning began to feel familiar. As she built up
speed, Poppy felt transported back to a time when spinning until
you were so dizzy that you couldn't stand anymore and bumping
into furniture and stumbling across the carpet until your brain
went straight again was a totally normal thing to do. Whipping
through the air, Poppy recalled her mother's voice telling her to
stop and she heard her young voice shouting back as she spun,
"I want to go home! I want to go home! I want to go home!"
Poppy remembered feeling weightless, like she was flying, until
her mother's hand yanked on her arm, pulling her to the floor.

"I want to go home!"

"You *are* home!" Poppy heard her mother scream.

Poppy was whirling so fast now that the memories floated up
with her hair and blurred with her arms and the room around
her. Then, unexpectedly and all of a sudden, Poppy stopped. Just
as the spell instructed, her fingers released the sticks as she fell to
the ground. Her head was a mushy, mindless mess. Her temples
throbbed. "I want to go home!" she heard in the far-off, remote,
unreachable past. As her brain began to settle, Poppy slowly raised
her head and opened her eyes.

It took a moment to focus. The sticks seemed to sway on the
carpet in front of her. Poppy blinked and then they stilled. She
had wondered how she would read them. She had thought she
would have to study the book to decipher their meaning. But
she saw it instantly, where Leo was. In her mind flashed an image of Leo, lying down, curling up against the cold, and shutting

his eyes against the dark. She glimpsed the shadowy shapes and structures surrounding him.

Leo was in the playground at the park.

With the spell completed, Poppy grabbed her coat and was hastily putting on her boots when her father opened the front door.

Without a hello, he immediately said, "Uh-uh. You're not going anywhere. Not at this time." Poppy put on her other boot. "And I had a phone call today from your principal recommending me a dog breeder."

Poppy paused, then straightened. "I just thought . . ."

"What did you just think, Poppy? That you can fool me like you did him?" Poppy noticed her dad looked more weary than angry, but she didn't have time to answer before he continued, "What did you do this time to end up in his office?"

"Nothing. Nothing big. I just wasn't concentrating in class. I was tired."

"Tired! I could hardly get you out of bed this morning." Poppy felt her father's eyes scan her face with worry. "If you're so tired, you better get to bed quick then. We'll see how you feel in the morning."

Poppy took off her coat, then her boots. She knew there was no persuading him. She couldn't bring herself to attempt any magic or clairvoyance on her dad. Somehow she sensed it wouldn't work anyway. As she walked up the stairs to her room, he called after her.

"Poppy!" She turned around and noticed suddenly how small her father seemed to her as she looked down upon him. "You've been doing so well since we moved. Don't let what happened to the cat . . . don't let it spoil things."

Poppy felt a pang of pity for her dad, for all his regrets, for ending up here on the edge of the country so far from home, for having a daughter like her, and so she nodded in understanding. Her dad sighed and padded off to the kitchen, and Poppy climbed the rest of the stairs to wait it out until it was safe for her to leave to see Leo.

By eleven o'clock Poppy could hear the low rumble of her dad's snores rolling across the landing. She waited another half an hour to be sure, then slipped silently out of the house. The cold night air felt fresh and illicit, and Poppy ran down the street, the adrenalin picking up her feet and making her feel more awake than she had been in days.

She reached the park more quickly than she'd anticipated. She climbed over the iron fence and jumped down the other side, her knees and feet soft for the landing. She had seen the playground from afar but had never been inside before. Her eyes pierced the darkness, looking for movement or just the shape of him. The place was eerie at night, like it was never meant to be empty or so very quiet. The slide, swings, and merry-go-round looked sad and desolate without any children on them. It felt to Poppy like it was the end of the world and she was the only person left upon it. Then she saw him, curled up beneath the climbing frame, nestled on the woodchip floor.

Leo didn't wake, not even when Poppy lay down beside him and got underneath the old blanket, burying her face in the back of his neck. He seemed to feel the warmth, though, and in his sleep, his hand took hers and tucked it underneath his chin. Poppy felt the tears form in her eyes that such a gesture could come so easily and naturally in sleep. She pressed her whole front against his back, her legs curling behind his, and let herself lie there peacefully, feeling this was where she should be. Nowhere else in the world but here.

Nothing was going to wake Leo that night. His day had been full and tiring. He'd walked across the hills to the next town inland to sell the bits and pieces he'd scavenged from the dell. A scrap-metal merchant, round as a truck tire, weighed Leo's paltry pieces of iron and copper and offered him a pittance for them. Leo took the money gratefully and said he'd be back with more. The man gave him a look of indifference, but Leo held the five-dollar bill up in the air triumphantly and told him he'd be seeing him soon. On the walk home Leo kept his hands plunged into his pockets, rubbing the five between his finger and thumb, thinking he would feast at lunch time. As it turns out, the chicken pot pie and the candy bar made him sick, and he threw them up down an alley, so his stomach was back to being empty once again. Leo had lived off leftovers for so long, it seemed he couldn't even eat normally anymore.

After gulping down some water he found in a half-finished bottle in a trash can, Leo took Ember's clock to Mr. Bryce. In all the drama with Poppy, Leo had forgotten his offer to Ember until late last night, when he had used his bag as a pillow and felt the edges of the clock digging into his head. Now that it came to it, though, heading off to the other side of town was the last thing Leo felt like doing. But a promise was a promise, and Mr. Bryce was the only person Leo knew who might be able to do the job.

His workshop, Bryce's Restorations, was a tiny antiques place on the corner of a terraced street of houses. It seemed a miracle that Mr. Bryce ever did any business from such an unlikely location, but his place was always full of ancient pieces of furniture and ornaments that people wanted him to repair. A few months back Mr. Bryce had found Leo sleeping in the back of his van. Leo, who had found the doors unlocked, had taken shelter there for the night, planning to be gone before dawn. Mr. Bryce was a very early riser. But instead of being angry or calling the police, he'd calmly made Leo a proposal—a little breakfast in return for a little help. He hadn't interfered or offered any pity or any charity—just a simple business transaction.

Before examining the clock, Mr. Bryce put on his spectacles, then held it right up to his long nose.

"Where'd you get this?" he asked gruffly, his eyes narrowing as he scrutinized Leo's face like it too was broken and needed restoration.

"It's not stolen. I swear it."

Mr. Bryce raised his eyebrows suspiciously.

"A friend gave it to me, to get it fixed." Mr. Bryce picked up a magnifying glass and peered at the clock again. "Look, can you fix it or not?"

"I'll give you fifty for it?"

Leo blinked. Fifty—that could last him for weeks. He could get used to eating pot pie and chocolate again. He could buy a sleeping bag from a store. He could buy Poppy dinner somewhere, act like a normal guy taking out a girl. But then Leo remembered Ember's face when she'd shown him the clock and how she'd trusted him to get it fixed, and he felt his mind soften and his purpose weaken. There weren't many people in the world who would trust him like that.

"I told you. It's a friend's," he said.

A look of surprise crossed Mr. Bryce's face, then one of irritation. "You tell your friend then. It's an antique, this one, a collector's item. Tell them to come talk to me, unless you can decide for them?"

Mr. Bryce held Leo's stare, waiting expectantly. As Leo stared back, he felt the few quarters he had left sitting in his pocket and thought how many quarters there would be in a whole fifty, how there'd be so many they wouldn't fit into both his pockets. Then Leo gave a slight shake of his head and Mr. Bryce said, "Give me a few days then," taking off his spectacles with liver-spotted fingers to reveal resigned, watery eyes. "I'll fix it up like new."

Leo spent the rest of the afternoon earning the fee for the repair, working in the storeroom, sweeping up, polishing the old pieces of furniture that Mr. Bryce had restored until they gleamed, unpacking boxes, and lugging the heavier items on and off the van out the back. He did all this so he could see the pleasure on Ember's face when her clock told the time again. Yet while he toiled, he thought of Poppy—how she was, where she was, when he might see her once more.

If his day had been long, Leo's evening had been even longer. He was shattered, every bone and muscle aching, and he longed to sleep early. But each time he laid his head down to get some rest something came along to disrupt him and he had to move on, searching for a new place to sleep. Mourners were keeping a vigil by a grave near the garden door, so he couldn't even enter there. In his other favored spot, someone had peed and Leo hadn't yet fallen so low to be able to ignore it. He then persuaded a couple of guys to let him join them under the arches, but ten minutes later he was woken up by yells that the police were coming. They all grabbed their stuff and ran for it.

In the next hangout, the crazy ranting of an old, white-haired street performer made it impossible to sleep, even for Leo, who had learned early on to block out noise. Finally he was uprooted by the jeers of an approaching gang of drunken office-types. He knew from experience the suits were the worst—so civilized and buttoned up by day but, at night, wild and vicious as savages.

Leo had never slept in the park before. It was considered too dangerous in there. A guy had been beaten up near the pond last year, and by the time he'd been found by an early morning jogger, it had been too late to save him. Leo preferred to have people around, safety in numbers, even if often they were out to cause trouble. But by now Leo was desperate and he could think of nowhere else to go.

When he entered the park, Leo realized immediately why he'd never ventured here before. It wasn't so much the danger than the utter loneliness of the place, like it was a habitat for ghosts, not for the living. But he was so exhausted, his lids drooping over his eyes, that he was almost asleep on his feet and could not comprehend turning back and starting his search afresh. He headed for the playground, remembering the one in his old town that Jocelyn used to take him to, how she used to push him on the swing and turn him on the merry-go-round. He saw her grinning face as she ran around and around, before she was ill and still had life in her, spinning him faster and faster, laughing as she went.

Leo lay down in the shadows beneath the climbing frame, telling himself that no one would find him there, telling himself he was invisible. He shivered under the blanket. The weather had turned properly cold now, and Leo knew with a sinking stomach that this month was just a small taste of the bad weather ahead. He would have to get his hands on a proper sleeping bag if he was going to survive the winter.

He always found it hard to sleep when the temperature was so low. The cold would keep nipping at him, biting at his skin, chilling in his chest. But tonight he was so shattered that, though his mind registered these attacks, his body refused to wake for them. In his dreams a warmth arrived from nowhere and spread down his back and through his limbs. It was so sweet and welcome that he held it tight, praying it would never go.

The birds started singing well before dawn had broken. It was still pitch black, and their song seemed out of place and out of time. For Poppy, they were her alarm, signaling her moment to go. Much as she longed to, she couldn't bring herself to wake Leo. He still looked so very tired, with shadows under his eyes and breathing that was heavy and slow, like even sleep was a labor. It seemed cruel to disturb him. So instead, very carefully, Poppy slid out from under the blanket. Leo stirred in his sleep, then shivered as he felt her warmth leave. Poppy took off her coat, stuffing the contents of her pockets in her bag, and laid it over him, satisfied he would recognize it and know she had been there.

Leo soon settled beneath it, his body still, his breathing steady. Poppy's teeth started chattering before she reached the park gates, but she didn't care. She had slept by Leo's side and this would see her through the day.

Sorrel watched the girl depart, wishing she could take her place next to the boy. He would hardly notice, one warm body for another. But what if he woke and saw her and realized it wasn't Ember next to him? The other girl had taken her chances. She'd been careful not to wake him, but then she'd left her coat. This puzzled Sorrel. The night was a cold one, to be true, but this would reveal her identity after taking such measures to keep him unaware. Perhaps the girl believed the boy would not recognize the coat but only wonder how it came to be placed on him.

The girl was light on her feet and she made no sound as she shut the playground gate and ran away down the path. When she had disappeared from sight, Sorrel moved closer to the boy, her eyes soaking in his features, so vulnerable in sleep. She realized with surprise that he was most likely younger than she and it made her feel like a fool for fearing his reaction to her. She could kill him right now, stop his breathing with a spell, and he would never have a chance to defend himself, let alone be shocked by her presence or disappointed by her looks.

Empowered by this knowledge, Sorrel laid down next to him and put her body where the girl's had been, stretching her arm around him as she'd seen her do. Sorrel held her breath and waited. Her body tingled with a feeling she'd never experienced before. It was more than excitement, more than anticipation. Then she breathed in his scent and felt dizzy with it. In these few moments she was not the future queen; she was not the daughter of the great witch Raven. She was merely like Ember, having a secret, making a mistake. Sorrel felt the boy's heart beating in time with her own. She heard the rhythm, so loud she wondered why it didn't wake him. But the boy didn't move a muscle. His hand didn't reach for hers. He didn't hold it to his chest. He just lay there, breathing, in and out, as if she didn't exist at all.

When she left, Sorrel took the coat. She did it to spite the girl whose hand he'd held. And she did it to spite him. She had gone to such lengths to find him, channeling all her power and knowledge as well as risking her mother's wrath for leaving the camp, and for so little reward. At first she hadn't wanted him to notice her, but as it turns out, not being noticed at all felt worse. Stinging with resentment, she stuffed the coat into a park trash can as she left. It would be found the next day by an old lady with newspaper shoes who would give a toothless grin of delight at her good fortune. She wouldn't think to wear it, just push it around in her shopping cart with the rest of her treasures.

CHAPTER NINETEEN

Poppy spent the following days working harder than she'd ever done before. Any spare minute, she would memorize spells and remedies so she knew them by heart and practice magic so it became second nature. Her mouth was constantly moving as she chanted charms under her breath, so much so that her classmates began to believe that Poppy had finally gone crazy. She wasn't scandalous or freakish anymore; she was just sick in the head. Poppy walked around school in such a haze that even the teachers couldn't fail to notice. Ever vigilant, they began to worry she might be under the influence of alcohol or drugs. A couple of them asked her to stay behind after class, hoping she would open up to them and offer an explanation for her behavior. They came away empty-handed, though, as Poppy stayed quiet and offered nothing. She just ever so lucidly and stone-cold soberly denied any problems.

Witchcraft was at the forefront of Poppy's mind, but at the back of it was Leo. He was always there, a part of her, and it felt odd she hadn't seen him for a while. She had expected him to return the coat and thank her for it. She had it all rehearsed—how she would refuse to take the coat back, showing him the new one she had bought from the secondhand store; how he would insist; how she would give him her old sleeping bag instead. She had needed to stand on a chair to reach it from the highest shelf of her closet. It was still in its plastic bag, never used, bought for a camping trip that, like so many of the trips planned with her dad, had never materialized. She had dusted it off and stuffed it under her bed where it lay waiting, as she did, for Leo.

As the days passed by and Leo still didn't show, Poppy allowed herself to drift further away from the day-to-day reality in which Leo and the coat and the sleeping bag existed and into the realms of her own mind, stretching it to the limits, venturing into the unchartered frontiers of her imagination. She dimly recognized that she was becoming obsessed, "training" like an Olympic athlete, needing her fix like a junkie, powerless to stop even if she wanted to.

And she didn't want to. Since Minx's death, something had taken hold inside of her. It was as though she had been empty of magic for so long that now that she felt full, she could never go hungry again. When Poppy succeeded in a spell, she felt complete, fully alive, like her whole self was present in that moment. And she felt triumphant—like she could fell a tree with her bare hand, or dive to the darkest reaches of the ocean and still have air to spare, or conquer the tallest mountain without tiring.

The only thing that could pierce this high was Leo. Whenever Poppy's mind strayed and touched on him, she felt her powers fade and found herself plummeting back down to earth. Magic didn't seem to hold the answer for the butterflies in her stomach when she thought of him or the confusion clouding her head when she remembered Ember's feelings for him. Leo was a distraction, an itch that if she started scratching, she would never stop. Poppy didn't want to spend her time wondering where Leo was and why he hadn't come to see her. She didn't want to doubt herself just when she was starting to believe. She wanted to climb back up to those dizzying heights where she felt like she could conquer anything.

Ember hadn't made it to the dell for days, but one evening she came over the top of the hill, picking a pathway down the slope, carrying in her arms a big bag brimming with treasures. She handed over the latest ingredients to Poppy and then, rather nervously, a new book. This one looked even older and more precious than the rest, and Poppy felt a thrill run through her when she saw it.

"It's my mother's," Ember told her in a voice strained with worry.

She seemed reluctant to let it go. Her fingers tightly clasping it, she made Poppy swear she would give it back soon and not leave a mark upon it.

"I know how precious it is," Poppy reassured her as she gazed at the book in reverence. She gave the book a slight pull so Ember had to release it. Quickly flicking through the pages, her eyes feasting on the ancient ink, Poppy could feel Ember wincing. It annoyed her, Ember's possessiveness. She tried to joke, "I am allowed to read it, aren't I?" but didn't bother to wait for Ember's reaction.

Poppy had already returned to the book, absorbed in what lay within. Simply seeing the words without even comprehending them transported Poppy to some higher plane that felt almost spiritual.

Ember, meanwhile, was feeling low, stuck in the mires of the mundane. Her complaints were of the coven—the cousin who wouldn't leave her be; the endless washing and mending clothes; the tedium of the long, lonely evenings; the reports of another foreign clan traveling closer, soon to be on these shores; fears of how this clan uprooted their tree and intended harm to her family. At this, Poppy's ears pricked and she looked up from the book.

"Another clan? How many are there? Are they everywhere?" Poppy could hear the excitement in her voice, and Ember heard it too and she looked at Poppy as if, momentarily, she didn't recognize her. "I'm sorry," Poppy quickly added. Then, for good measure, she continued, "I am sorry for the threat of this clan, I am. But your aunt will keep you all safe. You did say she was the most powerful, didn't you?" Then Poppy drifted off into her own imaginings for a moment before returning and finishing wistfully, "It's just I had never thought there'd be so many others."

"Why is that a good thing?" Ember remonstrated. "You wouldn't even like most of the witches I know. And the Eastern clan, they are truly wicked. They'd cut you down and boil your bones for their spells."

Even this gruesome detail sent a strange spark through Poppy. But she just said, "I like you, don't I, and you're a witch?"

Ember shut her eyes for a second, then gave a small smile. When she spoke next, it was of Leo and it became clear to Poppy this was what Ember had really wanted to talk about all along. Leo was the true cause of her anxiety—how she might see him again, when she might see him again, and why she hadn't seen him already.

With a shudder, Poppy realized how these thoughts mirrored her own. How pathetic she could become if she let herself. Poppy quickly glanced back down at the book, and soon Ember's words became as distant as the babbling stream beyond the dell and the breeze in the highest branches of the trees. Yet again, magic was her salvation. Poppy murmured some half-felt, sympathetic noises, and when finally she sensed a pause for breath coming, she pushed another list of supplies into Ember's hand. Ember looked at the scrunched-up piece of paper with dismay, and Poppy had to beg and plead that she try her best to gather them for her.

"It's working, Ember. I'm getting stronger. I can feel it."

Ember hung her head as she walked away, and Poppy felt a pang of pity. Perhaps she could find a spell to lift Ember's spirits and bring her better luck. Poppy's mind began to whir as different symbols and chants sprung to her mind that she might use. By the time she reached the outskirts of the town, all thoughts of her friend, or the sleeping bag for Leo, or the endangered cousin and foreign clan had evaporated. There was only the magic.

Leo, in the meantime, was pretending his feelings weren't hurt. He was fine that Poppy hadn't come to find him; he didn't need a thank you for all his help—he and Poppy, they were above all

that. She would show up when she was ready and he was happy
to wait until then. At least that's what he told himself, over and
over as though he were reciting lines from a speech that someone
else had written. However, it was hard to say the lines with any
real conviction when the disappointment of Poppy's absence kept
tripping him up and making him falter.

Leo spent a lot of his time beyond the graveyard walls, fig-
uring this was still his place, and if Poppy happened to be there,
then that was her business. He sat by the stream for hours, quiet
in the solitude that until recently he'd found comforting but now
just felt lonely, trying not to think forward or back, trying not to
have any expectations. It didn't work. His head kept turning at
the slightest noise. It was always simply the rustle of wildlife in
the bushes—a squirrel snapping a twig, a fox in a thicket, a bird's
cry splitting the air—but Leo couldn't help himself but look, just
in case . . . just in case it was her. And every night Leo left for
the town, feeling foolishly surprised Poppy hadn't walked through
the old, creaking door in the wall with an apologetic smile on
her face and a sheepish wave of the hand and that he hadn't had
the chance to forgive her instantly, despite knowing he should be
more aloof.

Leo wondered why Poppy didn't, at the very least, come to visit
the cat's grave. He worried she might have fallen into some kind
of trouble. Yet deep inside he felt it was important that Poppy
come to him this time. It wasn't a question of turns, or pride, or
resentment. Leo wanted the two of them to feel balanced, like
they fitted, like they could walk in step and in time. It was so very
tempting, though, to go to Poppy's house or school, just to get a

glimpse of her. But with his mind set, Leo waited, and the days ticked by and life just got slower and dimmer and grayer without her.

Ember's clock, however, was ready, and at last Leo had a purpose. He set off for the dell, walking faster and taller than he had done in days. He pictured Ember's face when she'd see the clock, and the thought made him feel brighter until his mind returned to the possibility that Poppy might be there and his face grew somber again and his step slowed. But, he reasoned, if they met today, it was not by his doing. It was beyond his control. Besides, it was Ember he was going to see.

As it happened, Poppy wasn't at the dell and Leo didn't turn around in expectation at any of the rustles or crackles from the woods, and when he left, he didn't feel disappointed. It was Ember who appeared there, whose face lit up with a smile upon seeing him, who raised her arm and waved in greeting. Her happiness, fresh and clear as the water that sprung from the mountainside, turned out to be the perfect tonic for Leo's troubles. The hours he spent with Ember felt as natural and simple as life should be, not distracted by the past or anxious for the future, no sudden highs or lows. What you saw with Ember was what she felt and what you received.

First, she helped him collect more scrap to sell, humming a tune as she searched. Then she showed him the river and lent him her homemade soap to wash his hands. The soap smelled of happy, carefree days. It smelled of Jocelyn. Chatting away so effortlessly in her singsong voice, Ember told him the names of all the plants and trees. There wasn't one she didn't know. She shared the nuts she carried in her pockets. They tasted so much better than any he had tried before. And when he shivered at the fierce north wind, Ember gave him a scarf she had knit. She wound it around his neck and looked so pleased to see it on him.

Only then did Leo realize that he hadn't given her the clock. Her face when she saw it was just as he'd imagined. And then she kissed him.

Chapter Twenty

Ember wasn't used to her dreams coming true, but she had dreamt of Leo and there he was. Not just a figment but real flesh and blood. He was standing in her dell, looking like he belonged there, rummaging for bits and pieces like he knew the place. She watched him for a while like she would a rare bird or butterfly, feeling blessed simply to have spotted him, committing to memory the feeling of having him there just in case he never passed this way again. Fearful of disturbing him, she didn't make a sound. She worried Leo would leave if he knew she was there, but at the same time, she longed for him to notice her. Ember knew she should call out to Leo, but the longer she left it to announce her presence, the harder it became. If she tried to speak, she wasn't sure she'd find her voice.

And then he turned and Ember smiled. Her lips moved of their own accord, and the joy they revealed was beyond her control to contain. She realized then, with a sense of abandon, she didn't want to contain it. She wanted Leo to know, to feel, how happy she was. She didn't want to hide in the shadows and watch. She wanted to talk to him and touch him.

He said her name. "Ember."

He said it warmly without question or expectation. She felt like hurtling toward him and jumping into his arms, but her legs moved slowly and nervously so she had to concentrate just to reach him. She grinned up at him, looking so intently into his eyes that she could see her own reflection there.

"Where's Poppy?" she asked, her pupils still fixed on his.

"It's just me," he answered with a bashful smile.

Just me. Ember nearly laughed out loud. A tiny, faraway part of her felt sorry she could so blithely forsake her friend, but she was too full of glee to feel any remorse.

"Are you looking for more things to sell?" Her voice sounded faint in her ears, but Leo seemed to hear her well enough and he nodded in reply.

"Metal, mainly."

"I can help you if you like."

Together they mined the dell for anything Leo considered valuable. It wasn't the things she would have chosen. Not the books, or pictures, or pieces of china. Though she was glad he didn't take those, for she had always hoped one day to have a home of her own in which to keep them.

An hour passed quickly and soon Leo had a stack of metal to carry home with him. He said he was thirsty and Ember took him to the river. It felt like a miracle to have him by her side, walking next to her along the path she'd trod all her life alone. She kept looking straight ahead, but she could hear his footsteps next to her own lighter ones. She could feel his closeness.

Without letting herself hesitate, she slipped her hand into his own.

"Cold," he said, and he held it tight as they walked. His hand was rough and calloused, and hers, which she always considered big, felt so small and soft within it, despite all the hours of laundry she'd been doing in the camp, working sometimes until her hands were raw.

At the river Ember watched as Leo cupped the freezing water into his mouth and how it ran like tears down his chin and neck. No woman's neck was like that, and she stared at the lump inside the front of it that rose and fell as he gulped the water down. She washed her muddy hands with the new soap she'd made, then handed it to him. He brought it to his nose and inhaled, shutting his eyes as he did so.

"Lavender," he said.

He was right, and by knowing that one detail, it was as though he knew the whole of her.

Then he scrubbed his hands and she watched them rub and intertwine and clasp, then plunge into the water. A shiver ran through her.

They sat on the rocks and she handed him some walnuts from her pocket, and they cracked them on the stone and delved inside the shells to pick out the kernels.

"They're good," he said, and she handed him another.

"Do you like jam? Next time I can bring you some. What fruit do you prefer? I have apricot, or raspberry, or greengage?"

"You make it?" he asked without answering her.

"Of course," she said. "There aren't any stores where I come from."

"Poppy told me not to ask." And with her name spoken out loud, the mood changed. Leo got to his feet but then reached out his hand and helped Ember up. Then he released her. She wasn't sure why.

They didn't hold hands as they wandered back to the dell, but Leo didn't rush and Ember was grateful that he talked and his words filled the silence.

"I don't have a proper home either, you know. I live on the streets. Doorways, benches. There are stores, but I don't have money to buy anything from them. I get what they throw out." Leo shrugged.

"You should have a caravan," Ember replied practically. "And a vegetable garden."

He laughed at her simplicity. "I should."

"It must be cold."

"It is. Especially the nights." And he shivered, perhaps at the memory or maybe at the gust of wind that whistled past. Ember reached into her bag and got the scarf she'd been knitting for her mother. It was almost done. She took her needles and swiftly completed two more rows before binding them off.

"Impressive," he said, and she glanced to see if he was laughing at her.

He wasn't, and she felt herself blush. Without looking him in the eye, she stood on tiptoes to wrap the scarf around his neck.

"For you," she murmured shyly.

Leo looked taken aback, and Ember suddenly worried she'd done the wrong thing without realizing it.

"I can't take it." His voice was different, awkward.

"Please, it's to keep you warm. I can make another."

Ember looked at Leo now and she saw how sad and troubled his eyes were and it made her own well up.

"Don't," he muttered. "Don't feel sorry for me."

"I'm not sorry for you!" she exclaimed. "Why, I'm jealous of you. I wish I were you. I mean," she said more hesitantly, "I wish I could come with you."

Ember watched Leo's face fervently, waiting to see if she'd said too much. His features slowly cracked, then softened.

"That bad, huh?" he said, and Ember realized he was talking about her own life, and she turned her head away but then looked back at him through the corners of her eyes. Leo took one end of the scarf and flipped it over his shoulder. "Thanks. It's . . . it's warm." Then he smacked his hand onto his forehead so Ember jumped back, startled. But Leo didn't notice, for he was busy rummaging in his bag and pulling something out to show her.

"My clock," she gasped.

"It's all fixed. Good as new."

Ember stared at the clock now resurrected and alive, the second hand ticking its circle. She put the clock to her ear and listened to it working, the clicks like a tiny heartbeat. And then she couldn't help herself. She flung her arms over the scarf around Leo's neck and kissed him, full on the lips.

In the kitchen Poppy was pouring a potion into a vial when her hand flinched and the potion dropped with a clatter. She stood there, stunned, looking at the precious liquid staining the tiles on the floor. She couldn't move. Her chest hurt too much. Her heart felt like it had been shattered too, all in shards, the blood seeping out of it. She breathed slowly through the pain, trying to claim it, own it.

As it eased, she felt like weeping. Not for the potion, though that had taken hours of preparation, but for another reason that she couldn't seem to drag from her subconscious and translate into thought. She glanced at the book and groaned out loud. Its pages were spattered with dark sticky blotches. Ember would be frantic. Poppy was already at fault for not visiting her, and now she had ruined the book she had sworn to look after. How would she ever gain Ember's forgiveness? The stains on the tiles came off with the strongest household cleaner. It would take something far more powerful to clean the book.

Poppy spent the next few hours trying to magic those spots away. When they finally lifted and she felt calm and could breathe properly again, that's when she saw it—the kiss. In her mind's eye, she saw how Ember's hands grasped Leo's face and how her body reached up so her lips could press against his. She saw it all in momentary increments—beat by beat, tick by tock. A second of surprise in Leo's eyes, the next second of consternation, a third of surrender, a fourth of receiving, a fifth of giving, a sixth of pleasure. Unable to watch any longer, Poppy picked up the book and hurled it across the room. It lay there wounded, just as she was, pages bent, spine cracked on the tiled ground.

❦

Leo was doing everything he had promised himself he wouldn't. He was outside Poppy's house, trying, hoping to get a glimpse of her. He didn't care about the balance between them anymore, that it was her turn, that she should thank him. None of that mattered now. He had to see her. Just for a moment. He didn't have any words to offer. He hardly knew what to think. Why he'd ever stayed away seemed baffling to him now, like that decision belonged to another boy with some other girl, playing a stupid game to save his pride.

Ember had kissed him and it had been a gift, a surprise, soft and sweet, and he'd felt grateful for it. It had come without the pressure of occasion, without the worry of rejection. But after, Ember's kiss made him think of another's and how that might feel. If it had been Poppy's lips on his, he would have kissed her harder, not so soft and sweet, but longer, deeper, never enough, never wanting it to end.

Leo kicked at the curb, then stared urgently at the house. He wanted to burst through the door and grab Poppy in his arms and do, right now, what he'd been imagining so vividly. But he didn't move. He stood there, wired with longing, not daring to even ring the doorbell.

Poppy knew Leo was close from the moment he arrived. He waited and waited, and it took all Poppy's strength to ignore him. She thought of trying another spell on him to make him go, to remind him of Ember. But Poppy found she couldn't concentrate as she needed to for witchcraft. It was as if Leo was in her way, his emotions emanating from him, every particle of his being summoning her, deafening her with his want and need. His guilt and frustration came seeping under the door and into her house, making her skin tingle and eyes water. Or was it her own feelings that were thickening the air, making it so hard to breathe? Having spent the last few days feeling so certain and assured, Poppy now felt weak with confusion.

Finally, when it grew late, Leo banged on the door. Poppy wished her father was home to deal with him and tell him to get lost. But, as usual, she was all alone. He shouted her name through the mail slot.

"I know you're in there. Poppy, please. Just answer the door. Just for a minute."

Poppy said nothing, and Leo banged with his fist again so the whole door shook.

"Why won't you speak to me?"

You know why, she felt like screaming, but she stayed silent.

Then Leo threw stones up to her bedroom window and she felt like thrusting open the window and slinging something back down at him. He stood in the front garden and yelled her name for all the world to hear. Poppy sat on the floor and scrunched her eyes closed, hugging her knees, making herself small and insignificant for she feared what was coming.

The rain arrived first. Hard and fast like tiny bullets, pelting down on Leo, stinging his face and soaking his clothes. He didn't move. The wind swept around his legs, the force of it so fierce it made him sway and threatened to lift him off the ground. Still Leo did not turn to leave. Not even when the thunder rumbled and the sky cracked and lightning bolts hit the ground to either side of him.

"Poppy!!!" he hollered defiantly as the water streamed over him and the wind whipped him like a lash.

He won't go, Poppy thought. *He'll never go.*

Trash cans, tricycles, and potted plants were being tossed around, skittering down the street like they were paper bags. But Leo stood firm.

Headlights appeared at the top of the street and a car wove its way around the carnage, windshield wipers flicking furiously back and forth, trying to combat the rain. The lights swept through her bedroom and Poppy heard the car turning into the drive. It must be her father. Only then did Poppy come to the window and pull back the curtains, worried what might happen next. Only then did Leo back away, stepping into the shadows.

But Poppy's father had already seen him. He jumped out of the car and shouted across the stormy, swirling air. Leo didn't respond, but his eyes glanced up to Poppy's bedroom window and he saw her there, watching. Within his imploring look, Poppy glimpsed layers of hurt, anger, desire, guilt. She didn't know which to respond to first. She didn't notice the lack of coat; she didn't question the scarf.

Then her father shouted again and Leo turned and ran.

Poppy's mood the next day was dark and angry. A bilious rage bubbled in her stomach. Electricity sparked in her fingers. In the hallways the crowds of kids parted to let her pass. No one said a word. It was as if they could sense the rabid fury running through Poppy's veins and knew that she might bite.

By lunch break Poppy had ratcheted up a triple detention for Friday night. In the dining hall she sat at one of the tables on the edge of the room, the chairs around her empty, like an invisible moat, the rest of the seats filled by the school's other loners. These kids sat together every lunchtime, connected solely by their strangeness. There was no love lost between them, only the neediness that alienation brings. Even with this bunch of anomalies, Poppy was the outcast.

They weren't the ones who threw the food, though. They wouldn't dare. The wet, lukewarm substance struck the side of Poppy's head. Normally Poppy sensed such attacks and knew how to dodge or divert them. But today she was distracted and this made her vulnerable. Annoyed at herself, she lifted her hand to wipe the food away and saw from her fingers that it was mashed potato—cold, white, and lumpy.

Another dollop was launched, and this time, it hit the back of her head. Poppy glanced at the others at her table. Their eyes instantly flicked down to their plates, offering no allegiance. Poppy shut her eyes. She was used to sending her tears inward to extinguish the fire that burned inside of her. But this time there were no tears to hose down the conflagration and Poppy liked how the heat in her belly warmed her, readying her for the fight. She wanted to stand up and let the fire shoot from her lips like a dragon, then watch as the culprits blazed and smoldered.

"Fire!" cried one of the dining staff as, inside the kitchen, a frying pan flickered with flames that rose up high to lick the ceiling. Within seconds the staff were stamping their shoes and flicking wet dish towels at fires that were cropping up all over the room.

Then the rats appeared. They crawled out of shelves and from under cabinets and scurried into the dining hall. Brown, gray, pink, and hairless, all with long worm-like tails that slithered

along the floor after their fat, wrinkled bodies. The fire alarm began to sound as the smoke lifted to form a thick layer of smog. Its
blare accompanied the screams of the kids, the voices of the boys
and girls both so high-pitched there was no telling which was
which. The rats ran up table legs and chairs and started feasting
on the lunches lying half-finished on the tables, their eyes red like
the fire from which they'd fled.

Poppy felt none of the horror or shame that her previous ca-
lamities had evoked. She took a moment, then smiled. And then
she laughed. She laughed and laughed until the tears streamed
down her face and her insides hurt from fatigue. The other stu-
dents ran from the room, jostling to reach the door, and the rats
followed after them. All they were missing was the Pied Piper
and his tune. Soon Poppy was all alone, and still she laughed, the
mashed potato dripping from her hair, the smoke receding, and
the flames flickering out just as swiftly as they'd begun.

Poppy had seen many school counselors in her time. They were
usually underpaid and underqualified. Often, it had seemed to
Poppy, they were in need of counseling themselves. Mrs. Silva was
different. She was full of life and vitality—big green eyes matching a glossy, emerald shirt; big hair and an even bigger bosom;
rings on her fingers and a pair of red pumps covering her toes.
Poppy wondered why, out of all the jobs in the world, Mrs. Silva
was doing this one, especially in this forgotten backwater of a
town. The woman looked as though she should exist in a faraway,
sun-kissed place that was as exuberant and glamorous as she was.

Mrs. Silva stood up, offering first a warm smile and then a warm hand to Poppy. And when Poppy shook Mrs. Silva's hand, she saw inside her and understood. Mrs. Silva was pregnant, only a few weeks, but definitely pregnant. That was the present, the here and now.

When Poppy released Mrs. Silva's hand, she knew the past. She saw all the pregnancies that had gone before. She saw the blood from the miscarriages and the tiny corpses of the two babies that had lasted longest but still not long enough.

Then, when Mrs. Silva put a soft, encouraging arm around Poppy as she led her to the sofa, Poppy felt it. The future. The tiny speck of an embryo sliding, falling, dying before it even had a chance to round its mother's belly or be announced to the world.

Knowing all this made Poppy more receptive to Mrs. Silva's advice, advice that actually made a lot of sense if Poppy were a normal girl with regular teenage issues and not a witch with supernatural abilities to cause fires and plagues of rats. In fact, Mrs. Silva's words were so sensitively and candidly chosen that Poppy wanted to listen to her. Her lilting, musical accent made everything sound refreshingly humorous rather than dour and depressing, so much so that Poppy suddenly felt the urge to tell Mrs. Silva everything. She didn't, of course. She couldn't. But she did go home determined to do anything she could to save Mrs. Silva's baby.

"*Buena suerte*," Mrs. Silva had told her. "Good luck, Poppy."

"You too," Poppy had replied meaningfully.

"Remember you are a very special girl. Believe in yourself and better days will come, yes?"

Poppy nodded, wishing she could offer some words of caution but holding them in. Muffling the magic and stifling the sympathy inside of her caused a pain in Poppy's side that ached right until the final bell of the day and all the way home until at last Poppy was able to open up her book of spells.

She realized at once this magic was beyond anything else she had tried. This was life and death, and only the darkest arts could hold such power. It would require courage as well as craft, for to save another, she had to give herself. Blood for blood. Bone for bone. Poppy chose the knife carefully. The sharpest she could find. Satisfied, she held out her left hand but it began to tremble. Quickly, giving herself no time to think, she placed her little finger on the chopping board. With her other hand she lightly placed the knife on her skin, picking a spot, just the tip, the tiniest part she could. It seemed the most unnatural thing in the world to cause herself hurt, but she had the best reason, the only reason. Muttering the words to the spell, she raised the knife. Then, like a guillotine, she let it fall.

For a moment Poppy felt nothing. Then the pain came, so sudden and savage that she had to scream. As she reached for the ointment and the bandage beside her, she tried to picture Mrs. Silva joyfully holding her newborn baby. Wrapping up her finger and pressing on it tightly, she recalled Mrs. Silva's kind words.

"Poppy, can it be? No boys, no alcohol, no drugs. What is it you told me . . . that you're different from the other girls here? Maybe you're right? God willing I have a daughter one day like you."

Poppy had felt like weeping as she realized how very unused she was to being liked by anyone at all. And Mrs. Silva's innocence had been so heartbreaking—the ignorance of what was to come and the eternal optimism despite what had already happened.

"Maybe you should talk to my mother," was all Poppy had been able to muster in return.

Mrs. Silva had let the words fade, right until they disappeared. Then she'd said, "Would you like us to speak about this? Your mother?"

Poppy remembered shaking her head.

"Are you sure? . . . Sometimes it helps to talk about it. No, always, I think it helps. Not to keep it . . . what's the expression . . . bottled up inside."

"Always? What if holding it in is the only thing that keeps you together?"

Mrs. Silva had sighed then, long and heavy. "Oh, Poppy," she'd said so very tenderly. "It feels like that. I know. You worry you will fall apart. I understand. But you're much stronger than this. Believe me."

The magic in the ointment was beginning to work and the pain was subsiding. Hardly bearing to look, Poppy grabbed the fingertip that lay like a scrap on the board and threw it into the pot. Then she cut a piece of hair and added that to the mix, giving different parts of herself to the spell—spit, mucus, wax—parts of *her* life to *give* life.

Poppy needed tears to add to the mixture. She thought of her mother, when she was young and fair and on her feet, and how she was now, unkempt and lying in her hospital bed. But no tears came. They never had for her. Poppy thought of her own life, broken into chapters, each one more fruitless than the last. Her heart was long since hardened to that, though. She thought of sweet Uncle Bob, dead in his grave, then of Minx all alone in hers. Still she couldn't cry. Her tears had run dry, her mind an arid, sandy desert. Then she thought of Ember, her only real friend. A misfit like her. So different from each other, but somehow the same.

As Poppy thought of Ember, her thoughts strayed to Leo, and Poppy realized with a pang that the two of them were connected in her head forever now. Poppy didn't want to think of Leo. It was too big, too much to cope with. He would spoil the spell, weaken her. It was too confusing. The throb of her finger. That was simple and straightforward. A pain you could expect and manage. Leo—that pain was unpredictable and had her reeling. She saw his hand in Ember's as they crossed the forest floor. She saw them as a couple, a beautiful pair of woodland creatures that looked too good together to ever be apart. She saw the scarf around his neck as he looked up at her window, and she saw exactly why and how he'd received it. And she saw the kiss. His lips on Ember's. Ember's lips on his. His lips on her own.

Poppy's hands went to her mouth as she felt it tingle with the touch and the warmth of it. She felt her fingers moisten and thought it was his mouth. And then she realized. It was her tears.

After the spell was done, Poppy felt drained like there was no more blood to give, like there was no more marrow in her bones. Dark circles had formed under her eyes, her skin had turned sallow, then deathly gray. Her hair lay limp on her head and her muscles ached like they had worked for days. Most oddly, there were blisters on her hands and feet as though she'd been toiling in the fields. She hadn't the strength to even wonder at them. She collapsed on top of her bed, fully dressed, and when she awoke her finger was almost healed, but a white streak had appeared in her hair.

Chapter Twenty-One

R aven was sleeping peacefully for the first time in days. Her body had healed and she no longer cried out in her dreams from the constant spasms and throbbing in her joints. She had stopped swathing herself in cream of arnica and wild lettuce and concocting sleeping remedies from hops and valerian, and painkillers from chili and devil's claw, skullcap and cannabis, turmeric and willow bark. She was able to eat again and she could feel her strength returning. But to sleep deeply and dreamlessly—this was bliss. So when she awoke, sharply and suddenly in the dead of night, she was angry first, worried second.

She sprang upright in bed and then her eyelids followed suit, opening wide. It took her a second or two to register she was awake and it was not yet near morning. Then she felt it, thick and tangible and acrid to taste. A deep, dark magic, the likes of which Raven had seldom come across other than during her own rare forays into the occult.

A few of the other elders felt it too. There was a tapping at her door just before dawn, and Raven knew it would be them, anxious and eager for discussion. She crept out, careful not to wake Sorrel, and saw the sisters gathered at her steps. She joined the huddle of old hags, and heads bent, voices lowered, they swapped theories on what had passed that night.

"Twas a powerful spell," said Sister Ada. "Not many about who can cast such magic as that."

The others nodded, noses long, dipping up and down into the early morning mist.

"The Eastern clan," murmured Sister Bethany fearfully.

There followed more nodding, accompanied by whispers of assent.

"Always the Eastern clan?" disputed Sister Morgan. "Can we for once look beyond the obvious?" Her eyes turned to Raven for support.

"It's obvious because it is most likely true," spat Sister Ada. "We are not fools."

"Hush now, I did not say that," Sister Morgan huffed. "But we jump to such conclusions like a toad jumping from hedgehog to cat."

"It is the year of the prophecy." Raven had kept her silence, but when she spoke it was a pronouncement and the others had to listen. "The spell this night . . . the great yew . . . the rumors of the Eastern clan—each and together, they must pertain to this. Sorrel is in danger from all sides, and we must keep her safe until the throne is hers."

The sisters clasped hands.

"So the Eastern clan it is." Sister Ada couldn't help gloating. Sister Morgan looked away.

"It is likely," Raven demurred, but for Sister Morgan's benefit, she added, "though we must be watchful from all quarters."

Sister Morgan turned her gaze to the center of the circle just like the others and they muttered spells of protection, for Sorrel, for the clan, and for themselves.

Raven knew, however, from the spit frothing at the back of her throat and the heartburn rising from behind her chest and searing her throat, that the Eastern clan was not responsible for the magic cast that night. She consulted all the usual omens to be sure, but she knew already what to expect.

It was the girl. She had been too ready to dismiss her. And now that lame, pathetic creature had somehow summoned up the most potent of spells.

How could she have done so?

Unless . . .

Raven could hardly utter this "unless," let alone follow on from where it led. She missed breakfast, unable to stomach food, and instead took some spiced rolls to Sister Wynne.

Sister Wynne was deafer than a white-haired ferret but partial to anything sweet, particularly if it contained cinnamon and clove. She knew astrology like she knew her own face with her star-specked eyes, orb-like features, and constellation of freckles. Sister Wynne spent little time with the rest of the coven, for she slept during the day so she could stargaze at night. Raven found her just as she was preparing for bed, her large rings of stomach covered by a long tent of a gown.

"Forgive me, Sister Wynne, for disturbing you."

Sister Wynne's face creased crossly, her eyes disappearing into the folds of flesh. "It's bedtime for me, Sister Raven. You know that well enough."

"I know and I am sorry for it. I need but a few moments."

Sister Wynne lumbered toward her bed. "Come back tonight when I have woken."

Raven held out the rolls. "These will be cold soon and hard. Perhaps you could toast them later?"

Sister Wynne's nose twitched. Her lips opened slightly as her tongue hit the roof of her mouth, then fell again. "They're warm?"

"Fresh from the oven."

"It's been a cloudless night, cruelly cold. I could do with some warmth, to be sure."

After Sister Wynne had wolfed down the rolls, Raven was able to persuade her to consult the charts. The elderly witch rustled and rummaged through boxes until she found the one, now yellow and creased, from the night of Ember's birth fifteen years ago. She then, at Raven's request, compared it to both the night of the great yew's destruction and to last night's.

The pattern was there. Raven didn't need Sister Wynne to point it out. Gemini, Gemini, Gemini. The babies, the girls, the truth. Sister Wynne couldn't decipher so exactly. Astrology could only hint and guide so that, if one tried hard enough, most could find what they willed. Even Raven, who knew what the zodiacs told of, found herself trying to think of an alternative truth to believe instead. Could this girl truly be the baby she exiled into ignorance—ignorance of herself, her family, her roots? The child she sentenced to life in the wilderness? Raven shook her head. It couldn't be. How could such a one have sprung from nothing to this elevated display of skill and strength? Not many witches, ever, could summon up such power. It was not possible.

Unless . . .

Unless . . .

The scent of the spell led Raven to Mrs. Silva. She dropped her basket of vegetables in the street and Mrs. Silva bent to help her as Raven knew she would. Raven touched her arm in thanks and saw, as Poppy had done, the tiny fleck of a baby, once so frail but now vital and healthy, holding on tighter and tighter to life.

"Thank you," Raven told Mrs. Silva, and she meant it, for she was indeed grateful. There was no denial now. No alternative truth. Only a ghastly secret that Raven had thought was safely buried, knocking on its coffin lid, ready to burst out and haunt her. Switching Charlock's baby all those years ago had been a precaution. Now it was an imperative. No one could ever know Ember was not a Hawkweed, that another far more exceptional contender to the throne existed. Raven must nail her secret back down and stifle it before it had its retribution.

Poppy excused herself from history because her head was pounding so much that each word Mr. Reed uttered made her wince. He usually got annoyed with pupils asking for bathroom breaks, but the white streak in Poppy's hair had caused enough consternation that morning, so he made no complaint. In the bathroom Poppy splashed water on her face and leaned against the sink, staring at her face in the mirror. Registering the pain in her eyes, she acknowledged she looked as bad as she felt. Her image began to swim in and out of focus, then she swayed on her feet.

Suddenly the hairs on her body stood on end. Even the hair on Poppy's head bristled. Before she could think what danger lurked, the attack began. First a punch, sending her flying across the room. Poppy looked around wildly for her attacker but there was no one. The bathroom was empty, just as it was when she came in. Poppy lifted her hand to her head and felt the wet stickiness of blood on her forehead. Then a blow to her ribs had her crying out and buckling over in agony. Lifted onto her tiptoes, she found herself being hurled into the door of one of the stalls. Fingers, strong and sharp, were in her hair, grabbing her head, knocking it savagely against the thin wall until the plywood cracked and dented.

"*Stop!*" Poppy registered in her head.

It wasn't a voice, nor a sound, more of a message she had to read out loud for herself.

Her nose cracked against the sink as she stumbled and fell.

"*Be gone!*" she deciphered this time.

"Who are you?" Poppy cried out loud.

She felt her body being drawn back like a slingshot and then her head was fired against the mirror, the glass shattering at the impact. Poppy melted to the floor like she was made only of liquid, then lay in a pool of clothes on the floor. As she slipped in and out of consciousness, she wondered what invisible force she had unleashed upon herself. Then all went dark and she could wonder no more.

It was Kelly Fletcher who found her. She bent down and peered over Poppy with thickly made-up eyes.

"What happened to you?" Poppy watched the gum stretch and shrink between Kelly's chewing teeth. She tried to sit up but couldn't. "I wouldn't try to move if I were you." Kelly reached into her bag for her phone.

"What are you doing?" Poppy croaked.

"Calling the police, whaddaya think? You been attacked."

Poppy sat up, her head swimming. "Don't," she said.

Kelly looked at her long and hard, then lowered the phone. "'Sup to you, I guess." She shrugged like she was more than used to finding someone battered and broken on the floor. "Ambulance?" she asked as a casual afterthought.

Poppy shook her head, holding onto the edge of the sink to get to her feet.

Kelly didn't offer any help, only words of experience. "Better clean yourself up before anyone else sees you. Otherwise they'll be on you like flies."

With that, Kelly reapplied her lipstick, licked her teeth, fluffed her hair, and headed back into the hall. Relieved that Kelly never asked her who or why, Poppy washed her face, pressing paper towels to her cuts, before opening the bathroom window and pulling herself out and onto the fire escape. The window banged shut behind her just as the school bell blared out and girls started pouring into the bathroom, pointing at the broken glass, shrieking at the blood, calling for a teacher.

Poppy had never felt so relieved to reach home. She'd pulled her hood right up and kept her head bowed on her journey, but still she'd received wary looks. The silence of the house felt like a sanctuary. Perhaps here she could think and understand what had happened to her. Then she heard it.

A woman's voice.

A murmur.

Then a giggle.

Then her father's voice, but sounding different—softer, happier even.

Poppy took off her shoes and climbed the stairs quietly, not wanting to disturb. She wasn't sure what she was going to do once she reached the top until she got there. Then she went to the door, still not sure why, and pushed it open. Perhaps if her ribs weren't cracked and bruised, perhaps if there wasn't a gash across her nose, a lump on her forehead, a cut in her hairline, perhaps then she would have stayed downstairs and waited, not been so impatient. But she had to see and feel the pain, get it over and done with quickly, for she'd suffered too many injuries already that day.

The woman screamed when she saw her and hid under the covers. Her dad looked shocked but, to his credit, more at his daughter's cuts and bruises than at his own predicament.

"Poppy, my God. Who did this to you?"

"Who is she?" Poppy heard herself ask.

"Poppy?" he pleaded, but Poppy was in no mood to be merciful.

"*Who is she?*" Poppy heard herself scream without realizing she'd raised her voice. Pain seared through her ribs and she clutched her arms around her chest. She could feel her cheeks red and hot and the blood dribbling down the side of them.

"John, you need to call a doctor."

Poppy couldn't look up and see the woman's face. It was impossible to straighten. But she detected the kind, sensible tone and felt strangely grateful for it.

"Now," the woman added firmly.

Poppy needed X-rays. She'd cracked a rib and had a mild concussion. The doctors said she needed to stay overnight in the hospital for observation. She didn't have the strength to argue. She dozed off, and when she awoke, her father was sitting in the chair next to her, the pale blue curtains pulled around them.

"What time is it?" Her mouth was dry and it was hard to form the words.

"It's late," said her father. He poured some water from a pitcher by her bed into a plastic cup and passed it to her. She sipped slowly. Even that was painful. "Are you going to tell me? . . . Who hurt you?"

Poppy shut her eyes as the irony struck home. "I can't."

"You can and you will. I'm your father. The police—they need to catch this person. Was it a boy? That boy I saw outside the house?"

Poppy's eyes shot open. "No!" Her father stared at her suspiciously. "No, I promise. Not him."

"Who then?"

"I don't know. Honestly. I didn't see them. It happened so fast. I'd tell you if I knew."

Her father hung his head defeatedly. Poppy felt a moment of sympathy, then steeled herself and went for the knockout.

"Don't you trust me?"

Their eyes met and a lot was said silently.

"I was going to tell you. Donna wanted me to but . . . " He shook his head like it ached. He sounded worn out, spent, so different from the man she'd heard as she'd climbed the stairs.

"Did we move here for her?"

"Yes." He said it quickly, relieved to get it out.

"But you let me think it was because of me, because I'd been bad?"

He paused this time before answering, looking out the window, thinking how best to answer. "I did. I'm sorry for that."

"What about Mom?"

Her dad lifted his head and looked her directly in the eye, and Poppy knew to brace herself. "There's a kid," he said. "A little boy. Your half-brother."

Poppy suddenly felt so tired, like she hardly had the strength to care.

"You'll meet him. Meet both of them."

"I have to sleep."

"I've told you now. Will you tell me?" Poppy felt herself sinking, her heart beating slower, her eyes drooping. "It's my job to protect you," she heard her father say.

You can't, she replied in her head. *No one can.*

Leo heard them before he saw them, the three rough voices grating against one another, mixing with the traffic, yet still so recognizable. He almost didn't want to turn his head to see them. He just wanted to run. But he kept himself still, his back against the doorway, trying to meld into the corner.

He thought he'd never see them again after he'd run from that apartment he had once called home. Yet here they were, as big and nasty as he remembered. Ever so slowly, he looked around to check. Their limbs were thick, hands solid and craggy like they were made of rock, bodies of stone chipped away by a clumsy mason, necks as thick as boulders holding up heads of cement. Their boots thumped onto the pavement, and Leo winced inwardly as he recalled the feeling of those boots thumping into his ribs and those fists knocking into his jaw. Only when they opened the door of the bar and barged inside, slamming the door behind them, could Leo breathe normally again.

Keeping close to the wall on the far side of the street, he crept away, wanting to walk right out of town, hitch a ride and get as far away as possible. He got as far as the circle road when a truck stopped for him. He wanted to climb on board. There was so much to run away from—not just them but Poppy too. He thought of her face looking down on him from her window as he weathered that storm, her eyes thunderous with accusation, as though she had known about Ember, about the kiss. It made no sense. Nothing did anymore. But just one step up into the truck's cab and he could leave it all behind him.

"You coming or not?" the driver barked impatiently.

Leo exhaled slowly, then shook his head, knowing all the while it was a mistake to stay, especially for her.

Sorrel, watching, had felt Leo's fear as the men appeared, just as she'd felt it so many times from a fox's or a falcon's prey. Leo was well practiced at hiding, Sorrel noted. He knew how to hush his breathing and turn his emotions inward. When he made his escape, he trod lightly for someone so tall.

The men Leo feared were wider than he, built like the bulls in one of the hillside fields. They had flame-colored hair on their heads and chins and red skin to match. They radiated heat and Sorrel longed to snuff them out. They were ugly, angry beasts, just as the coven's elders had taught her males would be. Sorrel yearned to use her magic but resisted until she could get closer.

She had never entered a chaff building before but now found herself following the men into a large room that was filled thick with noise and the heat of breath and sweat and the sour scent of hops and grapes. Her nose twitched at the stench and her tongue lapped against the roof of her mouth as she tried to rid herself of the taste in the air. She reached for a half-empty glass on a table, took a sip of what she thought was water, and nearly spat it out. The vile liquid fizzed in her mouth and burned her throat as she swallowed. Suddenly she wished to be home in the coven with her mother and friends close by. Then she saw the men, and the reason why she was here in this hole of a place came retching back to her.

She followed as the youngest, most pig-like of the three went out to go to the bathroom around the back of the building. A torrent of foul-smelling urine splattered onto the pavement and wall. Sorrel's lip curled in disgust and then she made her move.

"Pig!" she called.

He turned and looked straight at her, confusion flashing into fury. But she held him in her sights as she drew nearer, focusing her pupils on his, chanting her magic under her breath. When his eyes had gone misty, she pointed a finger at him and poked him hard in the chest.

"Tell me," she commanded.

He blinked but then he answered. "He's my stepbrother."

"Go on."

"He ran away. My dad—he wants to find him."

"To hurt him?"

"To end him."

"Why?"

"He had a knife. Tried to kill me."

Sorrel's eyes narrowed with suspicion. "Why?" she asked again.

"To stop us from killing him."

Sorrel shook her head at this typically senseless chaff aggression. "His mother?"

"Dead. But Jocelyn weren't his mother, not for real."

"More."

"His real ma gave him to her, made her promise to look after him."

"Who was she?"

"No one knows. She never came back."

"What about his father?"

"Even Jocelyn never knew nothing about him."

The exit door flew open with a clang and a man stumbled out, hardly able to stay on his feet. Sorrel tried a smile, not wanting to alert the man to any danger, but the drunk's face sobered up instantly and he hopped back inside like a rabbit into its burrow.

Sorrel released her finger from the other man's heart and brushed her hands against her skirt in distaste. She sensed there was no more she could learn from this pitiful creature. He swayed on his feet, still in a trance.

"I'm a brainless, useless fool," Sorrel instructed.

He repeated the words.

"I know nothing. I am nothing," Sorrel added, and he parroted the words back. Sorrel shook her head in disgust, then headed home, back to where the air was fresh and the women had their wits about them.

Chapter Twenty-Two

It was the lights that struck Ember the most. How bright the town was, as though day and night were one. The chaffs who had no knowledge of the craft had somehow conquered time and banished darkness. There were people up and dressed and full of life despite it being well past dusk. She had seen the lights from a distance once or twice and marveled at their prettiness, but now she was walking beneath them and Ember felt like a star was shining directly upon her, revealing her difference for all to see.

They'd tamed nature too, these ignorant chaffs. Trees planted one by one in neat, long rows; grass set in oblongs, short and trim; flowers running in strips; hedges shorn smooth and flat. Dogs on leashes and cats in collars. Ember felt awry and disordered in such a mathematical landscape of straight lines and pointy corners. The houses were tall with windows up high and roofs you couldn't see the tops of. Overhead, wires sliced the sky into parallel lines and many-sided shapes. Traffic followed the dashes in the road, car after car, stopping and starting and turning.

Ember had heard the tractors rumbling in the far meadows

and seen planes flying through the clouds, but this was the first time she'd set eyes on the cars that she'd been taught were so beloved by the chaffs. They puffed out acrid fumes that stung her eyes and left a strange residue in her throat, but there was something rousing about the roar of their engines and the sheer speed they traveled at. Even if she ran her fastest, she could never keep them in her sight.

Ember glanced at Leo, and he sensed it and looked back at her reassuringly. "Okay?" he asked, and she nodded, not knowing how to say all that she was thinking.

He had come to the dell again to ask her—it wasn't so much asking, more telling, like it was already decided, that he would meet her later by the gap in the thicket and take her into town.

"Show you the bright lights," he said as if he were joking, and Ember smiled, pretending to understand.

She had always thought Poppy would be the one to show her the place where she and Leo came from. But Poppy's time was taken up with magic now, and her once-daily visits to the dell were becoming fewer and further apart. So Ember didn't hesitate in accepting Leo's plan. She had to wait until her mother was soundly asleep, until her eyelids were sealed and sleep had eased the lines of age and lifted her face back into youth. And when Charlock's breathing was soft and quiet as mist, Ember tiptoed out, carrying her boots and putting them on her feet only once she'd left the camp.

As Ember darted through the forest, she kept expecting a hand to grab her and pull her back. She hardly dared believe she had managed to slip away undetected, and she couldn't let herself think what might happen if her absence were discovered. She accelerated, brushing through the ferns and ducking under the low branches, the holly and the thorns scratching at her clothes and skin. Whatever happened, it would be worth it, Ember told herself. She couldn't not go. To do nothing—that would be the worst fate of all.

Leo was there in the thicket already, and Ember felt a thrill of happiness that he had arrived first and been waiting . . . for her. She wasn't sure how to greet him, but he put his arm around her and roughly pulled her along.

"Come on. I've got it all planned."

He walked fast, faster than she, and sometimes she had to skip between strides sometimes to keep up with him. The moon and stars shone vivid and bright, lighting their way, and under her breath Ember sent a message of thanks to them. As they reached the town, it became harder to see the constellations, and nearing the center, Ember forgot to look upward. There was too much happening around her.

So many people. So many men. None like Leo, though. Ember felt foolish for expecting them all to be similar. They were all different shapes and sizes—some hairy, some hairless, voices high and low, some you could hardly tell were men at all. Ember clung tightly to Leo's arm and he looked at her comfortingly, like she was a child. She wanted to let go and show that she was like the other teenage girls she saw, with their high heels and short skirts and brightly painted faces. But her fingers wouldn't release their hold. She needed that contact with the one thing she already knew.

The town was loud and dirty and it smelled. Trash cans over-flowing, writing on the walls, buildings black with dirt—Ember couldn't imagine having to clean this place the way she scrubbed the caravan steps with a brush in one hand and a bucket in the other. Ember had waited to come here for so long, wondering if the day would ever arrive, and now that she was here, she felt overwhelmed. How could she tell Leo she wanted to go home where it was small and quiet and where night was night? Then, as they passed a store, doors open, heat blasting, she heard it. The song she had learned from Poppy's headphones. And suddenly Ember felt like she belonged.

"I know this one!" she cried out.

"What?" Leo said over the noise.

Ember pulled him inside the store and looked around at the walls, seeking the source of the music.

"I know this one," she said again, and as if to prove it, she started singing the words, not caring who could see or hear, all inhibitions swept away by the melody.

It took Leo a few moments before he could let go of the embar-rassment he felt as Ember began to sing so loud and free. Then his body relaxed and the tension left him as he realized nothing bad was going to happen. He didn't have to protect Ember from hu-miliation or teach her how to behave in public. People might stop and look, but no one was laughing or calling out names. And so what if they did? Ember looked happy, truly so. Nothing mattered to her right now but the music. The sense of joy and liberation was infectious, and soon Leo found himself smiling and wishing the song would last and last and the moment wouldn't end. But of course it did, and Ember turned to him and hugged him and he allowed his arms to wrap around her and squeeze her back, lifting her off her feet.

Leo felt glad, then, that he'd brought her. It had been a decision made in anger, and all the while since, he'd been regretting it. Rejected by Poppy, he'd felt furious at himself for feeling guilty when he had done nothing wrong. As if to prove his innocence, he had decided to do something good for Ember, something open and unselfish. So he had gone to the dell and told Ember of his plan. She had shown him the countryside, and in return, he would show her the town. It had sounded so simple and he had felt so sure. But then the evening came and she had seemed so nervous and out of place that his certainty had begun to crumble. Suddenly it all felt complicated, and Leo knew that he'd been kidding himself before about his good, unselfish deed. Then, just as he was trying to figure out how best to turn back, Ember had heard the song and started to sing and it all became worth it.

Now, as they walked around the town center, Leo felt like he was seeing it anew through Ember's eyes. The raucous voices and garish lights, the grumbling traffic and all the people in their many costumes—it felt like a performance staged and choreographed for their benefit and Leo wanted to applaud. Ember too seemed struck by the theater of it.

"Nothing's ever going to be the same again," she proclaimed, and instantly Leo felt the weight of what he'd put in motion. "You've changed my life," she added, and the burden of responsibility pressed down harder on him.

"You think that now," Leo replied, trying to make it lighter. "It's not such a big deal. Just a trip, a holiday."

Ember shook her head. "The dell—it's all different now. I understand it. I know where it all came from."

"It doesn't mean the dell's not a special place. I mean, I see that and I come from here."

"But I have to go back," she whispered. "How do I do that?"

Leo took her to the movies. He'd been saving it until last. They came in through the fire escape, and Ember gasped when she saw the screen with its giant super-race of people looming over her.

They sat on the steps in the aisle and watched until the hero and heroine kissed and the closing credits began to roll. Ember took Leo's hand, lifted it to her mouth, and rested her lips there. No sparks of electricity, just warmth.

The whole place emptied and the lights came up and Ember let go. A second later and she had grabbed a half-finished bag of popcorn and tried some. It startled Leo, how she flitted from one moment to the next.

"You like it?" he inquired.

"I know what it is, silly. We have popped corn where I come from. Not quite so salty, though." She offered him the bag. "Supper?"

He smiled and took a handful. "Not much of a meal," he apologized.

"What do you mean?" she said, getting to her feet. "There's tons of it here." And she collected more bags and poured them together to make two full ones.

Leo walked her home all the way to the edge of the woods, both of them munching on the popcorn. Then she gave him back the bag.

"No clues," she said. "We're not allowed into the town without permission."

"Will you get into trouble?" he asked.

"Not if I don't get caught," she smiled.

Leo looked at the trees thickening the dark woods. "How will you see your way home?"

Ember shrugged. "I could do it with my eyes shut," she replied confidently, but then she looked for herself and Leo thought he caught a hint of apprehension flicker across her face. Before he had time to question her again, Ember was putting her hands on his shoulders. "Thank you," she said.

"Anytime," he replied flippantly.

Then she stretched herself up onto her toes and kissed him. "You're supposed to kiss me back," she smiled gently. "Like the man in the movies."

Leo felt his face flush and his heart pound with panic, but Ember grinned, dimples appearing in her cheeks.

"Please," she said, fluttering her lashes like she'd seen the actress do.

Leo's mind scrambled for what to say, but then Ember was reaching up again and he found himself sweeping her into his arms, her back arching and her head tipping as his mouth covered hers. For a moment Leo even felt like a film star with his leading lady, like it wasn't real but a perfect act. And then, when he lifted her back to standing, Ember started to laugh with delight and he did too and it all seemed so effortless.

When Poppy's next session with Mrs. Silva was canceled, she knew immediately. The school secretary explained that Mrs. Silva was off sick and wouldn't be coming back for a while, but Poppy understood all that and far more. The baby was no more and Mrs. Silva would never be coming back. This would be the last loss Mrs. Silva could endure without losing herself. She would stop trying for a baby and instead try to live without that hope.

Poppy sat on the floor, in between the rows of books in the library, flicking frantically through her book of spells to find the one she'd used to keep the baby alive. She scoured the ingredients, the method. She had done everything it said. No mistakes. And she'd known it had worked. She'd felt it, seen it. The baby had been strong. It had been destined to live. Everything had been right. So what could have gone wrong? The book stated the spell could be reversed, but only by an even stronger, darker magic. Who would do such a thing? Why?

Poppy's mind was reeling and so she didn't notice the group of kids approaching. They were middle-schoolers, a mixed bunch. Some looked way off puberty, small and childish. Others were big and spotty, the potent cocktail of hormones bursting through their skin. And there were lots of them, filling the narrow passageway between the shelves of books.

"It's her," Poppy heard one of them say.

"Told you," said another.

She looked up and glared at them. She could hear the gasps. Her face still purple and stitched had been the cause of many stares and whispers since she'd returned back to school. Suddenly a small hand darted out and snatched the book.

"Give that back," Poppy demanded as calmly as she could.

"Or what?" challenged a bratty-looking boy.

"Or you'll be very sorry," Poppy said quietly.

"What you going to do?" another boy whined. "Set the rats on us?"

They all laughed.

Poppy leapt up and swung for the book, but they were too quick for her, passing it from hand to hand so it was always just out of her reach in a game designed to taunt her. Poppy's eyes narrowed. "Give . . . it . . . back." Her heart was beating in her chest, the rhythm getting faster and faster. She could feel the pulse in her neck quickening too.

She took a long, deep breath and then, just when she began to feel more in control, one of the girls piped up, "Your boyfriend's a hobo."

"Yeah, he's gross," added another.

"He's probably a junkie."

"Ought to be put away."

"Ought to be put down."

The kids laughed again, their faces contorting in depraved delight.

Poppy lunged for the book and was again defeated. They laughed louder and louder, some bent double from the hilarity. A spell to bring water flashed into Poppy's mind and suddenly all the kids began to pee themselves.

"Urghh!" cried one, staring at her friend. "She's gone and wet herself."

Then they all looked down at their crotches to see the warm, wet patches expanding. Now their eyes turned scared.

"Do I have your attention?" Poppy asked in a tone she recognized from her teachers. They stared at her mutely. "Now give me the book back and we can all go our separate ways."

The kids glanced at one another, seeking out consensus.

"No," said the most belligerent and bullish of the boys. He grabbed the book and held it tight in both hands.

"Give it back!" Poppy screeched, and with her words the book began to smoke, then burn, and the boy dropped it with a scream, staring at his blistering hands in horror.

The kids started to back away just as the books from the shelves came flying. Like a flock of birds, the books took to the air, their covers flapping like wings, beating so hard that some of the pages fell like feathers. At the sight of this, the kids began barging past one another to get down the corridor, their arms trying to protect their heads from the glancing blows of the books. One had a bloody nose, another a black eye. Only a couple escaped without a wound. Then, as the last of them turned the corner at the end of the row, the shelves came crashing to the ground in a final, thunderous boom.

Slowly Poppy bent down and picked up her book from the debris, putting it safely into her bag. Across the room the librarian stood stock-still.

"Those middle-schoolers," said Poppy, shaking her head. "No respect for literature."

Chapter Twenty-Three

That wasn't the end of it. Parents phoned and wrote in, complaining of bullying and describing an attack in the school library. Poppy was quickly pinpointed, her battered face and white slick of hair immediately identifying her.

"But books can't fly," she told Mr. Jeffries as she sat before him. "That's ridiculous!"

"Indeed," he muttered. "I was hoping you might offer an explanation."

Poppy looked stumped. "I can't."

"Many of the children have displayed injuries. One even has minor burns on his hands." Mr. Jeffries consulted a report. "One Simon Turner."

"I don't like to say . . ." said Poppy.

"Go on," encouraged Mr. Jeffries.

"Well, could they have hurt one another? Even accidentally. Pushing down those shelves like that. Running in the library. Throwing books."

Mr. Jeffries pushed his glasses firmly up his nose. "You're saying they vandalized the library?"

"Well, of course. It could hardly have been me. I'm not that strong. I mean, look at me."

Mr. Jeffries did look at her. He stared long and hard, letting Poppy bear the weight of his gaze. Then he exhaled noisily through his nostrils. "I'm not partial to mysteries, Miss Hooper. Not partial at all." The principal shuffled some papers on his desk, tapping them into a neat pile, and Poppy hoped this small restoration of order might signal the end of the meeting but discovered it was merely a pause. "So, Miss Hooper, what do you have to say for yourself?" Poppy looked down at her hands. "Well then, if you can't shed some light on the situation, perhaps your father can?"

Poppy's eyes shot up to see Mr. Jeffries's hand reaching for the telephone. She didn't care what her dad thought anymore, but she had been hoping to avoid involving him. He had been so irate about her refusal to speak to the police that the thought of yet another standoff felt exhausting. She stared hard into Mr. Jeffries's eyes—they were angry, frustrated, brown, no, not just brown, black pupils encircled with chestnut, ringed with a darker shade, the whites bloodshot and tired.

"I wouldn't bother, if I were you." She hadn't meant to speak, but the thoughts had come out of her mouth of their own accord. "He's too busy with his mistress and his child, the secret sibling I just found out about." Now Poppy had started, it seemed she couldn't stop. "So if you want to expel me, go ahead. I'm used to it."

Mr. Jeffries blinked, and it was then Poppy realized something strange was happening. His hand was still hovering over the telephone.

"Don't call him," she said tentatively, and she watched as Mr. Jeffries's hand returned to his lap. "You don't need to speak to anyone else about what happened in the library."

Mr. Jeffries stared back at her.

"Yes?" Poppy checked. Mr. Jeffries nodded. "It was just some middle-schoolers messing around. No one needs to be punished."

Mr. Jeffries's eyes looked blank.

"Okay?" Poppy prompted.

Mr. Jeffries nodded again. Poppy wasn't sure what to do next. She got to her feet, then racked her brains to remember a hypnotist that she'd once seen on television.

"I'm going to go now," she said authoritatively. "When I leave the room, you will wake up and go happily about your day."

Poppy wasn't sure why she said "happily," but it was too late to change it. She walked to the door, started to open it, then stopped and turned back to Mr. Jeffries.

"Bye, I guess. Oh, and you won't remember anything about this conversation."

She shut the door behind her and waited for a moment, wishing she could peek back inside. She couldn't hear anything until suddenly the telephone rang and the shrill of it made her jump. It rang and rang and Poppy started to worry until finally she heard Mr. Jeffries's voice say "Good morning" in a far cheerier tone than he was commonly known for.

Halloween in this town was limp and drab. By the time Poppy made her way home through town, the younger kids had done their trick-or-treating, most dressed in the same pumpkin or vampire outfits from the local supermarket. They were trailing home through the drizzle, picking candy out of their teeth, looking through the wrappers in their buckets for any missed treat. Here and there a few taller older skeletons and Draculas prowled, ringing on the odd doorbell just for the heck of it.

It irritated Poppy, this lack of imagination and flair. In the last place she had lived, the houses had been decked out like film sets, with gravestones in their front gardens and cobwebs coating the doors, scary mechanical voices shrieking and cackling, and pumpkins carved with great artistry and finesse. Here, even the shop windows could hardly be bothered to try to cash in on the occasion. Poppy knew she was being contrary. She'd always scorned all the effort before, but now that it was gone, she missed it. A few hours earlier she had looked the part at least. The white stripe in her hair and her bruises looked like a costume. But throughout the day they had faded. Poppy presumed the magic she used on Mr. Jeffries had somehow accelerated the healing. Now she just looked plain and ordinary, with not a hint of Halloween about her.

Poppy felt the frustration begin to claw its way out of her. She had just brainwashed another human being, and yet no one would ever know. She wanted to go up to the next ghoul and denounce them as some pathetic pretender. She wanted to whip off the next black witch's hat and shout out to all of them that she was the real deal. She wouldn't, though. She couldn't tell them, just as she couldn't stride into Ember's coven and introduce herself either.

Both were too petrifying a prospect. Suddenly Poppy felt sick of her own cowardly company. She longed for someone she could talk to, someone who would understand, so she stopped, just for a minute or two, outside the pharmacy where Leo had told her he'd first set eyes on her.

She searched for him, all around, in the costumes, through the masks. And then she saw his face, undisguised like her own, watching from a doorway. Poppy turned and walked the other way.

She knew, of course, he'd walk after her, that he'd catch up with her and pull her arm to stop her. She didn't know, though, that she would be so angry. She hadn't realized it was a fight she had wanted all along.

"Leave me alone," she hissed.

Leo let go of her arm and immediately she wanted it back there, hurting her.

"You were looking for me." He sounded angry too.

"Don't talk to me."

"Don't pretend. I saw you . . . you were looking for me."

Poppy stared into his eyes, so dark they were frightening. He put his hands on her shoulders, then her arms. "Don't touch me," she whispered.

She saw the uncertainty in his face and wished it away. Then his hands were in her hair, cupping her head. He was about to kiss her. She thought of Ember and it hurt so badly.

"I hate you." She said it and then ran.

Poppy's father came in the door around ten in the evening and Poppy didn't ask where he'd been. She could guess, but even so, it would sting to hear about his Halloween evening with his son.

"You don't have to come back, you know," was all she said.

He just grunted and grabbed himself a beer from the fridge.

Her dad was watching a scary movie when the gang of kids arrived so that, at first, Poppy thought the blood-curdling screams were from the television. Then there was laughter, the sound of a trash can being knocked over, more screaming, and Poppy's name being called, over and over.

"Poppy Whoo-whoo-hoo-per!" Like a ghost.

"What the? . . ." muttered her dad and he went to the window and opened the curtains.

Out on the street they stood, all in masks—devils and Frankensteins, warlocks and werewolves, witches and zombies, ghouls and grim reapers. Poppy saw her dad's face harden. He looked at her but didn't say anything. Instead, he strode to the front door and opened it.

"*Trick . . . trick . . . trick . . . trick . . . trick . . .*" came the chants.

"Get lost, you hear me?"

"*Trick . . . trick . . . trick . . . trick . . . trick . . .*" they continued ceaselessly.

"Right, that's it. I'm calling the police." He slammed the door and looked at Poppy. "Who the hell are they?"

"They're wearing masks."

"I can see that, Poppy. Who are they?"

Poppy swallowed. The chanting carried on, getting louder and louder.

"I don't know. Could be any of them."

Poppy's father shook his head despairingly. "Can I get the police involved now?"

"Just ignore them. They'll stop eventually."

Her father said he'd give them fifteen minutes. He and Poppy sat next to each other on the sofa, the television on mute, listening to the noise from outside, hearing the neighbors shouting and swearing at the unruly trick-or-treaters. Poppy shut her eyes and willed the gang to stop. *I can do this*, she told herself. *I can hypnotize people. I can make books fly. I can summon rats. Make fire. Start a storm. I have the power.*

Then, suddenly, the window smashed behind her and she was the one screaming and her dad was clutching hold of her as she cried.

That night Poppy stayed at Donna's house. Donna came to the door in her nightgown, looking far more ordinary than Poppy remembered. She told Poppy to be quiet so as not to wake Logan. *So that is his name*, thought Poppy. As she crept into the kitchen, she noticed traces of her father there. His newspaper on the table, a pair of his shoes in the corner, a tie slung over a chair. It felt like this was his real life, his time with her just pretend.

The house was small and Poppy slept on the sofa. In the morning she woke to Logan poking her in the side.

"Who are you?" he said in a voice husky with sleep.

"I'm Poppy," she said.

"Did you sleep over?"

"Yeah, I did."

"Cool," he replied, and his serious little face broke into a big grin.

"Is . . . is your dad here?" Poppy asked, squirming at the awkwardness.

"He's gone to work. He doesn't live here much."

Poppy pulled her legs off the sofa and sat up. "I'm sorry about that," she mumbled.

"Not your fault," he said so simply that it made her want to cry.

Poppy sat at the table with them, the three of them eating from matching bowls of cereal. It had been a long time since she'd eaten breakfast with anyone.

"Do you want to see some magic?" Logan suddenly piped up.

"Okay, sure," said Poppy.

"Quickly now, Logan. You've got school to get to," reminded Donna.

Logan rushed to the other room and came back with a pack of cards. He held them open to show Poppy, then put them in a neat-ish pile on the table, wiping aside some spilled milk with his hand. He got Poppy to cut them and turn them over, then do it again.

"Now I'm going to get rid of all the upturned cards," he told her.

Poppy watched as his little hands grappled with the deck until he found the card that was facedown and held it up to her proudly.

"This is your card. Memorize it." Logan paused for a moment. "Now I am going to read your mind," he said dramatically.

Poppy glanced at Donna, who raised an eyebrow. "Okay. Go ahead."

Logan shut his eyes as though thinking hard. "It's the queen of diamonds."

Poppy nodded. "Wow. You are a real magician."

"Do you want to know how I did it?"

Poppy smiled. "Isn't that a secret?"

Logan shrugged and Donna interjected, "Next time."

"What? Is she coming again?" Logan asked excitedly.

"Of course," Donna told him, and then she caught Poppy's eye. "If that's what she'd like."

"My dad's a magician too," Logan beamed. "He taught me that trick."

Poppy tried to keep the ache she felt from reaching her eyes.

"Maybe he can teach it to you," Logan suggested sweetly, and Poppy got up from her chair and started to clear the table.

At the door Donna took Poppy's arm. "Your dad's worried about you, Poppy," she said in hushed tones. "I know you probably don't want to talk to me about it, but . . . look, we don't want you to get hurt."

"A little late for that," Poppy retorted, then regretted it immediately.

Donna let go of her arm. "He's had a lot to deal with, your dad."

Poppy suddenly felt like crying. "I'd better go."

"I didn't mean with you, love," Donna said quickly. "I didn't mean that."

But Poppy was hurrying down the path.

"Poppy!" Donna shouted after her, and Poppy turned.

"Are you even going to tell Logan who I am?" Poppy called back, and Donna turned around anxiously to see if Logan had heard. By the time she looked back, Poppy was running down the road.

When she got home, their living-room window was boarded up, and it made the whole house look busted, like something from a war zone. Inside it was freezing cold. Poppy kept her coat on. She could see her breath on the cold morning air.

"Dad?" she called softly.

There was no answer. Poppy stood still and listened for a moment. When she was sure the house was empty, she went straight to her room and started gathering any money she had, even the smallest coins. Then she stuffed a few things into her bag and ran back down the stairs to the door. When she opened it to leave, she found Ember standing there, her eyes big and scared in a face that looked paler than usual.

"I've run away." It was only when Ember spoke that Poppy understood she was real, not some strange apparition. "I can't live there anymore."

Ember moved toward Poppy, arms outstretched for a hug. As Ember held her, Poppy was surprised at how good it felt to have that contact, how the hurt that had been chilling within her melted away in its warmth.

"Oh, I've missed you so," Ember declared, pulling back to look at Poppy's face. Then she noticed the bag on Poppy's arm. "Where are you going?"

"Running away," Poppy said jokingly. Ember looked confused and Poppy sighed. "I'm going to see my mother."

CHAPTER TWENTY-FOUR

They sat on the train, Ember gripping the edge of her seat. She had taken hold of it when the train started moving and it hadn't occurred to her yet to let go. She was too busy staring out of the window at the passing landscape, her brain hardly registering the new sights before they'd gone and been replaced by another and another and another.

"I've never gone so fast," she uttered to her reflection in the window.

"It'll go even faster soon," Poppy told her.

"Faster than this?" Ember marveled, not believing it possible, but Poppy was right, and soon the hills were flashing past them and Ember couldn't look anymore—it made her head hurt.

"So why are you running away?" Poppy finally asked.

Ember felt a little nervous about answering. For as Poppy had led her through the town to the train station, pointing out the various landmarks in a voice that expressed her low opinion of them, Ember hadn't confessed she'd seen them before. She wasn't entirely sure why she felt so reticent about admitting to her evening with Leo. She guessed Poppy might feel aggrieved. After all, Poppy had been the one to find her and teach her, to open her eyes to the world beyond the camp. In truth, Poppy should have been her guide that night, not Leo. So Ember kept quiet, and now her omission felt more like falsehood and the idea of that made her squirm in her seat.

"Are you okay? You're very quiet today." she heard Poppy say, and she broke out of her reverie to look up into Poppy's inquiring eyes.

"My mother—she's so angry with me." Ember hung her head, wishing she was quick-minded enough to come up with some other reason for having fled the coven, but her ears were still burning from the grilling Charlock had given her. Ember wondered now how she could ever have been so stupid to leave the camp for a whole night and not expect her mother to notice.

Poppy was looking at her sympathetically. "I know you're close with your mom, but that's what most parents do—tell their kids off," she said kindly.

"I broke the rules."

"So?" Poppy was smiling.

Ember shut her eyes. "It is forbidden."

Poppy sensed what was coming. Ember felt her withdraw, her smile vanishing and her face becoming serious and still. "What's forbidden?" Poppy asked quietly.

Ember took a breath. She couldn't lie. She had no magic, no sleight of hand or tongue, no illusions up her sleeve. Only the truth.

"I left the camp one night. I went to the town—with Leo."

She waited for Poppy to say something, but she didn't. The silence was too unnerving. Ember had to fill it.

"I saw the streets with all their different names. He told me where you lived. Twenty-five Wavendon Close. He showed me everything. Oh, Poppy. It was wonderful. So big, so bright, so—oh, I wish you had been there."

"Do you?" said Poppy flatly.

And Ember realized that she had done it after all. Lied.

"You don't have to be embarrassed," Poppy said coolly. "You're allowed not to miss me. You're allowed to live your life any way you want."

"What if you don't know what you want, though?" Ember whispered.

Poppy wouldn't or couldn't answer that.

Ember thought of all she had been blessed with—the sisterhood of a treasured friend, the comfort of a mother's love, the thrill of a boy's attention. She had never imagined she would have to choose between them. She looked out of the train window and felt the speed and saw the space that went on and on, further than she ever knew. The cities were as dense and vast as her forest but stronger and taller, so much taller even than the highest tree. It made her want to retreat back to the clasp of the coven. There were no choices there. It was too small and tightly knit for that. She felt sewn into the fabric of the camp, attached, and the further away she traveled, the more the stitches pulled and she could feel them fraying from her heart.

"Is that what you do?" she asked Poppy at last. "Live life how you want?"

"I'm trying," Poppy answered.

"And Leo?" Ember questioned.

"I think you should ask him that," Poppy said plainly. "It isn't easy. Life with no clan."

A man came down the narrow passageway between the seats, pushing a cart before him. From it Poppy purchased two soft, silver bags full of the thinnest fried potatoes and two drinks that fizzed from cans. It was like eating salt and drinking sugar, but it made the rest of the long journey feel better.

They walked for a long while to reach the hospital. The air was different so far from home, more contaminated with particles that Ember didn't recognize, and warmer too. Winter didn't seem so ferocious here. Ember saw some plants that were still flowering and many trees that were still clinging to the last of their red and golden leaves. There were none of the chalky gray and purple hues of the hills at home. Even the green of the grass seemed more primary.

The hospital, though, was the whitest place Ember had ever seen. It smelled sour and unnatural. Poppy went to the desk and gave her name. They had to wait for a while on a row of chairs, each one stuck to the next. Finally a woman, clean and stiff, showed them into a box that raised them up—an elevator, Poppy called it—until the number three in the list shone red. They walked along a hallway lined with identical doors, then suddenly stopped at one of them.

"She's sleeping," said the woman quietly.

Poppy nodded, seeming unsurprised even though it was still day.

Ember followed Poppy inside. In the bed lay a body, the face turned away so all that could be seen was light hair, fair and gray, fanned out upon a pillow. Poppy sat in the chair beside the bed. She put her finger to her lips as a sign for Ember to stay quiet. Ember moved quietly across to the window and stared out at the garden behind the hospital where people wandered aimlessly in white robes, drifting across the walkways like ghosts.

"Are you real?" The voice was croaky, as if unused to speaking.

Ember turned and saw a face staring at her, pale and drawn, but with eyes that shone like patches of blue sky among the clouds.

"Mom?" said Poppy from the other side of the bed. "It's me."

Ember could see that the woman heard Poppy but chose not to turn.

"Come closer," she said to Ember.

Ember did as she was told, and the woman's arm darted out from under the covers, grabbing Ember's hand and pulling her closer. She peered up at Ember's face.

"Mom! What are you doing?" Poppy jumped to her feet.

"You are real," the woman whispered to Ember, still ignoring Poppy. Her eyes blinked and blinked, as though not trusting it to be true, and then her face lifted with emotion and Ember realized she had once been young and very pretty. "I've seen you in my dreams." The woman smiled.

Ember felt a shiver ripple through her. The hairs on her arms were standing on end and she felt freezing cold. She wanted to get away but didn't know how to break free.

"I'm Ember," she said softly. "Poppy's friend."

She tried to pull her hand away gently, not wanting to do anything sudden. Poppy had no such caution. She leaned over and tugged sharply at her mother's arm. "That's enough. Let go of her now."

The woman just held on tighter. "It's my little girl."

"Mom, listen to me. It's me, Poppy. I've come to visit you."

Poppy spoke slowly, but her mother was still looking at Ember, addressing only her. "You're here at last," she said, and a tear rolled down her cheek.

Poppy bent over her mother's bed. "Mom, this is Ember. You've never met her before. You remember me, don't you? Poppy? Dad moved us away, but I'm back to see you. Like I said I would."

"My daughter!" Poppy's mother wept, more tears falling now.

Poppy perched on the edge of the bed. "That's right. I'm your daughter."

Poppy's mother shook her head vigorously and turned, for the first time, to look at Poppy. "No. No, you're not."

The woman raised herself up to look directly back at Ember, her eyes penetrating into her. Then she let go of Ember's hand and pointed a thin, delicate finger straight at her.

"She is."

CHAPTER TWENTY-FIVE

L eo felt like his heart would burst out of his chest. His lungs were burning and his throat was gulping down air in loud, rasping breaths. He leaned over, hands on his knees, worried they would hear him. They'd spotted him by the park. The first Leo knew of it was his stepfather's voice barking across the street. Leo hadn't even turned around. He'd just sprinted as fast as he could, dodging lampposts and cars, people and strollers. He took sharp turns and shortcuts down side streets and alleys. He jumped down steps and leapt over railings. When he couldn't hear them thundering after him anymore, he dashed onto the railroad line and climbed up onto the platform. Shielded by the commuters in their suits and their open newspapers, he held onto his legs to keep himself from collapsing and prayed he'd lost them.

Leo stayed put at the station, fearful of coming across them if he set out again. He sat in the dingy waiting room, reading a discarded section of a newspaper, trying to act like he had a ticket in his pocket and a train to catch. After a couple of hours a woman entered. Leo was used to keeping his head down, eyes averted, but this woman caught his attention. He couldn't help but steal a look at her. She was similarly dressed to Ember. Long skirt and cape with knitted fingerless gloves on her hands and a fur hat around her head. The hat looked like fox, Leo thought to himself. And her face—it was broad and smooth with a wide forehead, dark thick brows, and the most arresting yellow, oval eyes like a cat's. She was utterly strange, like a person from a distant land or time.

"I like your scarf," she said suddenly, and Leo's hand reached up to touch it.

"Thank you," he said shyly. "It was a gift."

Then he realized the wool was the very same yarn as the scarf tied around her neck. They matched. Leo felt his eyes widen. The woman's pale, full lips turned upward into a smile. Disconcerted, Leo quickly looked down.

"What are you named?"

It took a moment for Leo to work out what she was asking him.

"My name?" he said. "Leo."

"Leo," she repeated, trying it out, seeming satisfied.

The woman didn't speak again. She shut her eyes and sat there, upright and still. After a while Leo felt tired. He tried to keep awake but he kept nodding off, his chin dropping to his chest, until he'd jolt and lift his head and rub his eyes. Before long he'd doze off again, but each time he stirred he was aware of the woman still sitting there, so perfectly peaceful. At last Leo fell into a deep and dreamless sleep. When he awoke, he was alone. Outside the woman was standing on the platform, awaiting the train that was pulling into the station. Only a few people got off the train. Among them were Poppy and Ember.

Poppy had left her mother in the hands of the nurses, all struggling to restrain her like she was a wild animal needing to be leashed. The howling had started when Ember ran from the room and did not return. Each anguished cry seared Poppy's heart. She had thought there was nothing more her mother could ever say that would hurt her, but here she was, once again, having to hold in the tears and bite the inside of her cheek to stop herself from crying out.

Her mother was crazy. If she wasn't when Poppy was a baby, she certainly had become so. Poppy knew she should do as the doctors and nurses advised and pay no attention to what her mother said when she took one of her turns. And yet her mother's claims had been proved right. Poppy *was* unlike other daughters. She *was* strange and she *did* possess magical powers.

But what happened today with Ember was beyond even Poppy's comprehension. It made her head whirl so fast that she struggled to keep her balance and had to walk down the hallway with one hand on the wall, fearing that without it, she might fall.

She found Ember outside, wiping the tears from her reddened eyes and swollen face.

"That didn't go quite as I planned," she said, and Ember attempted a smile that quickly slumped back into sorrow. "I guess it's just what happens when your mom is crazy."

The tears welled up in Ember's eyes again while Poppy's remained dry.

"Why do you think? . . ." Ember tailed off.

"She's insane, Ember," Poppy said bitterly. "That's all there is to it."

The trip home felt so much longer without the urgency and excitement of the outward journey. Even the train seemed to be traveling more slowly now that the girls felt so subdued. They both sat in quiet contemplation until Ember finally broke the silence.

"I used to think I had another mother out there, in the real world, far away from the coven. One just like me but with soft hands and feet and white teeth and colorful clothes." Ember spoke so quietly that Poppy had to lean forward to hear. "I'm sorry I ran off like that."

"No," said Poppy firmly. "I should never have brought you. It wasn't fair."

Ember gave Poppy's hand a squeeze so Poppy spoke again. "You know . . . my mom . . . she's never been angry with me for going out. She never even cared where I was."

When they arrived, Ember's mother was waiting for her on the platform, just as Poppy felt she would be. Ember ran into her mother's arms and Poppy hung back on the edge of the platform. The air beneath the train rushed past her legs as it rumbled on its way, but she hardly noticed as her eyes were fixed on Charlock—how she pulled Ember to her, laying her cheek on her hair, how she looked at her daughter, talking earnestly, shaking Ember's shoulders, then hugging her again.

The contrast between this mother-and-child scene and her own almost made Poppy want to laugh out loud. But she stayed quiet, watching, fascinated. Charlock was the first grown-up witch Poppy had ever laid eyes on. She wanted so badly for Charlock to notice her, to recognize her as one of her kind, to beckon her over and take her under her wing. But Poppy's legs wouldn't move, and she stayed back and watched as Charlock set off, her arm around Ember's shoulders, keeping her close.

Poppy watched them until they disappeared. Ember turned at the last moment and gave a tiny wave and then they were gone. Poppy stood there for a while. She felt so very tired and lost. Then she heard his voice and immediately she felt found.

"Poppy!?" Leo called again.

Poppy turned and saw him and her heart filled like a balloon, lifting her spirits instantly. Slowly he walked toward her and gently put his arms around her. Poppy laid her head against his chest and wrapped her arms around his waist.

"I've missed you," he said.

No recriminations or anger. None of what happened before seemed to matter. Only this.

❦

They took the bus back to her house. Poppy paid and Leo said nothing, just climbed on board behind her. They sat close, legs and sides touching, hands enclosed together. Poppy shut her eyes and allowed herself to feel contented, just for this short while.

The house was dark and Poppy guessed her father wasn't home

but checked anyway before gesturing to Leo to come in off the street.

"What happened to the window?" Leo asked once inside the cold living room.

"Trick-or-treaters," Poppy said.

Leo took a moment before speaking again. "You all right?" His voice sounded tight with anger.

"I went to see my mother today."

It was Poppy's way of saying she wasn't all right, and he seemed to understand that.

"I saw a picture of her," he said. "That time in your room."

Poppy saw the blush appear on his cheeks and it made her flush too, guessing what he was thinking of. She went to the sideboard, really to avoid the awkwardness between them, and got out an old photograph album. She opened it up and saw the snapshots of her past. Putting it on the table, she looked down at the pictures and Leo came and stood next to her. The images were so familiar, and yet Poppy struggled to recall the time and place.

Leo touched a finger to a shot of Poppy's face. She was about five, alone in a garden.

"You don't look very happy," Leo said softly.

"Neither does she," Poppy said.

On the opposite page was her mother, so very young yet somehow aged by sadness, her shoulders slightly stooped as if she were carrying the weight of the world upon them. Poppy turned the page and suddenly there was her mother, smiling.

"A different woman," Leo remarked.

"It was before she had me," Poppy stated, trying to keep the tremor from her voice.

Melanie's golden hair had been blown by the wind so it fanned the air and a strand swept across her face. She was laughing, her eyes crinkled as her hand tried to hold back her hair.

"She looks like Ember," Leo commented casually.

Poppy blinked and then she saw it too. It wasn't just the shade of the hair and the eyes and the skin, though they were identical. It was the expression that clinched it, a look Poppy had seen on Ember's face countless times before, that she had thought was unique, yet here it was captured in a photograph from twenty years ago.

Headlights swept the room and Leo took a step back, panicked.

"Out the back," Poppy told him, and she ran to open the back door, her fingers fumbling with the key in the lock. The door finally opened and Leo leapt out. Then he turned back.

"Meet me later. In our place."

She nodded, more because he said "our" than in agreement to the plan.

He kissed her so quickly she hardly had time to feel it, and then he was gone and Poppy was shutting and locking the door just as her father was walking into the hallway.

"You skipped school today," he said.

Poppy realized then she hadn't given school a second's thought.

"Can't say I blame you," her father continued. "After last night." He went into the front room and looked at the boards on the window. "They'll be coming to fix that tomorrow." He blew on his hands. "It's like a freezer in here."

As he turned, he saw the album opened on the table. He looked anxiously at Poppy but didn't say anything, just walked toward it and looked at the photographs.

"Another lifetime," he murmured. Then he shook his head and closed the album. "It's no good looking back."

Poppy wasn't sure if he was telling her or himself.

"Isn't it?" she questioned.

It was agonizing having to wait, to watch the minutes tick by so slowly, powerless to do anything but sit there and stare at the photograph in her hands. Poppy had pulled it free of the sticky backing before returning the album to the cabinet. She searched her mother's face over and over again for confirmation. The truth was in Poppy's head, shouting out at her, but it felt too big and loud for her brain to cope with. And the doubts kept crowding in, making her temples throb. She had to be sure.

Finally her father slept and Poppy slipped out of the house with the few items she'd collected. She traveled fast, crossing streets and then fields to reach the spot she was looking for. There she gathered branches and sticks, stacking them to make a bonfire. It took longer than she thought to light it. She struck match after match, but their tiny flames were snuffed out the moment they touched the damp wood. Poppy smiled foolishly when she remembered she didn't need the matches after all. She had the power within her. Summoning a spell, she proclaimed it out loud, raising her hands so the fire ignited in a sudden burst, and soon

the bonfire crackled and roared like it was a living, breathing creature. Poppy felt the heat of it without and within.

She opened Ember's book of magic and read the words by the
glow of the flames. Chanting, slowly at first then faster and faster,
she threw in the items she had carried with her.

Something of hers—a book.

Something of Ember's—a white handkerchief Ember had
given her.

Something of her mother's—a pair of red high-heeled shoes
Poppy had smuggled into her bag when they came up north.

Poppy hesitated before hurling those in. They were all she had
of her mother. Life with Melanie might have been harrowing at
times, but it was the life she knew. Maybe a crazy mother was better than no mother at all. The fire gave a hungry snap and Poppy
released the shoes into its flaming jaws. Finally she took the photograph from her pocket, took a last look at the stranger smiling
back at her, and threw that in too.

Shutting her eyes, she cast the spell. When she opened them,
pictures began to flicker across the flames. In them Poppy saw
a story unfold, the story of her birth. Two mothers, their bellies
round and full. One rushing to a hospital, the other kneeling on
a wooden floor. Two babies born on the same hour of the same
night. Poppy one, the other Ember. Twinned, not biologically—
but magically. Melanie Hooper holding Poppy in her arms, looking so tenderly at her newborn. Charlock Hawkweed cradling
Ember, inhaling the scent of her. The images spun in the heat, the
two girls growing up as they turned—infant, crawling; toddler,
walking; child, running; teen, leaping. Around and around they
spiraled until the two figures met in the heart of the fire, clasped

hands, then melted away so it was just the bright hot light of the flames again, devouring the wood, licking the air.

Poppy's cheeks glowed red. Her childhood memories lay in ashes inside of her, choking her. She wanted to cough them up and out of her but she couldn't bear to let them go. After all she had discovered, she still couldn't say good-bye. Instead, Poppy reached her arm straight into the fire and retrieved the photograph. Her arm was ablaze. She watched it curiously for a moment. Then she blew on it, just gently, and the flames died away.

Poppy looked at the photograph of Melanie Hooper—she couldn't call her "mother" any longer. It wasn't even singed.

When Leo saw her, he felt the shock so hard he couldn't breathe. The happiness cracked open inside of him and his heart split into jagged fragments. He couldn't quite believe Poppy was here, running toward him. Good things didn't happen to someone like him. He was so unused to feeling such a high that he didn't know what to do or what to say. He was in uncharted territory with no idea which way to steer. His face wanted to smile but he had to breathe first. Before he could question any further, there she was, in his arms, and all Leo's thoughts disappeared. It was just about feeling. Feeling her against him. Touching her face, her arms, her body. Smelling her neck, her hair. Tasting her mouth, her skin, her tears.

"What's happened?" he asked her, his voice as breathless as he knew it would be.

Poppy looked up at him, her two eyes shining with emotion, the contrasting colors glittering even more brightly through her tears. Then she put her small, cold hands on his cheeks and kissed him so deeply, he felt he had the whole of her. He picked her up—so light, she was—and lay her down beneath the willow where his blankets were. Their limbs entangled, fitting together like they were part of the same being. All night they embraced and talked and finally slept behind the leafy curtain of the branches, and if Leo had stopped to notice for a moment, he would have sworn the winter air around them was midsummer mild and filled with the scent of jasmine and that wafting past on a balmy breeze came the sweet serenade of a nightingale's song.

Chapter Twenty-Six

Poppy didn't want to wake. She felt so safe and contented, and even through the haze of sleep she sensed this feeling might end the moment her eyes opened. So she kept them shut and tried to drift in her dreams for a while longer. Leo's arms and legs were heavy and warm around her. His breath was soft and steady on her hair. Poppy guessed he was awake too but didn't want to disturb her. Part of her wanted to turn around and kiss him, hear her voice saying his name, and listen to his reply. But instead she lay still and quiet. Leo's embrace felt like home and she didn't want to leave. She thought of him, the details of him, how he'd kissed her and touched her, and then she made herself stop or she'd have to turn around and make him do it all over again.

The dawn light peeked through the leaves and onto Poppy's closed eyelids, but still she didn't open them, just let the morning rays flicker on her face. Her mind was less obedient. Gently stirring, it took its own course away from Leo, and meandering this way and that, it settled on Charlock. Poppy couldn't bear to think of that. Not now. So then it traveled to Ember, and there it stuck and wouldn't shift.

Poppy's eyes blinked open. Ember. In front of Poppy's face, a cluster of aconite had sprouted, a lone patch of yellow brightness on the winter grass, the petals the same sunshine shade as Ember's hair. The flowers trembled before Poppy's eyes and closed their petals tightly shut. Suddenly Poppy felt cold. The warm glow of her happiness evaporated and she shivered from the chill. The air that had caressed her skin only moments before now nipped at it painfully, and the ground that had cushioned her all night became a hard and frosty bed. Rather than offering shelter, Leo's limbs felt like they were imprisoning her. Poppy wanted to itch at where his breath hit her hair. She wanted to push his arms away. She wanted to break free and run.

She gave another shiver and Leo kissed her neck.

"Morning," he murmured.

Poppy sat up.

"What's wrong?" he asked gruffly.

"I have to go and tell Ember. About us."

"I'll come with you," he said without an instant's hesitation, and Poppy felt her heart pang.

She turned and looked at him for the first time since they had awoken. Leo put his arms around her, and after a moment, she reached across to hold him back. "I have to tell her myself."

"Can you wait a while longer?" Leo asked. Poppy rested her forehead on his so their faces were an inch apart. "Just a while . . . " he entreated.

"She's my only friend."

"Not only." Their lips were so close she could feel his moving.

"I've broken her heart." She sighed and her mouth brushed the edges of his.

"We both have."

The jealousy was instant. A fraction of a second and Poppy was pulling away. She had caught the look of guilt in Leo's face and hated him for it. Not wanting him to know, she looked around for the rest of her clothes and started pulling them on.

"It's only ever been you," he said, knowing everything already. From his pocket Leo took a small, pink, translucent stone. "Jocelyn gave me this. Her favorite one."

He handed it to Poppy and she felt it cool and silky on her fingers, despite its rough edges.

"It's rose quartz," he told her. "The heart stone." Poppy glanced up at Leo and he looked embarrassed and then added a little skeptically, "The crystal of unconditional love—or so she said."

Poppy held it up to the light and saw it glow pink and warm inside.

"I don't believe in that stuff," Leo went on. "But I like the idea, I guess."

"I like it too," said Poppy softly. She offered it back to him, but he shook his head.

"It's for you." He smiled shyly.

Poppy felt the tears prick unexpectedly in the back of her eyes. "I can't take this—she gave it to you to show how much she loved you."

Leo nodded. "I know," he said. "That's why I'm giving it to you."

They kissed before she left, long and hard and urgent. Poppy tried to dismiss the idea, but it felt like good-bye and she knew Leo felt it too by the way he held her, not wanting to let her go.

"Come back to me," he whispered.

The hint of panic in his voice was there more unmistakably in his eyes. Poppy wondered how she was ever going to leave—and then it began to snow.

The flakes weren't fleecy or soft. They hardly seemed made of snow, more like cut glass. Spiky symmetrical perfect patterns that caught in Poppy's hair like elaborate decorations and sparkled on Leo's lashes. Leo gazed up at them, and Poppy saw the panic in his eyes had gone, replaced only by wonder.

Poppy found her way to the coven by instinct, letting her feet carry her where they willed. She had no idea of the route she was taking or how she'd get home. It felt like she had walked in circles, covering the same ground, yet traveling deep into the forest where the terrain was harsh and inhospitable. The snowfall hadn't lasted long enough to settle, but Poppy's boots were wet and muddy from crossing brooks and squelching through burping bogs. Her clothes were ripped by bushes so thorny that she'd left threads dangling from them. She realized early on that it was impossible for anyone to reach the coven without leaving some trace of themselves. Her footprints were everywhere, as was her trail of snapped twigs and broken ferns. Poppy hoped these clues might guide her way back.

The camp was hidden behind boulders that towered above Poppy's head like misshapen totems. Poppy gazed up at them and wondered at the age of their existence. It felt like they had been there since the beginning of time. She knew the coven must lie beyond them, so she walked around and around until an opening became clear to her.

Once inside, the low, dim light of the forest seemed to brighten. From behind a tree Poppy peered at the scene before her. There were caravans scattered about here and there with no sense of planning or geography. They blended into the surroundings, their wood matching the bark of the trees, strands of ivy wending their way across them. These homes seemed to have sprouted from the ground just like the plants that grew wild around them.

Closer to Poppy were wooden barrels, some full of water, others heavy with compost. Further off she noted a collection of beehives, and in another area stood a large brick oven with fire pits dug into the ground close by and grated with metal spits. Chicken and geese moved about freely, clucking and honking in constant conversation. A horse trotted through them, unharnessed and wild, and a bell jingled from a goat that was tethered to a tree. It was being milked by a woman—a witch, Poppy reminded herself. Poppy could only see the back of her, but she could just make out the faces of others who were walking about the camp, all busy with a job to do—carrying pails, or heaps of clothes, or bundles of kindling. Their clothes were much like Ember's, but that was the only likeness. Their hair was dark, and even at a distance they appeared stronger and coarser. *It was no wonder Ember had felt an outsider*, Poppy thought to herself, and her eyes scanned the camp again for any sight of her friend.

Suddenly a donkey brayed and Poppy jumped. Then an arm pulled at Poppy's elbow, dragging her back behind a boulder, and she looked up to see Charlock's disapproving face. Poppy angrily shook her arm free. Neither of them uttered a sound and, as the seconds ticked past, Poppy felt her temper easing. When it had subsided altogether, Charlock finally spoke.

"Don't tell her," was all she said.

Poppy felt the surprise streak through her. "Why not?" was all she replied.

Charlock shut her eyes as though deciding on something difficult. "He cannot be yours."

Poppy recoiled from the truth she saw in Charlock's eyes. She shook her head and tried to speak. "No," was all the objection she could manage.

Charlock stood as still as the silvery stone beside her and watched. Poppy's mind started to crack with fear. Desperately she tried to fill the holes with something concrete. When she was stable enough, she raised her chin and looked Charlock in the eye.

"I love him," she pronounced rebelliously.

Charlock gave a weary sigh. "What about Ember?"

"I don't want to hurt her."

"Then don't."

"She needs to know."

"She needs nothing of the sort."

Poppy felt the tears rising behind her lids. "I'm your daughter too," she cried.

Charlock took Poppy's hands in hers and Poppy stared at them—one pair older, browner, the other paler, younger, but the same hands.

"I know," Charlock said softly, like she cared. "Which is why I'm trying to help you."

So tender were the words that Poppy looked up into Charlock's eyes willingly, even hopefully.

But the words that followed were sharp, like razors cutting at her wrists.

"You are to be queen."

Metal on flesh.

"It is prophesied."

The blade pressing down.

"A queen can never mate. The chaff will die."

Slash.

"Their hearts break. The boy you love. It's already started. The arteries hardening, closing."

Slash.

"The longer you stay with him, the faster it will go. If you do not leave him, he will die."

Poppy tried to shake her head but it was her legs that shook. She tried not to believe, to walk away, but her legs would not carry her.

"I'm not a queen," she whispered.

"Not yet. But you will be soon," said Charlock.

"I won't do it then. I won't. You can't make me," Poppy argued, her voice raising uncontrollably.

"It's not a choice," Charlock stated firmly.

Poppy's head was shaking now, along with the rest of her, wanting to rid herself of Charlock's words. But more were to come.

"You'll kill him," Charlock repeated.

And with that, the last of Poppy's hopefulness bled away.

She couldn't remember much of what followed in the moments after that. She knew she had vomited because she could still taste the sour sickness in her mouth. Charlock had been talking, touching, guiding her, but Poppy couldn't recall the words or the feeling. Here she was now, on the fringes of the forest, her feet firmly on the path home, Charlock pointing the way. Poppy's face burned as she remembered her night with Leo—how she'd wanted to go further and how he'd resisted.

"You don't have to protect my honor, you know," she had whispered with a smile.

"I don't want you to do anything you'll regret," he'd said.

Poppy gave a loud sob and felt the bile rise up again from inside of her. Charlock swept her fingers gently across Poppy's forehead. It was soothing as Poppy always imagined a mother's touch should be. Poppy closed her eyes in despair.

"Tell no one who you are, that we've met. Not a word. And don't come looking for me," she heard Charlock say, and Poppy squeezed her eyes tighter shut so the tears wouldn't spill. "It isn't safe."

"How long have you known about me?" Poppy croaked.

"I've always known about Ember. Even when she was a baby, I felt it, that she wasn't my flesh and blood." Poppy's eyes opened and she looked at Charlock to verify the truth, though she already knew she was not lying. "I'm no fool," Charlock continued. "Despite what others may think. I love Ember, though, as my own."

Poppy searched Charlock's face for some clue to her affections, but her features were unreadable. If there was any love for Poppy within her, even the mildest sympathy, it was tightly kept in check.

"What about me?" Poppy wailed, and now the tears came gushing. "You're my mother. You're supposed to love me."

"I'm supposed to keep you *safe*," Charlock replied quickly, her voice harsh and dry. "The first day you came to the dell . . . so close, I could have seen you, talked to you, I could have told you everything . . . but then there would be no hiding you and they would come for you and they would destroy you."

"Who?" Poppy asked, the fear rippling through her as she remembered Minx and the unseen enemy who had inflicted all those injuries upon her.

"The ones who took you from me."

Poppy blinked. "I don't understand."

"The prophecy. 'In three hundred and three years hence, the Hawkweed sisters will yield a daughter who will govern all her kind.' So it is told. You are to be queen. Your enemies are manifold. And you are untaught and unpracticed, despite your power. The time will come to reveal yourself, but it is not now. Not yet."

There was such a force to Charlock's words, but still her face betrayed none of the passion that left her lips. Poppy looked away. She wanted to laugh it off, to mock it all as silly superstition. She wanted to find Leo and curl back into his embrace and pretend that none of this had happened.

"It is better not to know, is it not?" Charlock stated, and Poppy realized why she had kept her away and in the dark for so long. The truth was too big and brutal. It hurt to even hear it. "It is better for you. It is better for Ember. And for the boy."

"But he has no family."

"He will have Ember. They will take care of each other. This I think you understand already."

Poppy felt the last of her energy leave her. It took everything she had simply to stay on her feet. She leaned against a tree, feeling its rough bark against her back. How many winters had it weathered, how many storms had shaken it to its roots and it was still standing? Poppy thought of Leo, of all the hardships he'd suffered in his life and how he'd grown up so strong despite them. He was a survivor. *He will survive me*, Poppy thought, and

somehow her back straightened and her legs moved and she
started walking.

As soon as Charlock entered the camp, she sensed the atmosphere had changed. The energy was electric, and she could feel
the excitement surging through the air, touching her and tingling
on her skin. Voices were ringing out, high and choral with elation.
Arms and skirts were aflutter. Sisters were turning from one to
another in a quick, light-footed dance. It was Ember who skipped
toward her and told her the news.

"The queen is dying!" Ember's face shone with delight, her eyes
wide and pupils large as though she were intoxicated.

Charlock glanced around and saw others were struck with the
same fever. She felt a moment of shame that the great witch's de-
mise could be received with such euphoria. Then Raven touched
her arm. Charlock couldn't remember the last time she and her
sister shared a physical contact. In a flash it took her back to their
girlhood and it made her spirits sink even further to think how
times had changed them.

"There were those who doubted. But the prophecy—it's coming true, sister."

Raven spoke so evangelically that Charlock wanted to wince.
She stopped herself, of course. Instead, she muzzled her mind
and emptied her eyes as she always did when looking directly at
Raven.

"It is as you always said it would be," she responded graciously.
"Is Sorrel prepared?"

"I've told her to go and change into her best."

"It's what you've both been waiting for. She will be ready. Now, I myself must go and prepare for such a big occasion."

Having dismissed herself, Charlock hastened away. The secrets that swam soundless in her stomach were swirling and swishing, making her want to scream. She thought of Poppy and the wounds she'd inflicted on her own child. The girl had stayed so silent, so accepting. Charlock had expected argument and tears, but this had been far worse. She had underestimated her child's feelings for the boy. She should have delivered her message with more care. She should have shown her that it came with a mother's love.

But her love for Poppy had been held captive for a lifetime, deep within the pit of her being, and it felt too dangerous to release it. Over the years the love had begged to be let out. It had bashed against its bars and clamored against its confinement, only for Charlock to tighten the locks and block out the cries. She couldn't risk freeing it now. Instead, she had reported the news about the boy as calmly and clearly as she was able, knowing, all the while, it had to be done.

The throne was Poppy's destiny. The boy would be her downfall. He was not her fate, just a fleeting fancy that, in years to come, Poppy would be grateful to have escaped the consequences of. And yet the look on her face when she'd heard the news. Charlock had watched a part of her daughter die this day. *For the throne*, she reminded herself. *To be queen.*

"It had to be done." This was Charlock's mantra, the code by which she lived. She had known for many years now the lengths a mother would go to for her child, the lines she would cross, the hurt she would endure. She had left her baby in another's care. She had let her be raised by chaffs. She had learned of Poppy's presence in the town, her need for a mother, for identity, and yet she had withheld herself, keeping hidden. One motive was pure—survival. The other malign and murky—ambition. Charlock felt it like a tumor inside of her, growing and thriving as the years passed, feeding on her integrity.

As her guts tightened and twisted, Charlock hurried faster to the bathrooms. Her mind raced more quickly than her legs. *What if . . . what if?* . . . it asked. What if all those years before she'd spoken out? *This baby is not mine*, she could have said. What if Poppy had been found? What if she'd come home?

Charlock knew the answers all too well, and yet the questions hounded her still. She never knew which enemy had taken her baby from her, only that there were too many to choose from. Too many threatened clans. Too many jealous witches. Too many heirs apparent.

So many times she had thought of confiding in Raven. Raven could fix anything. But the sense was too strong, too nagging to ignore. *Bring your daughter home and you will lose her again*, it said. *Those who took her will come after her once more. Think of Ember*, it reminded. *The clan will expel her if they know the truth, and for such a sweet but feeble child, that would be a death sentence.*

With a grimace, Charlock squatted down low over the hole in the slatted ground and let her bowels spill and splutter. She breathed deeply, calming her nerves, telling herself to be patient—just a little while longer. Both girls were safe for now. The pain eased as Charlock's innards emptied, releasing with the waste all the fear that had been bubbling there. As she straightened and pulled down her skirts, she could hear the ovation as Sorrel made her appearance.

The cheers roused Charlock. *Let them think what they will*, she thought to herself. She knew better. It was her daughter who was taken. Not Raven's. It was Poppy who was feared. Not Sorrel. Charlock knew it to be true, just as she knew the earth lay beneath her feet and the sky above her head—it was she who had produced the chosen one.

Sorrel was chewing the side of her mouth jagged when she caught her mother's eye and immediately stopped. She'd received that very same look all through her childhood when she used to chew the ends of her braid. She'd nearly died from the ball of hair that had amassed and lodged in her throat. She remembered the sensation of choking, of gasping for breath. She felt a little like that now—that something was blocking her airways, that however hard she tried, she couldn't get enough air inside her lungs.

Sorrel looked around at the crowd flocking to her. All the sisters were there, young and old, even the infirm leaning on their sticks and the infants being held up to catch sight of her. Sorrel caught her Aunt Charlock's eye, her face tranquil as usual, as though nothing could ever trouble her too badly. Charlock smiled in encouragement, and Sorrel felt instant gratitude. But then she saw Ember there beside her, so beautiful in her happiness that Sorrel's teeth gnawed at her cheek once more.

"Look at the new queen," she heard a voice utter so reverently, as if the crown were already on her head.

A hand reached out to touch her skirt. Then another. *It's only me*, Sorrel wished she could remind them. But she kept silent, putting one foot in front of the other, moving forward to the designated spot, a circle scorched into the earth in preparation for this day.

The sisters joined hands to form a ring around her, behind them another band, and another that Sorrel was too short to see. They bowed their heads and hummed. One note, so soft at first, but then increasing in volume until it sounded like a giant whirring insect was in their midst. Sorrel felt the vibrations in the fabric of her clothes, in the hairs on her body that began to rise, and in her bones that suddenly felt light and hollow.

Ever so slowly, she ascended. Sorrel had heard of levitation but never dreamed she would experience it. Raised up by their voices, she lifted higher and higher into the air, until she hovered high above their heads among the trees. She stretched her arms out into the tangerine sky. Silhouetted against the sunset, she stayed suspended there, all the sisters so far below, their upturned faces gazing at her in awe.

Sorrel looked out over the trees and thought of the ancient queen across the waters lying on her deathbed of drying flowers. She would have had a day like this among her clan. She was a young woman once, heralded and raised up so high. That was over a hundred years ago. Sorrel's clan had waited so long for this day to come. Her own life had been mere incubation for now. In a matter of days she would be queen. This was her true beginning, Sorrel realized with a rush that seemed to elevate her further.

She shut her eyes and let herself breathe freely.

Chapter Twenty-Seven

Poppy let the spider crawl across her face. In her numbed state, she was vaguely curious to experience what it felt like. Yet even as the tiny feet tickled across her cheek and over her nose, tiptoeing onto her eyelid and through her brow, Poppy felt so detached from her body that it could have been someone else's face the spider was touching. She was supposed to write Leo a letter but hadn't found the energy either to fetch the paper or to pick up a pen. Charlock had given her strict instructions, but the longer Poppy procrastinated, the longer it wasn't over, the longer Leo could be happy and she could pretend. So she had laid down and waited, with absolutely no idea what she was waiting for.

The pins and needles had started in Poppy's feet, then crept up her legs until her body had become anaesthetized and stopped hurting altogether. She felt like she couldn't move, even if she wanted to. The spiders had been watching her for a while now. They had appeared as if from nowhere, gathering like dark clouds upon the ceiling. Then they began spinning. So swiftly the webs took their spiral shape, lacing the air above. Then slowly the spiders lowered themselves like spies on silken threads to take a closer look at her. Poppy studied them back and thought how ludicrously long and thin their legs were, like they'd been sketched in pencil.

Poppy was at Donna's house, where she knew Leo couldn't find her. Donna had given her a look of disappointment when she answered the door but had asked no questions and invited her in. She'd spent the night on the sofa again, unable to sleep, though she felt crippled with exhaustion. In the morning she'd told Donna she felt unwell.

"You do look pale," Donna had said and told her to go and lie down in Logan's room.

All day Poppy had stayed there, hiding from what must come next. Hour after hour she had laid on Logan's little bed, her legs hanging over the end. She'd watched the light change through the thin curtain as the day passed. She'd felt the temperature slightly rise over the course of the morning and then fall back again as dusk drew near.

Logan was back from school now. Poppy could hear him downstairs watching television. Part of her hoped neither he nor Donna would come in and see the infestation of spiders. Part of her just didn't care. She had no one anymore. Not Melanie, nor Charlock, not her dad, nor Ember—and most of all, not Leo. With him, she could have managed without the rest of them, but now he was lost to her too. And he didn't even know it yet.

The spiders glided back up to the ceiling and began a new and more frenzied piece of sculpture. Working together, each one sewed a section of this new embroidery. Poppy waited as they worked so studiously and silently. When they finished, they swung to the moldings to reveal their masterpiece.

Poppy stared. It was a bird. An ugly, evil-looking bird. So detailed was its image that it seemed to be in flight across the room, its wide wings outstretched, its sharp beak open, ready to swoop in for the kill. The adrenalin was automatic and acute. For the bird was unmistakably a predator and Poppy its victim. Poppy blinked once, twice, three times, then jumped to her feet.

She was waiting downstairs, a hunched, crooked woman with a beaky nose and a long, thin braid that slid down her back like a snake. Poppy couldn't tell how old the woman was, only how strong. The power radiated off her despite her slight and feeble frame.

"Take a seat, child," the woman told her. "Donna here is kindly making me a cup of tea."

"This is Mrs. Hawkweed, Poppy," said Donna brightly.

Poppy's throat narrowed and she had to swallow to be able to breathe again. This woman that she couldn't look at, that sent fear teeming through her, was her aunt. Ember had spoken of her with such awe. Raven, the most powerful witch in the clan.

"Miss," Raven corrected Donna.

"I'm sorry," Donna apologized and turned back to Poppy. "Miss Hawkweed found Logan outside on the street. He'd slipped right out from under my nose."

"The little minx," Raven added, and Donna laughed.

Poppy's heart jumped in her chest, and before she had a chance to stop them, her eyes darted to her aunt's and the look she encountered made the hairs on her arms stand on end.

"It's a dangerous world out there," Raven said. "Don't you agree, Poppy?"

Poppy said nothing, but the fear hit her bladder so hard she had to clench it tight before she peed her pants.

"Oh, yes," said Donna, oblivious. "He could have been killed, perish the thought." She put the tea down in front of Raven on the table. "We're ever so grateful."

"Oh, it was the least I could do," Raven said, but it was only Poppy who seemed to glean the menace in those words, for Donna was offering up a plate of chocolate-chip cookies. Raven shook her head and continued, "Children are the most precious of gifts, are they not?"

"Oh, do you have children of your own, Miss Hawkweed?" asked Donna, taking a cookie for herself.

"A daughter, much like Poppy here."

Poppy saw Donna's cheeks flush. "Oh, I'm not Poppy's mother," she said hurriedly. "She's from down south. Not been well."

Poppy felt the anger ignite inside of her. It gobbled up the fear like it was oxygen, and the heat made her brave. She shut her eyes and cast a rapid spell. Donna and Logan froze. Time stood still.

"Nicely done," Raven said.

"It was you," Poppy said. "You killed my cat."

"And I told you to go. And yet . . . " Raven paused to pinch at the tiniest speck of a spider hanging in the air. "And yet you're still here." She flicked the crushed creature onto the floor. "The little spy," she said with a thin smile that made Poppy want to recoil and look away.

Poppy couldn't do that, though. That would be a battle lost, so she kept her eyes fixed on Raven's. Instead, she wished hard, as hard as she might, for Charlock. For her mother. She didn't expect her silent cry of help to be heard or even responded to. She simply couldn't think of anyone else to wish for.

"The cat was a difficult catch. But these two, they'd be easy."
Raven gestured at Donna and Logan who stood there in mid-
motion like strange, expressive waxworks. "The child, so young.
Now, that would be a pity. As for that chaff you think you love,
that boy you swoon over"—Raven made a face of disgust—"I'd
enjoy hurting him."

Poppy gritted her teeth and dug her nails into her palms, tiny
reflexes but Raven spotted them.

"He'd suffer," she reveled. "Oh, I'd make sure of that. Keep him
conscious to the end. How he'd plead for his pitiful existence. A
buck without his antlers, a cockerel without his crow."

Poppy was trembling now, her whole body fizzing with fear
and rage. "Why?" she cried.

Raven gave a condescending shake of her head. "Just leave. Be
gone. There's nothing here for you but trouble. Every one of them
would be better off without you."

"You most of all," Poppy spat. Raven's stare was so acute that
Poppy almost lost her nerve, but she rallied her voice and her
words came strong and clear. "What have I ever done to you that
you must come here and threaten me?"

"Don't test me, child. You have talent but you know little."

"And yet you fear me so?" Poppy challenged.

Poppy felt the fury gather within Raven. "I should kill you
now," she threatened.

"Why don't you then?" said Poppy. "What's stopping you?"

Poppy waited to see if Raven would tell her about the blood
they both shared, about the family roots that tied them. But Raven's fury turned to ice, freezing any chance of such an admission.
When she spoke, her voice was glacial.

"I am giving you a chance. A last chance. Take it."

With a snap of her fingers she was gone, and Donna was biting into her cookie and Logan was watching the television again. Donna caught sight of Poppy standing there.

"Oh, Poppy. There you are. You feeling better?"

CHAPTER TWENTY-EIGHT

I don't love you.

Charlock said to write it like she meant it.

I don't love you.

Use your magic, she said. With it, you can make him believe anything. Even this.

I don't love you.

But Poppy's hands were trembling.

I don't love you.

Her head was hollow, the words bouncing off bone, echoing around her mind.

I don't love you.

There was no magic to be mustered.

I don't love you.

Until the ink began to weep.

I don't love you.

And the sentence sizzled.

I don't love you.

And each vowel and consonant burned their shape right through the paper.

Magic.

Chapter Twenty-Nine

It was for their own good. At least that's what Sorrel and Ember were told when they complained about their captivity. Hot on the heels of the queen's news came reports that other clans were on the move and heading in their direction. Last night's jubilation was quickly dampened by worry. The sisters took to their beds with a confusing mix of emotions and awoke certain of one thing: they must be vigilant. Rumors were rustling through the camp like a whispering wind sent across the seas from faraway lands. Rumors of spite and spells sent to hurt them. Rumors of other heirs to the throne, other young witches with extraordinary powers. Rumors of plans to wound and weaken the Hawkweeds before their queen was proclaimed.

The stories grew fatter and juicier with each telling, dripping their poison into ear after ear. The elders called for calm but even they seemed uneasy. You could see it in their stance and hear it in their voices. Even the very air felt heavy with foreboding. The trees stooped with the tension. The hens weren't laying and the goats' milk was thin and watery.

After breakfast Sorrel and Ember were told they must stay within the camp's circle. Every sister was instructed to watch that neither of them took a step beyond its protection. Since then Sorrel had worn an even sourer expression than usual, and when Ember tried to pick up their friendship from where Sorrel had left it, she found her advances rejected. Sorrel just looked straight through her and turned away.

So Ember was back where she started—all alone. Having tasted the sweetness and spice of friendship with Poppy, Leo, and even Sorrel, her loneliness was far sharper than she remembered. She looked to her mother for comfort, but even she, always so serene, now seemed distracted and jittery. Ember could tell Charlock was only listening to her with one ear while the other strained for snatches of conversations going on throughout the rest of the camp. Charlock wasn't looking straight at her either, her eyes wandering over Ember's head, scanning around in constant apprehension. Later Ember heard Charlock curse as she burned herself on the stove, then again as she tripped on the path. By lunch a sty had formed in Charlock's eye so she had to bandage a chamomile compress to it and now looked like she'd been attacked. Even to Ember, who had never mastered reading the auguries, none of this boded well.

"Do you think the Eastern clan have put a hex on you?" she asked her mother late that afternoon as they sat, both of them with bowls of cream under one arm while the other arm whipped vigorously until the yellow butter formed.

"Hush, child," Charlock cautioned. "There's still such a thing as bad luck, you know."

"I heard Sister Mabel say that they'd been sighted and they were traveling north."

"And I suppose Sister Mabel saw them with her very own eyes?"

Ember shrugged. Her forearm was aching, the muscles in it pushing through her skin.

"Keep whisking, Ember. This is no time for idleness."

"I don't see how more butter is going to help Sorrel."

"Busy hands make less mischief."

Ember flexed her fingers, then gripped the whisk once more, bowing her head to her work. The cream was at last thickening and she longed to dip her finger into its clouds and suck on its sweetness. To stop herself, she drew her mind back to their conversation.

"Are you scared of them? The Eastern clan?"

"I am scared of anyone with hate in their heart."

"That makes a multitude."

"Indeed it does."

"Why do they hate us so?"

"All the clans, even the ones we considered friends, turned against us when the prophecy was told. The Eastern clan is just the biggest and the strongest. And an Eastern sister has yet to be queen. It is their turn—their right, they believe—to be chosen next."

Ember paused before asking another question. Her mother had never been so forthcoming before, and she wasn't sure whether to press on and capture the moment or be gentle in case she broke it.

"Do you ever wish I could be queen?"

"No." Charlock's voice rang true and certain.

"Why not?"

"You are made for happier things."

"And Sorrel isn't?"

Charlock tutted under her breath but didn't answer.

"If only this queen would hurry up and die, then everyone would know for sure about Sorrel," Ember muttered.

"Ember Hawkweed—that is treason!" Charlock seemed genuinely aghast.

"I'm just saying what everyone is thinking. Just before the queen dies, Sorrel's name will appear on the stone and all argument will cease."

"There may be days before that happens."

Ember glanced at her mother and asked what she had wanted to ask all along. "The Eastern clan—what if they think I could be queen . . . what if they don't know Sorrel is the one and they are coming to hurt me?"

Charlock stopped whisking and looked up from her bowl. She answered slowly but surely. "You mustn't fret, child. It is Sorrel who is in their sights. But best be cautious nonetheless."

For a second the lack of threat—the lack of any interest from anyone—stung Ember, but the pain rapidly turned to relief. Then suddenly she was grinning with surprise.

"Look!" she announced happily, holding up her bowl. "The butter's ready."

Charlock smiled her praise. "Go and drain the buttermilk into the jar. Then rinse the butter well, better than last time!"

"Is yours not ready?" Ember asked, realizing her mother was still whisking. "I'm never first to finish."

They both peered into Charlock's bowl and then, before their eyes, the cream turned dark as charcoal.

Ember screamed as Charlock stared, struck dumb with shock. "Mother!" Ember cried. "Mother! What is it?"

Charlock got to her feet and grabbed her shawl. "Throw this away. Don't let anyone see."

"Where are you going?" Ember asked, the fear crawling across her skin.

"You are safe here but I must hurry." Charlock's hand was on the door when she turned around, "Tell no one, Ember. Promise me."

Ember nodded, then glanced down at the black bowl, wondering how she was ever going to touch something so vile. When she looked up, her mother was gone.

Sorrel knew where Ember was going when she alerted the others. It was immensely pleasurable to see her cousin stopped in her tracks as she was hurrying off to meet the boy. Sister Ada had Ember's ear between her bony fingers and Ember was wincing from the pain. Her cheeks were smarting too from the shame of it, being dragged through the camp and sat on the tree stump where usually the little ones were sent for punishment. The sisters had all gathered around Ember, their voices shrill with anger as they demanded to know what she'd been thinking and where she was off to and hadn't she heard the morning's instructions and did she think nothing of her safety.

Sorrel knew this was her chance and she took it stealthily. With all eyes on the humiliated Ember, Sorrel crept from the crowd, backing away to the edge of the camp. No one spied her and called the alarm, no voice shouted her name, no arm came out to seize her. It felt all too easy. As she stepped through the boulders and beyond the circle, Sorrel expected the crows to caw and the foxes to bark their hideous cry. But the forest seemed oblivious to her presence and off she ran, looking for the softest places to tread, moving as swiftly and silently as she could. She knew how fortunate she was that her mother was away scouting for news of the Eastern clan. And her aunt seemed to have disappeared also, perhaps to barter or comb for those supplies that the coven couldn't produce themselves. In any event, it was a rare day to have both of them absent at the same hour.

Charlock would not be happy to hear about Ember's exploits, Sorrel thought gleefully to herself, feeling the wind on her back, urging her forward. She almost laughed out loud with the thrill of her escape, reveling in the notion that it would be she, and not her cousin, who would find the boy. Perhaps this time she might show herself and say a word. She might shake his hand as she'd seen the chaffs do. She might tell him her name and hear his in return.

A queen could never do such a thing. A queen could never even contemplate it. If there were a last chance for a moment of freedom, this was it.

Sorrel wove her way through the trees, marveling at how fast she could travel when there was strong reason to. The hills soon stretched before her and there, nestling in their breast, were the sparkling lights of the town, beckoning her closer.

It took her some time to find him. The night air stung with cold, and the homeless were huddled in shelters and not at their usual street-side posts. It was when Sorrel was passing the church that she sensed him. The wind was whistling through the graveyard and Sorrel stopped to hear it. Led by its gusts, she passed among the headstones, each as varied as their inhabitants once were—old and crumbling, young and gleaming, tall and short, light and dark. But below they were all the same now. Bone and skull. Row upon row of skeletons lining up for the afterlife.

Even in death, the chaffs must attempt order, thought Sorrel. She came to the wall and waited, wondering if she had followed the wrong lead. Then she looked up at the dark cloud swirling against the cobalt sky. Coming to her aid, the moon appeared for an instant and a blast of wind caused a sudden bang. Sorrel turned and saw the garden door illuminated and knocking gently against its frame.

The boy was sitting before a tiny makeshift grave. Sorrel tried but couldn't sense the person buried there. She puzzled at who might be laid within that the boy might visit on such an unforgiving night as this. Then, in his hand, she saw a letter. The boy held it up and looked at it, feeling the folded paper under his fingers, turning it in his hands. Just one light sheet but so heavy with significance. The boy feared its contents, that much was clear. Once read, the words could never be unread. *Open it*, thought Sorrel impatiently. But still the boy just sat there, postponing the moment. *Open it*, Sorrel urged, longing to say the words out loud, to scream them. But he didn't dare.

Sorrel concentrated her mind and breathed slow and deep. As she exhaled, a breeze flurried around her. She sent it to the boy and it whipped around him, trying to pull the letter from his hands. The boy held it tightly, and when the wind tugged the paper from his grasp, he reached up and grabbed it with both hands. The gust gathered force and snatched the letter away, carrying it up and around so the boy was on his feet, running after it, turning and jumping for it. Sorrel smiled at this little jig and then, when she'd tired of seeing the boy leaping this way and that so foolishly, she had the air flutter the paper open and let it land in his hands.

The boy looked to the skies and shouted, "So you want me to read it, do you?" For a moment Sorrel felt a tinge of trepidation that he had somehow seen her, but his eyes were looking crazily up at the sky and then he cried out, "You can't come tell me yourself?" and she knew it was the letter's author he was berating. The boy held the letter up before his eyes. "Okay, I'm reading it. Happy now?"

Sorrel quieted her mind and let the wind soften. The boy shut his eyes for a moment, then opened them and looked at the words sprawled across the paper. Sorrel could see his pupils moving across the lines and she could feel it when the shock came. So strong it was that the tremors shot all the way through his body and into the ground, pulsing across the earth until she felt them for herself in the soles of her feet.

The boy read again and again and again, as though searching for some way to understand or hoping the meaning might change. Sorrel wanted to take the offending paper away. She wanted to start over and shake his hand and introduce herself. But then the boy fell to his knees and bowed his head low until it touched the earth. The paper crumpled in his fist and smudged in the wet, dark soil. The rain came of its own accord, pattering down on the both of them. The boy stayed curled up like that for a while, and when he raised his body, he unclenched his hand and looked at the paper, now sodden and torn, the blue ink smeared and running down it in tiny rivulets, washing the words away.

When he finally moved away, it was with purpose. His face was set hard into a single, unchanging expression. Through the town he strode, pulling open the doors to the bars and pubs, scouring the rooms intently, then slamming the doors behind him when he failed to find whom he was seeking. Sorrel watched from a distance, safe from view, as the boy never looked back, only forward, striking place after place on his hunt.

Sorrel's curiosity grew with every stop on the route. At first she felt a dread that it was Ember whom the boy was after. That lasted but a second. *The other girl?* Sorrel speculated. *Had she written the letter?* It was exciting, all this intrigue. As she waited in suspense for the boy to reappear, she became aware that she was enjoying herself, and with this came the realization of how rare it was for her to feel so entertained.

Then the door opened and Sorrel almost gasped with surprise. She hadn't seen it coming, though how obvious the boy's objective seemed now that it was revealed. The men's ugly features were twisted with delight at his appearance as their thick arms gripped him, pulling him and pushing him onto the pavement.

How could I have failed to anticipate this? Sorrel scolded herself. The boy's shock, the hurt, the need to lash out, the need for it to end. If Sorrel had been less fixated on the girls, if she had kept her mind at least ajar, she might have seen what was coming and been able to prevent it. Now she had to stay hidden in the shadows and wait until it was over. Part of her wanted to cast a spell, to magic the boy away, or armor him, or paralyze them. But the other part of her wanted to keep on viewing, appalled as she was by her own gratification. So she remained in her place, an audience watching as an evening's drama turned to tragedy.

Finally Sorrel could look no longer. The scene went on too long and, with it, the thrill of the fight abated. Even when the boy had stopped fighting back, even when he was broken and unconscious, still they battered him. Sorrel shut her eyes, but she could hear the ribs cracking and the thud of the back of his head on the paving stones and the voices of those pigs—that was the worst—squealing their excitement. She shrunk away and felt the brick of a building against her back. Wrapping her cloak around her, she hung her head in mortification.

Why have I come here? she questioned herself. *A queen come for a boy?* She was about to go when the attackers pulled back and left him there, splayed out on the ground, his body twisted and his face no longer his own. Even then Sorrel thought of leaving, knowing that no part of him was for any part of her. The show was over. Now that she saw the boy in pieces, she could hardly picture him whole. As she stepped closer toward him, she wondered how and why she could ever have held him in such thrall. Pleasure rippled through her, such was the relief she felt to be free of him. For with him went the jealousy, the insecurity too. She thought of Ember's beauty and found she no longer cared.

Then she thought of being queen, and for the first time, her fear had gone. Testing out her newfound liberty, she stooped down beside the boy and looked closely at the wreckage. His face was swollen and bumps bulged from his skin. Bruises were blossoming darkly, patterning his body. His nose was dented and a thick gash streaked his eyebrow. Sorrel searched for signs of his old looks but found none. Suddenly pity sprung up inside of her. She took his hand, limp and cold, in hers and shook it.

"Hello," she said. "I'm Sorrel."

He did not stir. Sorrel sighed and opened the satchel at her side. From it she produced a cloth and lotion with which to clean his wounds. When she touched him, it was like touching any other. Just skin and flesh and skeleton. She lifted a tiny vial to the boy's mouth and let the tonic seep between his cut lips. It must have stung, for he stirred. *That was a good sign*, she thought, and she spoke to him again to try to keep him awake.

"It's for the pain. It will help, you'll see."

The boy tried to open his eyes, but they were swollen shut. "Who are you?" His voice came croaked and cracked.

Sorrel looked down on him, so mangled and mutilated. "It's Ember," she said, because she knew she could.

"Poppy?" he murmured softly.

Sorrel felt her face tighten.

"Poppy?" he moaned, writhing as he became more aware of his injuries.

Sorrel poured the last few drops from the vial onto his lips. "It's me," she told him comfortingly, touching his brow. "I'm taking care of you."

His eyelids strained to open and he squinted up at her. "Poppy," he whispered. "Don't ever leave me," he sighed before sinking back into senseless sleep.

CHAPTER THIRTY

The girl hadn't gone yet, but Raven hadn't given up hope she would heed her words. The girl's powers seemed to have diminished in the last few hours. Raven could feel it, all the way from the camp, like the child was giving up on herself and letting the magic ebb away. For any witch, it took effort to stay strong. The girl had slumped into some kind of inertia that made Raven wish she had confronted her sooner. She had never guessed her words would have such a devastating effect.

Nonetheless, Raven prepared the potion. The accounts of the queen's fading had been confirmed, and Raven had returned to camp and immediately set to work. The other sisters had tried to speak with her about her niece but Raven had brushed them away irritably, demanding no interruptions. She had locked herself in the storeroom without even passing by her caravan to greet her own daughter. She had work to do and her mind was set upon it. She could not see or think of anything else. If the girl was not gone by daybreak, Raven would destroy her. As yet, the secret of this child's identity was still tied only to her, but Raven could feel the truth unknotting itself further with every minute that passed. She had done everything in her power not to resort to murdering her own kin, but the queen's death was drawing near and nothing could be allowed to get in the way of Sorrel's coronation.

It was an evil brew and smelled as such. Raven's eyes burned and her nostrils ran as the steam hit her face. Once ingested, the dark liquid would not stop the heart but slow it, so there would be no awakening from the coma. Still, Raven was determined to avoid the blunt instrument of murder. This poison required the most skilled sleight of hand and an exhaustive knowledge of the craft. Lobelia formed the base. Then hellebore, bloodroot, and apple seed. Added to that, the tiniest fraction of hemlock, juniper, mistletoe, and nutmeg. Only one ingredient was missing. Sap from a fig tree. There was one such tree that stood in the furthest corner of the orchard, pining for sunnier climes, a sickly slip of a sapling that shivered so from the winter's chill that even summer's rays could not revive it. It had never borne much fruit. *Now*, thought Raven, *finally it will serve some use.* Before she left, she bent over her potion and whispered to it a wish, a spell, a curse—all three in one.

> *Sleep a century's sleep*
> *Slumber silent deep*
> *No disturbance wake*
> *Or spell ever break*
> *Sleep a century's sleep.*

Then she gathered her skirts and hurried from the caravan, shutting the door behind her, searching through the darkness for that sad and lonely tree.

Sorrel knew there had to be trouble awaiting her. Raven would have returned by now and discovered her absence. Her fury would be mounting by the moment. Sorrel wasn't sure whether to hurry to stem the tide of her mother's anger or to slow down and delay being drenched by her wrath. For Sorrel had stayed longer in the town than she had meant to. She had dragged the boy to an alleyway and hidden him in the shadows there, patching him up as best she could and only leaving when she felt he would survive. When she departed, she knew she would not be seeing him again.

She took one last look, then headed out of town.

Suddenly Sorrel heard a rustling in the grass. Footsteps, she presumed. It must be her mother coming to track her down. Who else would be so far from home at this time of night? Her heart sank but she called out in greeting, "Mother?" Her voice sung clear on the silky air. "Is that you?"

There was no reply, just the echoes of her words against the hills. Perhaps her ears had deceived her.

Then Sorrel saw them—a pair of bright yellow eyes, gleaming fierce with ill intent. The fear she felt was shockingly quick and violent. She started to run. She could hear panting behind her. She could feel breath on her back.

Mother! she thought desperately. *I need you!*

The blow was hard to her back, knocking her to the ground. She hadn't time to brace her fall and she landed face-first. Her teeth cracked as they hit a stone and she felt them shatter to grit in her mouth. She turned around and found those searing eyes were pinned upon her. Others were appearing like searchlights glowing through the night, catching her in their beams.

Cats, they were, but like none that Sorrel had ever seen before. They looked like panthers, only larger, their faces wide and strong, their teeth like tusks. Every one of them was black, so their eyes shone out all the more. Their limbs were heavy with muscle and their paws were the size of Sorrel's hand. Sniffing the air, noses twitching, they closed in on her. Sorrel's hand went to her head. It was bleeding.

"What do you want with me?" she asked defiantly.

The first of them, her pursuer, put its nose to her neck. It felt warm and soft, nuzzling her, inhaling her scent. When the creature pulled back, Sorrel could see the flecks of gold in its eyes. Then it lunged, quick as a flash, and bit into her bicep. Sorrel screamed with the agony of it and clutched her arm. The creature seemed to be savoring the taste on its tongue, licking its lips. It turned to the others and addressed them. Sorrel felt no surprise when she heard its voice was that of a woman's.

"She is not the one," the creature said.

"Can you be sure?" another spoke.

"Taste for yourself."

Sorrel sprang back. "Please, no."

The second creature padded toward her as Sorrel tried to scramble backward, her arm unable to hold her. The cat pushed its nose into her clothes.

"I smell a male upon her," it announced. "She is no queen."

"To be sure. Look how she quakes with fear," came a voice from the pack.

"It must be the other child," said their leader, but there followed voices of dissent. That girl was weak, hardly more than a chaff.

Sorrel's mind was grappling, reaching for understanding when the leader interrupted the pack. "The other may seem weak, but perhaps that is a guise to put us off the scent."

"Who are you?" Sorrel whispered. The leader raised a paw and flexed its claws. Sorrel mustered the courage to continue. "The Eastern clan? Is that who you are? Name yourselves."

The creature lifted the paw to Sorrel's cheek. Sorrel felt a sudden sharpness pierce her skin and hang there like a trapped thorn.

"We have traveled far to find you. Tell your mother we are here and we are not alone. The clans are gathering. The prophecy is naught. No Hawkweed will be queen, not now or ever."

The rip was audible, like the tearing of cloth. So fast it was that Sorrel took a moment to register the pain. Then her hand flew to her face to try to stem the intensity of it, and she felt the warmth of her blood pouring through her fingers. The leader turned to the others.

"Sisters," she cried. "Shall we?" And together they turned and leaped away into the darkness.

The sap oozed slowly from the hole in the trunk. It had taken a long while coming. Raven had penetrated through the bark and the cambium, stopping well before she reached the heartwood. But the frail, leafless tree had nothing to offer. Sucking her teeth with irritation, Raven had moved lower down and tried her luck again. Finally the sap began to rise. Raven watched it drip slowly into the cup that she held to the bark. Drop by drop, how languidly it emerged, as though reluctant to leave its home. Shining and unctuous it seeped, glistening amber. Raven knew it would serve her purpose well.

Sorrel tore through branches and ripped through brambles to get home. Her hair was matted, her face covered with blood that camouflaged the multitude of scratches. Her clothes were torn and her feet were bare. She had lost her shoes a way back now. The soles of her feet were cut and bleeding, but onward Sorrel ran, desperate to reach home. It was only when she crossed the camp's threshold that she felt safe enough to collapse. Then she felt all of it, like a tidal wave crashing down upon her. Her chest, her face, her arm, her feet—her mind couldn't unscramble the signals fast enough, and Sorrel was unable to tell which pain came from where, only that she hurt like she'd never done before.

"Mother!" she cried with all her might, but her voice was cowering in her throat and only a faint squeak rose from her mouth. "Mother!" she tried again, but the sound was even tinier this time, no more than a flutter of a moth or the patter of a field mouse.

Sorrel's eyes wanted to close but she wouldn't let them. She wanted the pain to stop but she didn't want to die. She wasn't ready. It was too soon. *I am still a girl*, she tried to whimper. The pain was good, she told herself. The pain meant life. Garnering the very last of her strength, Sorrel crawled on her knees to the steps of a caravan. When the door opened, it was her cousin standing there, a white light, radiant and ethereal. *She is magical after all*, thought Sorrel. *She sparkles with fairy dust, as pretty as a princess. Perhaps the creatures were right and Ember will be queen. Perhaps it was a disguise. A trick.*

And then came Charlock, her aunt, so kind and capable, crouching at her side, instructing Ember to help, carrying her inside, laying her down, giving her water, medicine that trickled down her throat and soothed her so. She was safe. Sorrel felt the relief ease her tired, afflicted limbs.

I am safe, she thought, as she allowed her eyes to close.

The scream lacerated the night air. Savage and terrifying it was. It came from Raven's mouth without her intending it. The potion was gone. Her mind galloping, Raven frantically retraced her steps. She saw herself casting the spell, placing the potion down on the table before leaving for the orchard. She had been as fastidious as always, utterly precise, even carrying the sap so carefully from the tree, so mindful not to trip. Stepping back along the side of the orchard and around the back of the storeroom, she had reached the door and taken care to open it quietly without a creak so as not to disturb any of the sisters. Crossing the threshold, she had hurried to the workbench, eager to finish the task at hand. She had looked to where she had left the potion and seen it wasn't there. The shock of it had made her howl.

Now Raven's hands were moving to her head as if trying to squeeze an explanation from it. Not trusting her eyes, she looked again. Not trusting her memory, she searched around in other places. Had she left it in some other spot? On the bench, on the floor, on the shelves? Her hands felt for the container like a blind person, in case her eyes deceived her. But she found nothing. All the while her heart was pounding, faster and faster and faster.

The potion was gone.

Raven opened her mouth and screamed again.

CHAPTER THIRTY-ONE

L eo felt like he was walking on air. Above him the stars appeared as a map that only his eyes could read. One by one they flickered just for him, lighting up the way. Dimly, in the farthest reaches of his mind, Leo wondered if he'd died. If so, he didn't care. He felt like he was blessed, that the universe was wrapping itself around him and welcoming him in. Out of the blackness of the night sky came a swirling light display of blues and greens and purples, but in shades that he had never witnessed before. These were nocturnal, iridescent, alien hues sent from space.

He raised his arm up to touch the sky. His hand shone luminous, and when he waved it, a trail of shimmering powder sprinkled in its wake. Leo felt the enchantment, outside and within. He didn't hurt anymore. He wasn't cold. He wasn't unloved. He knew where he was going. He was going to find her and the light was leading him.

Charlock followed Raven's screams and found her standing in the storeroom, her eyes wild, her head shaking from side to side without pause as she muttered to herself over and over, "It's gone, it's gone, it's gone."

Charlock approached slowly as one would an injured animal. "Raven?" She reached out gently to take her arm, but her sister brushed it away.

"It's gone!" she gasped, looking up at Charlock, her face riven with distress.

"Raven, I need you to come with me."

"Someone's taken it."

So lost was Raven in her own panic that Charlock realized she hadn't heard her. "Raven, look at me."

"They've taken it," Raven said, grabbing Charlock's arms tightly. "They've taken it, they've taken it."

Charlock pulled free. "Enough, sister. You must listen to me."

"It's them. I know it. They took it."

The slap was quick and sharp and it hurt Charlock's hand as much as Raven's cheek. Raven stopped instantly and looked at Charlock in shock.

"It's Sorrel," Charlock said, and then Raven was falling and Charlock was catching her arms and trying to hold her up.

The other sisters watched as Charlock took Raven's weight, almost dragging her across the camp to the caravan where Sorrel lay. Their mouths fell open as they watched the giant among them so diminished. Raven stumbled on the caravan steps, and some of the other sisters moved forward to help, but Charlock gave a shake of her head. Bending down, she lifted her sister up and almost carried her inside. As soon as Raven glimpsed her child, her strength returned in an almighty surge and she flew to the bedside, pushing Ember roughly away.

Sorrel's eyeballs were rolling in their sockets. Beads of sweat trickled along her hairline and down her face and she was twisting and writhing from the pain. *If it was a creature lying there in such agony, you would put it out its misery*, thought Charlock.

"What can we do?" she said instead.

Sorrel tried to speak and Raven put her ear to her daughter's mouth. "Sorrel, my child, my life. Tell me."

"I'm not . . . the one," she breathed.

Raven turned her head away so no one could see her face.

Sorrel stared up at Charlock, her eyes glassy. "I'm not the one," she repeated, forcing the words out with such effort that afterward she seemed drained of any strength.

"Who told you that?" Charlock urged, but Sorrel's eyes were flickering wildly across the ceiling, no longer able to focus. Charlock touched her niece's face. "Sorrel, my sweet, who told you that?"

Suddenly Raven turned, her face savage with desperate rage. "The Eastern clan. Who else would hurt her so?!" Sorrel's eyes began to shut. Raven grabbed her face. "Don't sleep, Sorrel. Stay awake now." But Sorrel's eyelids had already fallen. Raven shook Sorrel's head and Charlock winced at her roughness. "Hear me, child. You must not sleep," Raven cried.

Sorrel's mouth was moving slowly but no words were sounding from it. Then the faintest noise.

"What did she say?" Raven turned to the others. "What did she say?"

It was Ember who had heard it. "The cats," she repeated. With Raven's black eyes fixed upon her, Ember trembled visibly and her next words shook in her throat. "She said . . . *the cats*."

Raven hugged the sleeping Sorrel to her. The girl's head drooped back and Raven had to cradle it and rest it on her shoulder. Back and forth she rocked her daughter.

"What can we do?" Charlock asked again. Raven didn't answer. Charlock caught Ember's panicked eye and made another attempt. "Raven, we must do something. Quickly."

Raven continued rocking her child, kissing her hair softly like Sorrel was her baby girl again, nestling in her arms. "There is nothing to be done," Raven said quietly.

Charlock took a moment before trying once more. "Sister," she said gently. "Use your magic. It is there inside of you. Summon it. There must be a spell. A charm?"

Raven looked at her, and Charlock saw her eyes were flooding with tears. She had never seen her sister cry before and that is how she knew all hope was gone. "It is too late," Raven confirmed. "It is no good." She laid her daughter down on the mattress and smoothed away the tendrils of hair from her face. "That potion came from my own hand. It misses one tiny element but is potent enough still. She will not wake, not for a hundred years."

"Like Sleeping Beauty," Ember whispered.

Raven swung around to face Ember, the most vicious of glares crossing her face. "You stupidest, most worthless girl," she spat. "No kiss ever woke anyone."

Ember's hands went to her face and she stepped back as though Raven's words had smacked her in the jaw. Charlock tried to send signs of comfort with her eyes, but Ember suddenly ran from the caravan.

Charlock sighed. Ember would have to tend her wounds alone for now. She looked at her niece, Sorrel's face so young and innocent in slumber. Not knowing what words to say, she put an arm across her sister's back, and to her surprise, Raven let it lie there.

"I am to blame. I did this," Raven wept, the tears now brimming over and cascading down her face, like a lifetime's worth of crying was happening all at once.

"It was the Eastern clan," soothed Charlock.

"I was trying to protect her. Oh, Charlock, look at her. My poor baby girl."

Charlock never thought she'd hear her sister sound so small and pitiful. She tightened her arm on Raven's shoulders and tried to keep her firm.

Poppy said her farewells to Donna and Logan that evening. The little boy begged for her to sleep over another night, but Donna picked him up in her arms, balanced him on her hip, and made him wave as Poppy headed down the path. Poppy saw Logan wriggle in his mother's arms and try to run after her. She felt sorry that she wouldn't get to know him as he grew up. Most likely he'd be too young to remember her and her image would sink to the sandy depths of his mind, one of those early childhood memories that would only resurface when he was a forgetful old man. Poppy looked back and waved. It proved the easiest of her good-byes.

When she reached the house on Wavendon Close, she saw the broken window had been fixed and her father was examining it, his face crumpled with concentration. His shirt was unbuttoned and his tie loose. His hair was thinning, Poppy noticed for the first time, and the skin around his eyes was grooved with lines. But he was still handsome. And his arms looked just as strong. Poppy remembered those arms lifting her up and putting her on his shoulders when she was small, before she stopped letting him or he stopped wanting to—Poppy couldn't recall which. How tall she'd felt. She'd had to duck beneath the branches of the trees.

Poppy had hoped she would find the house empty and avoid the necessary conversation with her father. But now that she saw him standing there, so serious in his middle age, she felt a deep relief to have the chance to talk to him one last time. He turned and lifted his head in greeting.

"They've put locks on them," he said. Such a mundane utterance, but to Poppy it was perfect. This was the ordinary banality she wanted for him, without a freakish child or troubled teen, without a lunatic wife to deal with.

"Why do you bother with this place, Dad?" she asked lightly. "Donna's place is nice enough and you could be together."

Her father looked startled, almost wary, like it must be a trick that she was playing on him. "I . . . well, I didn't think you'd want that," he said.

"I'm almost grown up now. But Logan, he's a sweet kid, and I bet he'd like his dad to be around."

"We'll see," he evaded. "You all right? Donna said you haven't been well."

Poppy shrugged. "Donna's been very kind to me. Tell her thank you, will you?"

"You look tired. You want supper?" her father asked.

"I grabbed something on my way. Why don't you go over there? See how they're doing." Her father observed her, looking closely for her reaction. "Whatever she was cooking smelled good," Poppy said persuasively.

"You sure? I wasn't planning to," he replied.

Poppy summoned up a casual smile. "Yeah, I'm sure."

He went into the hall and she heard the jangle of his keys. When he popped his head back into the living room, he was wearing his coat. "Don't wait up." He smiled.

"I won't."

"Bye then, love."

The rare endearment seemed to strike them both.

"Bye, Dad," Poppy said, and they waited, facing one another for a long moment until he looked embarrassed and quickly turned and left. Poppy didn't move as she heard the door shut, the engine start, and the car pull away. "Bye," she said again.

Up in her room she lay down on her bed, relishing the familiarity of it. It smelled like home. The pillows were so silky, the duvet so soft. She had no idea where she'd sleep next, but she knew it would be far from here and all this comfort. The thought made her weary, and she wondered vaguely how she would get herself up and out the door. She didn't have the strength for her journey, yet she had to leave.

The witch had meant every word she said. Her threats to Donna and Logan and Leo—they were all real, and Poppy didn't have the will to fight her. She felt no panic or despair, nothing so urgent as that. She just perceived the facts for what they were. Too many people were in danger because of her, and she felt too weak to protect them. Her departure was the only way to keep everyone safe. In that certainty, Poppy shut her eyes. *Just for a second*, she thought. *Only for a minute.*

An owl hooted late into the night and Poppy woke. She rose instantly and started to pack, stuffing as many of her clothes and belongings as possible into an old duffle bag of her father's. The sleep had done her good, and she moved quickly and decisively, leaving behind treasured items, refusing to be sentimental about her possessions. She pulled out the sleeping bag from under her bed and slung it over her arm. *At least it'll get some use now*, she thought. Then she went to her father's desk and took any money she could find in the drawers. She didn't feel bad. She was doing it for the best. He would be happier in the end, once she was gone and he was with them. Finally she raided the few bits and pieces from the fridge and the kitchen cabinets and stuffed the food in her pockets for later. She fed the cats before she left and they came to her, purring loudly, caressing her legs with their fur, licking her hands with their sandpaper tongues.

"I'll be seeing you," she told them, and she meant it. She knew they wouldn't be far behind.

There was only Ember left, and Poppy couldn't leave her forever wondering. Ember deserved to know all of it—where she came from, who she was. But Ember was in the camp and Poppy dare not get too close in case Raven sensed her there. She longed to see her friend's face, to hug her close and try to tell her everything she meant to her. She wanted to share all she knew and explain how they were twins of a sort, how their fates had collided at birth and it was their destiny to meet that autumn day in the dell.

And then Poppy thought to leave word for Ember there, in their meeting place. It wasn't nearly close to being enough, but it was something. So Poppy sat on the curb, and under the white light of the street lamp, she began to write.

It was the second letter she'd had to compose that day, and this one, though longer, came far more easily. The first had been torture, her mind stretched on the rack to its breaking point, never to be mended. She had stopped at the churchyard on her way back home that evening and left that letter by Minx's grave. She couldn't let herself think about Leo reading it, but somewhere, deep inside of her, she sensed he had. She couldn't think about Leo at all. Soon she would be far, far away. It wouldn't stop her thoughts from trying to travel to him, but it would stop her from ever having to see him again.

That she couldn't endure.

But there he was. Lying on the sofa in the dell, sprawled across it like he was sleeping. It hurt so much to look at him, just as Poppy knew it would. Her heart was beating its objection against her ribs and her stomach ached in protest. Time seemed to slow to a heavy pace. Poppy wanted to yank her eyes away but they were locked upon him. She noted impassively that Leo's legs were hanging over the side of the sofa. The angles of them—they didn't look right. Then sluggishly she realized. He was hurt.

Poppy's reaction to this came slowly too, bit by bit, in degrees. First, she looked around for Ember but the dell was empty. Next, it occurred to Poppy to leave, to pretend she'd never seen him. But she remained motionless, just standing there helplessly. Then Poppy remembered the last time they were there. The memory was hazy, sepia, like it happened a lifetime ago. Leo was tall and strong and smiling. *Leo*, thought Poppy.

Her legs began to move and everything sped up and, before she knew it, she was by his side and the tears were falling as she looked at his face, so cruelly damaged. He moaned when she touched his brow. He was barely conscious, barely breathing, but still he hurt. Poppy wanted to hold him and kiss him, the old urges rising up within her, but she stemmed them quickly with a snap and put herself to work. She had only a few of her remedies on her, but she used them all, tending only to the worst of the welts and cuts. He needed proper care. His ribs and collarbone were broken. His flesh was so badly bruised that she worried for his liver and kidneys. He needed a hospital; he needed a doctor.

Now Poppy was panicking. Her thoughts came rushing into her mind like a hysterical mob, clamoring for her attention. She tried to impose order, to prioritize. She needed help.

Ember. She could bring supplies. She must get Ember.

Ember was sitting alone on the caravan steps when the fox approached her. They eyed each other warily. The fox seemed loathe to get too close. It sniffed the air, then seemed to cringe at her scent. Reluctantly it took one step further. Ember leaned back, worried it would bite. Then the fox held up a paw and she saw it. Tied to its leg was a bit of paper. Ember reached out a trembling hand and untied the string from the fox's fur. As soon as the paper was free of it, the fox turned and sprinted away, vanishing into the darkness.

She unrolled the paper. It was just a strip, ripped from a larger page. On it, only a few brief words in a familiar hand. Three simple instructions, but acting on them could change a lifetime.

Come to the dell. Come now. Bring supplies.

Ember didn't hesitate, not for one second. She rushed to the storeroom and tried to recall her lessons and remember which ingredients were which. Her mind was a swirling, frenzied fog. The names on the bottles were all familiar, but not their purpose. Picking up an old sack from the corner of the room, Ember swept the contents of the shelves into it. The containers clinked and chimed as she swung the sack over her shoulder, but Ember knew the camp was too preoccupied with Sorrel to notice.

She tried not to think of Sorrel lying there. It had been terrifying to watch her cousin in such pain and to see her mighty Aunt Raven powerless to save her. But the four of them facing the crisis together, gathering around in support at such a time of need, there was also something good in that. It had felt to Ember like family should, like a moment to be cherished. None of the other sisters had dared disturb them, not even Kyra or any of Sorrel's clique. Instead, they all waited quietly outside for any news.

Ember had been right by Sorrel's side, though, part of the inner sanctum, until her aunt had so harshly discharged her. When she had run from the room and sat on the steps, the sisters huddled there had shaken their heads and whispered to one another.

"Go," Ember had cried sharply before the tears fell. "My aunt wants you gone."

The gathering had glanced at each other, but then, miraculously, they had followed Ember's orders. Even Kyra, her face blotched with crying, hadn't argued. Like a herd, they had moved as one back to their caravans. The doors had shut like a clatter of hooves and Ember was alone. The finality of it all felt paralyzing. As Sorrel's eyes had closed, so had Ember's future here. She had never before realized her place within the camp was so tightly wound with that of her cousin. The connecting thread had snapped. Everything had changed and nothing would be the same.

Ember's mind struggled to comprehend it all. She had looked into the darkness and it had felt like oblivion. She had hoped for a sign, something meant just for her, that she would understand. And then, as if on cue, the fox had appeared, its shock of orange fur so vivid in the gloom. Fearful, Ember had wished she could summon it away. But it had trod closer. It had to be an omen, Ember had thought, but what did it mean? The fox had lifted up its paw in answer . . .

"Ember?" It was her mother's voice, so Ember stopped and turned. If it had been anyone else, she would have made a run for it. She rested the sack on the ground for a moment. Charlock's wide-set, amber eyes caught it. She surveyed her daughter, waiting for an explanation. But Ember had experienced her mother's silences too many times before and she bit her lip to stop herself from talking. The seconds ticked by, and Ember, so desperate to be on her way, found it harder and harder to resist the temptation to speak. Finally, though, it was Charlock who yielded first.

"You're leaving," she said without accusation.

"I have to," Ember replied, keeping her voice hushed and low.

"It is not safe. Look at your cousin," Charlock remonstrated.

Never before had Ember defied her mother, but now it was different. She had to do what she thought was right, not what she was told. So she pressed her shoulders back and tilted her chin upward, standing up for herself in body and voice.

"The Eastern clan got who they wanted," she said firmly. "They have no interest in the likes of me, you said so yourself."

Charlock blinked, but from that tiny reaction Ember felt her mother's surprise. "If you leave, you can't come back."

"I know."

"Where will you go? What will you do?"

Ember trampled down the doubts that sprouted from her mother's questions. "You have taught me well," she said in a voice that didn't waver. "I will find my way."

Ember caught a glimpse of respect in her mother's eyes, but then they hardened for one last attempt.

"I could make you stay."

"You could." Ember didn't say anymore, but she knew her mother would comprehend the rest—that staying would be a kind of death, that she didn't belong, she never did, that Raven would not protect her anymore, and the camp could no longer be her home.

Charlock stepped toward her and Ember stiffened. But Charlock pulled her close and enveloped her in a hug, holding her like she never wanted to let her go. In her mother's arms Ember felt the love. In her kisses she felt the sorrow. Then, as suddenly as it began, it was over and Charlock was walking away. She never looked back. She never said good-bye.

Ember poured the contents of the sack onto the frozen ground. The tin and glass glinted in the moonlight. Poppy's hands rifled through the remedies, seeking out those she needed.

"Will he live?" Ember asked.

She didn't want to speak of Sorrel now when Poppy seemed so focused, but seeing Leo was like reliving the night's events over again. The same shock, the hope, the dread. Poppy held up a tiny vial, trying to catch the light and read the label.

Ember leaned forward. "Capsaicin." It was written in Sorrel's hand and Ember's heart contracted in her chest.

Poppy put the vial with the rest she had collected. "Are you all right?" she asked. Ember nodded, not wanting to lie out loud. "Can you stay with him all day?" Ember nodded her head again. "Your mother won't miss you?"

Ember looked away at that, scared Poppy would see her sadness. "I can be here."

Poppy started pouring, mixing, grinding the different ingredients. Her hands worked so swiftly, like they'd been doing this for years. Ember regarded her friend. She looked so much older and wearier, so different from the bold, rebellious girl she had met right here in this spot.

"Won't you stay too? Do you have school?" Ember asked.

Poppy shook her head. She glanced up briefly but then looked away again, seeming to withdraw even further. "I'm not going to be living here anymore." She announced this momentous news unemotionally, as though it held little importance.

"You're leaving?" Ember reiterated, trying to stir the notion into her mind and make it stick.

"It's not my choice," Poppy replied.

Ember started to cry; she couldn't help it. The tears fell for Sorrel, for Leo, for her mother, and mostly for Poppy. Then she pounced on an idea. How simple. How perfect.

"I could come with you. We could leave together. Just as we always wanted. Like swallows, remember?"

The mask from Poppy's face fell, revealing a countenance full of heartache and suffering.

"Oh, Poppy," Ember sobbed. "What has happened to us?"

From her pocket Poppy pulled out a letter. She lay it on the arm of the sofa. "Read it when I'm gone," she said. "It explains everything." Before Ember could object, Poppy picked up a jar and put it into Ember's hand. "He'll need these. Three drops, morning, noon, and night." Then she placed a paste in Ember's other hand. "This is for his bruises. Every hour." She looked over to Leo, so pale and ailing. "One of us has to stay with him. You cannot leave his side."

"It should be you," wept Ember. "What good am I to him? I don't know anything of herbs or healing. You have magic. You can cast a spell. You can look after him."

Poppy closed Ember's fingers around the remedies and kept her hands there, on top of Ember's. Cool, they were, but Ember felt a sudden warmth in her heart.

"I will make him better. Then you will make him happy."

Chapter Thirty-Two

Through the mists of sleep Leo sensed someone was caring for him. He felt their touch on his skin, tending to his wounds, easing his pain. When he felt the shivers convulse him, a body lay next to him, sharing their warmth and stroking his hair. The voice was soft and soothing, like an echo, calling across a vast distance.

"Leo . . . Leo . . . Leo," it pleaded. "Open your eyes . . . open your eyes," it begged.

Leo tried but he couldn't comply. His lids were weighted shut and all his energy was directed inward, consumed by healing. His bones were knitting together; his bruises going from black, to blue, to purple, to pink; his cuts scabbing over. Processes that took days, weeks even, were happening to him in a matter of hours. It was the medicine. Leo comprehended that. It was some kind of nectar. He tasted the sweetness on his tongue and felt it rush through his blood, magically mending him.

"Leo," the voice came again, but nearer now. "Can you hear me?"

He felt the breath on his face and then the heat of a mouth as lips touched his in a kiss. Very slowly he opened his eyes.

"Raven was wrong," said the voice. "About a kiss. Maybe it does have the power."

It was an angel, guarding over him, smiling down at him so lovingly. It was Ember.

"Ember?" Leo called, his voice weak and husky.

"Yes," she replied, her hand on his face.

"Where's Poppy?"

By nightfall Poppy had reached the hospital. A nurse with a down-turned mouth, thick lines to either side, told her sternly it was past visiting hours and that she'd have to come back tomorrow.

"Please. I'm . . . I'm her daughter. I have to see her. Just for a few minutes," Poppy pleaded.

The nurse pursed her lips. "Ten to noon tomorrow, or four to six p.m. It's hospital policy."

"I have to tell her something. It's important."

"I'm sure it's nothing that can't wait until morning."

"But it will help her." Poppy heard her voice rising with anger and battled to control it. "You do want to help her, don't you? Isn't that your job?"

"Do I have to call security?"

The nurse's hand reached for the phone but Poppy grabbed it. Eyes wide with alarm, the nurse tried to snatch it back, but Poppy clung on a second or two longer before she let it go.

"You want a real reason to be miserable? You have a tumor in your colon. Go home and be happy for the rest of the days you have left."

The nurse's mouth dropped open and Poppy strode past her, across the foyer, and into the elevator. As the doors shut, Poppy saw the woman sit down, her face white with shock. Poppy knew what she should be feeling—for herself, shame; for the nurse, pity—but she felt neither.

On the third floor a doctor spotted Poppy and called out to her, "You . . . miss, you can't be here."

Poppy whispered a spell underneath her breath, then walked right up to the doctor and looked him in the eye. Without blinking once, she gave him her commands. "You will go downstairs and see the nurse at the front desk. She needs a doctor." The man nodded. "Now."

Like an obedient dog, he turned and left.

Poppy walked along the corridor, looking for her mother's room. Inside was a man cleaning the floor with a mop. The bed was empty. The man saw her in the doorway and smiled. With that single, welcoming gesture, the grimness Poppy felt lifted a little.

"You looking for Mrs. Hooper?" he asked. "She's in the TV room."

"Thank you," Poppy said. "Thank you for looking after her."

"She's a nice lady. She your mom?" Poppy nodded. "Lovely lady."

Poppy nearly cried at that. She'd never thought of Melanie as lovely, but perhaps she was when she wasn't being reminded of her daughter.

"She won't want to miss her show, though," continued the cleaner.

Poppy tried to smile back at the man but her bottom lip was quivering too much. "I'll wait," she said.

Later Poppy hid in the bathroom while an orderly tucked Melanie into bed. It felt demeaning to be standing there, fully dressed, inside the shower, when she had something so important and life changing to say. She hadn't the heart to use her magic anymore, though, so she waited until her mother was alone and then she entered. Melanie looked up and saw her but didn't seem to trust her eyes. She squinted at Poppy as if trying to figure out if she were real.

"Poppy?" Melanie shut her eyes, then opened them and looked again.

"It's me," Poppy reassured.

"Is it really you?" Melanie asked.

Poppy came and sat down on the bed and took Melanie's hand. It lay limply in hers like it was anesthetized. "It's really me."

"Where's your friend?"

Poppy felt her ribs tightening against her chest. With everything she knew and everything she was about to say, the rejection still had the power to wound her.

"That's why I've come. I wanted . . ." Poppy faltered as Melanie sat up and leaned forward, her eyes shining brighter and, as they did so, becoming just like Ember's. Poppy swallowed and then tried again. "I wanted to tell you that you were right. You've always been right. About me. And about her."

Melanie sat back against her pillows. There was no sense of vindication or triumph. Instead, a tranquil look came over her face, as though she had found peace at last.

"You're not my baby," she said calmly.

"No, I'm not."

"Who are you?"

"I'm a witch." Melanie just nodded, as though it didn't sound utterly crazy, as though it wasn't impossible to believe, as though it was simply fact. "I was switched for your baby."

"Oh," said Melanie. "Your poor mother."

And for the first time Poppy really loved her. She squeezed Melanie's hand, wanting to say so much but finding herself too moved by this plain, quiet acceptance of all that had happened. The hand that had laid so lifeless in hers squeezed back.

"My friend, Ember, is your daughter, like you said. So you must get yourself well now and say good-bye to this place." Poppy recognized the fear in Melanie's face. "It's hard to start again. But Ember, she needs you."

An idea struck Poppy and she reached into her bag and pulled out Ember's clock. In her mind's eye she saw Ember running after her, clambering up the slope of the dell, out of breath by the time she reached the top, thrusting the clock toward her, insisting that she have it, that she loved her. It was Ember's most treasured possession and it had felt wrong to take it. But now Poppy knew what she was meant to do with it. She put it down on the bedside table so it faced Melanie. "She sent this for you."

Melanie stared at it, then slowly her fingers stretched out to touch it, ever so softly as if the clock and all it meant was so fragile it might crack under the slightest pressure. "It's so lovely," Melanie whispered. "Just like her."

Poppy smiled. Melanie was right. The clock was as pretty and delicate as Ember herself.

"Nine minutes past nine," Poppy stated. "Time to start again."

Ember had read Poppy's letter and then folded it up and put it in the pocket of her long skirt. She felt a momentous loss, like someone had died. It wasn't someone, though—it was her childhood she was grieving for. She hadn't liked it much, but it had been hers. And now that she knew it was based on lies, she was no longer sure what was true anymore or even who she was. The timidity, the softness, the lack of confidence and sense of failure— was that her or who the coven made her?

Who would she have been without the spell? Ember tried to see herself as a regular chaff girl, at home, at school, in town, with family, with friends, but it seemed like make-believe. Ember's past was still real, but all the memories she had stored away, high up on the dusty shelves of her mind, would have to be brought down, cleaned off and pulled apart. She felt exhausted by the very prospect of it.

Dusk was falling. Details were diminishing and shapes beginning to dim. Into the dark with them went Ember's ideas, of home and of herself. She looked at Leo, who was sitting up now and watching her silently.

"Aren't you going to ask me what she wrote?" Ember asked.

He shook his head. "Night is coming. We need to find shelter." Leo tried to stand and Ember helped him up. "Thank you," he said. "I owe you. Everything."

Ember thought of telling him about Poppy. How she had been the one to find him, to call her, to heal him. But then she felt her mind tighten and close as she stopped herself. It was just her and Leo now. Poppy was gone.

They walked toward the town, and as they entered the streets, Ember saw it all differently. Not as an outsider but as someone who belonged there, in the lights, the dirt, the noise, the scale of it.

"I want to go to Paris," she suddenly announced with a certainty that surprised her. "I want to see the Eiffel Tower and Notre Dame and visit the Louvre and buy some clothes." She held up her dirty skirt with disdain and glimpsed her muddy boots. "And shoes. And drink coffee. And get my hair cut short."

"No," Leo said suddenly, with a force that made Ember suspect he was thinking of Poppy and her short hair. Maybe she was being too sensitive, though, as then he mumbled, "Not the hair. It suits you like that," and she felt a little better. "How do you know about Paris anyway?" he asked, turning the conversation onto safer ground.

Ember's mind flashed to Poppy and how they had traded their books. She remembered lying on the ground, reading about all those other places in the world she thought she'd never see and looking at pictures of all those women she'd never be. And then her thoughts flicked unexpectedly to the image of her real mother, that ghostly lady lying so helpless in that bed, and Ember wondered if she had ever been to Paris and if she'd ever go anywhere else again.

Leo took Ember down a narrow street with homes stuck next to one another like one long house with many front doors. As they passed, Ember snatched glimpses of the lives within. She tried to picture herself like that, sitting and watching television, eating food out of a fridge, washing her clothes in a machine with a little round window. She could even have a car, a red one maybe, that she could park outside.

"Have you ever lived in one of these?" she asked Leo.

"I was in an apartment," he replied, and when she looked confused he added, "Like half of one of these."

"But better than a caravan?" she asked.

Leo shrugged. "Depends."

"You didn't like it?" she said, unable to fathom how that could be.

"Well, it wasn't Paris," Leo added, and for the first time since he had awoken his mouth turned up into the slightest and smallest of smiles.

At the end of the street they reached Mr. Bryce's workshop. Leo banged on the large doors and eventually an old, bespectacled man opened one of them just enough to peer out. He didn't seem at all happy to see them. Leo ignored the scowl and introduced Ember. Mr. Bryce's unblinking eyes were round like an owl's through his glasses as he scrutinized her. Ember stood straight and still, wishing that she was cleaner and that her hair was washed.

"A newbie?" growled Mr. Bryce, and Leo nodded.

"First night. And it's a cold one. I think it'll snow."

"I'm not even going to ask what happened to you," grumbled Mr. Bryce, but then he pulled open the door with a creak and muttered that they could stay but one night only and not to come asking again.

Inside, the room was piled high with furniture and ornaments. It reminded Ember of the dell, only you could tell this stuff meant something to someone. Giant mirrors with frames of gold and silver leaned against the walls. Before them sat furniture with velvet seats and tassels and feet like animal claws. On the shelves danced

china women in big skirts, and next to them posed painted creatures of all descriptions. It all seemed so fanciful and frivolous, so
far from the coven, where nothing was just for show and everything had a use.

Mr. Bryce brought in some tea and pieces of bread and butter. The tea was very sweet but Ember gulped it down, relishing
the warmth. The butter wasn't half as good as her own. After, he
showed her where the bathroom was and Ember looked around
the tiny room with wonder. She turned the taps and watched
the water pour and gurgle down the spout. Then she twisted the
knob for the shower and marveled at the miniature waterfall that
rained down. She pushed the running soap out of its container.
She flushed the toilet and jumped back at the sound. And then
she caught sight of herself in the mirror. Disheveled and dirty, she
looked like something that belonged in the dell, not Bryce's Restoration. Staring at her reflection, Ember thought of the river that
was both her looking glass and her bath and remembered how she
used to dream of letting it wash her away to a better future. And
here she stood; her future now become her present.

She went back into the workshop with a new sense of purpose.

"What is this place?" she asked Leo, running her fingers over
a table that gleamed. Ember had never thought wood could look
like that.

"Mr. Bryce fixes things up. Makes old things new," he replied,
and the idea of that felt pleasing to Ember, like she had come to
the right place. "He mended that clock of yours for me," Leo remembered, and Ember thought of Poppy and missed her. Again
she felt like speaking of Poppy and again she stopped herself,
clenching her jaw shut, proud of her resolve.

They found another sofa to sleep on, this one deep and velvety soft. Ember shifted over as far as she could to leave room for Leo. He hesitated, though, and Ember saw that he looked nervous.

"You have to lie down," she told him practically.

Leo shuffled awkwardly from one foot to the other. "I can sleep on the floor. I'm used to it."

"Don't be a silly goose," she laughed, sensing what was needed to persuade him. "I laid next to you in the dell."

"That was different."

"Was it?" Ember asked, his nerves flitting across to her like fleas. "I don't think I understand."

Leo opened his mouth to explain and then seemed to think better of it as he came over and laid down. He made sure not to touch her, and the gap between them felt so wide that Ember had to bridge it. She didn't allow herself to hesitate, just moved her head quickly and surely onto his shoulder. A second later his arm came underneath her back and around her waist to hold her. Ember could feel Leo's heart tick-tocking in his chest.

"We have to look after each other," she whispered. And then, finally, in the comfort of the dark, she let herself speak of the one they loved who wasn't there yet lay between them. "It's what she wanted."

Poppy sat bolt upright, eyes open. She had been sleeping in Melanie's room on the chair in the corner and she felt the crick in her neck as she turned her head to look around. The hairs on her arms and the back of her head were bristling. All her senses were on high alert. Poppy checked Melanie first but she was sleeping soundly. Then she went to the window and the door but she could see nothing amiss. But something was wrong. Of that she was sure. She wouldn't make the mistake of ignoring her instincts again. Something was terribly wrong.

"Help me," came the voice, entering Ember's dreams. "Help me, please." Ember shifted in her sleep, not wanting to wake.

"Ember," the voice came again. "You have to help me."

Poppy, thought Ember, through the blanket of her slumber. Her body moved of its own volition, lifting itself so lightly from the sofa and treading so carefully to the door as though careful not to wake her mind. For still Ember slept, even though her eyes were open and her legs were carrying her across the room. Like a ghost, she drifted up the street. It was snowing, but her bare feet didn't seem to feel the cold. They left a line of meandering footprints in the white powder, proof that she was no apparition.

"Ember," called Poppy's voice plaintively. Ember followed it, all the way out of town and into the hills. The sky turned from black to white, matching the snow-covered earth. The sun must have risen but it never showed itself. Still the snow fell, up to Ember's knees in places. The trees in the forest seem to strain under the burden of their new load, and occasionally a thump would sound as clumps fell and landed. But Ember slept on.

After hours of walking, she reached the furthest edge of the forest. She had never come this far before. It was the end of the country, where land met sea. The ocean flashed like steel before her, like she could walk upon it. Ember moved to the very edge of the cliff, her toes touching air. She felt a sudden urge to fly, to swoop down and skim the sea with her skirts.

"Poppy?" she called out at the empty horizon. No response came. "Poppy?" she questioned again, unsure which way to go.

"Ember?" sounded Poppy's voice again.

Ember turned with a start and nearly fell as the snow beneath her feet dislodged, then toppled down and down before being gobbled by the hungry sea.

"Mind your step," came the same voice again as Ember straightened and peered into the mist, her eyes still glazed.

She stared and stared but could not make sense of what she saw. It was not her friend she found across the moor, standing tall and dark as the trees behind. Instead, Poppy's voice came from another's body.

"Aunt?" Ember questioned. "What are you doing here?"

"The same as you, child," answered Raven, this time in her own voice, her lips a shocking red scar upon her pale face. "I am waiting for her to arrive."

CHAPTER THIRTY-THREE

When Leo awoke, he was alone. It didn't come as a surprise, though he felt the disappointment dropping down into the depths of him. He knew Ember was gone, but he checked the bathroom and the street outside anyway. He felt no hope of finding her in either place, but he looked just because he felt he should. He had slept restlessly, haunted by images of Poppy, a ghostly figure that kept slipping like a shadow through his hands so that, in the end, he turned to Ember, curled up next to him, for her warmth and solidity.

His body was healing but his head, thick with painful thoughts, still hurt him. Ember had been a salve to that—her optimism and constancy. He didn't question why she had left. It seemed to him to be a part of life, his life anyway. His mother, then Jocelyn, next Poppy, now Ember. All these women were connected, but when he tried to work out how, the answer eluded him.

The person he wanted to ask, Jocelyn, was dead.

The other, his real mother, he had never known. Not a picture, nor a belonging. He had no clues of her existence. Only himself, his features, his expressions, his character.

And one other fact. She had left him with a woman who had loved him as her own. She had chosen well but, other than that, she was nothing to him. The mother who loved him, who had held him and fed him and taught him, had been cremated. All that was left of her was a jar of ashes and an ache in his heart.

Leo plumped up the cushions on the sofa just as Jocelyn used to, then did some lifting and carrying for Mr. Bryce by way of a thank you. When he stepped out onto the street corner, he looked both ways. He could turn right, go back to town and pick up where he left off, sitting in the same doorways and benches, scouring the same trash cans for food like nothing had happened, like his life hadn't been spun around and he wasn't sick with dizziness from it. He chose the other direction. This time it was his turn to leave.

Ember was shivering so much that her teeth were chattering. She wasn't sure if she was asleep or awake, so when she saw Poppy arrive she wondered if she was dreaming. But then Poppy was next to her, cradling her and rubbing her hands over her body, trying to warm her.

Ember tried to speak, just one word, but her jaw wouldn't stop shaking.

Go, she tried to tell her friend.

Go, she yelled inside.

But Poppy was muttering spells and rocking her and breathing her warmth onto her neck.

Go.

"Just in time." Poppy turned and saw the witch, Raven Hawkweed, standing before the trees. "She wouldn't have lasted much longer."

"I had left," Poppy shouted. "Just like you wanted. I was gone."

"I know." Raven opened her arms at the futility of Poppy's actions, and her black cloak flapped in the wind, threatening to carry her high into the air.

"Then why?" Poppy cried. "Why did you bring me back here?"

Raven didn't answer. Her eyes had caught sight of something behind Poppy and she was staring intently at it. Poppy turned to look and saw Charlock approaching on a horse.

"Sister," said Charlock, dismounting. The horse had no bridle or saddle, and Charlock kept a hold of its mane as it tossed its head and stamped its foot.

"Take her," spat Raven. "She's served her purpose."

Charlock looked to Ember, then to Poppy.

Poppy knew what was being asked of her. She scooped Ember up and stumbled over to Charlock, who lifted Ember easily and lay her on the horse's back like a sack. With a flick of her hand, Charlock slapped the horse's rump, then again two more times, following it until she was sure that the animal was heading away, gingerly picking its feet across the icy snow as it went.

Charlock made her way back to Poppy. Raven's eyebrows drew together like curtains to become one.

"Be gone, Charlock. This is no more business of yours."

Charlock stood beside Poppy, facing Raven. "But she is the one I came for."

Poppy saw the thoughts race across Raven's eyes like clouds on a windy sky. "How long have you known?"

"Since I gave birth and another's baby was put into my arms. Since she came to town and I felt her near. Since always." Charlock's words were crisp and cold as the snow beneath them.

Raven shrank back for a moment. Then she straightened. "I spared her then. I won't again."

Poppy wanted to leap behind Charlock and shield herself, but she kept her feet rooted and her body still. She saw Charlock's hands clasp together as if to stop them from lashing out.

"I knew Ember wasn't mine, but I never thought, not for a moment, that *you* were responsible. I presumed it was one of the other clans who hurt me so. Never you. Never my own sister. Perhaps I am the fool you take me for."

"A secretive fool," spat Raven.

"And then you visited her. You went to the chaff's house and you threatened her."

Poppy's head snapped around to look at Charlock. "You were there?" she gasped.

"You called for me," Charlock explained. "I came too late. I'm sorry. But I saw Raven watching you, waiting for you to leave. And then I knew it all. Motherhood—it makes us mad."

Into the virgin snow appeared lines, slicing the white frosting. The lines touched and connected until they spelled two words.

THE PROPHECY

Now Poppy did move behind Charlock. This magic, out here, in the open, before her very eyes—it made her feel small, a pretender. Charlock's eyes bore into the words and a line began and crossed through all the letters, chopping them in half.

"Your daughter cannot be queen, so no Hawkweed can. Is that it, Raven? This one is your niece. She is your flesh and blood."

"It was supposed to be *my* baby!" shrieked Raven, her voice so pierced with pain that Poppy had to put her hands over her ears to muffle the sound.

"Who said?" challenged Charlock, low and fearless.

"I looked after you. I wiped your nose, I dressed you, I led you by the hand and carried you on my back. I've always had to look after you."

"That's what you chose. And I let you. Long after I stopped needing you, I let you."

"I am the greater witch."

"You are. But your daughter is not."

Raven flung her arms upward in fury, her hands pointing to the sky. Angry clouds gathered at her command, and as Raven clenched and released her fists, a volley of hailstones were unleashed upon their heads. Raven stretched out wide, her head tipped up to the sky. On one side of her the sea roared with rage, and waves, cresting from the flatness, rose and fell with a crash, over and over. On the other side the wind whipped through the trees so their trunks swayed in a frenzy and their branches lashed out at one another viciously. Raven stood at the center of it all, a crazed conductress, lost in her music. From the sky came the percussion, a rumble of drums, a crack of thunderous bass and a clash of cymbals as lightning struck.

It should be terrifying. Poppy realized that. She should want to turn and flee. Raven had summoned nature to vent her wrath. But Poppy didn't feel the threat and she didn't feel small anymore. Instead, the elements surged within her and she felt more alive than she had in days. She focused her mind and the tiny missiles of hail landed to either side of her, missing their target. The wind swept her hair from her face so she could see all the more clearly, and the storm made her cheeks glow, her heart race, and her hands tingle. It was exhilarating. She stepped forward and past Charlock's arm, which had reached out to stop her.

Above Poppy's head the clouds parted and light shone down through the gap between them. She waited a moment longer, until the wind stilled around her and the music faded. Then she spoke, strong and clear.

"Take your prophecy. Take your throne and your crown. Fight between yourselves, cause more misery, tell more lies. I want no part of it." Poppy turned around and called to the sky, the sea, the snow. "I will decide who I am and who I will be!"

The animals came first, even the hibernating creatures awoken from their winter sleep, peering out from the forest to see what had disturbed them. Hedgehogs, mice and hamsters, snakes and frogs, badgers and bears, all bleary eyed and lethargic, marking the perfect snow with their paw prints. Next, swooping down from the clouds and the treetops came the birds, hovering in the air to watch. Then the witches arrived, stepping through the forest and into the field like they too had been there all along.

Poppy stared in amazement. There were so many of them, with different shades of skin and garments, some pale and meager, others bright and lavish, each come to see this show. They approached steadily, in no rush, neither their pace nor their demeanor giving any hint of their intentions. Then, all at once, as if rehearsed, they stopped. Every muscle in Poppy's body tensed as the silent seconds ticked by.

At last a voice rang out, bold and clear. It was a striking woman with inky hair falling straight and silky to her knees who spoke. Behind her stood the rest of her coven, eyes set and bodies poised for battle. More notable, though, were the two giant panthers, fur black as night like their clan, sitting to either side of their leader, still as statues. "You hear that, Raven? She does not *want* the crown."

"The Eastern clan!" Poppy heard someone mutter beneath their breath.

But it was Charlock who answered. "It is not the girl's decision. It is her fate. The prophecy tells that my sister or I would bear the next queen. This girl is my daughter. She is a Hawkweed."

Charlock looked to Raven, expecting her retort. But Raven's head was lowered as though she were studying the ground. She seemed diminutive and frail, but Poppy could feel the electricity surging and sparking within her and wondered if the others could feel it too. When Raven looked up, staring only at the Eastern clan, her face seemed mutilated by her madness. Her voice was just as distorted and came in a savage, scarring shriek that hurt the ear.

"You . . . poisoned . . . my . . . girl!"

The panthers came to life, pawing the ground and hissing savagely. But it was too late. Already Raven was lifting her hand and flinging it toward their leader. From it came an electrical current that cut across the air like blue lightning and hit the witch in the chest, throwing her back against a tree.

The Eastern clan stepped forward, raising their hands in response, and Raven held her head back and laughed.

Chapter Thirty-Four

E mber's face knocked gently against the horse's stomach, its hair soft and warm against her cheek. She had been awake for some time now but was too weary to lift herself up and nervous she would fall if she tried. She had been watching the world from upside down, the icy ground her sky, the billowing drifts of snow her clouds. They passed through endless pines, and Ember observed how the lowest of the branches were flopping and drooping just like her, the green needles pricking under the white weight of winter. And then, at last, Ember saw the glassy river and she knew she was nearing refuge. The rhythm of the horse's steps had become comforting to her and she missed it as soon as it stopped. Then there were hands around her, reaching for her and pulling her down. Ember looked up to see Sister Ada's baggy features hanging over her.

"Child, what has happened to you?"

Sister Morgan elbowed her way in. "Get her warm first, sister," and a cup was being lifted to Ember's lips and hot liquid was slipping down her throat.

"Where are Sisters Raven and Charlock? Have you come from them?" Sister Ada persisted.

Ember tried to speak but couldn't think what to say.

"What do you remember?"

"Poppy?" she said. The sisters looked at one another confused. Then she suddenly remembered and spoke again. "The sea."

"What were you doing there?" Ember heard another voice ask.

"Were Raven and Charlock with you?" questioned Sister Morgan gently.

The horse snorted and stamped its foot impatiently, answering on Ember's behalf.

"We must go," said Sister Bethany.

"Quickly," ordered Sister Ada. "Gather the clan."

Leo's arm was aching from holding out his thumb. Not a single vehicle had stopped. He must look even worse than he felt. His jeans were stuck to his legs from the slushy spray of speeding wheels and his skin was raw from the cold. The next car to approach was smart and clean, a suited man at the wheel, no passengers. Leo didn't even bother trying to signal. The car passed him like all the others but then it slowed to a stop. Leo peered at it in astonishment. Suddenly it revved into reverse and leveled with him. Leo thought of the soft seat, the heat, the stereo. The window rolled down.

It was Poppy's father. "Get in," he barked.

Leo thought of the warmth, then looked at the man's face and thought again.

"Get in," Poppy's father commanded.

Leo opened the door and sat down. It was as plush and comfortable as he had predicted.

"I know you, don't I? You're Poppy's friend." Leo nodded. "Do you know where she is?" Leo shook his head. "Do you speak?" Leo nodded again. Poppy's father gripped the steering wheel with frustration. Leo could see his knuckles turning white. "Look, you're the only kid I've ever seen her with. Ever. I've no idea why she picked you, but now she's gone and I need to find her."

Leo looked up in surprise and his eyes met Poppy's father's for the first time.

"You didn't know? Terrific." Poppy's father hit the steering wheel with the heel of his hand. "I've given that girl so many chances and this is what I get for it."

Leo reached for the door handle.

"Wait," said Poppy's father, his voice softening slightly. "Where are you heading?"

"Away." Leo shrugged.

Poppy's father shook his head like he was wrestling with an idea. "I'm going to see her mother. Figured Poppy might have gone there. If she has, maybe you can talk some sense into her?"

Leo's hand rested on the door handle, waiting for his brain to send the signal for what to do next. Poppy. He was supposed to be running away. He should open the door. He wanted to open the door. But his fingers released, his hand moved back to his lap, and the car started moving.

Bats and birds filled the sky above the cliffs. From their view up on high, the battle looked breathtaking. Bolts of fire, flashes of light, crackles and sparks of electricity streaking across the air like a fireworks display. Beneath that, crimson patterns were brightening the white snow like art. But down low and up close, it was an ugly picture. Trees had been felled, their stumps sizzling. Witches too lay twisted on the ground, missing limbs. The crimson was their blood, trickling from their wounds, their eyes, their noses, seeping into the snow. Many witches fought on, despite their injuries. Boils and pustules bubbled and burst on some unlucky faces. Others had lost hair, from their heads, their eyebrows, and lashes. Spells whizzed like bullets, often hitting at random. The sound of chants and curses came like a chorus so it was impossible to distinguish one from the other.

Poppy was defending, dodging, and blocking, with no time for any attack of her own. Every sense she had was magnified a thousand-fold. Her reflexes worked faster than she had ever believed possible, her limbs moving before she even had a chance to think, her body one step ahead of her brain. The magic that was usually such a silken, slippery thing now felt solid and hard. It had become a sharp-edged weapon, and Poppy felt its shadow on her, darkening her mind. The thrill and release she had felt at the fire in the dining hall and then again in the library—that was nothing compared to this. This was all-consuming.

Poppy could see it in Charlock too. The expression on her face was frightening—eyes burning, cheeks hollow, hair wired with electricity. Poppy wondered whether her own features were just as savage. But she was grateful for Charlock's transformation. Time after time her mother would defend her, shielding her from blows both magical and physical, repelling those who tried to hurt her. As for Raven, she hardly seemed made of flesh and blood. She fought as one not born of this earth. Single-handedly she was laying waste to whole strips of the enemy. She seemed unstoppable, but Poppy feared what might happen to them if she tired.

It was merely a momentary misgiving, but with it Poppy felt her strength suddenly dwindle. She looked around her and saw only death and destruction and it felt terrifying. A witch, monstrous in her fury, ran toward Poppy, screaming, and Charlock blasted the assailant back. The witch lay on the ground with her ribs jutting out of her chest like railings, but her eyes stayed open and still she stared in hatred at Poppy and her lips kept on chanting.

"Look!" shouted Charlock, and Poppy turned her head to see a new group of witches joining the fray. "Our clan!" cried Charlock.

And with these two words Poppy felt her mind re-engage and her energy surge.

Straight into the conflict the clan went, firing spells and rallying behind their leader, Raven Hawkweed. They were still massively outnumbered, but these witches were fresh and ready for the fight. The young among them bristled with excitement; the more experienced gritted their teeth in grim determination. There was no time for them to question Poppy's presence. She was with Charlock and that was enough. Besides, the air was thick with malice, droning with spells of the wickedest kind, and it would take all their effort to stay unharmed.

Close by, a girl not much older than Poppy was quickly knocked to the ground. She lay there gasping, clutching her side, as her attacker loomed above her, lifting her arms to strike again. A bolt of light shot from Poppy's hand and pierced the witch straight through. Before she fell, the witch looked down in curious surprise at the hole where her stomach once sat. Poppy stared in horror at the damage she'd done, a perfect cauterized circle without a drop of blood.

The girl she had saved sat up and regarded Poppy with newfound admiration. "How'd you do that?"

"I don't know," Poppy told her, reaching out a hand to pull her up.

"What do they call you?"

"Poppy. My friend, Ember, have you seen her?"

"She's safe," said the girl, and Poppy shut her eyes in momentary relief.

"Watch your back!" cried the girl, and Poppy turned to see another witch advancing. Again she attacked and hit her target. She nodded to the girl in thanks.

"Are you Sorrel?"

The girl shook her head but not before Poppy caught the light change in her eyes. "Kyra," she replied.

Holding her wounded side in her palm, the girl charged forward with a war cry bursting from her lips. Poppy watched her go, quickly losing sight of her in the flying hands and turning torsos of this frenetic, frantic, deadly dance that Poppy found herself a part of. The battle was far from won, but now Poppy felt they had a chance—if not at victory, at least at survival.

At the battle's raging, bloody heart was Raven. She cut a swath through the skirmish, like she was merely slashing down the brambles in the forest that got in her way. So fast she moved, intent on reaching her destination. For a moment Poppy feared it was her that Raven was aiming for, but Raven shot past without a glance in her direction.

Then Poppy realized. There was but one witch in Raven's sights, the leader of the Eastern clan. This witch knew that Raven was coming for her and she was ready. There was no surprise on her face, no trace of panic.

Hands outstretched like claws, both witches released their magic. The Eastern witch was a match for Raven, thwarting her spells, deflecting and reflecting her powerful attacks. Enraged, Raven breathed fire upon her. The witch cried out as she fell to the ground. But instead of staying down and beaten, her body folded and curled as her back lifted up and her limbs reached down so she was on all fours and growing still. Poppy blinked, and suddenly the witch was a panther, even greater and more fearsome than the others.

"You think your sorcery scares me?" cried Raven. "You dare attack my child?"

The creature roared, displaying its huge teeth, then lunging for a bite. Raven smote it away with the back of her hand. Poppy hurried to Charlock's side as the panther raised its head again.

"Ask yourself, Raven. Why would *we* bother with your daughter when she is not the one?"

Raven flinched, but then opened her mouth and let it become a beak—long, pointed, and deadly. "You lie!" she shrieked, and her head darted forward, stabbing the cat in the eye.

The panther's paw flew to its face as it howled with pain. "Look to your sister," it cried. "Or do you have the brains of a bird to match that beak?"

It took one look of doubt to end a lifetime's trust. Raven locked eyes with Charlock. So intense it was that Poppy could feel the beam of her stare. She could see Charlock's cheeks start to burn with the effort of holding that gaze. The seconds ticked. The battle slowed as all faces turned to watch. Raven's stare was searing, but still Charlock met it with her own.

Poppy squeezed her mother's hand, and as she did so, she saw it—Charlock slipping into the storeroom, taking a potion from a table. Sorrel stumbling through the woods, her face cut, her body trembling. Charlock scooping her up into her arms, tending to her wounds, giving her something to calm her nerves to help ease the pain. Charlock's hand cradling Sorrel's head. "Sip carefully now."

The liquid flowing into Sorrel's mouth, dribbling down her chin. Charlock tenderly wiping it away, helping Sorrel to lie back. Sorrel whispering her thanks, asking for her mother.

Poppy let go of Charlock's hand. She couldn't help it. Her mother's hand hung there, empty and limp for all to see. Raven's eyes didn't waver, though. Her focus remained set only on Charlock's face.

And then it happened. Whether because of Poppy's hand, or Raven's stare, or simply that the truth will out, Charlock's eyelids blinked shut, and in that moment Raven knew. She saw it too, and the horror of it ravaged her. She shut her eyes in pain and bowed her neck as if waiting to receive the blow. When it came, the panther's strike caved in Raven's head like it was made of plaster and swept her body up like it was foam that lifted in the air, then floated to the ground.

Charlock cried out in anguish and clutched her head, as though she felt the blow upon her own face. She flew to her sister's side and all made way for her. Kneeling down in penitence, she took Raven's hands. Her tears fell and washed away the blood and the hideous beak, healing the broken bones and fixing the ripped skin.

"I'm sorry, sister. I didn't know the potion was so strong. My only want was to hurt you as you would me." The words gushed forth in a flood of sorrow. "Forgive me," Charlock lamented.

"If only the past were so easily mended," cawed Raven.

Charlock sobbed. Her face, usually so flat and still, creased and crumpled with emotion. "The prophecy!" she cried as if by explanation.

Raven's eyes flickered up and what she saw there made them close. "Don't cry," she said softly. "You are a Hawkweed. You are the mother of a queen."

Charlock took in a sudden gasp of breath just as Raven exhaled her last. "My sister," she wept as Raven's hands slipped out of hers and into the cold, wet snow.

Chapter Thirty-Five

Everything about her was pale like clouds. Her hair was so fair, it was almost white. Her eyebrows and lashes too. Her eyes were a faded denim blue, same as the veins running like streams beneath her bleached skin. Leo wondered how a woman so light and airy could have produced a daughter as dark and fiery as Poppy. The two of them seemed to belong to different species.

They were in a hospital room, and Mr. Hooper had been questioning his wife, Melanie, about Poppy and she had answered openly and clearly. She was sitting upright in a chair by the window. A book lay open on the small table next to her and her eyes seemed bright and alert, not at all what Leo had been expecting. Mr. Hooper commented on how well she looked. There was a faint tremor in his voice, and Leo noted that Poppy's father seemed nervous.

"Thank you," Mrs. Hooper replied graciously. "I'm feeling much better."

Poppy had been to visit her, she told them. She had seemed fine but she hadn't said where she was going or when she might come by again. Mr. Hooper looked disappointed.

"Don't worry," Poppy's mother advised calmly. "She's a strong girl. She knows what she's doing."

Mr. Hooper actually stuttered on his next few words. He was going to ask around, he said. Take a look in town, and if there was no sight of her, he would head home. "At least if she returns, I'll be there waiting," he shrugged.

Looking a little lost, he waited for some acknowledgement, but Mrs. Hooper just nodded serenely, and this seemed to make him feel even more unsettled as he turned and tripped over a chair and then had to pick it up and reposition it by the bedside.

It was then that Leo saw the clock.

"Could I stay?" he asked suddenly, and they both turned to stare at him. "Just for a bit longer?" he added.

Mr. Hooper looked at Mrs. Hooper, and she said kindly, "Well, that would be lovely."

After that, Mr. Hooper was in a hurry to leave, but he tried to give Leo some money before he went. Leo refused, but not taking no for an answer, Mr. Hooper thrust it into the pocket of Leo's jacket along with his card.

"To get you started," he said gruffly. "You hear anything . . ."

"I'll call you."

When he left, Leo picked up the clock.

"You like it?" asked Mrs. Hooper. "It was a gift."

"Poppy gave it to you," Leo said.

Mrs. Hooper looked around furtively, then whispered, "She did, but it's not from her. It's from my baby girl. I'm getting well so I can be with her."

Leo looked at Mrs. Hooper, so pale and fair, then looked at the clock. "Ember," he said.

Mrs. Hooper's eyes lit up and she leaned toward him. "Do you know her?"

"Mrs. Hooper, will you tell me about Poppy? Tell me everything?"

There was blood in the panthers' mouths. Poppy could see their fangs, yellow like their eyes, oversized like their giant, panting tongues. They had pushed her back to the cliff's edge. She could go no further. Only Charlock had tried to defend her, but she had been quickly overcome. The rest of the Northern clan were no help, despite Charlock's rallying cries. They had lost all spirit and nerve after Raven's death and had shrunk back in shock, allowing Poppy to be surrounded. Now they could hardly bear to look at her. Their backs were stooped with defeat, their eyes lowered as if searching for their feet within the snow. Only Kyra met Poppy's gaze, but the message she sent her was full of remorse.

"So you are to be queen?" came a witch's voice.

"No clan," came another.

"No schooling."

"No knowledge."

"No experience."

"Why should we have you?"

"Why?"

"Why?"

"Why?"

The voices stabbed at Poppy like knives. The panthers growled and snapped their jaws at her. Their saliva hit her arms. She felt the sea air on her back and tasted the salt of it on her tongue. How easy to let go, to run away for good.

"Are you sure she's yours, Charlock?" cackled a witch. "She doesn't seem a Hawkweed."

Hooper or Hawkweed? Poppy wanted neither.

Another witch spoke out, this time addressing the leader of the cats. "You said she was the one we had to fear. She's nothing but a chaff!" she cried scathingly.

The panther turned its head toward the witch, and as it did so, Poppy saw the blackened, clotted socket from where its eye had fallen and almost gagged.

Chaff or witch? She thought of the fire and the rats, of the broken glass and the books in the library. She remembered Mrs. Silva's baby and Minx and Margaret Bryant's eyes. She saw Melanie and Charlock, Ember and Leo. It had to be for something.

The panthers stepped closer. Poppy was on the very edge of everything. She reached inside her pockets, feeling, needing, hoping. Her hands grasped the smooth, glossy curve of the chestnut Ember had given her. Poppy brought it out and looked at it, glimpsing her reflection in its shine. Then, in one swift move, she threw it down before the witches.

As soon as it hit the earth, great trees rose and spread around her, forcing the enemy back and shielding her from them with their thick branches and lush greenery. Poppy's legs gave way with relief and she sat in the snow, feeling lucky to be alive. But the fire came fast and furious, blasting the trees, devouring their leaves and turning their wood to cinder. Poppy hung her head in dismay.

"Poppy!" she heard Charlock cry. "Again!"

Quickly Poppy delved into her pocket once more, and this time she found a piece of paper. She pulled it out and her spirits sank when she saw that it was Melanie's photograph. She couldn't see how this could ever come to her aid, but she tossed it toward them and waited. Nothing happened for a moment, and Poppy felt ridiculous for even trying. But then the paper folded and tucked and folded again until it became a paper boat, and beneath it the snow melted into a pool and the pool became a lake, spreading its bank wider and wider, pushing the witches further and further away. The witches started to murmur to one another and their voices grew louder. Poppy could see the consternation spreading from face to face.

"Is that magic enough?" she shouted to them. "What other tricks do I have to perform?"

The leader of the cats roared and the water began to evaporate into rain that disappeared into the clouds above until the ship sank into the puddle that remained.

"Is that all you've got, girl? You are but a pretender to our throne. A fraud, a fake! That is all you are!"

Poppy felt the familiar stirrings of resentment and injustice within her. She got to her feet and stood tall and proud. "And yet you have all left your homes and traveled so far because of me. If I'm a fake, what, tell me, does that make you?" She could feel the wave of anger rippling among the witches, and they stepped toward her threateningly. Poppy's eyes gleamed as she reached inside her pocket, praying for one last chance.

"Give up, child," scorned the panther. "There's nothing you can build that I can't destroy."

Poppy's fingertips touched something cool as glass. She groaned inside. Not that. Of all things, not that. The witches were staring, waiting, and so she clasped it and held it up high. The heart stone. *Unconditional love*, those had been Leo's words.

"This," she cried. "This is everlasting."

Released from her hand, the crystal spun through the air, flickering rainbows of pinks and mauves and magentas on the snow. It landed like the tiniest iceberg in a sea of white. Then it grew, more monumental and magnificent by the second. The witches gasped in awe, and even the cats moved back to stand and watch until they were lost from Poppy's view as the ridge of rose-tinted crystal mountains towered higher and higher into the sky. They sparkled and shimmered in the light, and as Poppy marveled at them, one thought was in her mind. *Leo.*

And then she started to climb.

Her hands and feet gripped the jagged clefts and crevasses as she pulled herself higher and higher away from the hurt and the loss, away from her past. It was all she could do just to put one hand and foot before the other, dragging herself upward. The sun burned through the white of the clouds and the crystals glittered all the more, Poppy but a tiny spot of dust upon them. Finally she reached the peak. To one side the tops of the trees spread out for miles, uphill and down. To the other draped the ocean, with all its blues and greens and its promise of other shores too far for her to see but, with her magic, Poppy could make them out in her mind—the beaches, the meadows, the spires and rooftops, the mountains, cities, deserts, jungles. On it went, and with it the endless possibilities of new experiences and fresh encounters.

Poppy looked down at the witches and their battle, so small and feeble beneath her. *The world is so much bigger than this*, she thought to herself.

From her summit she addressed them all. "I am both witch and chaff. Both Hooper and Hawkweed. This is who I am and this is what I can do." She stretched her hands out wide.

The Northern clan knelt and, directly, other clans followed. One by one, they bowed before her. Only the panthers refused, growling their dissent, scratching at the snow in protest. Poppy lowered her gaze upon them and muttered a simple spell, and mewing kittens they became. Soft and fluffy and harmless.

Charlock stepped forward until she reached the leader of the pack, distinguishable by its single blinking baby eye. Charlock picked it up and it fitted in her palm. She stroked its head and scratched its chin, and despite itself, it began to purr.

"Go back to the East," Charlock said. "And leave my daughter be."

CHAPTER THIRTY-SIX

Poppy only felt the magnitude of what had happened when Ember hugged her. Her mind and her muscles had been wound so tight for so long now she felt she might snap. But in her friend's embrace, finally she could soften.

"You're safe," whispered Ember. "We're both safe now."

The wounded were being treated, and Raven was not the only sister to be lost that day. Yet still the coven, fired up by their victory, wanted to celebrate.

"All in good time," Charlock said, her face and demeanor having returned to their inscrutable placidity.

The color was restored to Ember's cheeks and her hand felt warm in Poppy's as she led her to the camp's table. They sat there for a while, sipping broth from large spoons.

"Already they're looking at me differently," Ember said quietly from behind her hand so only Poppy could hear. "I've heard them whispering."

Never before had a chaff been allowed within the coven's circle, and Poppy could tell the witches were wary about Ember's presence. They didn't dare speak of it, though, not to Charlock and least of all to her. So Ember stayed another week to ensure her full recovery, sleeping in the caravan in which she had spent her life so far, but this time with Poppy lying next to her.

The winter days were short, night creeping into the afternoons, curling around the camp and coaxing the coven to their caravans. More time was spent in bed than out, more sleeping than arising, and so the time passed quickly, too quickly for Poppy's liking, until it was already Ember's last night. That evening neither girl could sleep. Instead, they talked long into the darkness, speaking of what had happened but also of what might come.

"Never in all my dreams did I think you would be here with me," Ember said softly. "I'm so glad we had these days together."

"Do you want to stay?" asked Poppy, suddenly hopeful, then wondering how she might make that happen.

"I can't."

Ember sounded so rigid that Poppy felt the rasp of rejection. "You don't want to," she argued in response.

"I can't," Ember said again, this time more gently.

Charlock entered the room, shutting the door quietly behind her. They heard her undressing and slipping under the covers, neither of them shutting their eyes, both waiting for her to fall asleep. Poppy could see their breath lift like smoke on the cold night air, but the blankets were thick above and beneath her body, keeping her warm, the material scratching slightly at her skin. No light came in through the little window. There was no need for curtains; it was pitch black outside and Poppy's eyes had to work more keenly than ever before. Occasionally the clouds would allow the moon to show itself and then she could see the little caravan with its wooden floor and painted door, the family of copper pans hanging from the ceiling, the sheepskins strewn across the chairs. But when the moon disappeared again, they were plunged back into darkness and Poppy was reminded of the poem she'd learned at school of the moon *"wandering companionless among the stars that have a different birth." Like me,* she thought, and then Ember whispered, "You could come with me?" and Poppy recognized the wishing in her voice.

"I don't think I belong out there," Poppy whispered back, glancing to the other bed to check that Charlock's eyes were closed.

"And you do here?" Ember blurted, her voice rising so Poppy had to put a finger to her lips to hush her. Ember tried to speak more quietly but she couldn't keep the fervor from her words. "You don't know what it's like inside this place," she stated.

"I know," Poppy soothed. "Truth is, I don't know where I belong."

Ember reached out and clutched Poppy's hand. "They'll make you queen."

Poppy felt herself freeze, then made herself relax and thaw. "The prophecy," she said with a small smile. "Did you ever think it could just have been a bunch of meddling women long ago who wanted to cause some trouble, make themselves feel important?"

Ember's forehead furrowed as she tried to fathom that. "It's come true, though, hasn't it? I heard what you did on the battlefield. You have the greatest power of all of them."

"It was the most alive I've ever felt, apart from . . ." Poppy fell silent.

She couldn't talk of Leo, not to Ember. How could she explain that her power was also her curse? For it meant she couldn't love him or feel his love in return. Poppy gave a shiver as she remembered Charlock's words about Leo's heart and how she might have harmed it. If she'd stayed with him any longer, he would have died. The thought of this made Poppy's face drop, and she felt Ember gripping her hand tightly in response.

"What are you going to do?" Ember asked desperately.

"I'm going to take you home," Poppy replied, trying to find a confidence she didn't feel.

"And then?"

"And then we'll see."

Poppy felt Charlock's eyelids blink in the blackness.

The next day Poppy and Ember left for town. Charlock made Ember a bag full of her old clothes, but Ember shook her head.

"Those are Poppy's things now," she said softly.

Charlock gave a small nod, then turned her eyes to Poppy, fretfully searching for signs. Poppy kept her face still under her mother's gaze. "You will come back," Charlock announced.

It sounded like a statement, not a question, but then Charlock waited for an answer and Poppy felt her insecurity. She didn't know what to say, so she replied with a question of her own. "Will I know it?" she asked. "When the queen dies?"

Charlock nodded. "You will feel it." And then she said it again, this time as an order. "Come back."

A few of the sisters gathered to see Ember leave, but most, especially the young ones, went about their business, wishing to avoid any awkward good-byes. They had wanted Charlock and Poppy to make Ember forget. *For her own benefit as much as ours*, they had said. But Poppy refused to let Ember go lost into the world, not knowing her past, not understanding herself. And though the witches shook their heads, they didn't challenge her. Surprisingly, Sister Ada was among the few to see Ember off. When she approached, Ember's eyes automatically widened anxiously. But the old witch took Ember's chin between her bony fingers and spoke with what came close to affection.

"You take good care out there."

"I will," promised Ember.

The two girls stayed at John Hooper's house for a while. There was a For Sale sign outside and he had already moved most of his belongings to Donna's. He still looked a little sheepish when he talked about her and Logan, but knowing that Melanie had come out of the hospital and that he had both her and Poppy's blessing had freed him to begin his life again. It suited him, this new life. He seemed relaxed, softer in the shoulders, with the weight of all his worries having lifted from them. And he smiled more, deepening the lines around his eyes and mouth but looking younger for it.

Poppy introduced Ember as her friend, and Ember's eyes welled up and she hugged John, clasping him tight, even though she and Poppy had agreed she would try to stay calm. Neither of them could imagine telling John the truth—or him believing it. Poppy knew it would be too much for him to comprehend and he would only feel hurt and bewildered by it. For Ember's part, she worried that John would think her crazy, just as he had her mother. The coven had taught her that most couldn't and shouldn't turn their minds to the irrational and extraordinary. For her, it was enough simply to spend some time with him—her father . . .

"Poppy's told me so much about you," she said as her hands held onto John's back.

John gave Poppy a look of surprise over Ember's shoulder. "Not all bad, I hope," he joked awkwardly.

"Oh no," said Ember so sincerely that her eyes shone. "Only the best."

As for Poppy, she wasn't sure she would ever stop thinking of John as her father, especially when he was so relieved to see her and got so mad at her for worrying him like that. She explained that she'd be going to live with her mom for a while. It was as close to the truth as she could get, and he nodded, then kept on nodding while he rubbed his eye and cleared his throat.

"You're a good daughter, Poppy," he said, and it was her turn to hold back the tears at these words she thought she'd never hear. "I don't like to think of your mother alone," he added, and Poppy wished she could tell him about Ember and Melanie just to comfort him. But then he was standing up and phoning his work and her school and arranging for them to spend their last few days together.

One morning he took the girls shopping, and Ember asked to have her hair cut.

"Not too short," she told the hairdresser firmly. "Just different."

She sat in the chair and let her head hang back into the sink and seemed to relish the feeling of the shampoo upon her scalp and the bubbles in her hair. Then it was dried by what Ember whispered looked like a weapon that shot hot air at her head but made her hair bob and float upon her shoulders.

Afterward, dressed in jeans and boots with a heel, with color in her clothes, makeup on her face, and layers in her hair, Ember looked like someone new. She walked and talked differently too. Poppy had seen her studying the other girls in town and on the television, but she still was surprised at how fast Ember took to her new part in life. Then, when they traveled on the train a few days later, Ember behaved as though she had done the journey a hundred times before.

It was Poppy who didn't fit in, who never would.

Melanie had moved out of the hospital and into a small house in a village nearby. It had a garden in front and behind, Ember noted, and the door was purple like violets. Ember had expected to run into her mother's arms, but when the door opened and she saw Melanie standing there, she found her legs wouldn't move. Poppy had to shove her inside and pull her into the kitchen. Melanie seemed just as dumbstruck and would hardly look in Ember's direction. Instead, she busied herself by making the tea, but her hand shook so much as she poured it into the china cups that Poppy took over the task, chatting all the while, trying to bridge the silence. Ember felt like weeping.

Then Melanie got out the cake she had made. Her cheeks flushing with embarrassment and her voice shaking with nerves, she presented it on a little stand. Upon it was written Ember's name. Ember stared at the cake. It was white and pink and perfect, and when Melanie cut into it, Ember nearly cried out for the shame of spoiling it. They sat on sofas, balancing tiny plates awkwardly on their knees.

"It's delicious," said Poppy, urging Ember with her eyes to speak. "Don't you think so, Ember?"

Melanie glanced up and Ember nodded, and then Melanie looked away again.

After they'd cleared the plates, Poppy suggested firmly that Melanie show Ember the house. While Poppy waited in the living room, Ember walked up the stairs, following her mother. She stared freely at Melanie's back, observing how her hair fell on her shoulders, how her cardigan hung at her waist, how her ankles flexed on the steps and her feet fitted into her small, cream shoes.

Upstairs was a neat, blue bathroom. Next to it sat Melanie's bedroom, yellow and white like daisies. And then they came to a second room. It was light and clean and there were books upon a shelf and a stuffed bear upon the bed.

"Do you like it?" murmured Melanie so quietly that Ember could hardly hear her.

"It's lovely," said Ember, and she saw the relief fill Melanie's face, softening her lines.

"Do you think you'll be comfortable here?" Melanie asked, and suddenly Ember couldn't breathe. "We could change the curtains or the duvet cover. I wasn't sure what colors you'd prefer," Melanie added apologetically.

"It's . . . it's for me?" stuttered Ember. "This room . . . it's for me?"

"If you want it?" Melanie's voice was so tentative it almost cracked. "I mean, I want you to have it. I mean, I would very much like it if you stayed."

The tears started to roll down Ember's cheeks and she wiped them away with the back of her hand, feeling ashamed to be crying when she felt so very lucky. Then she saw Melanie was crying too and her arms were opening and she was stepping toward her and hugging her.

"My baby girl," Ember heard her mother say, and she felt like she had finally reached home.

When they went back downstairs there was Leo, standing across from Poppy. His hair was growing back upon his head and his bruises were fading. He looked less scrawny than usual. Ember couldn't stop the grin from spreading across her face.

"Leo," she called out to him, and he turned and she ran and jumped into his arms. "You're here." Then she looked around. "You're all here."

It wasn't to last long. Despite Ember and Melanie's protestations, Poppy insisted on leaving. Ember couldn't help but notice how quiet Leo stayed, not lending his voice to the attempted persuasions or to the emotional good-byes.

"You will come back?" Ember heard her voice echoing Charlock's, though hers was more fraught with pleading. Then, when she caught Poppy's second's worth of hesitation, she begged more desperately, "Promise me!"

Poppy hugged her close and Ember recalled how guarded Poppy used to be about such displays of affection and how open she was now. As if to prove her right, Poppy went to Melanie and put her arms around her. Poppy's eyes closed in that embrace, but Ember saw how Melanie's hands spread across Poppy's back and how her lips moved in words of heartfelt thanks.

Poppy had thought about running and hiding when she sensed Leo approaching the house. She looked around for somewhere to go—out the back door if it wasn't locked, through the window if she could heave it open, down into the cellar—but then Leo was at the door and a key was turning in the lock and he was in the hallway and walking toward her. He stopped in the doorway. She could see in his eyes he was expecting her. He had known she would be coming with Ember.

He didn't speak, though, and neither did she. She hardly dared to look at him for fear of hurting him. Charlock's warning blared inside her mind like a siren wailing: "you'll kill him," "you'll kill him," "you'll kill him." Poppy wanted to put her hands to her ears to silence it, but instead she stared at Leo's chest, trying to peer through his skin and beneath his ribs to find his heart. As she did so, she felt it beating, fast but strong. There was no damage yet.

Faint with relief, she glanced up and saw Leo's eyes were looking at her, as if reappraising her, trying to see her differently. Her own heart thudded against its ribbed cage even faster than his. *Let me out. Set me free.* Poppy lowered her eyes to Leo's feet and noticed he had new shoes and that his trousers were clean and ironed.

"You've been staying here." She spoke her thought out loud without intending to.

"Melanie's been looking after me the last few days," Leo replied, not realizing Poppy hadn't meant to start a conversation.

"I'm glad," Poppy said truthfully.

Leo walked into the living room, but perhaps he could see the panic in her eyes because he stopped on the other side of the sofa and didn't try to come any closer. "What about you?" he asked. "Who's looking after you?"

Poppy shrugged. Leo shut his eyes for a brief second as if struggling with his thoughts. Then he opened them and spoke with a passion that he tried to hush so only Poppy's ears would hear it.

"I won't stop, you know," he said. He didn't need to elaborate. Poppy understood completely. "I've tried so hard, but I'll never stop."

Poppy met Leo's eyes, and in that moment, suspended in time and place where only the two of them existed—no one else—she allowed herself to feel how much she loved him, despite the risk it posed, despite everything. It only lasted a second, maybe two. That was all she dared. Before it could injure him any further, she blinked and lowered her eyes.

"I'm sorry," she whispered.

And then the others were there and Ember was running toward Leo and holding him and talking, so much talking, and Poppy knew it was time for her to go.

He didn't say good-bye. She didn't want him to. She wouldn't have been able to say the words, and she knew he felt the same.

She didn't even glance at him again, as if not wanting to dilute that last look, the one that had said everything.

So Poppy was on the road, alone again, drifting. She slept in a cheap hotel that night, using money her father had given her when she'd left. The walls were thin, the mattress too. *Is this all there is?* she thought. *Is this my life now?* And then she heard it, a meow from the rooftop. A smile spread across Poppy's face and she ran to open the window. The cats were all there and they came in, one after the other, curling around her on the bed, enthroning her with fur.

The train was ready to depart. The seats were filling and doors slamming. Poppy was on her way back to Charlock, having stayed away far longer than she'd promised, though it was more the cats that had made her decide to return to where the witches were. She wasn't sure how she would like her life there. It seemed more convent than coven. A life of abstinence and sacrifice, a retreat from modern life and all its comforts. And yet she was a witch. The cats last night had reminded her of that. So perhaps she should be with her own kind and learn their ways, however harsh that might be.

A whistle blew, and in that second Poppy felt the magic hit. It shuddered through her, and looking around, she saw everyone had stopped. Everything was silent. The train's engine had died; the guard still had the whistle on his lips; a businessman stood with arms outstretched, his briefcase just balancing on the luggage rack; a woman held a coffee in front of her, about to take a sip; a dad held a baby, midbounce, on his knee. Poppy got to her feet and stared down the platform. Crowds of people looked as though they had been turned to waxwork, expressions stilled upon their faces but their eyes empty of life.

Then the birds arrived. Pigeons first, followed by the robins; the snow buntings and redwings; jack snipes and sanderlings and even geese in formation, swooping down from every angle of sky to perch upon these people posts, landing on their arms, their bags, their heads, their hats, flying in to watch her. Poppy felt the hundreds of tiny eyes focused on her and dimly wondered what they might be waiting for.

As soon as she posed the question, the answer came. So acute and sudden was the insight that it lanced right through her mind. Her hands flew to her head to try to shield it from the pain.

The queen was dead.

Poppy bent over in her seat and the truths hit her skull like they were hammering their way in.

The queen was dead.

She was now queen.

She was of the Northern clan.

Charlock was her mother.

Raven her aunt.

Sorrel her cousin.

Ember her friend.

Leo her love.

Leo her love. Poppy sucked in air, then blew it out, over and over, trying her best to breathe as the knowledge kept pummeling her. Leo her love.

She could see it now. His heart was whole! He was no chaff. Witch blood ran through his veins. His mother—a witch bearing a boy, not bearing to kill him, but hiding him with a lady who would take in a baby and love him as her own. Leo's heart wouldn't break. Poppy could love him. He could love her.

He was her love.

With that, time began again. The birds took to the skies once more. The guard let the whistle fall from his lips, the businessman settled his briefcase on the rack, the woman drank her coffee, and the baby resumed its bouncing. Outside, the crowds went on their way and all noise resumed. Only Poppy changed direction, jumping suddenly to her feet and pushing past the other passengers. The train had begun to ease away from the station and the platform was disappearing quickly.

Poppy opened the door and leapt.

As she ran back into town she thought only of Leo. Not of being queen, or being a witch, or being magic. Just of him. She thought of his face as she told him she loved him. She would make him believe it again. The gates of their lives had swung wide open once more, and Poppy ran faster and faster to reach her destination.

When she felt the stitch start in her side, she thought of Leo's joy, his relief, his thankfulness, and it spurred her on. When she felt the burning in her lungs, she thought of Leo's kiss, his face, his hands. When she felt the ache in her legs, she thought of how she could kiss Leo back and touch him and tell him everything. And she thought of their life, together, away from it all, away from everyone, and she ran even faster.

Then she saw them. And she stopped. Stopped moving, stopped thinking. For there was Ember, just as she had once foreseen. Ember in her new clothes and face and hair, holding onto her boyfriend's hand, walking out of the café. Gone was the girl who would run down a hillside and marvel at songs and be interested in the migration of birds. Poppy had predicted it. She had envisaged it so exactly. But she had been blind to the most important detail.

The boyfriend—that was Leo. Her Leo. Ember's Leo. His fingers were clasped in Ember's, his words were for her ears, his smile for her eyes. This was the future Poppy had seen for them all those months ago back in the dell when all was new and innocent and full of promise.

It had touched her heart then. It broke it now.

She stood there watching, gasping for breath, as Leo and Ember, a couple who fit together so easily, who made so much sense, who looked so right, walked along the pavement, past the shops, across the road, through the crowds, and disappeared from view.

CHAPTER THIRTY-SEVEN

It was hot in Sorrel's room, stifling, and Poppy longed to open the door and the windows and put out the fire. The rest of the coven was freezing cold and the contrast was hard to bear. But still Poppy sat there beside Sorrel's bed and next to the stove the witches kept stoked with wood in fear of their patient catching a chill. Roasting, Poppy wondered if her cousin felt the heat. There was no sign of perspiration on Sorrel's forehead, but she was covered in a thick, heavy quilt and it was hard to imagine she wasn't sweltering beneath it. Suddenly Poppy couldn't resist the urge any longer and she pulled back the quilt in one quick movement and folded it at the end of the bed. Instantly she felt a little better.

Poppy had come here for the silence, and as she cherished it now, she stared at the patterns on the quilt and pondered on how many hands it had taken to stitch each piece to the next. Since her return to the coven, she had been impressed by the sheer industry of the witches. They were never idle, always busy with work or study. Magic was just one small part of life, and even that demanded craft and discipline.

There had been so much talk already that day, so many words about what must happen next, so many questions that needed answering. Charlock, especially, was consumed with making plans and reminding Poppy of her obligations. She acted as though she had forgotten their previous conversation, as if pretending all was well would make it so. For when Poppy had entered the camp, Charlock had flown to her side and embraced her. Poppy had known it was an uncharacteristic display of emotion, and it had moved her. *My mother loves me*, she had thought to herself, and it made the hole inside of her less cavernous. But then Charlock had pulled back and held onto Poppy's hands and looked her in the eyes.

"You're here," she said, and that's when Poppy saw it. The lie.

"You knew," Poppy blurted.

Charlock's grip lessened and fear shadowed her face.

"You knew," Poppy accused. "You knew he wasn't a chaff, that he wouldn't die. You lied to me."

"Because I love you," Charlock whispered.

Poppy shook her head. "Because you want me to be queen!"

"Because I am your mother." Poppy let go of Charlock's hands and walked away. Charlock called after her in a voice shrill with guilt, "Why aren't you with him then, if you love him so? You want to be queen, that's why! Well, let me help you. Poppy! . . . Poppy! Don't walk away from me!"

All night Poppy had tried to summon up the anger that had fueled her over the years, but none came. The tank was empty, so the next morning she just parked herself there in the camp and pretended to listen and look like she was interested. After a while even that became hard. With every word spoken and every plan made, Poppy switched off a little more.

She just wanted to be left to be. She needed time, time to grieve, then time to be a witch before she became a queen. The idea of ruling and governing and being responsible for so much and so many and sitting above all these other venerable women with their lifetimes' worth of experience seemed inconceivable to her. Who was she compared to they? *Nobody*, came the answer in her head.

Sorrel's eyelashes never flickered, and even the eyeballs were motionless beneath their flimsy lids. Her muscles never twitched. For a moment, even two, Poppy longed for such escape—a neverending, dreamless slumber. She felt so weary, like she had aged and her youth was drifting away, a chick's down on the breeze, never to return. How easy it would be to sleep and never have to wake again. And then Poppy felt guilty wishing for such a thing when this girl was lying there, sleeping her life away. *All because of me*, she thought. *Another victim of the prophecy.* She had tried so hard to undo the damage done. Melanie, John, Ember, and Leo. Now, she realized, now it was Sorrel's turn.

Poppy shut her eyes and stilled her mind, stopping ideas before they could become thought, hushing the conversation in her head until there was only her heart beating, pumping the blood through her veins. Poppy wasn't aware of the light that started to glow around her. She wasn't conscious of any of it. But this aura shimmered and sparkled like sunlight on sea and fireflies in night. The colors radiated green and blue, yellow and purple, red and pink like a rainbow, each blending into the other and spreading beyond Poppy to Sorrel, surrounding her sleeping form. Its warmth touched every nerve on Sorrel's body, permeating her skin. Slowly, so very slowly, Sorrel's gray and pallid features became infused with life and a pinkness returned to her lips and cheeks, like a sketch transforming into a watercolor.

Sorrel's eyes moved beneath her lids and her lashes flickered.

As she walked away from the camp, Poppy could hear the cries of jubilation growing louder with each step she took. She couldn't help but feel a swell of pride as she imagined them gathering around Sorrel, marveling at her recovery and tending to her needs. For the healing that had happened that day was not just Sorrel's; it was Poppy's too and theirs. Limb by limb, organ by organ, Poppy felt revived. The same warmth and glow that ran within Sorrel's veins ran within her own. The energy that had seeped away on seeing Leo and Ember now came surging back to her. It got her to her feet and walked her to the door. It sent her out of the camp and through the forest. It grasped her destiny and made her stretch and shape it to her own will.

When Poppy reached the cliff tops, she stopped. There were no signs of the conflict to be found, as if all traces of the violence and suffering had melted away with the snow. Only small patches of white remained; otherwise the landscape seemed untouched. There were no corpses, no debris or broken branches from the trees. Even the sea winds seemed calm today. It was as if the battle had never happened, as if it were all a dream. So unreal, it felt, that Poppy had a sudden urge to go back into town, to that house on Wavendon Close, to check if life was as she had left it in September. A troubled teenage girl moving into town, starting a new school, friendless, naive, and ignorant.

Then Poppy saw it, a glint of pink among the bracken. Never letting it out of her sight, Poppy crossed the ground until she reached it. Stooping down, she picked it up. Leo's heart stone. Her heart stone. She held it up to the light and watched it shine.

Poppy went to the cliff's edge and looked out over the ocean. She remembered the view from up high on her crystal mountaintop; all those places across the waves she could discover and get lost in; how vast the world, how insignificant her troubles. Tilting her face to the sky, she stretched her neck upward, readying herself for her journey. Then, swift and sure, she bent and tore a strip from her skirt and, with it, tied the crystal to her ankle. Standing tall once more, Poppy shut her eyes and her mouth began to move, though the words were silent. The wind swirled around her, blustering fiercely until she wasn't there anymore, only a pile of clothes lying on the ground where she had stood.

From the clothes emerged a bird—a swallow, small and slight. Its tiny feet pushed upward; its wings unfurled. Off it flew, over the cliff, diving downward, falling fast, carrying on its leg a twist of cloth. Then, just as it neared the water, too fast, too hard, upward it soared, skimming the surface and carrying droplets on its feathers as it floated through the air, out over the sea, gliding into and beyond the clouds.

Acknowledgments

Thank you . . .

Weinstein Books for your belief in this story, especially Amanda Murray, Cindy Eagan, Georgina Levitt, Cisca Schreefel, and Brianne Halverson. I feel so lucky to be working with you.

The team at Orchard Books, especially the brilliant Megan Larkin and Sarah Leonard.

My fantastic agents Catherine Clarke at Felicity Bryan Associates, Catherine Drayton at InkWell Management, and the team at Andrew Nurnberg Associates.

Livia, for the stay in Italy that gave me the time and rest to come up with this idea. And my kind and encouraging early readers—my gorgeous friends, Michelle Coulter, Carolyn Drebin and Debra King; my beautiful niece Atalanta Kearon; and my fabulously talented Write Club ladies, Kathryn, Courtney, Tash, Camilla, Jess, Vicky and Michelle—thank you all.

My darling mum, Voula Tavoulari-Brignull, for the resounding faith she has always had in me and my dad, Tony Brignull, the master wordsmith, for passing on his love of poetry and storytelling.

Most of all, my children for providing the magic in my life and my husband, Billy Radicopoulos, for the love and the madness and for keeping me writing through all of it. I might have written more without our brood but it wouldn't have been this.